ACP... YO-BVQ-649

DISCARDED

DO NOT REMOVE
CARDS FROM POCKET

SNAKE IN THE HEART

Publisher's Thanks

The publishers gratefully acknowledge
the kind assistance received from
the following organizations
towards the publication of this book:

The Arts Council of England

Dansk Litteraturinformationscenter,
Copenhagen

SNAKE IN THE HEART

a novel by
HENRIK STANGERUP

translated from the Danish by
ANNE BORN

Marion Boyars • London • New York

Published in Great Britain and the United States
in 1996 by Marion Boyars Publishers
24 Lacy Road, London SW15 1NL
237 East 39th Street, New York NY 10016

Distributed in Australia and New Zealand by
Peribo Pty Ltd, 58 Beaumont Road, Mount Kuring-gai, NSW

British Library Cataloguing in Publication Data
Stangerup, Henrik
  Snake in the Heart: Novel
  I. Title II. Born, Anne
  839.81374 [F]

Library of Congress Cataloging-in-Publication Data
Stangerup, Henrik
    [Slangen i brystet. English]
    Snake in the heart : a novel / Henrik Stangerup : translated
  from the Danish by Anne Born.
    I. Born, Anne. II. Title.
  PT8176.29.T3S513   1996
  839.8 1374–dc20   95-22923

ISBN 0–7145–2996–6 Cloth

Typeset in 11/13 Nebraska and Avantgarde
by Ann Buchan (Typesetters), Shepperton
Printed by Redwood Books, Trowbridge, Wiltshire

PART ONE

Self-disgust is a snake that
constantly pierces and gnaws at the breast,
sucks the lifeblood out of the heart
and blends it with the poison
of despair and the hatred of humanity.

FROM THE STUDENT ESSAYS OF KARL MARX

CHAPTER ONE

Of course he *would* have to meet Lund at the entrance to the Elysée Palace. They went through the gate together, past the guards with machine guns and across the courtyard with the rows of black ministerial Citroens.

'This is going to be an important conference,' said Lund as they went up the steps, 'we'd better keep our ears pinned back, mon vieux!'

'I've got a hunch he won't say anything particularly new,' Mollerup replied gruffly. 'This and that about the Franco-German pact, Southeast Asia, the French atomic capability . . .'

Mollerup was irritated by Lund's superior knowledge. As time passed there was just nothing the man didn't know about French politics; he was always on top form, never lost for an answer, the perfect correspondent, an eye on every finger, the last published book on de Gaulle or the history of the French Communist Party or the causes of the failure of the Fourth French Republic under his arm, pages half cut and a bookmark in his place. Darling of editorial secretaries who could find a striking headline in a flash and get as much out of an interview with a bistro proprietor as with le Ministre des Rapatriées. The scent of Tabac shaving lotion clung to him, his flowered handkerchief curled in a suitably Bohemian fashion from his breast pocket, his shirt was white and there wasn't a single spot on his tie. Mollerup instinctively buttoned up the neck of his checked shirt. He knew Lund had noticed he was ready for a scrap or anyway feeling sour. With an exaggeratedly courteous gesture Lund waved him ahead into a row just behind some American journalists who already had their note pads out to describe the auditorium:

the gilt chairs, the huge glittering chandeliers, the red curtain behind the platform where de Gaulle would shortly take his place.

When was it Lund had started to get on his nerves? He couldn't recall the exact moment, but there had been a coolness between them for at least a year. Lund had been in Paris for two years as correspondent of a conservative Copenhagen evening paper. But it was not politics that had divided them. Mollerup was accustomed to mixing with people of every possible political stance, at one time he had played skittles every Friday with a journalist from a radical right tabloid. During Lund's first months in Paris he had even helped him in all kinds of ways, such as finding a flat with a reasonable rent in a central arrondissement, getting accredited as soon as possible, making contacts with a couple of French daily papers and giving him advice on how he could keep his tax down to the lowest possible level. Lund had been stationed for five years in London and had made a distinguished name for himself. Mollerup remembered how during his first months in Paris Lund had looked rather too much the Englishman, as pale blond Danes like to resemble Englishmen, with Dunhill pipe and tweed jacket, not realizing that surprising numbers of Englishmen are small and blackhaired and don't wear tweeds or smoke Dunhill pipes. After his arrival Lund had a perpetual bad conscience, he felt he wasn't doing enough for his paper and thought he had not the least understanding of France. But as time went on he caught up with it. He began to enjoy Paris and no longer said 'old boy' but 'mon vieux' after every other sentence. Above all his articles grew longer and appeared at shorter intervals. Perhaps it was this gradual change from English to French, from Dunhill pipe to Gauloises, from white handkerchief to flowered, from Burberry to Cardin, which irritated Mollerup — this rather too facile sloughing off of a skin? Or did the irritation stem from what he had heard — that back in Copenhagen people talked more of Lund than of him, of this

Lund's amazing ability to settle into a new situation, a new country? Was the coolness between them purely due to the fact that Lund no longer needed his help and could even take it into his head to instruct *him* in French politics and one day, on the staircase of the Danish embassy, had caught him out in a couple of notorious mistakes in an article? Was it envy he felt? If it was — why didn't he get shot of it and look behind the caricature he had formed of Lund and resume a normal friendly relationship with him? But to make such a reconciling gesture, an invitation to dinner, for instance, required him to be in a stronger position than he held at present, to recover his old journalistic self, his old rhythm, turn out some articles that would earn Lund's respect. At this moment he could kick himself for not sitting on his own in one of the front rows, and he was on the point of asking Lund if he would mind not humming, but stopped himself and instead took out his note pad and began to draw the head of one of the American journalists.

The ministers entered one by one and seated themselves at the side of the platform. At once the assembled journalists lowered their voices. Fouchet stood up after first sitting down, he looked across the hall, thumbs thrust into his waistcoat pockets, as if searching for an acquaintance or assessing how many journalists were in attendance. Then he sat down again. Malraux had taken a place in the front row and was pulling violent grimaces. Seeming to sink down into himself he picked bits of skin off his upper lip with nervous fingers. He blinked unnaturally the whole time and then put a hand over his eyes as if the light hurt them. Would he soon fall asleep as he usually did at press conferences? Mollerup leaned forward to study him better between the Americans' cropped heads. He looked as if he was really asleep and Mollerup wondered if there might be a chance to get an interview with him when the press conference was over and he woke up. He pictured it already. Prominently placed on the front page of the second section of the Sunday paper. With a framed reference on the front page of Section One. Our correspondent in Paris interviews André Malraux. Headline: GREECE IS HERE AND NOW. Sub-heading: *France's renowned Minister of Culture speaks frankly on the possibilities of building a bridge across the culture gap.* Paragraph: The first time a Danish journalist has been received by André Malraux he spends four hours talking about his writings, his two ministerial appointments, de Gaulle's historic mission, the left wing which no longer has anything to believe in, and about a Danish Bornholm clock found in the flea market for 15 new francs (or some other amusing detail of the kind editorial secretaries usually put in the sub-paragraph to balance the bombast).

Mollerup felt the blood rise to his temples. Then it occurred to him that the sub-paragraph might be wrong. *Was* it the first time a Danish journalist had interviewed Malraux? Wasn't the last one a piece Ussing had sent to Denmark before he had retired to an apartment near the Pigalle, a conversation with Malraux after he was hailed on the Place des Invalides as Colonel Berger? And hadn't Malraux signed the accompanying photograph of himself in uniform, with the eternal cigarette stub between his nicotine-stained fingers, the smooth hair carelessly brushed back from his forehead: *To the Danish freedom fighters with hearty greetings?* In any case: no Danish journalist, probably no Scandinavian one, had visited Malraux in his time as minister of culture, that was what mattered. Had Lund tried? Or Munk, the student who after a study period of four months with a freelance job for a few minor papers thought he knew everything about France and much more than the whole Danish colony? Mollerup glanced sideways: Lund sat with his hands in his lap rolling a gas lighter between his fingers. On the end chair, a couple of rows in front, Munk had seated himself with a little tape recorder. How their eyes would widen when they saw the interview with Malraux. All being well Lund would get a reprimand from Copenhagen because he had not done it and thus caused his newspaper to lose prestige in Francophile eyes.

He started to write down a series of questions, after turning to make sure Lund could not peek at them. What does M.

Malraux consider the possibilities are of taking culture to the people? Are cultural centres the way forward? Theatres in the suburbs of Paris? Why has M. Malraux stopped writing novels and treatises on the theory of art? Is he writing his memoirs? If Malraux turned out to be approachable and willing to talk, he might ask him some more pressing questions. Is it true what they say, M. Malraux, that as a young man you brought back treasures from the temples in Indochina? (To ask straight out if he had *looted* them would be too much.) He could also grill him with quotes. What does M. Malraux think of this assertion: 'He who is at one and the same time active and a pessimist is and remains a fascist, unless he has an old allegiance in his body?' That quotation was one of the few he knew by heart. He had used it the first time in a term paper in the spring of liberation year. 'Is nihilism the philosophy of our time?' had been the title of the essay, with reference to Nazism, which his old Danish teacher used to call 'active nihilism.' He got good marks for the essay, and afterwards it was read out to the whole class by the teacher, who repeated the quotation twice, as if he had never heard it before, as if he was delighted with this find he first read it to himself, then to the class: 'A *Frenchman* would express it as precisely as that,' he said later, arranging the knot of his tie. '*Just* as precisely, I tell you.' Did his old teacher read his Paris reports now as he in his time had read Ussing's, he wondered. He recalled how some mornings the teacher came into the classroom without saying good morning, gasping for breath, went straight to the lectern and lumberingly sat down and opened a newspaper, then in a tone of reverence and after getting his voice back asked for silence so he could read out one of Ussing's famous whole-page interviews. A few days after the liberation there had been one with Camus in *Combat*, made nine months previously, shortly after France was liberated, followed by a portrayal of Camus watching a football match. There had been one with André Gide in carpet slippers with a cold and one with Sartre, made at the Bar Royal. The teacher did not care for Sartre, and the interview with him was not read out with quite the same respect allotted to the others. 'There's a touch of the

Prussian in that man — but *enfin!*' was the teacher's comment after the reading. But he would not dream of having a Malraux interview read out. He must have read it for himself since he had remembered the photograph with the hand-written greeting to the Danish freedom fighters.

Mollerup tore the sheet of questions from his note pad and put it into his breast pocket. Better to be well prepared in case he could arrange the interview after de Gaulle's address. If he succeeded in getting hold of Malraux and having the inter-view in a major position in the Sunday newspaper, on the front page, his old teacher would undoubtedly arrive at school on Monday morning with the paper under his arm and make straight for the lectern in one of the senior classes, call for silence and read out the interview with the same reverence as in his time he showed to Ussing's interviews. If he was still working, that is. And if he hadn't made the change to reading conservative newspapers in his old age. Perhaps it was Lund's Paris reports he regaled his pupils with now, his recent conversation with Simone Signoret, his important survey of de Gaulle's military and political career in four feature articles, which confirmed Lund's reputation as an expert on France. He dismissed the idea as absurd. His old teacher belonged to the diminishing race of old-style radicals who would rather go without a newspaper than read a con-servative one. For his sake if for nothing else he would contact Malraux after the press conference. He would carve his way through the throng, catch Malraux's eyes, fell him with a compliment — *M. Malraux, in the current debate in Denmark on the gulf between culture and the people you are playing a vital part. You are in fact the central figure in your capacity of artist and minister!* — and the interview would be landed. You had to grab the French with flattery. Mollerup isn't half coming on! they would say in the editorial office in Copenha-gen. I knew Mollerup would go far, his old teacher would say to his pupils, I knew it from the day when he used the right, the absolutely right, quotation in a term paper: 'The man who is active and a pessimist is and will remain a fascist unless he has an old allegiance in his body.'

'Say what you will: he's a personality now!'

Mollerup was only half listening.

'I said: he's a personality now!' came sharply from Lund.

'Who?'

'Malraux! *André Malraux!*'

'He *was* one at least,' he replied quietly. It struck him suddenly that Lund had been contemplating an interview with Malraux too, and worked out the tactics for getting it, and even though he could hear how inane his reply sounded he hoped it might have cooled Lund's enthusiasm and sowed doubt in his mind as to whether Malraux was really worth an interview after all.

A movement ran through the assembly. Sporadic applause around the hall from journalists who had risen to their feet. Others remained seated, some of them with ostentatiously crossed arms: de Gaulle had entered and seated himself in front of the red curtain, at the table on the platform.

'Le grand Charles himself,' said one of the American journalists.

'Wonder if he's going to attack us this time,' replied his companion.

'Just listen!' said the first and burst into a dry neigh of scornful laughter when de Gaulle rested his fingertips on the table and made a long pause in the middle of his speech, followed by a sudden obstinate enunciation of the words: 'Independent Europe has — consciously or unconsciously — been dismissed by many adherents to the idea of Europe. They consider it to be normal and satisfactory that policy on Europe should be decided in Washington.' Each word, each sentence seemed modelled in neon, thought Mollerup and visualized a drawing by Steinberg in which the word NO emerged from a man's mouth like something gigantic and immovable and momentous. Then he started to fill his pad with notes on de Gaulle's address and manner. *Looks like a dinosaur!* he wrote in the top corner and paid scant attention when Lund, who had not written a single line but sat with hands in lap still rolling his gas lighter between his fingers, sarcastically let drop out of the corner of his mouth the comment that they would be able to read the speech word for word in *Le Monde* before telephoning a report back to Copenhagen.

Feeling Lund's eyes standing on stalks straining to see what he wrote, he replied after a few moments: 'I'm writing about the mood in the hall, about everything that gives colour.'

'You're an expert at that sort of thing, of course,' said Lund. 'Our man in Paris! Monsieur Jean!'

A dinosaur. The resemblance was striking. The small head, the long neck, the little blinking eyes. The ancient monster in the rose bed, the magnificent one. *Like a dinosaur de Gaulle settled himself in his chair in the Elysée palace yesterday afternoon to hold his half-yearly press conference while outside the sun rose high in the sky. As expected, de Gaulle spoke on France's attitude towards the USA, on French independence, on south east Asia, on the Franco-German pact. (France is firmly resolved to build up an atomic arsenal as long as the two giants, the USA and the USSR, do not disarm in earnest. France's first airborne atomic missile is already operational.' 'After eighteen months of the Franco-German pact it cannot be said to have led to any common line of action within NATO'.)* Mollerup had finished planning his report when he gradually began to have doubts about the appearance of a dinosaur. Did it look saurian, slimy? Was it hairy? Did it have little blinking eyes or big and all-seeing ones? Was it herbivorous and amiable or carnivorous, a terrifying beast of prey? Was the dinosaur the one with spikes on its back and a lashing crocodile-like tail and a grinning mouth with sharp teeth or the one with the huge body, long neck and small head? Did de Gaulle in fact have a long neck? Did he blink his eyes? And anyway, whatever it looked like, could a dinosaur settle itself into a chair? He crossed out the word dinosaur. He decided to write a concrete report, leave out all these 'likes', omit the mood-painting, the messages: *yesterday de Gaulle warned the USA and West Germany* or *de Gaulle warns USA and Germany* or just *de Gaulle warns.*

'Seems you're right,' said Lund.

'What do you mean, "right"?'

'Yes, that . . . that he's not saying any more than we'd expected, the old buffer.'

'Well, I think it's a pretty important speech,' he replied and suddenly felt anxious because he could not get the idea out of his head that nothing was easier than to make an attack on de Gaulle. Nothing would be easier than jumping up and leaping through the rows of chairs and on to the platform, pressing a pistol against de Gaulle's chest or sticking a knife in his neck or merely strangling him. He leaned back and took hold of the back legs of his chair. A drop of sweat ran from his armpit all the way down his ribs, down to his waistband where it slowly evaporated. Suddenly he felt as he had done when he was small and sat at the table when his parents were giving a dinner party, and in the middle of the meal, without knowing why, perhaps because one of the guests laughed in a sinister manner or he grew restless because it took so long for the grown-ups to finish eating, he felt a violent urge to get up and do something that would make the assembled guests scream and rush from the table with their hands pressed to their temples, an urge he could only subdue by clutching the seat of his chair so the blood was pressed out of his fingers. He didn't have a pistol on him, or a knife, and what could his hands do? But the compulsion continued to possess him, it filled him, it *became* him: in a few minutes, in a few seconds, he would rise and push his way out of the row while everyone thought he was going to the toilet. He would run up the centre aisle while one or two people stirred in alarm because they sensed what was going to happen. Then he would throw himself at de Gaulle and a gathering chorus of voices would rise in panic and all the ministers would get to their feet with Malraux at the head to rush to de Gaulle's aid accompanied by the shrilling whistles of the gendarmes and officials. He would throw himself at de Gaulle and perhaps it would succeed, perhaps de Gaulle would fall backwards in such a way that he broke his neck or his head struck the floor, and a few hours later the announcement of his death would have spread around the world and the name of Mollerup would be on the front pages of all the

newspapers that had named Oswald nine months ago, long
articles would be written on this Max Mollerup and his life,
on the secrets he might be hiding, this unknown Paris correspondent. Countless theories about his character would
circulate. Was he a communist fanatic masquerading as a
liberal? A right-wing radical fanatic who saw danger in de
Gaulle's clash with America? Was he a religious maniac or
merely insane? No one knew. No one knew anything more
about this Max Mollerup or Monsieur Jean than that he had
lived in Paris for ten years, was the son of the world-famous
Danish actress Marianne Mollerup, that when young he had
been a moderately promising poet who lived the life of a
bohemian in the Latin quarter of Copenhagen and belonged
to the group around the anti-bourgeois erotic poet Schade,
that he was unmarried, had an apartment with modern
paintings on the Avenue de Wagram, spent his summer
holidays either on the west coast of Denmark or in the glove
town of Millau in the south of France, dressed informally in
sweaters and checked shirts, and wrote articles that clearly
indicated a certain weary penchant for the lyrical and sloppy.
No, no one knew anything about him that could explain his
sudden, demented action and during the consequent court
proceedings they would know still less: for did not the puz-
zling Dane explain clearly and plainly, with conviction in his
voice, that he had nothing against de Gaulle, on the contrary
he considered him to have been of great benefit to France?
Did the sudden urge that had made him run up the aisle and
throw himself at de Gaulle with all his strength reveal anything sensational in his nature — an urge similar to those he
had as a boy and was on the point of jumping up to do
something that would make his parents' dinner guests run
screaming from the table? Could not everyone suffer urges?
He *had* to do it. That was all he could say. Was it because he
felt desperate at being among so many journalists? He did
not know. Was it because he felt like committing the
unmotivated murder, acting meaninglessly for lack of an old
allegiance to the body? Crime without cause? The negative
revolt? He really did not know.

His neck and chest grew damp as he fantasised on how the affair would develop after the first weeklong, panicky commotion, after the papers no longer wrote about the death of de Gaulle on the front pages but transferred the meaningless assassination to page four or five: he would be condemned to death and then the sentence would be changed to life imprisonment because he was a citizen of Denmark, and after a few years in a French prison he would be extradited to Denmark. The Danish papers would announce that he had been brought home, but the rest of the world would gradually forget his name because it was not connected with cold war fanaticism like that of Oswald and perhaps because it was harder to pronounce. He would long since have grown accustomed to de Gaulle's absence, Pompidou or Fouchet or some leader of the opposition would be president of France and the reign of de Gaulle a piece of history like the Fourth Republic or the popular front. He himself would sit in his prison cell or in a remand institution, and as the years passed he would find it harder and harder to comprehend what it was he had done on that July afternoon in 1964 when, like hundreds of other journalists, he had attended de Gaulle's press conference in order to report on it. For it was not he who had murdered de Gaulle, but an alien power that had taken up residence in him in the form of an urge. Why should he, Max Mollerup, be enlisted in the brigade of obscure president-murderers?

When de Gaulle moved on to take questions from the journalists and one asked if the general saw any serious possibility for France to play the part of mediator in Vietnam, another if the door of the Common Market would ever be opened to England, Mollerup relaxed his grip on the chair and tried to see his fantasies, his idiotic childish fantasies, in a comic light. He unravelled them one by one, starting from the last, the imprisonment, the court case, the articles about him, until he reached the starting point: that he was sitting here on a routine assignment, with Lund beside him, and had merely been seized with a daft idea. As the obsessive thoughts faded his muscles slowly relaxed and a momentary violent relief made him stretch his arms over his head, clasp his hands behind his head and thrust his legs under the seat of one of the Americans. Then he grew restless again. Pulled his legs in, removed his hands from his head. The man going round with a microphone for those journalists wishing to put questions nodded affirmatively at him; he must have thought he wanted to ask a question when he stretched up his arms and put his hands behind his head. Mollerup shook his head and waved a hand in negation, but the man had already disappeared to the back of the hall and had passed the microphone to a woman journalist in man's dress who stood up and in a marked East European accent asked de Gaulle if he had adopted any definite attitude towards the German voices claiming that the Munich agreement ought to remain in force. When de Gaulle made no reply the woman turned pale, and when the man with the microphone left her with a shrug of his shoulders she began to shout questions at de Gaulle which made a couple of journalists near her shush her in irritation, and the man, who was now making for Mollerup's row, turned once or twice and told her to sit down again. When she repeated her question for the third time de Gaulle glanced sideways at her with a swift scornful toss of his head and snapped:

'Et alors!'

'Hope he gives you a better answer!' said Lund, making way for the man with the microphone. 'Hope *your* question's a better one!'

Next the grapefruit-shaped microphone was planted in front of his mouth and the man leaned over him chewing a licorice pastille with his left side molars. Mollerup tried to fend him off with a look; he had newly cut hair, polished nails, his little finger, pointing straight up while the other fingers grasped the microphone, bore a big gold ring with an aristocratic crest on it. Mollerup continued to stare at the man and discovered he had a little pimple under one eye that grew redder and redder as still no sound entered the microphone. Silence followed, a tense expectant silence all over the hall. Lund cleared his throat abruptly and clicked his teeth, the two Americans turned round and studied him curiously, the man with the microphone pointed his stiff little finger at him with a commanding gesture. It was so close that Mollerup thought he could hear his own breathing over the sound system. When after a moment he heard his own voice asking if it was possible to put a question to M. Malraux, if de Gaulle would permit the minister, the minister of culture, to reply to questions from the assembled journalists, he could hardly recognize his breathless inarticulate voice uttering mistakes in grammar he had not made since he first arrived in Paris. The man with the microphone opened his mouth in astonishment and balanced his licorice pastille on the tip of his tongue. Malraux shifted slightly in his seat but kept his hand over his eyes. And de Gaulle . . . for a fraction of a second he met de Gaulle's eyes, his small, distant yet penetrating eyes, looking at him as if he was a mere nothing. Then the whole thing was over. The man with the microphone was on his way to an African journalist waving from one of the front rows, the two Americans mumbled something to each other and shook their heads. Lund kept quiet and looked straight ahead of him. But from somewhere far back in the hall came faint laughter, faint laughter that continued until the African journalist rose, tugged his white cuffs down over his wrists and in perfect French asked whether the planned atomic weapons might not result in a reduction of aid to 'le tiers monde'.

Mollerup zigzagged through the crowd to be one of the first to leave, but soon the crush at the exit was so great that he was squashed in among a group of chattering Germans. He had got away from Lund by striding over some chairbacks so he emerged a few rows behind, but Munk with his tape recorder was suddenly in front of him in conversation with the press attaché from the Danish embassy, towering a head or two above the crowd polishing his bald pate with one hand. Munk raised his eyes to heaven, the press attaché flung his arms out. Mollerup ducked so they could not spot him, they must be discussing him and during the afternoon the press attaché would have told the whole staff of the Danish embassy about his misfortune, a misfortune that in the eyes of the embassy and the Danish colony would become a scandal, the scandal of the year. Munk held up his tape recorder before the press attaché's eyes and tapped it pointedly. Would they use the tape against him?

In the courtyard the crowd quickly dispersed. Munk and the press attaché bade each other a courteous farewell and vanished out of the gates. Small groups of journalists stayed in the courtyard chatting with their jackets slung over their shoulders. Mollerup walked past the parked ministerial Citroens and came out on to the Rue du Faubourg Saint-Honoré, then turned left. The hot sun shimmered in the dense petrol fumes, from a café came the noise of a jukebox. Outside a boutique on the opposite pavement three models in Persian furs were posing in front of a photographer. They alternately held their furs tightly gathered to their bodies with one hand to their necks and faces turned sharply downwards, or pulled the furs aside and kept their legs wide apart and their faces in profile, under the furs they had nothing on but lingerie. A police officer did his best to direct the pedestrians around them, but soon the circle of spectators grew so big that the models could no longer be seen. Mollerup could not help smiling when he saw Lund had joined the crowd. Then he turned up towards Rond Point after buying *France-Soir* and *Le Monde* at a kiosk. Soon afterwards he sat down at a café table and opened the newspapers. There he could read all about de Gaulle's address. Then Lund stood before him, sun on his forehead, hands in pockets.

'By your leave?' asked Lund and sat down at the table.

They drank Pernod together without speaking. Mollerup read *Le Monde*, Lund looked out at the traffic. Then Lund broke the silence:

'Now, shouldn't we get together properly one day, either at my place or at Chez Georges?'

'That's a good idea,' he replied.

'Over a little calva à la Maigret, maybe.'

'Fine!'

'Let's say that, then.'

Two children ran about playing in front of them, under the trees at Rond Point people thronged among the stamp stalls. The sun had gone in.

'You'll give me a ring, will you?' Lund said.

'Yes, I will. Or you ring me.'

Lund nodded and held out his hand to Mollerup, who stood up and put the money for his Pernod on the table.

He was soon out of sight along the Champs-Elysées, past the Panhard and Citroen firms, past the première cinemas and the big pavement cafés crammed with people. He pondered on why Lund had not said a word about his misfortune, then tried to forget everything that had happened. If he hurried he could get his report written and phoned to Copenhagen in a couple of hours. The sooner it arrived the better it would be placed on the front page. He was no longer in doubt about the headline: DE GAULLE WARNS.

CHAPTER TWO

There was an exhibition of modern drawings at the Maison du Danemark on the Champs-Elysées. At the entrance on the second floor stood the press attaché shaking hands, the ambassador stood in the furthest corner near a temporary lectern reading through his speech, his glasses slipping and his French wife helping him with the pronunciation of a few French expressions with her index finger on his typescript. Most of the guests were members of the Danish colony in Paris, artists and students from the Danish Students Hostel at the Cité Universitaire, journalists, specially invited secretaries from the Ministry of Culture in Copenhagen and various members of staff from the Danish restaurant on the floor beneath the exhibition room availing themselves of the chance of a free glass of champagne.

Two French critics in red corduroys and beige suede shoes arrived half an hour after the opening while the ambassador was reading his speech on the podium. He outlined the centuries-old cultural links between Denmark in the north and France, from the Danish students who had been sent by Bishop Absalon to study at the Sorbonne, to the equestrian statue in Copenhagen by the French sculptor Saly of King Frederik V from 1771 and on to the Danish ballet dancers and artists who had made brilliant careers in twentieth century France. The ambassador stepped down to sporadic applause. Conversation resumed and champagne glasses were refilled. Immediately after the speech the two critics went round the exhibition. Before the various series of woodcuts showing people falling down endless staircases to the infernal regions or entangled in exploding tramway wires, they issued a running commentary on the Scandinavian penchant for exaggerated symbolism. They expanded the commentary into a brief analysis of the Scandinavian character, delivered with machine-gun rapidity, Scandinavian pantheistic innocence, the light nights, the dark winter: the manic-depressive temperament wrapped in a drapery of Germanic mysticism. Then they disappeared, past the press attaché at the entrance whose face they enveloped in the smoke from their Gitanes made of maize paper as he was offering them glasses of champagne. As they went down the stairs without so much as saying goodbye he was momentarily confused, not knowing what to do with the glasses. Then Mollerup, who had stood outside watching the incident, came through the door and relieved him of one of them.

'You should get your glass from the table over there!'

The insolence of the remark dawned on Mollerup only slowly. Champagne glass in hand he made his way across the room to a wall hung with pictures by an artist he had known in his youth in Copenhagen. He saw at once that Ellesøe had not made any progress during the past fifteen years, anyway not in drawing. The same small black miniatures of streets in the city centre, with a single resentful lamp hanging under the November rain. The same shit-brown, smocked brooders in foot-shaped shoes, collapsed on steps. To begin with he had greatly admired Ellesøe, his first encounter with art in Copenhagen and his first interviewee, after he had been taken on by the radical press bureau. It had been a long, glowingly intimate interview about art and social solidarity. But after a time he disengaged himself from him which brought about a violent row at three in the morning in Amagertorv Square. Thinking about Ellesøe made him look away from the pictures: suddenly he heard what the press attaché had said to him, he heard the remark right in his ear: *You should get your glass from the table over there!* He turned round feeling eyes on his neck. The press attaché could only have addressed him like that because his misfortune at the de Gaulle press conference was now an official secret, and he had been made ridiculous in the eyes of the Danish colony and was one of the 'written-off' — the stock expression for those Danes in Paris who had drawn undesirable attention to themselves and were best avoided. The first person he caught sight of when he turned round was Lund, being greeted with a hearty hand-shake by the press attaché. Lund whispered something in the press attaché's ear, the attaché nodded and with a hand under his arm led him over to the champagne table. A little way away a group of artists had surrounded the ambassador. They pressed him with questions on his attitude to modern art, and when he made evasive replies, a six-foot-four tall painter with a full red beard started thumping him on the shoulder in a comradely-corrective manner so his champagne glass splashed over and his wife uttered a little shriek.

'You never rang up, you bounder!' Lund suddenly shouted at him across the room.

'Neither did you!' Mollerup shouted back, relieved that the eyes on his neck had been sheer imagination. As if at a word of command they started to walk towards each other. They met in the centre of the room.

'You certainly did get plenty out of de Gaulle's address,' said Lund, straightening the flowered handkerchief in his breast pocket.

Mollerup was well aware that his headline DE GAULLE HITS OUT did not exactly cover the actual content of the speech. But on the other hand: a hint is seldom misunder-stood, and the newspaper's leader writer had in fact followed up his report with a leader stating that de Gaulle undoubt-edly aimed at withdrawing France from NATO.

'It was one of his minor speeches,' Lund went on. 'You know that perfectly well, Mollerup. But you do like to write in meter-high letters every time . . .'

He could not interpret Lund's smile. Did he mean to hurt or was he merely in a convivial colleague's mood?

'Tameness is journalism's worst enemy,' he replied and heard the all too clichéd tone. But now he had to take care not to beat a retreat:

'And surely there was no need to belittle de Gaulle's speech the way you did with your mean little reference like some unimportant news item at the foot of the page! What was your headline for that day now?'

He couldn't quite remember. He tried:

'Something about quintuplets on Lolland? Or foot and mouth in Godthåb?'

'I thought you'd stopped reading any papers but your own,' said Lund with the same smile.

Mollerup scrabbled for a comment that could get him out of the tight corner he had been driven into. He was trapped in a situation where almost everything he wrote took on some or other concealed reference to Lund because he knew that much of what Lund wrote concealed a reference to his own articles. If he had written, under the pseudonym Monsieur Jean, one of his slightly ironic pieces on the ingrown indifference of the French to other nations, a day or two later in the reading room of the Embassy he would see an article signed Monsieur Dupont, on French receptiveness to other cultures behind their mask of apparent indifference: where did the Danish film director Carl Theodor Dreyer have more admirers than in France, for instance? And once when he had written an alarming essay about the latent danger of a coup from the right, instigated by French industry magnates and generals, soon afterwards Lund wrote in his own paper that the rumours of a coup from the right were unfounded, even though the French were Bonapartists, as individualists they would never in the long run allow themselves to be governed by Fascists.

Lund lit a cigarette:

'But great things will soon be happening! Whether de Gaulle will go as far as to withdraw France from NATO, is another thing . . .'

'That's the one thing he's after,' Mollerup exclaimed.

The press attaché came between them:

'So you two correspondents can't agree?' he asked.

'Mollerup knows from 'reliable' sources that de Gaulle wants France to be withdrawn from NATO,' said Lund.

The press attaché passed his hand over his pate and bit his cheek:

'You know how we all appreciate your aggressive reporting, Mollerup. But aren't you exaggerating slightly? The General plays his cards with an eminent sense of tact, we can surely agree on that. The General is a Frenchman. The General is a nationalist. He is everything we Danes value, in favour of the Atlantic alliance, a European. But does he aim to take France out of NATO? Hardly. Never! Remember, de Gaulle may be anti-American, but above all he is anti-*communist.* Read his memoirs!'

Mollerup grew bitter. Each time he put Monsieur Jean aside and launched out on a detailed report of the Portuguese workers' inhuman living conditions in the shanty towns of Paris or the scarcity of places at the Sorbonne, he was always accused by the other Danes in Paris of being aggressive. Just because he tried to get behind the facade and present another view of France than the accepted one? Because he did not, like Lund, sprinkle his articles with elegant, man-of-the-world idioms?

'Well, we shall see who is right,' he said stubbornly and was about to tell the press attaché and Lund that certainly, de Gaulle was anti-communist, but in his heart he wanted to revive the classical French-Russian alliance, when a whiff of perfume blended with the smoke of Lund's cigarette and a young black-haired woman paused near the press attaché. Over a wine-coloured dress she wore an unbuttoned thigh-length raincoat casually belted. Her long hair was tied back at the neck with a tortoiseshell slide with a silver fastening. As the press attaché did not notice her she cleared her throat quietly with a finger to her lips. When he turned to her she explained in a low voice that she was Italian, from Venice. She studied ethnology in Paris and earned her keep as cultural correspondent for one or two Italian newspapers who wanted to send her to Denmark. She was not going yet but needed certain information as soon as possible.

'To Denmark!' said the press attaché, brightening.

The Italian woman smiled in surprise at his reaction:

'I am only going for a week, and I am afraid that . . .'

'That a week is too little to get to know a foreign country!'

The attaché nodded agreement: 'Absolutely! I am only just beginning to know France and I have lived here almost twenty years. Mademoiselle? Madame?'

'Madame,' she replied, blushing slightly.

'Madame, you are welcome to come to my office at the Danish Embassy whenever you need help. Now, unfortunately, I must look after the other guests, but you are in good company with these two gentlemen, who are colleagues of yours: Denmark's two leading Paris correspondents!'

He took the Italian woman by the elbow and led her closer to Lund and Mollerup. Then he turned on his heel and clapped his hands to the staff to pour more champagne.

'Isn't ethnology becoming the fashion among French students?' asked Lund, offering the Italian woman a cigarette as he watched the press attaché's back, as if he was aggrieved at being left behind and forced to start a new conversation. As the woman at once took up the thread and enthusiastically described her subject, which thanks to Lévi-Strauss had become the leading *science humaine,* Lund's attention was seized, his annoyance was replaced by an obvious pride at having begun the conversation well and he told her he had had great benefit from studying Margaret Mead in his time. Then he was distracted by the appearance of his wife and two small children who were looking round for him.

'I shall have to leave you now, unfortunately,' he said. 'Do you have children, Madame?'

'Not yet . . .'

Lund kissed her hand and went over to his wife and children by the door.

'Et vous?' she asked.

'Me? What?' Mollerup was nonplussed at being left alone with her. Now he would have to go on with the conversation.

'Have you any children?'

'No, I haven't . . .'

'You are not married, perhaps?'

She looked at him curiously. Then she opened her handbag, took out a powder compact and dabbed her nose with a powder puff. Mollerup felt embarrassed on her behalf, embarrassed because she must feel she had been intrusive by her last question. He could actually feel her registering silence in every nerve, and he thought of rescuing her from the dilemma by asking her whether she used Shocking or Caleche or Magriffe or whether they should go out to dinner.

Instead he came out with: 'Marriage is a meaningless institution.'

Her embarrassment vanished in a clear scornful laugh. She did not restrain it, then she stopped with a self-reproachful look on her face, as if she were afraid at her own unexpected openness. She looked away. Half to herself, half to him she praised the exhibition hall in a professional manner. But she did not think much of the drawings. She took her glasses out of her pocket and went over to the picture of a man pressing his hands to his ears as a bomber in the background dropped its load. She put on the glasses and with a finger bearing a long unvarnished nail she drew a quick circle around the picture and criticized the poor composition.

Her perfume had excited him and he was sure she wanted to go out with him. When he got around to asking her to have dinner with him at the Relais de Venice he immediately felt less sure. To start with she appeared not to have heard, she went from picture to picture, the tip of her tongue playing at the corners of her mouth, tossing her head to make her hair fall smoothly over her raincoat collar. Then she turned to him after pushing her glasses on top of her head with an uncertain expression in the dark pupils as if she had heard what he said quite well, but was still in doubt over the sense. Mollerup was overcome by a sudden sensation of heaviness. Everything was heavy, around him and inside him. Heaviness and immobility, with the Italian woman like an agent of disquiet just before his eyes. Her way of crossing her legs. Her posture. Her clothes, the thigh-length raincoat over the wine-coloured dress, the pale leather boots to mid-calf. The glasses on her black hair, the jewel at her neck. Her slim hands with unpainted nails. She was out of place here. She came from a world where everything depended on appearance and awareness of situation. If only he had gone down to the street with her. If he had found an excuse to leave the exhibition with her and they were on the Champs-Elysées and he had waited to invite her until then. Then he would have been able to quell the increasing uncertainty he felt at her lack of response, he could quell it by taking her arm and leading her to a pavement café, as if everything he did was perfectly natural to him. Here he was helpless.

'Well, maybe,' she replied at last. 'But . . .'

She tightened the raincoat belt and looked down. Then she opened her bag and took out a small orange card and wrote down her address and telephone number with a big Montblanc fountain pen. She handed him the card and vanished from the room. He slipped the card into his breast pocket. He felt chagrined by her 'but'. Not until one of the artists from the group around the ambassador and his wife winked at him and shaped a naked woman in the air with a pair of big hands did he realize what had actually happened, the Italian woman had written her address and telephone number on an orange card that now rested in his breast pocket. He went over to the window and saw her take the pedestrian crossing at L'Étoile and disappear into the drugstore on the opposite side. He stayed by the window for a while waiting for her to come out again.

As she did not reappear he suddenly decided without really knowing why to follow her. He nodded goodbye to the press attaché and crossed at L'Étoile just before the green lights changed. As his hand reached for the glass door of the drugstore he caught sight of her. She stood with her back to him, in the pharmacy, where an assistant was putting several small packages into a carrier bag. He went inside and went quickly up to the newsstand to buy a paper to hide behind. With his eyes over the top of the paper he saw her leave the shop, cross the pavement and put her carrier bag on to the seat of an open green sportscar. He followed slowly and stood on the pavement holding the paper up in front of him. Not until the car had reached Rond Point did he lose sight of it.

It was late afternoon and more and more people entered

the drugstore, girls in trouser suits with deathly white make
up and thick black lines around their eyes, young men in
checked shirts, elderly ladies with artificial flowers in their
hats, and businessmen in dark suits, one or two nuns and,
sitting round four tables joined together, a group of boy
scouts from Scotland. For over an hour he sat at a table by
himself beneath some framed front pages of *The New York
Times* and *New York Herald Tribune* with the Armistice announcement from the First World War. He had a couple of
brandies and found himself going over various disconnected
impressions. The rounds of applause in the Elysée Palace
when de Gaulle walked in and sat down at the table on the
platform. An evening trip on the Seine in the torpedo-shaped
plastic boats. The scent of thyme from a restaurant on the
Left Bank. Gradually he felt calm stealing over him, a calm
that came from a pleasant feeling of indifference. Of stand-
still. A thin middle-aged man sat opposite him. He was
probably ten years older than Mollerup, about fifty. He had
been trying to make contact, but not until he sat down right
beside him did Mollerup notice him. He had a carnation in
his buttonhole. His cufflinks were in the form of two little
gold anchors. His temples were greying and he wore greenish
snakeskin shoes. His skin was as transparent as parchment,
and when he opened his mouth and said 'Goedendag' you
saw the flash of one or two gold teeth.

'Goedendag,' he repeated and leaned towards Mollerup.

'Hoe lang blijft U hier?'

'Pardon?'

'Hoe lang blijft U hier?'

'I am Danish,' Mollerup replied in English. 'Not Dutch!
Danois!'

'Oh, so you are Danish,' said the stranger, pointing to the
newspaper which he had put down beside him on the leather
seat. Mollerup discovered he had bought *de Telegraaf* when
he wanted to hide from the Italian woman.

'I *am* Danish!' he repeated and thought the Dutchman
obviously had the same objectionable habit as Danes: to take
any fellow countryman they met abroad for a relation.

'Waar kunnen we ons vermaken?'
'Sorry, I don't understand.'
'De toneelspeler!'
'What?'
'I said: you must be an actor.'
'And I told you I am Danish!'
'Well then. Then I am Chinese! Goedendag Menneer!'

The stranger got to his feet after taking another look at the newspaper. He threaded his way through the tables and sat down at a new one, not far from a young man in a wig. Little by little he moved closer to the young man and then addressed him, this time in French. The young man smoothed his moustache closer to his cheeks after moistening his fingertips with saliva, ignored the Dutchman and nibbled the nail on a little finger. Then he suddenly smiled, put his hands on his lap and leaned back as if interested. The Scottish boy scouts made bubbles with their straws in their lemonade. The two nuns discreetly summoned a waitress. At the bar an American turned on his transistor radio so loudly that a waiter nearly dropped an ice cream out of sheer fright.

Several days later when he let himself into his flat on the Avenue de Wagram he found letters waiting from his mother and his publisher. 'I'll be arriving in a week's time, then, dearest,' announced his mother's letter, 'you've no idea how much I'm looking forward to seeing Paris again after all these years. I expect the town has changed a lot since your father and I were there in the mid-thirties.' His publisher warned him that if he did not get the manuscript of his book on Paris finished within a month it would not be ready for the booksellers in time for the Christmas market. The letter contained just a few lines and was signed by a secretary. It irritated him immensely. About eighteen months earlier when he had written suggesting a book about Paris in 'a different style', without all the clichés of a travel book, a book about modern Americanized Paris whose reverse side was a mass of wooden hovels and holes in the ground among barrack-like tenements. A book that would give a disturbing quirky slice of the Chicago Paris had turned into during the last ten years, when he had written the letter in an inspired moment and also spiced it with his own experiences, he had received an effusive reply from the publisher who thought that if he could 'capture the vision' that 'lay veiled' in his letter, this would be *the* book about Paris. And he was offered a fat advance. But for one reason or another he got no further than cashing the advance and writing less than half of the chapters and a preface in which he presented himself as guide through an unknown labyrinth. So the book was not published in time for last Christmas as he had promised when he wrote a receipt for the advance, and the letters from his publisher grew curter and curter and now only filled a couple of lines with the secretary's signature. He had a month in which to complete the book. Thirty days.

When he went into the dining-room he found his Spanish maid squatting in front of the television set. She had made herself comfortable on the floor, on a rug she had dragged in from the hall, and with wide open eyes was watching the pop singer Claude François leaping around with a gold microphone on a beach in Africa. He noticed she was really quite nice-looking in profile, and wondered whether she had a regular boyfriend or was a virgin. Her plump body and hanging lower jaw indicated that she still lived in the enclosed world of a young girl, anyhow she didn't dream of doing anything about herself. When she realized he was standing in the doorway she sprang up and put the rug under her arm.

'You're quite welcome to watch television,' he said. 'I've told you you can watch when I'm not in the dining room!'

'Merci, Monsieur!'

She bobbed and held the doormat in front of her with her arms around it as if it was some precious object she was afraid he would take away from her. He shook his head, went into the study and sat down at the desk. Thirty days. Thirty days of at least three pages each. And then in the thick of it all his mother was about to descend on him with her bulky old cabin trunks. Last time he had seen her over a year ago she had been in hospital and no one had expected her to survive. But by a miracle she had recovered, and after a brief convalescence on an estate in south Sealand she had returned to Copenhagen full of her old energy to run her fashionable central cinema. She gave big interviews and was photographed as the one-time world star, holding a scrapbook. She talked about her recovery, about how she was approaching seventy-five and still all there, about her memories of her stardom in the tens and twenties and thirties, and about the films she planned to show, chiefly French films. This was the reason for her visit to Paris. She wanted to see what was going on in the French cinema, as she wrote in her letter, which meant she wanted to see Gabin films and more Gabin films. And he would be obliged to take her around, get contacts for her in the French hiring companies, see films with her from morning to night. Their old disagreements would be sure to flare up again. For the first few days she would be all sweetness and kindness, but then she would start to question him about everything under the sun. Whether he was doing anything. Whether he organized his life in the right way. She would advise him to marry some daughter or other of a barrister she knew in Copenhagen, and finally she would go on about how his father had known when it was time to stop dreaming his way through life.

An impulse made him go out into the corridor where some reference books that had once belonged to Ussing were packed away in a big cardboard box on a shelf beside the gas meter. It had not been opened for twenty years. It had been bequeathed to Ussing's successor who had passed it on to Mollerup in the mid-fifties with the message that somehow or other the contents should be preserved as the property of the newspaper. Among other old volumes was an *International Who's Who*. He cleared the desk and opened the box. On top were some Danish-French and French-Danish dictionaries, he might find them useful, of course, but the rest of the stuff was useless, a *Who What When* from 1942 with the Danish fleet in silhouette and old cars and radios, two volumes of a twelve-volume encyclopedia from the same year, some news-sheets from the Danish and French resistance. Next came several packets of yellowed typing paper headed with Ussing's name in Gothic letters, and an address book in which most of the names and addresses were half illegible because they had been written with one of the first bad ball pens on the market. Malraux was listed as one of the last names under M and André Gide was further on, for some reason under S, but the rest of the names had vanished into oblivion. At the back of the book there were some postcards with naked girls and inside a Danish-French dictionary seven numbers of *Paris Secret*. Some of the pages were missing and on one of the models, a black girl with a fair wig, Ussing had amused himself drawing glasses and moustache and military style boots.

He felt tempted to put the whole lot aside and to act now at once on an idea he had had simmering a long time: to try to track down Ussing in the Pigalle district. If he could find him and perhaps get himself invited to his flat his story would be *the* story in the Danish colony and at home in the Copenhagen office, which had long since given up hope of tracing him. He would be able to quash the countless rumours still current after twenty years, that Ussing earned his living as a brothel-keeper, that he was a member of a smuggling ring that operated from Stockholm to Rio, that he was writing a mammoth novel that would not be published until after his death, or simply that he had died of drink. He would reveal the truth — the truth he was sure covered the case of Ussing: the old man had just grown tired of journalism and in particular of the intrigues of the Danish colony.

There was much to indicate that Ussing had been a very lonely man, the porn magazines bore out this theory of Mollerup's: only a lonely person could find satisfaction in these and kill time by drawing glasses, moustache and military boots on one of the models. Perhaps these magazines were Ussing's sole contact with the other sex. Perhaps he had not been the international correspondent he seemed to be, the journalist for whom every door was open, with tilted hat and scarf wound twice around his neck, but a repressed and desperate person who kept some secret that barred him from contact with other people. Then his eyes fell on *The International Who's Who* for 1937. Its pages were only slightly yellowed, they smelled faintly of damp and age and by imagining that the book had just been published he gave himself the feeling of being in 1937. 1964 was a science fiction year, not so far from the year 2000. Somewhat non-existent, nightmarish. 1937 was now, insistent and present, a reality he was in the midst of, holding a newly printed handbook containing names that some time in the future, in the fifties and sixties, would appear in the history books or vanish mercilessly into oblivion. Names that ruled the world, names renowned in the spheres of art and science, managers of large firms, counts, barons and diplomats. He was well aware that his mother was named in the book, she had often pointed out that there was no international reference book that did not mention her as one of the greatest stars of the silent film and later as one of Denmark's greatest actresses, but he titillated himself by not immediately looking her up and instead, calmly and expectantly leafing through the book and letting his eyes move down the endless columns of names. *Adamski*, Stanislaw, Polish ecclesiastic and politician, Christian-Democratic mem. of the Seym, Bishop of Silesia. Katowice. *Brisker*, Sydney S., South African politician, mem. South African Nat. Party. 129 Cato Road, Durban, Natal. *Clair*, René, French film director, during the last few years has become known as leading French film director. Paris VIII, 44, Champs-Elysées. D E F G H. *Hitler*, Adolf, German politician, Chancellor of the Reich Jan. 33, proclaimed Leader of Reich and Chancellor for life after death of Pres. Hindenburg Aug. 33. Berlin. *M. Mollgaard*, Danish physiologist, Copenhagen, Charlottenlund, Esperanceallé 15. *Mussolini*, Benito, Italian statesman. Resigned all Portfolios except Premiership, Air, War, Navy and Interior June 36. Rome, Palazzo Venezia. And finally, a couple of columns back, *Mollerup*, Marianne, Danish actress. Copenhagen, Østersøgade 96.

He wanted to read on, there were masses of names he

would like to meet, Johannes V. Jensen and Martin Andersen Nexø, the Danish writers, and Stalin and Chamberlain and Goring. Each of these celebrities walked around their rooms, finished a book, had a cold or engaged in transactions, prepared wars, undercut opponents, telephoned, telegraphed, affected the life of the world, wrote the year 1937 into history. Perhaps Hitler inaugurated a gymnastic rally with enormous searchlights at a stadium in Flensborg, Mussolini battled with a plague of mosquitoes on the banks of the Tiber. These dead pages, these alphabetical names made a living pattern and he wanted to learn it down to the smallest detail. But only a chance starting-point remained, a tiny scrap of the pattern, the address Østersøgade 96. His mother and father had only had the apartment for a short time, they moved in in 1936 and he and his mother left it in the summer of 1937 after his father's death. Before that they had lived in a small flat in the city centre, and from that summer on he again lived with his mother in a flat in the centre, just above the cinema whose management she had taken on. During the last year or so he had frequently thought about his childhood, but not until now, when he was looking at the handbook, did he really think about the apartment in Østersøgade. He could not recall much about it except that there was an immensely long corridor and that he had his own room with a view over Zinnsgade, while the view from his father's study took in the lakes, the Sortedam enbankment on the far side of the water, Østerbrogade with its trams and in the centre the little artificial island with hundreds of noisy ducks on the small stone jetties and seagulls in constant circling movement over the trees on the island.

Summer 36? Yes, it was summer 36: the three of them set off early one morning in their new open Citroen that had long been the object of admiring comment in the neighbourhood, and drove up the coast road to the summer cottage in Espergærde. And then followed a summer without end. He recollected it now as filled with sunshine, with his mother as hostess at a long series of dinner parties with guests from Sweden and Norway. In the mornings his father would wake him as early as six to go and bathe. His father taught him to swim and to make rafts out of driftwood. Later in the day when they went to the beach again his father would take books with him that he had to review, usually newly published novels. He could remember his father talking about one particular novel about unemployment and the despair of the young people who could not afford a good education. He could not recall the name of the leading character or who the author had been. But he could clearly remember the mood of the book through the way his father had spoken of it — the atmosphere of rain, November in the Vesterbro quarter of Copenhagen, billiards saloons, tax collectors and scuffles among the waste bins, and the day to day feeling of anxiety about the war that lurked around the corner and made some of the book's characters buy gasmasks. His father would lie with his back against a sand dune while he talked. He spoke quite quietly with sudden strange pauses between sentences. He said he would always be grateful when life was good to him, no one knew what the future might bring. But he only half listened because everything was as it should be and there was nothing to be afraid of. But one day when his father paused for an unnaturally long time and suddenly bent over as if he was in pain he did feel fear, he discovered what it was to be frightened, an unexpected and terrible thing might happen. When they returned to Østersøgade his father had to stay in bed all the time, and when unemployed people came and rang the bell and asked for money he grew so weak that he could not get out of bed to open the door, but put a certain sum of money in a jar in the hall specially for them. His father never discovered that the money did not go to the unemployed but was spent on licorice and toys, for he was already in hospital. He died in the middle of winter and in the summer his mother moved back into the city centre. The open Citroen was sold, he did not have his own room any more but had to share one with his aunt who had come to be near his mother and comfort her. His father was not buried. He was cremated and the urn with his ashes was placed in an Old Catholic reliquary in a niche in the new living room, where it had remained ever since. He was strictly forbidden to go near the window sill where the reliquary was kept, and when he once tried to force it open with a penknife his mother was beside herself, and as he got bad marks and failed his exams at that time and found friends who taught him to break into cigarette slot machines, he was sent to boarding school. Some time after that he was dubbed 'the theatre rat' because at the headmaster's invitation his mother had given a poetry reading in the gymnasium to the pupils who had been sent to the school by the authorities. They giggled at her because she put her hand to her heart and turned her eyes to heaven during the sad poems. But that must have been in 1938 or 1939.

1937 was Østersøgade. The few months they lived there. The apartment changed after his father died. The study with its view over the lake was locked, and in the living room covers were put on the furniture and cords tied over the sofas so no one could sit on them. 1937: Hitler was immersed in his work as Chancellor of the Reich, Mussolini was living in the Palazzo Venezia, and when programmes were broadcast on the wireless saying war was coming, his mother sighed that it made no difference whether there was a war or not. Whatever happened, life was tragic. She sat by herself in a corner of the dining room, in an armchair brought in from the living room, reading his father's obituary notices over and over again while his aunt cooked and kept house. Yes, 1937 was autumn in the city centre, but above all 1937 was those months in Østersøgade with the smell of naphthalene and damp linen. A smell like the smell of old paper, like the reference book when he pushed his nostrils down between its pages, a smell of the past and death, of something nightmarish.

He suddenly felt afraid of the book and put it down. This non-existent present filled him with a feeling of timelessness. He had to touch the writing desk. Had to feel the firm wood with his palms and fingertips. He had to go round the room and touch things, the paintings, the chairs, the stove, the cascades of flowers on the wallpaper. He had to go over to the window to make sure life was going on, that the cars moved along as they should, and the immigrant Spanish workers strolled up and down outside the cafés. But it was as if everything around him was cracking, as if at this moment there was neither anything called 1937 or 1964 but only a carefully crocheted pattern he couldn't see but whose stitches and tentacles never loosened their grip on him and stopped him from being himself, from choosing. Now and again a piece of the pattern would be lit up, as if in a blinding magnesium flash, the smell of naphthalene, the years at boarding school, the bohemian period in the Minefield when he had become a student, the poems he had published in the Sunday supplements, the first years in Paris when he at long last felt something was happening in his life, that he had control over it. There were the years when little by little he lost his grasp of things and grew more and more irritable and his articles grew sloppier because he avoided everything that had previously engaged him. Instead he took up the role of causeur with an occasional major feature, as Monsieur Jean who generally wrote short ironic essays on being a Dane among Frenchmen, essays he despised while he was writing them, but were usefully quick to throw out and also suited the 'popular' slant of his paper.

Perhaps some calculations would throw light on the whole pattern. He could reckon up how many articles he had written, that he had had between ten and fifteen girlfriends since he became a student, that during the last three or four years he had visited Paris brothels about once a month, and had seen at least 2,000 films and leafed through a similar quantity of books, that in total he had been round the world a couple of times, that he had telephoned away two or three months of his life, that he had drunk — how many? he totted it up on a piece of paper: 24,000 cups of coffee since secondary school and half as many cups of tea and had smoked about 10,000 cigarettes a year in the last twenty years, which came to 200,000 cigarettes in all. He could tot up a huge score.

It took him a long time to fall asleep. With a whisky beside him he lay in bed looking at the orange visiting card: *Claudia Benedetti*, 34 Rue de Dragon, Paris 6ème. Tel: LIT 3501. The pains in the back of his head returned in waves. It was almost morning. A milkman clinked his bottles down in the street. Half awake, half asleep he fantasized about gigantic dinosaurs wandering around primeval swamps while a series of suns exploded on a black sky, all around the horizon, to the sound of laughter like the laughter in the Elysée Palace when he put his question to de Gaulle.

CHAPTER THREE

Rolf Hauge was the best-known Danish artist in Paris. Shortly after the war he cycled with his wife in tandem from Denmark to France, with his painting tackle on the carrier and the Dannebrog, the Danish flag, painted on the coat-guard so he wouldn't be taken for a German refugee. For ten years he lived on porridge and chips and red wine in a gypsy caravan in a Paris suburb inhabited by Arabs and negroes, with his studio open to the sky, without money and — according to the interviews he gave the Danish press — with nothing but a pair of trousers, two shirts, a handknitted sweater, a pair of pre-war shoes with holes in he could not afford to have soled, and a good dollop of the Copenhagen spirit of enterprise. But the years of hardship came to an end. In the mid-fifties he was discovered by French art critics who saw in his stone sculptures and paintings with gothic themes a hitherto ignored world of roots going back to ancient Germanic arts and crafts, a world that had every chance of breaking down the circle of academicism French painting had ended up in. He began to sell to American collectors who loved going to visit him in the Arab suburb and being offered pommes frites fried on the primus stove. Soon after this he was taken up by a fashionable gallery on the right bank, and when he met a rich French woman interested in art at a private view, the time had come to split up with his wife and move into a castle south of Paris with ten acres of apple orchard around it. Beside the castle he built a barrow with four large windows, one looking out to each of the four corners of the world, so he could arrange his studio down underneath the tombs.

While the barrow was under construction a scholar from

the National Museum in Copenhagen fuelled the myth about him in Denmark, the myth of the spontaneous and generous Scandinavian from the back streets of Vesterbro, who after several years of inhuman existence in a gypsy caravan had been discovered by stringent French art critics and one morning woke up to find himself world famous like another Hans Christian Andersen. Rolf Hauge swiftly became the great ideal for all the young Danish artists in Paris, an example of the phenomenon that talent always wins through in the end. He faithfully attended exhibitions of Danish art to dole out censure or praise. If he did not like the paintings he could assail anyone he met for weeks afterwards to tell them Denmark had turned into a province with no idea of continental sophistication. But if he liked what he saw he lost no opportunity of developing his favourite theories: that the renaissance of modern art would come from northwest Europe. He had made himself the spokesman for these theories in numerous articles and books that he printed at his own publishing firm, which all concluded with a tribute to the Celtic-Scandinavian temperament that was superior to the Latin in sincerity, depth and visionary strength — indeed, he thought, perhaps there was no such thing as the 'Latin temperament'. When he was asked why he stayed in France if he found the Latins so unsympathetic, why he did not go back to Denmark, he replied that France had always given back their souls to rootless artists because the country itself did not have what was understood by 'soul'. Nowhere was one more oneself than in Paris. Russian artists became more Russian, Danish more Danish, Norwegian more Norwegian: had not Hamsun, in fact, written *Pan*, his most Scandinavian novel, in Paris, during a heatwave summer, in a hotel room, stripped to the waist with his feet in a bowl of water? In his eyes too it was typical that Chiang Kai Shek had studied in Moscow, Chou En Lai on the other hand in Paris: which of the two in the course of their political careers had shown themselves to be more *Chinese*? It is true that he had not made the last comment directly, Mollerup had put the words into his mouth during an interview, but after it had come out and he was accountable, so to speak, for the words, he adopted it completely.

As thanks for the interview he gave Mollerup a serviette on which he had drawn rock carvings: at last here was a journalist who had found his way to him. Although on the same occasion he announced that on the whole the press were a pestilence, that did not hinder him from figuring in other interviews: a conversation with Rolf Hauge was a sought-after assignment for all the Danish journalists in Paris, and when six months later Mollerup saw the statement on Chiang Kai Shek and Chou En Lai appear in a conversation Lund had had with Hauge, actually in the subtitle, he decided to avoid him and never mention him again in articles. It was purely and simply because he was looking for material for his Paris book, for which he had just had yet another six months' deferment, and also to escape being with his mother, who was now staying with him for a second week, that just for one evening, he had accepted an invitation. Rolf Hauge was holding a big reception for Scandinavian artists in the barrow because the exhibition at The Danish House in the Champs Elysées, which had stimulated a critic for a cultural weekly to conjecture that 'something' was happening in modern Danish graphics, had ended.

'You really *miss* Denmark down here!' was the first remark Mollerup heard as he went down the slippery stone steps to the barrow where tobacco smoke floated in thick clouds below the ceiling and was sucked out of the four sky-facing windows in rectangular blobs like cottonwool. In one corner a bar was set up, with beer and red wine and calvados and pottery bowls of chips and crackers. Hauge's finished, half finished and just started sculptures served as chairs, while his paintings had been hung up from cords below the ceiling so they should not be damaged during the evening. The draught from the windows made them sway to and fro like flags in a seamen's church while the tobacco smoke increased their impression of elfin mystery.

Mollerup was one of the last to arrive and he had to edge his way through the guests to get to the bar. Hastily he scribbled on his note pad: 'You really *miss* Denmark down here!' The remark had come from a young man sitting on the lowest stair running his hands through his huge mop of hair. Without doubt he was a painter or sculptor too, only an artist could make the word *miss* resound to such an extent with nostalgia, with unbounded longing: the remark did not express anything offhand and chance and conversational, it was the expression of a violent visionary passion, it came from the depths, from the roots, and in all its apparent banality it was just what Mollerup needed. He intended to take particular care over a planned chapter in his Paris book on the Paris of the Danes, the Paris which met the Danish women students who lived with French families as au pair girls, but above all the Paris of Danish painters and sculptors. The chapter would have an ironic and distancing undertone, and the remark, 'You really *miss* Denmark down here!' was the perfect introduction, allseeing and appetizing. He would divide the Danish artists into two groups, those who after a short time in Paris turned against everything Danish and viewed Denmark as a dull backward province, and those who were never able to establish real contact with the French and for whom Denmark, after a short period of exile, glowed in their memory as a land of dreams swathed in a ruddy sunrise, for whom everything Latin, everything French, served merely to show Scandinavian sensibility in flattering relief. It would be too crude to describe Rolf Hauge by name as a kind of ringleader of the latter category, that would only result in legal action and years of intriguing. But no one would be able to accuse him of anything if he portrayed a group of the nostalgic artists gathered for a Wagnerian orgy in a faithful copy of a Danish village church which a masked Rolf Hauge, a Rolf Hauge under a false name, had built outside Paris, a Rolf Hauge who did not publish books on the *Celtic-Scandinavian* renaissance but on the *Gothic* or the *East Nordic*, a Rolf Hauge who sculpted in iron instead of stone and did textile printing instead of paintings.

He looked curiously around the barrow, sniffed the atmosphere, took careful note of the various faces, tried to catch snatches of conversation. The chapter swelled within him, fed on impressions, insistent to be written and published. The church would appear as another Xanadu, a Gothic-Celtic-Old Scandinavian Xanadu with rock carvings painted on the arches, with a copy of the sun chariot hung from the roof and flint axes for bottle openers. Instead of the four windows looking out at the four directions, a glass mosaic would filter a ghostly light down over the guests like the light on a Jutland marsh on a midsummer night after sunset. Instead of bagpipe music (Rolf Hauge climbed on to the bar counter and asked for silence while one of the men guests with a goatee beard and tartan cap walked into the centre of the round floor and tuned up his bagpipes) he would instal an organ in the church. The chapter would be objective, nothing would be exaggerated, the description would speak for itself. He would capture the party in the country church from every direction, like a camera. The conversation would sound as if recorded on tape. 'You really *miss* Denmark down here!' — in the course of the evening he was bound to collect a supply of that kind of comment. By retouching and camouflaging he would have most of the chapter on a plate. All he needed to do was to use his eyes and ears.

Rolf Hauge sat at the bar continuing to demand silence. Once or twice his voice seemed about to crack with irritation because the young man on the steps was making sounds like a hungry hyena in a zoo. Another guest wanted to prove he could lift a sculpture with his outstretched arm, a third was throwing crackers about, a fourth, a fifth, a sixth — no one seemed to take any notice of Hauge's orders, and not until he yelled for all of them to keep quiet did the guests move unwillingly to the sides so the man with the bagpipes could be seen. He obviously cared less and less for the whole thing: now and again he threw a beseeching glance towards the bar, he was most unwilling to perform. He put his bagpipes under his arm, removed his cap and took a couple of steps away from the centre, but immediately Hauge jumped down from the bar and pushed him back, replaced his cap and put the bagpipes to his mouth. After he had played a thin tune, with half-closed eyes and reddening ears, Hauge announced that the tune was from Brittany, like the man playing it, who was a close friend of his. The melody was so simple that everyone could hum along with it, he went on, and in case anyone wanted to sing it he would be happy to recite the refrain in Breton:

> *O Breiz, ma Bro, me gar ma Bro!*
> *Tra ma vo mor'vel mur'n he zro*
> *Ra vezo digabestr ma Bro!*

'And once more — in Danish!' shouted a woman.

'In Danish!' chorused more voices. 'In *Danish!*

'Jack and Jill ran up the hill!' shouted the lad on the bottom step. Taking no notice of the voices Rolf Hauge went on, with affected dignity:

> *Ra vezo digabestr ma Bro!*
> Oh, Brittany, my fatherland, I love my fatherland!
> as long as the sea makes a bulwark around it
> stay free my fatherland!
> *Ra vezo digabestr ma Bro!*
> *Ra vezo . . .*

But only a few listened. The bagpipes player was told to start again, but when he realized the party was dissolving into small groups he approached Hauge shaking his head and put his bagpipes down on the bar counter. Hauge put his arm round his shoulders consolingly, he too had now realized that no one intended to listen let alone hum along, and instead he walked around among the crowd with a bottle under each arm making sure everyone had plenty to drink.

For most of the time Mollerup had been standing in a

corner, half hidden behind a three-meter-high painted sculpture with three large holes in it. Through the middle one he could study the company undisturbed. He decided not to mingle, not to take part in discussions and draw attention to himself. He preferred to have only a couple of drinks and keep a cool head. Least of all did he want to meet Rolf Hauge. If he kept to himself it would be far easier for him to describe the party dispassionately, if he had been face to face with Rolf Hauge and looked into his blue eyes, his boyish blue eyes, it wouldn't be so straightforward to present him in the chapter without a pang of conscience. Mollerup put his notepad into a hole in the sculpture, in another hole he put an ashtray and the welcoming glass a young woman with amber beads round her neck had given him at the bar when Hauge turned his back for a moment. He felt in fine form, the post behind the sculpture was his Archimedes point. But if he was not eager to meet Hauge, Hauge was certainly eager to meet him: a little later, to his horror he heard Hauge's voice quite near, behind a group of guests, asking where he was. A lady's arm promptly indicated the sculpture, and before he could escape Hauge poked a hand through one of the holes and patted his cheek while with the other hand he seized his collar and pulled him out of his hiding place with a 'Mollerup, for God's sake — what are you *hiding* for?' He succumbed to a hearty embrace and Hauge whispered in his ear that they must do something about a new set-up, the two of them, in peace and quiet, over an extra special dinner and with no untimely interference from others. By set-up he meant a new, well-mounted Sunday interview because in a few weeks he was to have his biggest ever exhibition in the gallery on the Right Bank, a retrospective from the thirties to today. It would range from his first paintings made on old cloths stretched over apple boxes in a bicycle basement in Dannebrogsgade, Copenhagen, up to his latest work, an eight-meter-wide and four-meter-high painting that had taken several summers in Brittany to finish and was now hanging above them in the centre of the barrow's vault.

'Can't you *see* it, man! An exhibition such as only Picasso and those boys get the chance of! With my whole artistic development on display, from the time I trudged around like Mr Nobody in Copenhagen up to now when . . . ah, how things *move*, don't they, and now . . .'

Hauge came to a stop, thrown by the fact that Mollerup was not evincing enthusiasm and did not at once, as every other journalist would have done, express the deepest gratitude at being chosen to make an interview with *le patron*. His pupils flickered uncertainly, with one hand he took hold of an ear and rubbed the lobe between index finger and thumb, with the other he feverishly scratched his chest under his shirt. Then he regained his self-confidence, found his foothold. After measuring Mollerup from top to toe, in a silent complaint that journalists and Mollerup in particular never had any understanding of serious matters, he went behind the bar where the cords he had used to hoist up the paintings were bunched together. He detached one from the bundle and started to let down the large painting, as if it were a backcloth in a theatre and he was setting the scene for the second act of a dialectic drama. A few people came over calling out excitedly and expectantly, which made him speed up the lowering process. When the painting was at eye level he took up position beside it and held forth on its 'content,' a word he apologized for using — what is content? What is form? Is there anything other than form? Nevertheless: he regarded the content of the painting as the most comprehensive expression of the dialectic between Scandinavian and Southern which had marked his art throughout a long life. Beneath the apparently 'wild' surface of the painting, a channelled and controlled wildness, lay Scandinavian unease in a space of stillness; the formless but self-conscious figures that appeared in thick layers, applied by hand after the canvas had been initially backgrounded with quiet colours, depicted the fateful and destined meeting between form and fire, between creation and destruction.

And the light. The light was the most important thing. The light that itself was the raison d'être of the paintings. This indefinable, this deeply irrational light that both enveloped the figures in the painting and made them stand out more clearly, this light that was not affected by the struggle between form and fire, could be found by a painter in only two places in the world, on Bornholm, the Danish island in the Baltic, and in Brittany. Nordic light, Celtic light. The light that implied an acknowledgement that nothing lasts, that all struggles remain unresolved and that only stillness remains, cosmic stillness. A light that was as alien to the Mediterranean person as the dark grey Atlantic ocean. He had called the painting 'The Light over Saint-Aubin du Cormier,' where in 1488 six thousand Bretons led by Prince Jean de Rohan fell in battle against the French, because he wanted to pay tribute to this light that was the contrary of the continental light — *that* heroic light beneath whose tragic glow for centuries the Scandinavian and Celtic free man's spirit had grown up allied to rigorous fatalism. In short, the painting depicted the break between the fatalist free man's spirit and the Latin barracks mentality. '*Barracks mentality?*' Hauge repeated the words and made a long pause, he looked deep into the eyes of every single guest, the question mark was written on his face. As a good producer he knew it was important to present his points and surprises at the right moment, after carefully leading up to them. 'I can well understand some of you are startled!' Another pause, more expectation among his listeners. Then he concluded his lecture in a hurry, with instructive glances at Mollerup:

'Go to Brittany and you have the entire divergence between the Nordic mentality and the Latin. A garden in Brittany is wild, luxuriant, it grows as it will. A French garden is geometric, with clipped tree crowns and gravel instead of grass. Visit the villages of Brittany, Plougoff, Plouhinec, Plozevet. Study the weather-beaten houses, talk to the weather-beaten natives. You feel it at once. Brittany is Scotland. West Jutland. Bretons are *us!*'

'*Painters!*' someone shouted.

Rolf Hauge looked around in astonishment.

'Painters should *paint . . .*'

Hauge's expression was transformed into anger:

'Who said that?! We are not accustomed to talking behind people's backs here!'

A youngish man with unframed glasses wearing light summer clothes stepped forward while Rolf Hauge demonstratively began to hoist up the painting again with excited little jerks. When he had pulled it right up, he turned to the young man and received, at first grudgingly, then more benevolently, his apologies. His heckling had not been malicious, rather a corrective, the guest assured him. There was an ironic sparkle behind the unframed glasses as he emphasized that his personal view did not agree with Rolf Hauge's: on the contrary, the Scandinavian idea of a free man's spirit was none other than a conforming slave mentality — he had to admit he had scant knowledge of the Celtic spirit. Who were more lacking in independence than Danes and Swedes, more *fearful*? Who were more themselves than the French? Was there a more tyrannical religion than the Protestant, with its preaching of guilt and still more guilt, was not Catholicism far more mentally hygienic and *liberating*? Was it not significant that psychoanalysis had most followers in guilt-ridden Scandinavia? Rolf Hauge listened without interest. He looked as if he thought it would be senseless to reply to what the other had to say and glanced distractedly up to see if the painting was hanging correctly. He strolled around, studied one of his sculptures, made a young woman jump by patting her behind. Then he suddenly made a 180 degrees turn on his heel, as if he was in a saloon in a Western, and felt danger behind his back:

'Protestantism here and Protestantism there!' he let fly. 'The difference between Nordic and Southern has nothing to do with religion. The difference is simply the same as between dream and common sense, a Nordic garden has a dreamlike quality, a French one is purely matter-of-fact. Again, the difference between a French garden and a Nordic one is the same as between Racine and Shakespeare. French people do not *understand* the magic in *A Midsummer Night's Dream*! They want the whole thing carved out in blank verse, or whatever it was Racine wrote in . . .'

He paused and then went on:

'In the end it is all a question of feeling. The French can't feel as we can, can't have visions! Take a word like *Götterdämmerung!* You can't bloody well say that in French! *Les crépuscules des Dieux!* It just doesn't go!'

The young man in summer clothes listened in a friendly way and jingled some change in his trouser pocket. He mumbled something about not having thought about it like *that*: Racine versus Shakespeare, Shakespeare versus Racine, it sounded convincing. But the ironic glint that still sparkled behind his glasses did not seem to mean he was convinced, rather that he found it unnecessary and impolite to provoke the host of the evening further. When Hauge asked who he was he revealed that he was a secretary in the Ministry of Culture in Copenhagen on a visit to Paris to see the exhibition in The Danish House. That seemed to reassure Hauge who dropped a closing remark to the effect that it was not surprising that he had revealed ignorance. What did peasants understand about cucumber salad, what did secretaries understand of intellectual life? Hauge was pleased to have had the last word, the stranger retired.

But all around discussion was in full swing, for or against France, for or against Denmark. A well-known woman author in a hairnet and jeans, in Paris to write a series of articles on French family management, criticized the way French parents brought up their children, the mothers were always on at them, they were never allowed to be themselves. That led to another guest castigating the French educational system. Because she had not wanted to send her son to boarding school in Denmark she had sent him to a French school, and if it were not for the fact that he was quick to learn and adaptable he would already have suffered lasting harm; not only were the pupils allotted marks according to a medieval grammar school system, but the bottom of the class had to (here she tightened her lips to emphasize her contempt) wear a *dunce's hat* when the marks were given out. Would you believe it? What would become of a pupil like that, from the purely human point of view? At once others came to the defence of the French system, among them a commercial attaché at the Danish Embassy who was convinced that Denmark, thanks to the new educational methods, was heading for moral dissolution. As he saw it, French schools were the best in the world, the strictest, admittedly, but the best, the talented pupils went to the top, the less gifted were weeded out. 'In Denmark it is a handicap to be clever,' he rounded off.

'*Expat!*' hissed the author.

Bottles were emptied, tobacco smoke gathered in several layers under the dome. Mollerup, who had found a new hiding place from where he could study the party, was relieved that Hauge had forgotten to go on insisting on an interview, and his note pad was already bulging with comments, overheard conversations, facial expressions and descriptions of the guests' clothes. Then Madame Hauge came down the stairs and announced that there was smørrebrød and hot meat balls in the adjoining castle. Mollerup put his note pad into his inside pocket. He had written AMONG NORSEMEN in big letters on the outside of the pad. He had his chapter.

A horse-shoe shaped table was laid in the largest of the reception rooms. Dancing was going on in an adjoining room, a stereo played American folk music. At one point a girl of little more than seventeen buttonholed Mollerup. She told him excitedly that she had been given a leading part in a French film.

'Why should they always be Swedish?' she asked, scratching a blob of crab salad from his lapel with her little fingernail.

'Who should always be Swedish?' he asked.

'The Swedish girls . . . I mean the Scandinavians, here in France. Do I look Swedish?'

She did not wait for an answer and insisted he must do an interview with her, it wasn't every day that a Danish girl got a chance like hers. He took her telephone number and promised to ring her very soon. Then someone clapped him on the shoulder. When he turned round he was looking right into Ellesøe's face. Yes, it was him. He was slightly thinner, with hollow cheeks and a goatee instead of the big full beard he had worn twenty years earlier. Mollerup wondered why he had not seen him at the private view at The Danish House.

'It is you, isn't it?' asked Ellesøe.

'Yes, it's me,' replied Mollerup and thought he must have changed as much in Ellesøe's eyes as Ellesøe had in his. Soon he would doubtless comment that he had got fatter. Fatter and older. Should he leave? He had not the least desire to renew contact with Ellesøe after all these years. What could they have to say to each other?

'You really have changed,' said Ellesøe.

'You too!'

A moment's silence. Then Ellesøe went on:

'Actually I noticed you just now when you were prowling around down in the barrow with your paper and pencil. Are you making notes for an ironical article on Danes in Paris?'

'There's always fieldwork to be done, isn't there?'

'Nulla dies sine linea?'

'That's right.'

'Did you see my wall at the exhibition, by the way?'

'No,' he lied. 'But there's still time to see it, isn't there?'

'The show finished yesterday . . .'

'Oh, so it did!'

Mollerup tried to sound really disappointed while nourishing a suspicion that Ellesøe had been at the opening day and thus could catch him out in an outright lie. To lead his mind on to something else without delay, Mollerup took him by the arm and took him around the various rooms, which he knew from earlier visits. Ellesøe told him he had got married just over ten years ago, in the middle of the dreary fifties, at the town hall, naturally, with a couple of friends from the Minefield as best man and usher — and you can bet his friends grinned when he suddenly went in for holy matrimony. Now he had three children, a girl of twelve, a boy of ten and another girl of two. A consolation child. The result of a reconciliation with his wife after a year when they had considered divorce. Ellesøe ended by saying he had grown tired of tavern socialism and that things changed as you got older:

'Can you remember that morning?'

'The morning in Amagertorv?' Mollerup asked.

'You were bloody intolerable! You suddenly reminded me of one of those toffee-nosed Ordrup boys . . .'

Mollerup pretended not to have heard. He had a feeling that now was the time for old scores to be settled. So it would be best if he sounded glad they had met again, but at the same time regretted he had a lot of work waiting for him and needed to be fresh to deal with it in the morning. Why on earth then did he hear himself asking if they should finish the evening with a couple of drinks in Paris? Why had he once again put himself in a situation when he thought one thing and said another?

'Delighted!' came the reply.

But Ellesøe was hiding something. The tone of his voice revealed it. His ironic tone. And his look, his searching, curious look: how have you been getting on? Are you happy with yourself? that look asked. The look he hated and as time went on sensed in everyone. But why didn't he go, then? Nothing was easier than avoiding a painful end to an evening in which for the first time for ages he had been in control of himself and not given himself away. For the first time in months he had played the role of spectator perfectly, and then he had gone and given away his cards and felt like two different people. The assured and the unassured, the self-controlled and the vulnerable. And more and more the latter took away strength from the former. As they went around looking for Hauge to say goodbye, Mollerup only faintly heard the voice inside him that said it would be foolish to arrange an interview with Hauge just to impress Ellesøe and perhaps make him jealous. He knew Hauge had always been the object of jealousy to all the other Danish painters, and by appearing to be in league with him he could pay back the remark that in his time he had been like an Ordrup boy.

Perhaps Ellesøe would humble himself and beg for an interview too.

They met Hauge in the great hall of the castle. He was glowering at some guests who were sliding down the banisters from the first floor. When he caught sight of Mollerup he pushed himself off with his back to the stairpost and staggered towards him. His eyes were bloodshot, his hair rumpled and in one hand he had an empty beer bottle.

'What's the matter with me?' he asked in a thick voice when he came up to Mollerup. 'What's the *matter*?'

'What's the matter?' Mollerup asked coolly, 'what should be the matter with you?'

'Everything! The people, the castle, everything!'

'You've just had too much to drink. You'll see: next Sunday when we do the interview you'll be fine again. As strong as a lion.'

'Then we'll give it all we've got!' Hauge tried to deafen the music: 'We'll give it them right in the eye! That's the only language they understand in Copenhagen!'

Hauge had cheered up when they said goodbye and insisted on kissing Mollerup on the cheek. He merely shook hands with Ellesøe, he was just one of the crowd, a chance Danish artist on a visit to the famous Rolf Hauge. Mollerup smiled: he knew Hauge's methods of reducing colleagues. A handshake with the eyes directed elsewhere. A hello and goodbye with an inbuilt question mark, er, have we met somewhere before?

'Is he always like that, Hauge?' asked Ellesøe as they were driving in to Paris soon afterwards.

'What do you mean, "like that"?'

'Giving himself away, pathetic . . .'

Mollerup laughed inwardly and turned corners extra sharply. His little tactical manoeuvre had succeeded, then. All the way in to Paris Ellesøe must have thought of nothing else but that interview, time and again jealousy must have surged up in him, but he had controlled himself, had not wanted to give away his feelings before this moment when he could no longer keep them down and tried to camouflage them behind a casual tone.

'That's about the size of him, yes, I mean . . . when your name is Hauge you can allow yourself quite a lot,' replied Mollerup, finding a parking place in one of the narrow side roads off the Pigalle. 'Are you game for a bit of fun?'

La Belle Ondine was Mollerup's favourite bar in the Pigalle. He often came here when the loneliness of his flat in the Avenue de Wagram grew too much for him; he was on first name terms with the hostess and knew most of the girls. They sat at the bar and soon had two girls on each side, Ellesøe sat between a black girl and a white one, Mollerup between two Vietnamese. The girls bit their ears and asked for a drink. Mollerup leaned across the decolleté bosom of the black girl and initiated Ellesøe into the girls' stories. The two Vietnamese came from Hanoi but had fled, at first to South Vietnam, later to France because they were Catholics. That was obvious: they wore gold crosses around their necks. Ellesøe blushed and scratched his beard, did not know what to do with himself between the black girl and the white girl who played with his ear lobes and poked silver-laquered nails into his ears. Was he thinking of his wife back home? Did he regret the loss of his bachelorhood? First the business with Hauge, now the bar and the girls who tackled him blithely, confused him. Mollerup leaned across the bar and ordered whisky for them all.

Yes, they would like to see striptease privée. When they could not decide whether they wanted to go to bed with all four girls, the two Vietnamese took over and offered to undress for them. That didn't sound half bad, Ellesøe thought, and soon after they found themselves in a double room in a nearby hotel. The bed stood on a small stage, there were mirrors in the ceiling and the light bulbs were red. A record was put on the gramophone while they were laughingly ordered to sit in a pair of armchairs from where they could see the show. The girls began to undress, they slipped out of their shabby silver lamé dresses to reveal black underwear. At that moment the hostess came in. She had brought towels in case they wanted to make a foursome of it after the performance, and demanded money in advance. Mollerup pulled out his wallet and gave her three hundred new francs. Normally he paid between a hundred and a hundred and fifty for a quarter of an hour. But the madame demanded four hundred as this time it involved striptease privée.

'Four hundred! But I've only got three hundred on me . . .'

His uncertainty immediately affected the girls, they held the towels up in front of them and picked up the lamé dresses, gazing suspiciously at him with offended murmurs.

'The price is four hundred,' replied the hostess. 'Two hundred a girl.'

'Yes, but you *know* me, don't you . . . I can pay next time . . .'

'That's what they all say!'

The record was stopped and one of the girls clicked a switch, the red light went out and a naked bulb threw a sharp white light over the room. The girls were already fully dressed.

'You and your brothel-romance!' said Ellesøe when they were out on the street again. 'They were only out to cheat us!'

Mollerup had the idiotic feeling that now he was going along with Ellesøe and not the contrary. He was once again thinking one thing and doing another: he should have said goodnight as soon as they left the hotel and gone home after remarking to Ellesøe that he surely had enough at least to get himself a taxi.

'Brothel-romance or not, no need to make such an issue of it!' was what he said without conviction.

Ellesøe glanced at his watch and was about to offer his hand to Mollerup, but something held him back. He looked at him with the same searching look as earlier, a nerve ticking in one cheek, with his left hand he played with the keys in his pocket. Mollerup could see there was something he wanted to say.

'Why wouldn't you admit you had seen the exhibition, by the way?' he asked at last.

Mollerup was not really surprised at the question, it did not come as a shock. But had Ellesøe actually seen him, alone or with the Italian woman, or was he just guessing that as a correspondent he would naturally represent his paper at a private view of Danish art? Then Ellesøe hailed a taxi:

'Nice to see you, anyway! Give me a buzz next time you're in Copenhagen!'

He went into a bistro and downed two beers at one go, it dulled the consciousness of having been made small. When he went outside he was befuddled, he bumped into people and several times stumbled over his feet. Once he found himself in the gutter and got wet up to his ankles, and one of the girls in the doorways grinned at him. It was past three but there were still many people about. Hundreds of faces came towards him, closed faces with inquisitive spying eyes, Arabs, negroes, American tourists, a single Dane — you can always recognize a Dane, he thought, that self-effacing air, the half German, half English dress, blue blazer and sandals. Where did all these people come from, where were they going? What kept them upright, instilled in them the necessary minimum of self-confidence? He knew it — knew that way of thinking was really too banal to contemplate. The anonymous mass. The lonely crowd. He himself an anonym among anonyms. A face among the faces. Anonymous! He savoured the word, turned it around. a-n-o-n-y-m-o-u-s. Where did the word come from? Was it Greek? Was it of Latin origin? For a moment he felt happy, happily self-commiserating. He was alone. He was no one. He was free! Condemned to be free as Sartre, in fact, maintained everyone was, all these people who passed him or whom he overtook. Then the happiness vanished as suddenly as it came: certainly he was alone, anonymous, a face in the crowd, but he was also the Mollerup whom at this moment Ellesøe, after the space of twenty years, had again formed a picture of and was no doubt smiling tolerantly about in the taxi on the way to his hotel. He suddenly thought of a negative he had once seen, the negative of one of the first pictures taken of Hans Christian Andersen. It belonged to a film man who had shown it to him with pathos in his voice: this *is* Andersen, Andersen's own physical emanation! The picture Ellesøe had formed of him corresponded to that negative: it was him and yet was not him. Ellesøe held a negative of him that he believed was his true self. And Lund held another negative, and the press attaché a third. The journalists at de Gaulle's press conference all held a negative of him as the over-eager Danish journalist who had made a gaffe such as no one else had made at de Gaulle's press conferences. And his mother owned a negative of him that she was convinced was him even though he was forty years old, a negative that was exactly the same as the one she had made of him when he was very young and she used to exclaim 'I know you!' when he did something that did not suit her.

He crossed the boulevard to the side street where he had parked his car. He was suddenly alarmed at the idea that his mother had made use of his absence to poke around in his flat. It would be like her to search for his hiding-places. To read his letters, and among them the letters from the publisher pushing him for the manuscript of his Paris book. And suppose she had found the box with Ussing's papers and books and porno magazines and thought those belonged to him . . .

In the corridor he tripped over his mother's cabin trunk rushing to get into his study. The cardboard box of Ussing's things stood where he had left it after rummaging through it. His letters were in the right order, under the cannon shell from 1864. If she had been through his things she had left no trace. He walked around the flat restlessly, listened at the door of the bedroom where his mother was asleep whistling loudly through her nose. Through the crack in the door wafted a faint scent of perfume, powder and talcum. The Spanish maid had made up his bed in the study. This was the only room his mother had not yet taken over. The trunks were in the corridor, in the living room were several smaller bags and baskets, in the dining room various flower and plant pots she had bought during the last couple of days because she did not think the flat was 'homely' enough were on the floor by the open door to the balcony. But the study still belonged to him. He sat down at his desk, he didn't feel like going to bed, still had that nagging unsatisfied feeling. He thought of going back to the Pigalle to find the two Vietnamese girls and give them enough money to go to bed with him and so counteract their contempt. But it was past four o'clock. Instead he sat on the edge of his bed with the whisky bottle, looking through the notes he had made at Rolf Hauge's party. He could not disentangle the various items, 'You *miss* Denmark down here' and the other scattered remarks were totally meaningless, the words made no sense to him, the evening and its atmosphere were gone. And if he could not recall the atmosphere he would not be able to write the satirical chapter about Danes in Paris.

When he took off his tie and lay down fully dressed he recalled the Vietnamese girls again. Their shabby silver lamé dresses, their black lingerie. The traffic started to move in the street below. He still could not fall asleep. How long had it been since he slept with a girl? One month? Two? What was it like to hold a naked woman's body? He got up. Drank some whisky and wandered around the flat watching morning creep over the neighbouring rooftops. He went into the corridor and opened the door to the Spanish maid's room. She was fast asleep, one leg outside the duvet, her hair in disorder over the pillow. He smiled at the numerous colour photographs of Johnny Halliday and Claude François above the bed. He crept right into the room and sat down on the edge of the bed and let one hand slide up her uncovered leg. Little pale downy hairs, the beautiful knee. The scent of warm body mixed with a hint of underarm sweat. He only wanted to touch her. Wasn't intending anything else, not really. But suddenly she was awake, and when she saw him she uttered a shriek and pushed herself up against the bedhead holding the duvet to her breast for protection, as if she had dreamed of a monster and now saw it alive before her eyes. He tried to hush her, spoke to her reassuringly, patted her cheek, turned to go. But already his mother stood in the doorway, in a tattered old Japanese kimono, without her wig, her scanty white hair tousled, and without make up her deep wrinkles were like a net over her face. She looked straight at him:

'*Max!*'

The Spanish maid sat bolt upright in bed and began to howl.

CHAPTER FOUR

The worst thing was that she did not say anything. At the breakfast table she did not say a word about the night's episode. She sat opposite him pouring out tea and cutting bread as if nothing had happened. She wore the Japanese kimono over a salmon pink petticoat, with black eye-shadow on, the white wig with its fringe looked so natural it was impossible to tell the hair was not her own, the deep wrinkles in her sunken cheeks were half obscured by the thick layer of powder, and her lips outlined in red — heart-shaped after the fashion of the thirties. She did not look much more than sixty-five or seventy, and he could not help wondering whether he would be equally spry in his seventies, that is, if he lived that long. Were women slower to get hardening of the arteries than men?

'You're looking at me,' she said.

'Am I? I'm a bit sleepy, that's all . . .'

'Haven't you anything to do today?'

'Nothing for the paper, but . . .'

'But?'

'Nothing. There are always one or two irons in the fire . . .'

He thought of the Paris book that was still hanging fire. He hadn't even thought of a title, and on his desk were the piles of finished chapters and notes and jottings for the chapters to come. He could still manage to finish the book on time, he visualized it as a blend of objective reportage and subjective irony, but each day wasted, each hour, each minute, made it harder to get going, to take the final leap into the material. And if his mother began to pry and question him about the 'irons' he had in the 'fire' she would immediately, with her usual intuition, discover his wound and rub salt into it. Fortunately, she again began to talk of the thoughts that came to her on returning to Paris for the first time since the thirties. The soul of the city had not changed at all, even though so much, so infinitely much, was different! She leaned over the table so the kimono fell open a crack and revealed part of her wrinkled, liver-spotted neck and breast. She gently patted the wig and poured a last cup of tea: '*Paris!*' she said, looking dreamily out of the window and over the rooftops. After a few minutes' silence in which she apparently sank into memories of the twenties and thirties, she lifted her cup and slurped a mouthful or two with steam rising from the cup. Then she went on talking of Paris, this town that never changed, she said that since her arrival she had felt twenty, yes, thirty years younger. Meanwhile she brushed crumbs into a little pile and screwed the lid on the marmelade jar. Finally she announced that the director of one of the biggest cinemas in Paris was going to hold a reception in her honour. She had had a phone call from the press attaché who had discovered she was in town.

'You are invited too!' she said.

'I'll . . . I'll look forward to that . . .'

'Of course!'

Not even when the maid came in to clear the table did she make use of the opportunity to mention the night's mishap. She told the girl to clear the table, at first in English, but when the girl looked uncomprehendingly at her she resorted to gestures and sign language. The table was cleared in no time. He noticed that now and then the maid looked at his mother with a little smile on her lips, an intimate little smile, as if there was something between them, as if they had talked over the breakfast table about what had happened during the night — even though they could not express themselves except by gestures and sign language. He wanted to break in, to draw attention to himself and try to put a wedge between them. But at the same time he was afraid they might merely take the opportunity to scold him, with his mother as spokesman. He looked at his mother again, she was sweeping the last crumbs together with the corner of her napkin. It was as if she knew that he knew but did not want to . . . only wanted to keep quiet for his sake. That was what she must be thinking: 'I am not saying anything for his sake. He knows well enough that his behaviour last night was disgraceful.' But then this business with the press attaché? Why was he being brought into the picture now? Was it a conscious ploy on his mother's part? Did she know at this moment that he knew she had heard from the press attaché about his impossible behaviour at de Gaulle's press conference? It all started to go round in circles and his hand holding the glass of orange juice broke out in a sweat. Then he drank it and put it on the tray which the maid held out to him.

'You *are* looking at me,' his mother said.

'No, I'm *not* looking at you.'

'What are you doing then?'

The old hair-splitting. The old clinging to absolutely nothing. The old tone-of-voice duel.

'*Look* at you!' He rose.

'Yes, that's what I said!'

'Yes, that's what you said.'

He agreed with her. But with a certain offhandedness in his voice that he knew irritated her, an indifference that clearly showed he only agreed with her for the sake of peace.

They had visited five arrondissements in the past week. One day they went to a museum, another climbed a church tower, they sailed down the Seine in a plastic boat, they had lunch together in the Eiffel Tower or drove slowly up and down the Champs Elysées looking at the pedestrians. In the Place de la Bastille his mother consulted a fortune teller in a little wooden hut and was promised ten more fit and youthful years, in the flea market to her astonishment she found a bundle of old film programmes with framed art nouveau pictures of her in her great roles of the twenties and thirties, as Miss Julie, as a circus princess, as an Egyptian queen, as Mary Stuart. When she arrived she had demanded that he should set aside at least every other or every third day to show her around Paris, according to a plan she had spent weeks working out back in Copenhagen, inspired by old postcards and diaries. From the outset she let him understand that in all probability this would be her last chance to visit the city of her youth, the city where she had lived for nine months with his father when he was preparing his doctoral thesis on Danish writers in Paris, when she had taken time off from her theatre and film work, a city that had always received her with open arms as an artist. The Parisians had been the first to see the quality of her first silent film, where the Danes had merely scorned it, and it was in Paris that she had her greatest success as a guest actress when, shortly before the war and shortly before she retired, she had appeared on the stage of the Comédie Française. When she mentioned that guest appearance he realized that she had in fact grown old, that the seventy-five years had taken toll of her memory: how many times hadn't he had to hear about her appearance at the Comédie Française. About his father sitting in the first row listening to the enthusiasm of the audience, about the role she had mastered completely even though she did not understand a word of French — she had quite simply learned her dialogue by heart with the aid of a secretary at the French embassy in Copenhagen. But he let her run on. He thought that after all it was only just over a month he was obliged to house her. When all was said and done, it was his duty to make her stay as pleasant as possible. And while the Spanish maid washed up in the kitchen and the water hawked in the rusty pipes, he offered to show her the St Germain-des-Prés quarter. Instantly a change came over her, she forgot the bad feeling between them — perhaps she had forgotten about the night's events? — and said that she knew about that artists' quarter where young people gathered, as in their time they had gathered in Montparnasse with Hemingway and the famous painters.

Suddenly he regretted his offer. His place was at his desk and not at his mother's side as a tourist guide. But if he withdrew his offer the rest of the day would be a resumption of hair-splitting which would probably culminate in a shower of admonitions and reprimands over his sneaking into the maid's room. When his mother, humming to herself, had gone into her bedroom to get ready, he sat at his desk and tried to gather his thoughts and the piles upon piles of notes. In the middle of the desk lay a newly published book on Paris. *That's what they're like — those Parisians!* it was called. The author was a well-known German Paris correspondent for a paper in Hamburg. The book had been published first in Germany, but now it had been translated into French and had reached the top of the bestseller list. He had already read the German's account and intended, if need be, to use a couple of chapters from it if he was still unable to get going. The German had turned everything upside down and drawn a picture of Paris which was the opposite of the traditional one. He presented Paris as a gloomy heap of stones, as the morbid centre of a modern, technocratic and conformist Prussia. Gone were the happy Parisian days, the old, riotous Parisian atmosphere when the weeks rushed by with no thought for the future and people danced on the boulevards and sang revolutionary songs and the girls were a garland of wanton femininity. The German correspondent presented the modern Parisienne as a steamroller of ambitions, solely intent on earning money. The young people of Paris were depicted as the most energetic but least charming in Europe, with no interest in politics, no feeling for anything other than the state of the market. Possibly the book exaggerated when it denied the importance of Paris as a centre of culture, but its attacks on the modern French novel and new-wave films seemed by no means unfounded: it dealt well with the clash over novels that never depicted real life but concentrated on their own process of creation, and the films that limited themselves to showing the activities of petit bourgeois anarchist groups on the Left Bank of the Seine. The German had a good eye for the Paris snobbery most people accepted. The chapter on sexual liberation in Paris was the liveliest. Liberation and Paris? No, those words didn't rhyme, he himself had discovered that time after time. A woman could only get hold of a diaphragm after going through the third degree at the doctor's, and the majority of students did not have sexual intercourse with each other before the age of 28. The statistics confirmed this in black and white. Finally there was a chapter of special interest to him, about the Paris of the Germans. The chapter made no bones about brutally ridiculing the German colony who thought everything was much better in Paris than in Berlin and Bonn. The German had various bones to pick with his countrymen who after a short or long stay renounced their ancestral assets and liabilities in their desire to be more French than the French, more Parisian than the Parisians. This chapter in *That's what they're like — those Parisians!* made him feel really at home.

He held the book up to his nose and sniffed at the scent of printer's ink and paper, leafed forwards and backwards in it and stroked its back. Then he put the book down and turned it around to see it from various angles, imagining it was the first copy of his own book. He took a step backwards to look at it at a distance with the drawing on the cover of a French petit bourgeois looking at himself in the mirror catching sight of a Jacobite in a blood-red cap holding a pitchfork, with the decapitated head of an aristocrat in his hand. Finally he put the book on the letter scales. His book would no doubt weigh the same when it was printed, not too much, not too little. His own book.

He felt in command of himself again and gazed critically around the room feeling like tidying up. First he arranged all his notes in one heap, then he emptied the ashtrays into the waste bin. The books on the windowsill, the desk and the table were placed back on their shelves. He put the exercise books filled with glued-in articles into a pile on the shelf under the table. He emptied the contents of the desk drawer into an easy chair and sorted them out, he threw away old bills, cinema tickets and menus he had stolen from restaurants, put paperclips in one bundle, elastic bands in another, ballpens in a third. Finally he dusted the windowsill with a handkerchief and cleaned the typewriter with a toothbrush before putting a new ribbon in it. Then his mother came in, in an ankle-length dress and thick brown walking shoes. She had a shawl over her shoulders and wide antique Indian silver bangles on both wrists:

'Well, then, *now* I'm ready!'

Everything was 'wonderful.' Everything was 'just as it was in my time.' Youngsters who dressed as they pleased and didn't care a hoot what anyone thought, the Arab carpet sellers and the din of traffic, the kiosks bursting with all manner of newspapers and the *scent*, that absolutely special, unique Parisian scent of metro and garlic and petrol fumes. 'Copenhagen is a *nice* enough town, but Paris . . .' she said as they walked down the Boulevard St-Germain. She held his arm and he had to take small steps so she could keep up with him. Sometimes she would stop suddenly and turn round to look at some young people in fancy dress, or point with her black-laquered stick at a poster advertising a Picasso exhibition; this made her ask him why he did not write more articles about art in Paris, which always welcomed the experimental and modern: Picasso's name had been on everyone's lips in her time too. She would go up to a little girl in confirmation dress holding a gold cross, pat her on the head and smooth her dress so the parents beaming with joy clasped their hands together and asked whether she had grandchildren of that age. He translated the parents' questions and then his mother's answer: no, her son hadn't even plucked up the courage to get married! The weather was on its best behaviour, not a cloud in the sky, a light breeze made the tree tops whisper to the leaves. Only when American tourists passed did his mother express displeasure, turn her face away almost as if ashamed, and hiss that only Europeans, Germans and Scandinavians had any feeling for Paris and its beauty. Just as the Americans had shown no understanding of her films, which were serious and lacked tacked-on happy endings, so they undervalued the tragic significance of Paris, to them the city was merely a collection of backdrops they dreamed of tearing down on a whim and taking home with them. 'Americans have no *respect* for things,' she instructed him, and then told him, for the umpteenth time, the old story about the time the Americans were naive enough to believe she would accept an offer of a great career in Hollywood's soppy films, with the result that they revenged themselves by digging up some or other little Texas floosie who was the living image of her. That was how 'The false Marianne Mollerup' came into being, and for the two years the impostor usurped the screen she was obliged to defend her honour and her name, she brought one case after another, she wrote to the international press and made a series of famous European directors demand a veto on the American and false Marianne Mollerup films, but then the floosie — luckily — was killed in a motoring accident because success had gone to her head.

He noticed his mother growing more and more agitated as she talked and how a little later red spots came up on her neck when they stopped in front of a bookshop, and in a box of film books on the pavement she at once discovered a book on the great stars of cinema history and almost at the same moment a picture of the false Marianne Mollerup in the chapter devoted to her, the real Marianne Mollerup. She put down her stick with a vehement gesture and looked about her nervously, then her face assumed a fierce expression and she tightened her mouth so her lips wrinkled like old leather:

'My God, you can hardly *see* the difference!' After making sure no one was looking she tore the picture of the false Marianne Mollerup out of the book and threw it in the gutter.

They played bowls. He hadn't dreamed she would accept when he offered her a game in a bowling alley in a side street to the Boulevard St-Germain. He only did so to distract her, and especially to stop her snarling more and more loudly about the American tourists at café tables. But her agitation over the false Marianne Mollerup had livened her up, she really felt like a game of bowls! She wasn't so ancient! Quite a crowd gathered around them when they had been playing for some time and each time she threw the ball and sent it rolling erratically down towards the ninepins they slapped their thighs or cheered enthusiastically. A black man offered to help her with a straight throw, but was rejected with a shrug. She had always managed by herself. To start with she obviously took the attention as a compliment, as if she was no more than twenty, beautiful but helpless, outwardly concentrating on throwing straight but in reality only interested in attracting the men's attention. But gradually, as the spectators started to chuckle with their hands to their mouths, the skin of her cheekbones tightened and with a great effort of will she succeeded in getting a ball to roll fairly straight towards the goal so two outside ninepins vanished and the scoring board allotted her four points out of a possible 80. Then she straightened up, held her aching sides and looked the spectators straight in the face so they stopped giggling and instead grew respectfully silent over this remarkable old lady in her ankle-length velvet coat and hat with artificial flowers. With her stick held before her like a weapon she made her way out of the alley. Now she wanted to go to an art exhibition. So they went to an exhibition of African death masks. Then she wanted to see the hotel where Zola had lived. She wanted to see statues and churches, she was indefatigable.

'You were created in this town!' she said suddenly as they were leaving a church.

He stopped short, not understanding.

'You were created in this town! Yes, that's what I said!'

It was as if she had hit the nail on the head. Every time he said anything about Paris not being so marvellous and artistically inspiring after all, that this city too had its disagreeable nightside, she countered by saying that he probably had some nightsides as well. She would not tolerate any contradictions, she had come to Paris for an experience and it was not to be spoiled. 'You should be happy to be living here!' she said time after time. 'This is where it happens, this is where beauty meets with tragedy.' She must certainly have taken this from his father, which made it sound still more blasphemous when he questioned her enthusiasm. It was his plain duty to love Paris, to see it with *her* eyes, to take possession of it as a treasure. And now he learned something else: he had been created here, in some hotel or other in 1925, he was the fruit of his father and mother's Parisian love-bliss. From now on he could no longer permit himself to argue. If she saw a statue that she liked, he must like it too; if she thought a girl looked Parisian and the fact that she looked Parisian meant something special only granted to a select few, it was his duty to agree that the girl looked *Parisian*. This town was her town, and if he opposed it he opposed her. Pointing with her stick, hanging on to his arm, she let herself be led up one street and down another, nothing escaped her attention and if they met a beggar she merrily opened her pearl-embroidered purse and gave him a suitable gift of coins. But after a time her breath grew short and as they turned a corner little beads of sweat suddenly appeared on her forehead. With a slight shudder he felt her fingers dig into his arm.

'It's my back,' she said.

He caught himself smiling. He couldn't help almost taking pleasure in her discomfort though he felt increasing dislike of her fingers digging into his arm. He thought she actually deserved to be left alone on the spot this moment so she could experience how particularly unhelpful Parisians are when one is foreign and unknown and falls ill in the street. She could beseech passers-by for help, no one would listen. In the eyes of the passers-by she would not be Marianne Mollerup who was one of the world's greatest film stars during the tens and twenties and thirties, she would be a completely unimportant and insignificant old lady; there were thousands of them in Paris, a porter's wife, a Miss Daisy, a drunkard. Then he stopped thinking when she demanded they should go somewhere where they could sit down and rest. But there were no benches near, only steps. She said she must have a glass of water at once, holding a pillbox she had taken from her bag. With difficulty he got her to sit down on the steps of a block of flats and knocked at the concierge's door, but when no one came to open it and he was ashamed to approach the residents, he hailed a taxi. They drove down towards the Boulevard St-Germain.

She seemed to be getting worse. She bit her lips when she sat down on the sofa just inside the door of a big café, and when she drew breath he could hear whistling in her lungs. He quickly asked the waiter for a glass of water and explained that his mother was seriously ill. But the waiter refused to give them the water if they did not order something more. Appealing to the waiter's sympathy had no effect, he was forced to order at least a cup of coffee or tea for himself, for which he had not the slightest desire. The people at neighbouring tables followed the little scene attentively, a model groaned loudly with disgust and an elderly man sitting beside her with his hair combed into little Roman kiss curls, wearing a red checked suit with a chrome yellow silk handkerchief hanging from his breast pocket, took her by the shoulders and explained that that's how tourists behave sometimes, rude, no manners. Germans! came a whisper from another table. But these reactions did not seem to make any impression on his mother. She was still holding the pills in her hand with whitened knuckles. The sweat kept running down her forehead making little stripes in the thick layer of powder, her eyes were bloodshot around the dark pupils and the nerves in her neck quivered with agonized longing for the glass of water. Now and then she glared at the waiter who was now standing by the buffet brushing fluff from one trouser leg. As he was obviously not coming back straight away she grew really impatient and struck the table top with the knob of her stick so the elderly gentleman in the check suit clapped his hand to his brow.

In the mirror he saw his mother's neck and his own face, as if she was an interviewer in a television programme and he was the interviewee, the victim. His mother's agitation transplanted itself to him. What was he to do? Get up and go and fetch the glass and reprimand the waiter? Stay in his seat and feel his mother's eyes like flies over his face, burning with rage and accusation, as if everything was his fault, that she was ill and that the waiter still didn't bring her the water? Her eyes went on loading him with blame, and when he looked in the mirror and behind her neck caught sight of his own face with the cheeks porous and swollen with too much whisky, he could almost understand why she chose to make him the guilty one and why she had to make herself a negative of him corresponding to the negative she had made of him ten years ago and twenty and thirty years ago and still further back. In her eyes, of course, he was not in the least changed, he was still the more or less unsuccessful result of hers and his father's love. He could sit here and be the one he was and yet be a third, something quite different. He could be this perfectly different image in his mother's mind, an image that was as alien to him as the glimpses he suddenly got of himself when he caught his profile in a mirror far off that reflected itself in the mirror just in front of him with his mother's neck and his own face seen from in front. A strange profile, obviously not so young, a profile he refused to take possession of, refused to acknowledge as his own, with scanty hair, a hint of a double chin and flabby pale cheeks. Not since two years ago when he had ordered a new suit from his tailor and was frightened to look at himself in the tailor's side mirror that reflected itself in the mirror in front of him had he made a similar acquaintance with himself. But he had lost even more hair, was even fatter in the cheeks. Ten years ago when he came to Paris for the first time and sat in cafés for hours observing the customers, he would have smiled to himself at such a face with the scorn of youth, the pleasure of the spectator.

Anxiety made his breath come quickly, gaspingly, and every time he moved in his seat, leaned forwards or backwards, he saw himself doing exactly the same thing in the mirror, only in another way, like a caricature or a jumping jack, as if he was struggling to escape from an invisible net.

Again his mother struck the table with her stick:

'Where in heaven's name is that glass of water?!'

Something was happening to him. He could no longer restrain his malice. He let her go on banging again and again and even felt some sympathy with the waiter who still did not bother to bring the glass. And he prolonged his exaggerated smile and made no reply when she ordered him to go and fetch it. She looked at him in amazement, her brow wrinkled so her wig shifted slightly at the hairline, then she again told him to go and get the water at once and at the same time speak to the manager and demand that the waiter be fired. He still did not reply, the smile stuck to his lips. Then he started humming and looking around the café absently, as if plunged in his own thoughts, unaware of what was going on around him. An almost childish joy tickled his midriff. And a little later: a feeling of freedom came over him and suppressed the anxiety. The elderly gentleman with Roman kiss curls realized something painful was taking place and started to stare out both him and his mother. But this time he felt no irritation at the stranger, did not feel his eyes as something unpleasant and sticky and instead of turning away he nodded to the man making him start and became the one who had to turn his face away.

'Do you know that man?' asked his mother, her mouth half open.

'No!'

'Then perhaps you could go and get that glass of water instead!'

He started to polish his nails on his lapels. Then he took out the contents of his pockets and put them on the table, the cigarette packet, notebook, pipe, tobacco pouch, handkerchief, a note pad, fountain pen, two ball-point pens and his address book. He arranged them all in a tidy pile. He did this without knowing why, but he had to move his hands about. After a bit he put the things back in his pockets so the cigarette packet and pipe went into the pocket where the address book and note pad had been, the tobacco pouch in the inside pocket where the notebook used to be, the notebook into the back pocket, the two ball-points and the fountain pen into the breast pocket, the breast pocket handkerchief in one side pocket after he had first demonstratively blown his nose on it. He pushed his chair back a meter and looked at his shoes. They needed a polish, he gave them one with a paper serviette.

Then he took a straw from a little tin box and blew into it

so the paper cover flew off like a toy rocket and landed on his mother's shoulder.

She did not speak to him for two days. If she was not out contacting film distributors or seeing Gabin films she locked herself into his bedroom, deeply aggrieved. They met only at mealtimes. Her eyes followed all his movements as he was eating, but he held on to his strength and avoided meeting her gaze, instead concentrating on *France-Soir* or *le Monde* which he kept beside his plate or on the few pages of the Paris book he had managed to write. He had spent some hours at his desk in an attempt to get going, now it was neck or nothing, there were barely two weeks before the manuscript had to be finished if the book was ever to be published. He had taken a chapter on the French sex-debate from the German book, retouched here and there, an amusing chapter, snarling and savage. He had trouble with the chapter on the Paris of the Danes. He recalled Rolf Hauge's party, but every time he tried to write about what had really happened that evening, he found himself on the wrong tack, the characters would not come alive: not the woman author in the hairnet nor the Breton with the bagpipes nor Rolf Hauge. He could hear the discussion on Denmark versus France in his head but not even with the help of his notes could he reproduce the dialogue dramatically enough. The chapter turned out either too much of a parody or too little.

On the other hand he had landed a chapter on demonstrations in Paris. His scrapbooks had yielded some six years' old reports describing the period just before and just after de Gaulle's accession to power. He was very surprised on reading through these old articles; they were written with a light hand, full of small precise detail, lively and unpretentious. Unwillingly but curiously he compared them with the latest articles he had sent off to his paper. It seemed to be quite a different person who had boisterously evoked the atmosphere of the Paris in which de Gaulle assumed power, with one demonstration succeeding another, and Sartre, in front of four microphones, in which the wind made a fluting sound like that in empty beer bottles, spoke to a crowd of thousands, from the one ten years later, who, as Monsieur Jean, wrote casual little pieces on Parisian unpleasantness. The reports had been written during a period of his life when fatigue had not yet set in, when he was still filled with curiosity and loved nosing around the boulevards and using his eyes and ears. He had just moved into his flat and was happy to have left the hotel rooms he had occupied for several years. The reports were the high point of his career, and the editor-in-chief had sent him a big cheque as an encouragement in addition to his normal salary. But today no one remembered those reports, he hardly did himself until he found them and with an uncomfortable feeling that they were someone else's work wrote them out and inserted them into his book.

Why couldn't he get the same life into his description of the Paris of the Danes? Why couldn't he describe the idiotic Rolf Hauge's party with the same stylistic intensity he had used when he pictured Sartre in front of the microphones and the police surrounding the Sorbonne? It must come down to a question of technique. Of recalling the Hauge party down to the last detail and finding an angle to describe it from. In the past he could look down a street on an early spring morning when the cafés were opening and the watercarts were hosing the road and afterwards go straight home, sit down at his typewriter and describe that street, the cafés and the watercarts and the light filtering down through the trees so he could not tell which was most real, the street or his description of it. The world around him was not something aggressively overbearing, it was lightly and unconcernedly present as something to be made use of, written down. Surely it could be like that again. It must be possible for him to get Rolf Hauge and the woman author with the hairnet and the Breton with the bagpipes and all the others to live on the page.

During the next few days he made no progress on the chapter and it was with a feeling of hopeless futility that he accompanied his mother to the cinema where the reception was to be held. Hauge's party had exploded into fragments he could not tell apart, and his nerves were on edge over the smallest detail. Every sound pierced his ears, and when his mother opened her mouth for the first time since the episode at the café and announced that this was the day of the reception, her voice sounded like a loudspeaker. He was constantly in a sweat and frightened because perfectly ordinary objects came and jostled him. He could sit for minutes just staring at the ashtray beside the typewriter with its heap of butts, ash and used matches. He could pick up a match and scrape off the burned sulphur with little quick movements until the tip was as sharp as a needle and then heap all the stubs into one corner of the ashtray and spike them on to the match in a row. He felt imaginary pains, one moment above his eyes and in his temples, the next in his stomach. He smoked at least three packets of cigarettes a day, his fingers were stained yellow to right above the knuckles and each time he took a breath it felt as if something cracked in his bronchial tubes. Having a bath helped. When he lay in the bath with only his nose and eyes above the water, looking up at the ceiling with its big black sooty patches from the geyser, he had a moment's peace, he was nowhere, things around him lost the supernatural feeling, sounds disappeared into the blue and the chapter on the Paris of the Danes stood out clearly in his mind. Usually he stayed in the bath until the water was cold and he was chilled through, but when he was back at his desk again both the pains and the sounds came back and Rolf Hauge's party broke into the fragments and scattered impressions he could not synthesise. It was while he was sitting at the desk spiking cigarette stubs with a match that his mother came in and reminded him of the reception: 'But you don't have to come for *my* sake!'

She was in top form. Even before they reached the cinema she had embarked on new tactics. Instead of resentment she now chose to give an impression of effortless ease. Controlled, cool, both acid and friendly, she behaved as if nothing had happened, and he had to listen to a stream of praise for Jean Gabin, how he was still so wonderful and masculine. But when they entered the cinema's spacious vestibule she grew distant and turned away from him, and when the Director came up to them she made a point of not introducing him as her son so he soon found himself on his own while she put her arm in that of the Director and allowed herself to be drawn into a circle of film people. A waiter in white evening dress pushed a small trolley around serving sherry and madeira. The conversation that had fallen silent the moment they came through the door, resumed, and among the guests he recognized, from photographs in the press, various young actresses and directors. The young producers, wearing smoke-coloured glasses and Mao-jackets, stood in a group by themselves, the older ones walked around with cigarettes hanging from the corners of their mouths shaking hands and laughing with assumed vitality at the occasional witticism while directing stolen glances at the young ones. Then the Director called for attention. With a discreet cough he stood on a chair and clapped his hands so the company fell silent and the waiter stopped his trolley with its clinking glasses, then he lifted his eyes to the ceiling for a long intense moment. Then he looked at the walls with a distant expression, next dropped his head suddenly to inspect his shoes and their shiny toes, and put his hands in his jacket pockets so only the thumbs remained outside. He began to speak. He spoke of when he was young, when he became aware of film as art and for the first time, in a small side street in Montmartre, at a cinema otherwise only frequented by pimps and newsboys, saw Marianne Mollerup's magical face: *'Now, forty years later, as if destiny had shuffled the cards, you, Madame, stand amongst us. You run a great cinema in the centre of Copenhagen — you, the first lady of your country. But whether you incarnate Mary Stuart, Queen Christina, Marie Antoinette or just run a cinema in Copenhagen, in that Copenhagen that is all too far away, you will always be the seventh art's faithful servant, unforgettable and majestic as actress, invaluable in the role of cinema director with — for this we know, rumour has already told us — a preference for*

French *film. The calibre of a human being is measured by the magnitude of their passion. Your passion for the seventh art is unrivalled.'*

Renewed silence followed his speech. Then one of the older producers spoke of how it had always been his dream, his secret but now expressed dream, to make a film with Marianne Mollerup, 'who knows, perhaps it isn't too late yet!' One of the young producers with smoke-coloured glasses took over and talked about the lasting spiritual relationship between the new French avant-garde film and the silent film. After an actress with an empire coiffure and a soft voice had praised Marianne Mollerup as a living example of how devotion to a cause always pays, the speeches were at an end. The waiter pushed his trolley around and refilled glasses.

From where he stood he could see his mother. Her flower-decked hat towered over the crowd, and when the circle spread out a little he saw how she smilingly received one kiss on the hand after another and how, with her hands constantly in movement, she tried to answer various questions. It was all very correct, no one raised their voice, no one looked as if they had had too much to drink. It occurred to him how different the French and the Danes are at gatherings. But the correctness did not prevent a discussion between the young and the older producers starting up. One of the older ones happened to pass the group of young ones and let drop the remark that their admiration for silent films was not only romantic but also absurd. The older man apparently did not expect an immediate response, apparently expected his remark to stay hanging in the air as food for thought, and was already on his way when the leader of the group, a lean and Germanic looking young man with blond curly side whiskers, called him back in a low but military tone. The young men at once let fly: admiration for the silent film must be seen in context with natural contempt for the films of the intermediate generation, for the works of burnt-out directors of the fifties and sixties. The older man unbuttoned his jacket feverishly and buttoned it up again, sniffed at the flower in his buttonhole, trying desperately to master an outbreak of fury. He laughed in ironical resignation, patted the young man on the shoulder and said he was well aware that it was a law of life to turn against older but not yet dead artists. It was easy enough to admire those!

'Dead and dead,' the young man replied smiling and looking across at the guest of honour.

'Oh, well, you know quite well what I mean, young man! But don't overlook the fact that it was my generation that put the voice into film!'

'Yes, worse luck!' replied the young man and made all his friends in Mao-jackets laugh by numbers.

No one was taking any notice of his mother now. The argument soon drew the attention of the assembled guests. He saw his mother take a step or two towards the discussion. But then she suddenly stopped and made straight for him instead.

'Talk to me!' she whispered commandingly.

She looked at the group as if at a loss and started to laugh hilariously. He could not repress slight admiration for her when her ruse succeeded and various people turned back to make a circle around her. Still more came up, glass in hand. Now it was the turn of the young producers to be left alone and one or two of the older ones remarked quietly that they were really not worth wasting time and energy on. Then between the shoulders of two of the older producers Mollerup suddenly caught sight of the Danish press attaché. He must have arrived after the others or else he had been in the lavatory. Now he was involved in conversation with the Director of the cinema. He had his hands behind his back and kept on rocking forwards. A little later the press attaché and the Director made their way towards him between the two producers.

'Now then, Mollerup! Just the man! As a journalist you can tell us: what's *happening* to Dreyer?'

'He must be waiting for the last payment on a new film,' he replied without hesitation, wondering where in heaven's name he had got that from. He had to give a swift answer.

'Yes, that's what I thought!' said the press attaché, and
turning to the Director:

'You see, Monsieur le Directeur, Dreyer is a remarkable
man, you know, something of an eccentric, not especially
Danish, at one and the same time naive and a genius . . .'

'All geniuses are naive,' came from the Director. 'Not
excluding the Danish ones!'

'Exactly! And that's probably the reason for Dreyer not
making all the films he might have liked to do. On numerous
occasions the Danish state has . . .'

What came next happened faster than he was aware of.
When those listening realized that Dreyer was the subject of
discussion his mother was left to her own company for the
second time. A young actress picked a hair off the press
attaché's collar and described how she literally swooned over
The Vampyr. Since then she had seen that masterpiece at least
four times a year. The eldest of the producers clearly recalled
how as a young man Dreyer had sniffed around the Paris
studios and made interviews with French film makers. Even
the young producers came out of their invisible holes to hear
news of the great Danish producer. That was too much for his
mother. Now she no longer tried to be the centre of attention. She buttoned her coat, straightened her hat and took
his arm to indicate they were about to leave. Age! she said,
smiling sweetly to the Director, in her broken English. Age!
She permitted the astonished Director to kiss her hand and
her cheek despite his efforts to keep her from leaving.

He was not surprised that she was in a savage mood when they
got home, but when she kept it up the next day and the next
so he could not get anything done, he saw nothing for it but
to pick up one of the pot plants she had put in the dining
room and hurl it to the floor to make her leave off her
ferocious recriminations against Paris. Suddenly nothing was
as it should be any more. Paris was an insolent town with
insolent inhabitants, the French film people at the reception
had shown no more tact than the waiter who refused her a

drink of water, the Jean Gabin films she had seen were worse than any Danish musical comedy, and it was only because *he* had published them in the six-monthly programme of the cinema that she was obliged to hire them. The apartment was either too cold or too hot, the bathroom too damp while the air outside was so dry and full of dirt that it gave her a pain in the lungs. But after he had thrown the pot plant on the floor she kept quiet for several hours and settled down to crochet or do crossword puzzles in the Danish newspapers that were scattered around on his chairs and sofas.

'A village in four syllables,' she asked after a long silence.

'Don't know,' he replied curtly.

The village in four syllables became the starting signal for fresh recriminations. This time they were directed at him. He made himself immune and let her ramble on about how deeply disappointed she had been over their reunion, which had been very different from her expectations because he locked himself away the whole time and regarded her as if she was air. And since they had last been together in Copenhagen a year ago she had thought about him every single day and talked about him to all her friends. But how often had he written to her in that year? Once?

'Twice!' he corrected her.

If he kept out of her way in the apartment he could get a few hours' peace, but if they met in the dining room or the corridor there was trouble at once. Either his shirt collar was threadbare or he needed a haircut. His shoes were not polished, his trousers needed pressing. If they had a meal together he looked out of the window and gave one-syllable answers when she upbraided him. At last the day came for her departure for Denmark. In the morning he excused himself by saying he had to go out to get material for an article, and just before lunch he left the apartment to avoid getting mixed up in the hectic muddle the packing of her luggage would involve. He strolled around the Right Bank most of the afternoon, bought a couple of new books on de Gaulle's foreign policy or inquired about prices of the latest models in car showrooms.

When he went home she was sitting in the hall waiting for him. She did not say hello, and he knew at once there was trouble in store. She followed him as he went through the rooms into the study. There she sat on the sofa and held his eyes. Hands solidly on her knees she recounted, at first slowly and didactically, then faster in a voice that broke over the stories he knew by heart, the old but to her unforgettable stories of how as a boy he broke the reliquary holding his father's ashes, and how he only got through school because she telephoned the teachers and how later he had caused the greatest sorrow of her life by giving up his studies at Copenhagen University to live like a seedy bohemian. He had to listen to how he had kept her awake night after night and finally to how happy she had been when he sent his first articles home from Paris and she thought he had changed and found his feet in a way that would have made his father happy for him. He knew what she was after and tried to control himself. There were only a few hours left of her stay and he was not going to let her go home in triumph because she had got the better of him.

'But look — look how you have ended up!'

'Where have I ended up?'

She made no reply.

'*Where* have I ended up?' he repeated.

'That business with the maid is merely a symptom,' she said in a low voice, 'and your childish behaviour at the restaurant . . . but do you really think people are not *talking* about you in Copenhagen? Saying that you . . . that you haven't *got* anywhere!'

He knew what was coming next before she had uttered it.

'You know it's only for your own good that I mention it!'

He had fallen into the trap. She knew she could always lure him out of his lair by talking about what 'people' said about him, even if these 'people' only existed in her imagination. Who could they be, these people who talked about him in Copenhagen? Her women friends, her doddery old friends with their bird brains? It would only make it ten times worse if he cross-examined her. He gave her a long look, with a lethargic expression meant to cover his defeat. But when she rose to go and put the last few things into her hand luggage, the certainty of victory was written on her back.

The sounds came at him again from all directions. The ticking of the clock on his desk, his mother trying to call the maid in the hall, footsteps from the family overhead, cars in the street, a cistern running somewhere and the telephone that kept on ringing. He put out a hand and lifted it. Copenhagen came through. A sub-editor was on the line. He roared so loudly that it hurt Mollerup's ears:

'Damn it all, Mollerup, where the hell is that interview with Jeanne Moreau?'

Jeanne Moreau. That was all he needed.

CHAPTER FIVE

Autumn was on its way. The first carts selling roasted chestnuts appeared on the boulevards. The wind cut into people's cheeks and fallen leaves heaped themselves in big piles in the gutters or stuck fast to the roads when a sudden squall came and made pedestrians take shelter in doorways and beneath the awnings of cafés and shops. The restaurants had long since passed their holiday closing period, and the numbers of tourists dwindled by the day. The newspapers wrote about the steadily increasing dissatisfaction with de Gaulle after his press conference in July, about the mercenaries' intervention in the Congo and about the war in Vietnam. There were rumours that de Gaulle intended to send a mediator to Hanoi. Many thought it would be Malraux.

Mollerup had been closeted in his study for two weeks. A few days after his mother left he started work in earnest, after first doing a long interview with Anna Karina whom he had succeeded in contacting. For the eighth time that year he gave up trying to get hold of Jeanne Moreau. He worked on his book from morning till night and finally took yet another chapter from the German author's book and altered it slightly here and there. He actually had the manuscript ready on time and in the same breath wrote a lecture on the transformation of France which he was to give at the Danish Club. He sent off the manuscript by express post to Copenhagen and a couple of days later a telegram came from the publisher: *MS received stop splendid work stop anticipate big sales.* The weeks of concentrated work had exhausted him physically and when he went to a café he almost dropped off the whole time as the events of the past few months came back to him. He knew everything had been mere coincidence, but he still felt as if he had been the victim of an invisible conspiracy. He smiled at the word. Conspiracy. If he revealed his thoughts to others they would think him infantile. But suddenly she was there again, his mother. Just beside him. Her searching and reproachful eyes. And next he was at de Gaulle's press conference again listening to himself putting his question and faint laughter coming from the back of the otherwise silent hall and the man with the microphone stopped chewing his licorice pastille and the two American journalists in the row in front of him turned round and gave him a resigned look. He blushed. He could sit here alone at a table at the back of a café and blush like a schoolboy although no one was looking at him, neither the waiter behind the counter busy putting glasses in place nor a man putting coins into the juke box near the door. And then above all, that Ellesøe who must appear like a jack-in-the-box and make a fool of him. But the thought of the publisher's telegram bolstered him up. *Splendid work stop.*

As he grew less tired it dawned on him that the book would mark the long awaited turning point in his life and that he had merely been through a crisis that lasted longer than normal. The mid-life crisis? He determined to start a new life at once. He would begin with a thorough spring-clean. He sacked the Spanish maid, who had been so much on her high horse since his mother left that she would scarcely answer when he called her. Instead he took on a cleaning woman for four hours every morning. The apartment was soon so sparkling he could hardly bear to be in it, either at the newly-polished desk or on the sofa by the table. The final part of the clearance was what he looked forward to most. He had collected all his scrapbooks in a pile and carried them down the kitchen stairs and out into the middle of the yard. He poured petrol over the pile and put a match to it. The flames quickly took hold and page after page with glued-in articles 'from our correspondent in Paris' curled up and blackened. On top of the pile he threw the exercise books he used for smaller articles, the chatty articles signed Monsieur Jean. The burning of these in particular gave him a feeling of liberation. From now on he would no longer use the pseudonym Monsieur Jean. From now on he would be called Max Mollerup again.

The money from his publisher enabled him to re-equip himself. He drove around the boulevards in his new clothes and amused himself closing his eyes for a long second before opening them again while he told himself that this was the first time he was in Paris. Behind him like a stage he had surmounted months of hopelessness and lack of self-confidence, before him was a new unknown place to take possession of, a town where he would find himself and live life as it ought to be lived. The Italian woman came to mind. He had forgotten that for weeks he had gone around with her orange visiting card in his wallet and that she had obviously been interested when he invited her out, when she had given him the card and vanished without saying goodbye. But what did she look like? He remembered the impression she had made on him, an impression of something almost demonstratively graceful, at once present and not present. Her black hair, he could remember that. Thick black hair with a tortoiseshell clasp. And he could remember her light-coloured calf-length leather boots and her thigh-length raincoat with the belt loosely fastened and under it the wine-coloured dress. Was it wine-coloured? Red, anyway. And her modern tea-cup-circular glasses, he would be able to distinguish them if he saw them. And he could picture her hand when she drew a circle slanting down over an engraving by Ellesøe, a slim hand with long unlaquered nails, and while he thought of her hand he heard her voice, her non-committal voice with a nasal Italian accent explaining that in her view Scandinavian art was far too heavy. He could recall everything about her with the exception of her face.

He pulled up when he found a parking space and took out the visiting card. Her big upright hand somehow did not fit the impression he had formed of her. She ought to write with small, backward leaning letters. The Rue de

Dragon where she lived was only a few minutes from where he found himself. What if he went round there? No, it would be better to ring, after all, and he soon found a café with a telephone. The walls of the kiosk were covered with pencil drawings and abusive words about de Gaulle and his ministers. After trying to make out some of the messages he plucked up courage and rang her. But the moment the ringing tone stopped and a woman's voice answered he fell dumb. The air in the kiosk soon grew so stifling from his heat that he couldn't breathe. *Alloo!* the voice said again and now he was sure it was hers and a strange urge to irritate her rose in him. He let her go on asking again and again if there was anyone there and heard her clicking the telephone irritatedly before he rang off. And then came a feeling of humiliation. He hated telephone boxes and always had trouble calming himself after ringing people in Paris he needed to contact as a journalist. Each time he saw himself in the role of the eternally pushing foreigner with a placard saying 'Excuse me, here I am!' on his back. Then he dried the sweat in his armpits with his handkerchief, straightened his tie and struck his fist hard against the wall to beat the feeling of inferiority out of his body, and when he rang the second time he made use of the old trick of telling himself that a simple phone call wouldn't kill him, for God's sake. He found his voice when the Italian woman answered again, without a quaver he asked her if she could remember him, and of course she could. 'Oh, it's *you*,' she said, and he laughed aloud and began to draw on the wall with a stump of pencil that lay on the crumpled telephone directories. When she said it was a long time since they met and she had been expecting him to ring before now he grew quite confident, and when he laughed again it was partly at himself for his timidity. Holding the receiver firmly between his shoulder and his ear because he needed his hands free to get out his diary he told her he had had a lot to do since the exhibition at the Danish House, he had had to shut himself in to finish a book, and you can't get through a book in a weekend. 'I understand that,' she interrupted. And then he asked her out. She agreed to the date he suggested.

'By the way, was it you who rang just now?' she asked.

'Was it me who . . . no!'

He glanced at a drawing of Sartre embracing a nude Brigitte Bardot with his trousers round his ankles. *That's all he wants,* was written above the drawing. *The shit.*

'It's such a childish thing to do, to ring and then put the receiver down,' she said, and he had to agree with her.

She was in a brown checked trouser suit and had left her hair free so she had to keep brushing it back from her forehead with two fingers. They had arranged to meet at the Deux Magots and their table was only a few meters away from one where some Danish students behaved as if they owned the place. He thought of telling them that French people who did not know what the Danish student's cap meant would take them for members of a Visiting German choir, but then he would probably have to join them and give them good advice on what to do in Paris, and he didn't much want to do that just then. The Italian woman took a gold cigarette case from her large portmanteau-like bag and leaned forwards across the table to get a light from him. His nose caught her perfume. The same one as last time? He was about to ask, but instead she was the one to get their sluggish conversation going. He himself was on his fourth cigarette in a quarter of an hour.

'How long have you lived in Paris?' she asked him.

'Ten years,' he replied.

'You're a native then!'

'And you?' he asked.

'Four years. I lived in Spain for a few years after leaving Italy. And then four years here in Paris.'

The Danish students had a bet on about how old the Italian woman was. They measured her from top to toe and made loud comments on her appearance. He had to listen to all kinds of comments on how good she must be in bed, how her hair would be lovely to bury your nose in and of how she must be aristocratic because she was so beautifully dressed. 'And her make-up!' said one. 'Danish girls look like dishcloths compared to her!' 'Thirty!' came from another, the smallest and fattest of them with prominent frog-like eyes. 'Thirty-five at least!' said a third. Mollerup was scared that they would soon start discussing him, as men out with attractive women are discussed. Forty-five! No, forty-eight, at least! An impulse made him push his chair back from the table so he could dash outside. At the kiosk close by he bought the previous day's Danish newspaper and pushed it into his jacket pocket with the headline showing. On his way back he wondered which of the students had guessed right, if the Italian woman was thirty or at least thirty-five.

'I just wanted to see if I had an important article in the paper today,' he said when he went back and put the paper on the table as a clear indication to the students that he understood every word they said. It wasn't long before they caught sight of the paper and turned their faces away whispering.

'Oh, yes, of course, you're a journalist.'

Was she annoyed? Had his action offended her, made her feel superfluous? She took a diary from her bag and wrote something with a little lady's fountain pen with a silver tassle on the cap. She spent some time leafing through the notebook. Then she put it back in her bag, gave him her attention again and looked at him ironically, as if to say that now they were on equal terms.

'Have you ever been to Spain?' she asked.

'I spent a month there some years ago. But I don't care for it much, maybe because of the heat. The south of France, on the other hand . . .'

'And Italy?' she asked, biting the nail of her index finger.

'No.'

He noticed she was taken aback. Of course it must sound pretty silly that as a journalist he had never been to Italy, and he should have found a way of explaining to her that he had always had an irrational aversion to Italy that went back to the years just after the war when a student friend went to Italy for a summer holiday and would go on for months afterwards about how cheap things were in Rome. He came to associate Italy with the Square of Our Lady in Copenhagen, where the main university building lay, and where he and his friend exchanged enthusiastic travel stories while putting on their cycle clips. In his mind Italy became a place where enterprising Scandinavian academics took their recreation dressed in khaki shorts and sandals. But how could he explain to her that his aversion to Italy was linked to his student friend's cycle clips? She would laugh. Or shake her head.

'There's a powerful upper class in Italy, isn't there?' he asked, out of the blue. Desperately searching for a remark that could lead her mind elsewhere.

'Isn't that so everywhere?' she replied.

They said nothing for a long time. He was sure their relationship was already doomed, that they had nothing to say to each other and that it had been a mistake to even ring her up. She knocked the ash off her cigarette into the Martini ashtray, he rolled the bill the waiter had put down on the table between thumb and index finger so it was no bigger than a match. Now and then she stole a look at him, and he felt that at any moment she would put on her sunglasses, slide her fingers through her hair and find some excuse to leave him sitting with the Danish students and their giggling girl friends. Suddenly she smiled:

'You should have met my father . . .'

'I should have loved to,' he said, bewildered.

'He's dead,' she said. 'He was exactly like one of those Italians you see in American gangster films from the forties. He never had any education and I really believe he never opened a book. But he had the knack of making money fall from trees. I came to think of him when you asked if there was a powerful upper class in Italy . . .'

She spoke in a low well-controlled voice, without having to search for words or any sign of natural uncertainty from having once more to initiate the conversation. She started drawing little black dolls on the back of the bill. For fun he took out his own ball-point pen to draw as well, but she pulled the bill away, her smile becoming clear laughter:

'There's not room for us both!'

She stopped laughing:

'But tell me about your parents.'

'My father is dead too,' he replied.

She had filled the back of the bill with black dolls and unfolded the wrapping from a piece of sugar to use that. Now she drew abstract patterns.

'Forgive me, I didn't mean . . .' she went on, with her eyes on the table.

'Oh, it doesn't worry me,' he answered. 'My father died ages ago. But my mother is still alive. She is an actress. Or rather, was. Marianne Mollerup, you may have heard of her.'

'Is *she* your mother!'

She looked up from the table, put down her pen and crushed the sugar paper into a little ball which she put in the ashtray. She seemed both surprised and impressed and asked again if Marianne Mollerup really was his mother. Her reaction braced him, suddenly all his uncertainty blew away, he had taken the lead without realizing it and had no difficulty finding the right words as he told her he had just had a visit from his mother. He described their game of bowls and the black man who offered a straight throw, but was rebuffed because she said she could do it herself. The Italian woman laughed a lot at that and put her pen back into her bag so as to concentrate on what he was saying. He went on to tell her of his mother's energy in going round visiting film distributors and spiced his narrative with little anecdotes about her putting margarine on her bread to prevent hardening of the arteries. He smiled to himself over a picture of his mother that had suddenly become sympathetic, but now she had gone there was no need to saddle his date with unpleasant details — details relegated to his past crisis. It must be a good sign that a gloomy period of his life was over and done with that he did not feel any pain and could even talk about his mother with a trace of pride in his voice. Right out to his fingertips he could feel he had caught the Italian woman's interest, for the first time she saw him as other and more than a chance person she had made a date with. He could not stop talking, and even the story of how his mother had once appeared on the stage of the Comédie Française although she could not speak a word of French seemed full of meaning as he recounted it:

'She simply learned the French dialogue by heart — with some help from a secretary at the French embassy in Copenhagen!'

'How *well* you describe it . . .'

'If you like . . .' he hesitated, then went on: 'If you like I could get you an interview with her. You told me you were going to Denmark to write some articles . . . or perhaps you've already been?'

'The trip has been postponed till Christmas time,' she replied. 'But an interview . . . do you think she would really . . . that your mother would agree?'

'Of course! I shall be glad to introduce you . . .'

'I'm looking forward more and more to my visit to Denmark . . .'

She was still regarding him with curiosity:

'I've always longed to see Scandinavia. I've been told the Scandinavians are very friendly people, but that it's only the Danes who have a sense of humour?'

He shrugged his shoulders deprecatingly. But as she was waiting for an answer he had to admit there was something in it, that the Danes were jolly folk. And soon he was carried away by his words again. Denmark turned into a friendly, smiling land where you always had time for a pleasant chat about life. For a moment he felt ashamed to serve up the old jokes about the Danish attitude to the Germans during the war, but suddenly he had launched into various anecdotes. The first of them fell on good ground, the next he recounted with a touch of nervousness in his voice. He felt he might be boring the Italian woman who had started to fold the sugar papers again. He paused, then finished with the story of the

German soldier on guard at Amalienborg, the royal palace in Copenhagen, in an armed guardhouse. The German could not understand why the Danes always nearly fell off their cycles laughing when they rode past him until another German explained the reason: *He's got no trousers on* had been written in chalk on the guardhouse. He shook his head when he finished the story and did not laugh at it, as if to avow that he didn't think it was specially original and funny though probably typical. But now she was smiling surprisingly broadly and repeating that she was looking forward to going north when there was snow in Denmark and lighted Christmas trees outside all the houses. He suggested happily that they should go to the Danish shop near the Arc de Triomphe. There she could get a little feel of Denmark.

Meanwhile the students were on their way out. At the door they turned and looked at him. Lipreading he saw they were saying: 'He's Danish.'

In one of the windows she admired a big round table topped with orange-coloured tiles, but when he said the table would cost at least a thousand francs she giggled a bit and pulled him along to the next window where she pointed at a set of coffee cups in various bright peasant colours with little pegs instead of handles. While she was enthusing over them he caught sight of the lame proprietor inside the shop. He had once made himself unpopular with him because he had done an article for the back page accusing the shop of spoiling the world renown of Danish decorative art by selling inferior goods. He had written the article in the form of an open letter to the Danes responsible for this, from the average French citizen Monsieur Jean who had bought articles for his daughter and in the sincere belief that Danish goods meant quality had been palmed off with a lot of useless furniture. To his great surprise the proprietor's face lit up with a welcoming smile, he reached for his stick and came limping out onto the pavement saying the open letter hadn't been so ill-placed after all, it had put the fear of God into his suppliers in

Copenhagen. Wouldn't he like to take a look round? He remarked to the Italian woman that prices were particularly advantageous at the moment.

Before leaving them to themselves the proprietor let drop that he wouldn't mind if Monsieur Jean wrote another open letter pointing out that the Danish furniture wasn't as bad as he had thought. Mollerup promised to think about it. The last thing he wanted was to tell the man that Monsieur Jean no longer existed, and he hurried over to the Italian woman, who had not understood a word of the conversation; she was holding some pieces of silver jewellery up to the light and trying them on her wrist and fingers. He opened his wallet behind her back to see how much money he had on him, then waved to an assistant to come over and asked her to wrap up a bracelet, but without letting her see. The assistant caught on at once and took the bracelet from under the nose of the Italian woman on the pretext that it was to be sent to the south of France. After he had taken the package and they eventually left the shop his companion was full of praise for what she had seen. How she would like to furnish her home with Scandinavian furniture. Danish furniture. Her home? It struck him: was she married? Hadn't she originally introduced herself as Madame? Maybe she was divorced. When they had been out on the pavement for a while she wanted to go back to the window with the orange-topped table. He walked a step behind her and slipped the package with the silver bracelet into her pocket.

Her reaction was not at all what he had expected. Had he expected her to fall on his neck with gratitude? Whatever it was, he thought it strange that she opened the package and unwrapped the bracelet without turning a hair. She fastened it on her wrist and put the velvet-lined case back in her pocket after crushing the wrapping paper and throwing it into the gutter. Eventually she looked directly at him, the hint of a smile spread across her delicate lips. She looked at him as if to say he should not have done that. For a moment he cursed his impulse. She could at least say thank you. Behave as if she liked the gift.

Then she took him by the arm:
'I know a really good little restaurant.'

There was thick flocked wallpaper on the walls. The tables were set close together, and the Indian chef, standing beside the door turning iron skewers holding pieces of meat and peppers over a pan of charcoal, yelled excitedly when he was pushed by a group of guests waiting for tables in a crowd by the entrance. The two waiters and a younger, Yul Brynner-bald man behind the till carried on a loud shouting conversation. When the bald man caught sight of the Italian woman he rose and found a table for her. Some of the people waiting grumbled at the special treatment. They had certainly been standing there much longer than she had.

'This lady has *booked* a table!' the bald man shouted back.

As thanks for his little white lie he got a kiss on both cheeks and one on his forehead. Mollerup felt more and more sure there must be something between them. The bald man was the self-confident, Latin type, slim and sporty, unshaven without seeming distasteful, the type who rode and played tennis and went on weekend trips to Brittany. When he left them to fetch the menu he came back with a whole series of jokes. The Italian woman clutched her mouth with laughter. People laughed at the neighbouring tables as well, and a young man he vaguely recalled from his mother's reception called to the Italian woman, so she turned her face towards him and rounded her lips into a kiss. He felt that everyone in the restaurant knew each other. The feeling grew stronger when his companion told the people nearest them that he was the son of no less than the world famous Marianne Mollerup. He had to nod around at people for a long time. Then they were left to themselves. They agreed to have grilled corncobs as a starter and then brochettes with cocktail sausages and pieces of mutton.When she had given their order to a waiter sent to their table by the bald man she rested her chin on her hands.

'Why did you give me the silver bracelet, actually?' she asked quietly.

He poured wine for them both.

'Because it suits you,' he said. Pretty stupid.

She quickly dropped the subject. She looked as if she regretted the question and instead joked at the fact that pieces from the corn on the cobs, which the waiter had put in front of them, stuck in their teeth. She split a match lengthways and gave him one half to clean his teeth with. At first he thought this distasteful, but she insisted and pointed at other diners picking their teeth, and for the first time she seemed to him to be suddenly frank and relaxed, as if in her eyes it was a completely normal event that they should be sitting eating corncobs together and she pass him a split match to pick bits of corn out of his teeth. At that moment it seemed they were intimate with each other down to the last detail, the few hours they had spent together might be several weeks. And yet. Why did she still say nothing about being pleased with the bracelet? She must be pleased with it since she kept it on and kept caressing the clasp. Why didn't she regard his having given her a silver chain in memory of their visit to the Danish shop as something as normal as her splitting a match and giving it to him as a toothpick?

She poured more wine for them both and put the half eaten corncob back on her plate before pushing it away with the back of her hand. Then she opened the box of matches and shook out all the matches on to the table. No, we don't need so many matches for that, she said gaily when he looked at her in surprise and said he really didn't have any more bits stuck in his teeth. She just wanted to play something with him. She arranged five matches to look like a dustpan. Four made a closed square, the fifth was the handle. She put the sulphur from a sixth match into the square. By taking away three matches he must get the dustpan turned round the other way so that the sulphur was not enclosed. The dustpan must look exactly the same as before, a closed square with the fifth match as a handle. For a long time he tried various possibilities, but each time the handle was left inside the square if the matches did not fall into a pattern which had nothing to do with a dustpan.

'I'm not allowed to move *four* matches?' he asked.

She shook her head. In the end he gave up when the handle once more came to lie inside the square.

'No, no . . . like this.'

She put all the matches back in the box when the waiter brought the next course and took away the corncobs. While they pulled the mutton and cocktail sausages off the metal pins he racked his brains for a match trick to surprise her with. But he could see from her expression that her thoughts had moved on. She studied her plate absently. Then she met his eyes: 'Are you married? As far as I remember you said you weren't when we met the first time . . .'

'No, I'm not married,' he replied and pondered what meaning she had put into the words 'first time.' It was as if she emphasized that from now on they would be seeing each other regularly. He pushed his plate aside and lit a cigarette in high spirits.

'You must have plenty of opportunities. I mean, with the job you have.'

'You shouldn't get married just for the sake of it.'

'I didn't mean it like that.'

'Are you married? As far as I can remember you introduced yourself as Madame . . .'

'I am married,' she replied, biting her cheek. 'And yet I am not.'

'What do you mean?' he asked when she paused.

'I am officially married to a Spaniard. He is a painter. We separated a couple of years ago, but in Spanish law we can't be divorced. That means I can't marry again even if I want to.'

'That might be an advantage,' he said, trying to sound ironic.

Suddenly a business-like note had sprung up between them. Every time she had asked him a question he felt he had to ask her one in turn. Their conversation seemed to have become a mutual cross-questioning.

At the next table a young man was trying to make sounds like a Jaguar sportscar going down a mountainside in second gear. Then he made the noise of an atom bomb exploding while forming the shape of a mushroom with his arms. When he had finished various people applauded him. The Italian woman joined in the clapping.

'But I suppose you know many women?' she asked, in a different tone, jokingly.

'Many and many. Of course I've had a few girlfriends in my time . . .'

'But no one you wanted to live with?'

'There was one. I met a girl, she was Danish and she lived in Paris and worked at the Danish embassy. We decided to move in together, and we might have got married . . .'

So far what he said was right. Eight years previously he had met a Danish girl. Their relationship lasted six months. They were both lonely, he was living in hotels on the Left Bank for the second year running, she had a little attic room in the home of a French family. Neither of them knew anyone else and they met by chance while they were both drifting around town. They actually bumped into each other on a street corner, and when he said pardon she replied with a pure Danish *undskyld*. They went out together a couple of times a week. When they made love, as a rule in his hotel room in the early hours, it was without any special emotion, let alone love. It was the natural need to break out of the loneliness of being in Paris which bound them together, and they also shared the same kind of humour and could amuse themselves for hours mocking the French and their solemnity. When they decided to move in together it was still purely on grounds of convenience rather than emotion. They found a flat near the Place de la Bastille with a room each. They agreed that both should be completely free, if he brought a girl home or she had a man friend in they would just put a note on the front door warning not to disturb. But one day when he went to fetch her and help move her things to the flat he was told she had been killed in a car accident near Versailles. He was shocked and at first refused to believe what the lady of the house where she lived told him with a sorrowful face and a voice choked with tears. But as time went on he met other girls, casual relationships that might last a week or a couple of months, and he began to forget her. Years could pass in which he did not think of her, but in the last six or eight months she had returned to his mind. When he was alone in the apartment he would suddenly start to experiment with wondering what his life would have been like if she had not died, if their friendship had grown into passion and passion into love. And now while he was telling the Italian woman about her, he felt how for the third time that day words took control over him. He described his lost Danish friend as something infinitely beautiful, something poetically Nordic. He described feelingly her fair Jeanne d'Arc hairstyle, her freckled nose, mother-of-pearl coloured eyes and gentle nature. When he got to the day when he heard of her death he tried to put a damper on himself but inevitably began to dramatize, so that the Italian woman looked at him with the same expression as when he told her about his mother. He could feel himself again becoming *interesting* in her eyes. At last he came to an end. He offered her a cigarette.

'And there hasn't been anyone since then?' she asked diffidently, winding a lock of hair around her finger.

'There has,' he replied. 'But not in the same way. Falling in love . . . that seems to be something I have finished with.'

They paid and left the restaurant. On the way out she blew a kiss to the bald man. They walked down to the Seine. Not until they reached the booksellers did he dare take her arm. They did not speak, but when a river boat, with washing fluttering over the cargo, sailed past she pointed at it rapturously and followed it with her eyes until it disappeared under a bridge. She leaned against him and did not resist when he took her by the shoulders. A little later his arm was around her waist. They still did not speak, but she laughed several times while she tried to match her stride to his.

Then she said she had better go now, she was expecting

visitors and had a lot to do, putting out glasses and making supper. She would like to invite him, but the guests were close friends and relatives from Italy. He was annoyed with himself not to have been the one to suggest parting, in half an hour he had to give his lecture on the Transformation of France at the Danish Club. She moved away from him a little, twisting her bracelet. When he took hold of her arms and cautiously drew her towards him, she made no resistance. He kissed her. Her lips were just as soft as he had imagined them. Her tongue played with his teeth for a moment, then she freed herself and shook her head as if regretting the kiss. She vanished over on to the opposite pavement. When he called to her that he would ring her one day she did not reply but went down a side street. A few moments later she came back and called across to him that she was in every morning until eleven.

He hadn't expected such a crowd to turn up. He glanced warily in at the window of the clubroom situated behind the Danish House. The audience filled the whole room, mostly country girls employed as nannies by French families, who all knew each other. The club was run by the Danish pastor, who invited lecturers at least twice a month, either from Copenhagen or from the circle of Scandinavian artists and correspondents in Paris. Mollerup had been on the list of lecturers several times during the past year, but each time the day approached when he was to speak on 'The Metamorphosis of France From Anarchy to Technocracy' he cried off at the last moment because he had not finished preparing his lecture. Now at long last he had succeeded in finishing it, and in the passageway leading to the clubroom he stopped and read it through for the last time. Then he noticed his name on the notice board: *Max Mollerup on the Metamorphosis of France. Danish coffee and layer cake.* Somebody or other had amused themselves by adding an *at last* in front of his name. A hum of voices came from the clubroom and he opened the door and looked in. In one of the front rows he caught sight of Rolf Hauge. He could also see the proprietor of the Danish shop and Munk, the student he had not seen since de Gaulle's press conference. He felt a stab of disquiet. Munk had obviously come along for the sole reason of embarrassing him, of criticizing his talk no matter what he said. He was so cocky he was convinced he was the only person to have any understanding of what France was like. Mollerup shut the door again and sat down on a bench rolling his script together. He could still manage to disappear and phone an excuse from a kiosk. No one had seen him yet. He could say he was ill. But no. That would be contemptible. And besides, it was time he showed the rest of the colony what he was worth.

It went much better than he had expected. To start with his hands shook and his throat felt dry, but after a while he noticed his audience was really listening. After a short introduction in which he explained that unfortunately a lecture that spanned more than twenty years of French history could not go into depth, hc made a good impression straight away with a description of the existentialists he had met when he came to Paris in the mid-fifties. He talked about the long-haired young people who established themselves as a group in the Paris sewers. There they lived, day and night, they swore they would never go back to the rotten society above ground. Now and then food was lowered to them through one of the entrances to the sewers, but if they had almost starved for some time they thought nothing of slaughtering the meter-long, snow white rats that ran around their legs. 'Are they still living down there?' a girl asked, shuddering. 'Who, the rats or the existentialists?' he replied, looking up from his script. 'The existentialists,' said the girl. 'I'm sure they are!' he responded with a smile.

Then the lecture changed character. He left the exotic and neared the point when de Gaulle came to power. He gave a succinct outline of the character of this coup d'état, and then the way was open to a general description of the astonishing change that had taken place in France during the past six years. From being an impoverished house divided against itself, France had become the leading nation in Europe. This had altered the French people to such a degree that they had acquired a completely different character. Where before young people lived in the sewers and listened to Juliette Greco's nihilistic songs, today they were the most bourgeois in Europe. He ended with a paradox: if you want to experience Paris, the Paris beloved of generations of foreigners, decadent Paris, the art capital of easy virtue you must go to — London.

His lecture was received with enthusiasm and as soon as he had finished a lively discussion took place. It turned out that most of the girls had known a Jean-François or Jean-Luc at some time or other who had deserted them after making them pregnant. And why did they desert them? Because they had to take exams, of course. The girls were loud in their complaints, and one went so far as to demand that articles should be published every year in the Danish newspapers warning nice friendly Danish girls not to go to France. When the discussion threatened to become a shouting match Mollerup felt obliged to say that his lecture was not meant as a general slating of France. Paris was still the city where everyone could find what he wanted, could live his own life as in no other place. He admitted that Frenchmen's sexual morals were more cynical than those of Danes, but on the other hand it could hardly be inaccurate to maintain that Danish girls in Paris were too gullible and blue-eyed. Silence fell in the hall, but a few girls grumbled that he should just try being a girl in Paris, it was worse than being a negro in the USA. But maybe he was right to say the Danish girls were too naive. After all, he knew more about Paris, having lived there for so long. This last remark came from the minister's wife. Then the chairs were pushed aside to make room for the coffee tables and layer cake.

Now was the psychological moment to leave the gathering, he said to himself, gathering up his script. Rolf Hauge was engaged in convincing a group of girls that Paris was still the place for anyone who wanted to get on, to be famous, internationally renowned, like Anna Karina and himself. Munk, who strangely enough had at no time made any attempt to argue with him, was helping the minister's wife to put out the layer cakes on the long pine trestle tables that were arranged with much clattering in three rows facing the yellowing photographs of the Danish king and queen. As Mollerup went through the hall he nodded courteously to the gathering, no, he wasn't leaving, he was just going to the toilet, that's everyone's right! He went into the passage and closed the door carefully behind him. The Danish newspapers for the day lay on a chair, just delivered by the postman. He leafed quickly through them. In his own paper he saw a sizeable article announcing that Monsieur Jean, our well-known Paris correspondent, would publish a book about Paris before Christmas, a book unlike any other Paris book. Paris From The Shady Side *was a shattering description of a town which from being the home of lovers and art had become a melancholy heap of stones offering no shelter for human kindness*. Above the article, clearly written by one of the apprentice journalists, was a youthful picture of him. His hair was thick and curly, he sported a small moustache and his cheeks were hollow. He wore an open-necked shirt. Had the picture been taken in the summer? And when? Suddenly he felt nervous at seeing himself in the paper as the author of *Paris From The Shady Side*. He grabbed the paper Lund worked for to see if his book was mentioned there too. It was: a brief paragraph on the culture page noted that the Parisian Dane Max Mollerup would soon publish a book on his experiences of the French. While he snorted at being described in Lund's paper as a Dane living in Paris, it made him wonder whether the book could measure up to the appetizing preview in his own paper, whether it would be run down by the bilious critics, whether in short he would be laughed at for it. Would they also spot that two chapters of *Paris From The Shady Side* approximated closely to the German correspondent's description of Paris? He put the idea away from him. Of course the book would be a success. *Laughed aloud several times stop*. Then he felt a hand on his shoulder. He turned and looked straight into Rolf Hauge's watery blue eyes:

'Mollerup! Old sport! What about that interview you promised me? Bloody hell!'

He tried to put him off by saying he would phone in a day or two, although he knew that was the last thing he intended. From now on he would have nothing to do with Danes in Paris. From now on he would choose his friends for himself. Then the proprietor of the Danish shop appeared as well:

'Now you won't forget that open letter with the assurance that my goods are top quality again?'

He looked from Rolf Hauge to the proprietor and back to Rolf Hauge.

'Has he promised *you* PR as well?' asked Rolf Hauge.

'I'll ring next week,' Mollerup repeated. 'Then we'll do both the interview and the open letter, and all three of us will be happy.' Then he turned on his heel and vanished with a smile.

Down in the courtyard restaurant, packed with Parisians under the umbrellas in red and white Danish colours, he turned round for the last time and looked in at the windows of the Danish Club where a few groups of girls were still gesticulating wildly. It made him think of an aquarium at his fish shop. At one end of it the fish would crowd together around the chromium air pipe so they looked as if they would be smothered, but at the other end there would always be a single fish swimming around with plenty of room to frisk in. While the others at the club from now until long after midnight would be smothered in discussions on Paris, with Rolf Hauge and his family on one side, the au pair girls on the other and the minister and his wife as mediators. While the stored-up aggression towards Parisians would give rise to fresh violent salvos and the longing for Denmark would pass like a ghost through the hall with the pine trestle tables, the photographs of the royal couple and the minister's wife's home-made layer cakes, he was already on his way into Paris, the Paris nobody could cram into a formula, that vanished like a shadow every time you thought you had grasped something of the town, which transformed itself from day to day, from hour to hour. You could agree with someone that Paris was this and that, but when you were out on the boulevards the next moment the words didn't fit any more. It was with a feeling of wordless relief that he emerged into the Champs-Elysées where thousands of pedestrians hurried past. He slipped into the crowd and let himself be carried along with it. With each step that separated him from the Danish Club an awareness rose in him that now he had brought a chapter of his life to an end, that he had put a section of suffocating past years as a member of the Danish colony behind him. He was on the way to something new.

A sudden rain squall shook the tree tops by the Rond Point. A fur-clad prostitute in a sports car drove along beside him and waved. He smiled at her and walked on down to the Seine. He picked up an old walking stick from under a bench and when he passed a tree he struck it with the stick. With each tree he hit he shattered a piece of the past, he struck his mother's visit out of the world, and Rolf Hauge's party, and de Gaulle's press conference, he struck Lund out of the world, and Munk, and the proprietor of the Danish shop. They all vanished, one by one, and when he reached the statue of King Albert at the Place de la Concorde and there were no more trees to hit he threw it with all his might into the middle of the river. Although he again had trouble recalling the Italian woman's face he was filled with a tingling physical warmth, a warmth he had not felt since he was a student and in love for the first time. As he went past the National Assembly he felt liberated as never before, and he could have sung for joy, could have shouted it out over the street. The Boulevard St-Germain lay before him in the misty nocturnal autumn light. People in restaurants were having dinner, most of them were at the coffee and cognac stage and looked satisfied and mellow. He stopped on a metro grating and took the dry scent of trains and human sweat and cigarettes deep into his lungs. He was happy. And Paris responded to his happiness by suddenly opening out to him with its houses, its balconies, its rushing traffic, its beautiful women walking past him in the twilight, its cats in doorways and its quiet rain falling on the treetops, dripping from the branches to fall on the gratings around the tree roots. He undid his raincoat so the rain fell on his neck and down his shirtfront. The rain was as warm as summer rain but the growing heaps of yellowed leaves showed that winter was near. He had come to the Rue du Dragon where the Italian woman lived at Number 34. He turned into the street and stopped opposite her street door. He looked up at the façade. There was light on the third floor. He went into a shadowy doorway and in one of the lighted windows suddenly caught sight of the bald man from the restaurant where the Italian woman had taken him for dinner. For a moment he thought of going up. When the bald man was there she could not be entertaining only the family from Italy. But perhaps he was more than a friend, perhaps he was her cousin or half brother? He just wanted to see the place where she lived, see the door he would pass through when he went to fetch her in future to take her out to dinner or the cinema or theatre, or for weekends beside the Atlantic. Then shouts and screams came from one end of the Rue du Dragon. A crowd of young people came lurching towards him. Too late he realized they were the Danish students from earlier in the day.

'There he is again,' one of them shouted, dancing around tipsily. 'There he bloody well is again. *The Dane . . .*'

He retreated right inside the shadows of the doorway.

CHAPTER SIX

The dance floor was closely packed with young men with sideburns and girls in strap shoes and almost see-through thin dresses. Black waiters sidled among the guests while four turning projectors in each corner threw a yellow, a blue, a red and a green light over the hall. The Italian woman was sitting on a red 1890s sofa. She sat between a fat writer with frameless glasses and a tall gangling painter whose most striking feature was a thick tuft of hair sticking out of each nostril. Earlier in the evening she had explained to him that they were old friends of hers — like the bald man. No, he was really neither her half brother nor cousin, she assured him when he insisted they were like each other. They had not talked about much else that evening, and he wondered when the conversation would really get going.

During the weeks since he had met her they had phoned each other regularly and chatted about all kinds of things. Mostly she was interested in hearing facts about Denmark. Each time he said he would help by showing her around Copenhagen when they were there together at Christmas. Eventually what he had been hoping for all the time came about: she invited him home. But when he arrived he was disappointed to find the bald man and the one with the crewcut, whom she introduced as a writer, already installed. Soon afterwards the painter arrived too. But perhaps it was not yet time to get to know her better, he thought. With a southerner's feel for the rules of the game, she probably wanted to test him out for a while, and he tried to seem relaxed when they all sat on her bedroom floor playing Wagner on a record player. He assumed the same mien as the others, an expression that said that very little in the world affected him while at the same time he made himself out to be familiar with Wagner. When they were walking to a night club later it seemed as if none of them knew each other. The bald man walked by himself on the opposite side of the street, the crewcut writer vanished for a time into a late-night bookshop. Now they had been sitting near the band for a couple of hours, the bald man with his hands to his temples and his eyes fixed on the black marble table, the crewcut writer with his hands behind his neck and his legs stretched out so his feet rocked on the heels of his shoes, the painter was engaged in sketching the dancers and only the Italian woman exhibited some restlessness when she took a mirror out of her bag and re-applied her lipstick.

Mollerup found it hard to keep quiet. He badly wanted to make more contact with the others, although he well knew that their silence was not coldness so much as lack of interest in him as in any other foreigner. After a while he went and sat at the bar by himself. He started to talk to a broad-shouldered fair-haired man, who turned out to be Swedish. When Mollerup said he was Danish the Swede leaned towards him and told him the story of his life. He had lived in Paris for five years as a correspondent and the whole time he had asked in vain at restaurants and shops for the cowberry jam you could get in Sweden. Now he wanted to go home, back to Stockholm, to his apartment on Söder that was free now his divorced wife had died. Mollerup reckoned the Swede, who was getting more and more drunk, must be about the same age as himself.

Suddenly the Italian woman was standing between them. Mollerup was surprised and didn't know whether to introduce her to the Swede, but she took the glass from his hand and said she wanted to dance, and before he knew it he was in the middle of the floor. From the start she held him close, with both arms round his waist and her forehead against his neck. His heart beat so hard she must have felt it. He put one hand on her back and let it slowly slide up to her neck so her hair fell over his hand.

'Were you surprised?' she asked in a low voice.

'Surprised?'

'Yes, because I . . . wanted to dance with you?'

'I hadn't quite expected . . . .'

'I suddenly wanted to. And you didn't come to me, so the mountain had to . . .'

She leaned slightly back and looked straight into his eyes. He tried to hold her gaze by looking straight between her eyes, at the top of her nose. For a long time he did not move his pupils, and in the end she gave up and shook her head when her eyes started to water from staring at him through the tobacco smoke in the place. She put her forehead to his neck again so his chin was just over her head. She pressed closer to him, put an arm round his neck and gently scratched his nape.

Suddenly he caught sight of the Swede; arms rotating like windmill sails, he brutally shoved the dancers aside and came straight towards him. He seized the Italian woman round the waist so they could hide behind some of the dancers, but the Swede came nearer and Mollerup saw with a faint shudder that he must be at least two meters tall and almost a meter across the shoulders. It was impossible to hide from him. The Swede loomed over him with a broad grin, he took a few clumsy dancing steps to show he wanted to join in. They must dance with arms round each other's waists and show the other boring people how Scandinavians could go to town in the right way. He grabbed Mollerup's waist and the Italian's, both were lifted into the air and swung around to the accompaniment of the Swede's laughter that swelled from a suppressed clucking in his larynx to a hilarious roar. The Italian woman kicked out with her legs and punched the Swede in the neck, but not until she had lost one of her earrings and uttered a shrill shriek did he calm down and let them go, looking at them with sorrowful eyes as if he could not understand why they didn't enjoy the fun as much as he did.

When two of the toughest black waiters went over to him and seized him roughly under the arms to throw him out, he tried to resist for a moment. He shook off the two waiters like fluff and stood there swaying. Mollerup expected him to crash to the floor. But he pulled his jacket into place, buttoned it and strode with huge strides towards the exit. When he reached the cloakroom he turned round and yelled as loudly as he could:

'Bloody French!'

Not far from the nightclub they went into a restaurant that stayed open from seven in the evening until six in the morning, and ordered onion soup. His head buzzing after too many whiskies, Mollerup pondered, as the beginnings of grey morning light filtering through the windows more and more, over who the Italian woman's friends really were and why he had been invited along. Too late he realized he had crumbled a piece of bread into a hundred pieces in an absurd semicircle at the side of his plate, and he kept restraining himself from blurting out some idiotic comment or innocuous question to get the conversation going, make the others open up just slightly. Who was the bald man? Why didn't he know more about him than that he owned a restaurant or perhaps merely managed it, wore a black sweater and looked like a sporting type? And the writer — why had he only noted his crewcut, as if he had no other characteristics, and the painter with tufts in his nose? Who were those two? Was the crewcut man any good as a writer, anyway?

Who, what, how. He was tired. Just that and no more. He ascribed his increasing nerviness to that: he had been up since ten in the morning and was no longer at the age when he could stay awake for twenty-four hours without noticeable effect. His eyes were quite painful when he looked around at the old posters on the restaurant walls. The posters urged every fit young Frenchman to volunteer for the colonial forces. One poster showed an oasis in the Sahara with a French soldier holding a coconut, another a cavalry battle between a horde of Bedouins and a small company of French. The largest poster showed three faces, a Vietnamese, an Arab and a Frenchman. *Three colours, three continents, one empire* was printed at the bottom. Liberty, equality and fraternity. He looked from the poster over to the Italian woman. She returned his gaze with the smile he was beginning to know so well; a smile that perhaps might express a great deal, perhaps no more than the desire to flirt with no strings attached. But there was something inhibiting her. Something stopped her from speaking freely to him as she had the last time they met. The presence of the others?

Suddenly the crewcut writer put down his spoon.

'I was once in Sweden,' he began. 'It struck me that there is a strange *atmosphere of death* in that country. Now, the way your countryman behaved in the nightclub, his drunkenness, his craving to have a good time with other people, his shouting . . .'

Mollerup realized slowly that the man was addressing him.

'My countryman?' he tried.

'Yes, the tall Swede,' the writer went on, 'it was obvious he wanted to escape from something . . . I only once met a spunky Swede while I was in Sweden, and she was a woman. She told me, directly: being Swedish is the same as having a chronic bad conscience!'

The crewcut writer did not seem really uncongenial, thought Mollerup. There was even a certain good humour in his eyes when he took off his glasses and massaged the corners of his eyes with two fingers. His voice was high-pitched and hoarse and as he warmed to his subject he revealed a fiery nature: he gesticulated with his hands in the air, threw out his arms and laughed aloud when he described something he found amusing. It was impossible for Mollerup to break into his monologue and correct the image he had formed of Sweden as the homeland of inarticulate guilt feelings. The others listened interestedly to what he was saying but obviously believed him. Eventually he stood up, unzipped his trousers, took out his penis and held it over the plate. Mollerup was instantly wide awake because of the sudden astonishing manoeuvre, he stared fascinated at the organ. The wrinkled skin round the head, the protruding veins and the little eye-like duct opening. Then the writer stuffed the penis back again and sat down. No one in the restaurant appeared to take any notice of him, and he himself seemed restrained and natural as he remarked that the freedom the Swede prided himself on had not been acquired by exhibiting his willy.

They went up to the Boulevard St-Germain where only La Pergola was open. The juke-box there could be heard far off in the morning air. The birdsong pierced Mollerup's ears and the grey-white light of the sky beat down on the walls of the buildings and ricochetted from them into his eyes. The clock at the Mabillon showed ten past six. Some way along the boulevard, almost as far as the Deux Magots, they caught sight of the Swede with his jacket slung over one shoulder handing a handful of notes to a black girl. They all stood there for some time unsure whether to go in or not. The Italian woman had black circles under her eyes, the bald man squatted on the pavement and the painter planted his arm heavily round the crewcut writer's neck and let himself go limp. Standing there Mollerup suddenly felt amiable towards them, mutual weariness seemed to put them all in the same boat. He looked from one to the other and each time was rewarded with a friendly smile. He felt on particularly good terms with the crewcut man despite the nonsense he had talked about the Swedes. His stubble had grown and it was only now that Mollerup really noticed his face. The hard morning light revealed his porous skin with cuts here and there from shaving. He had not put on a clean shirt for days and one side of his nose bulged out in a strange way as if he had pushed a big lump of cotton wool up the nostril. Then they all agreed to make an end of the night. The Italian woman, whose eyelids kept on dropping down, kissed the painter and the bald man on the cheek. Mollerup offered his arm so they could go some of the way together, he was going her way, he wanted to pick up a taxi at the cab rank opposite the Deux Magots. But the crewcut writer, who had got into his mini-jeep that was parked nearby, waved her over and they drove off together in the middle of the road, with the horn blaring. The painter soon went off too, and Mollerup was left alone with the bald man.

It ended up with him going home with the bald man who lived only a few minutes from where they were and had half a bottle of vodka waiting they could have a go at before going to bed. On the way up the staircase they met the first residents on their way to work, and from all around came various sounds of the morning; an electric coffee grinder, a bath being run, a lavatory plug pulled and a child wailing with hunger. Mollerup moved like a sleep-walker and hadn't the energy to wonder why the bald man, who had been the most obviously on guard when he danced with the Italian woman and followed him with his eyes every time he smiled at her, had invited him back. There was only a shabby staircase in front of him to climb step by step. There was a door with a worn name plate he had to enter. There was a messy apartment with a leather sofa full of holes on which he could sleep. The sun blazed at full strength through the window and flashed like steel in the vodka bottle the bald man put before him on a table. He himself sat on a pile of old newspapers opposite with hands folded on his knees.

'How did you come to meet Claudia?' he asked from somewhere far off.

Mollerup didn't manage an answer. He fell asleep as if pole-axed with the sun right in his face so his eyelids grew red and hot. He did feel himself falling on to his side so his head struck the armrest of the sofa but then he was insensible to further impressions. He sank down and down through layers of air and velvet-soft water until everything around him was dark. When he woke up many hours later he still lay in the same position, but he had a quilt over him and a pillow under his temple. His shoes had been taken off and his shirt unbuttoned at the neck. He was sweating all over. His beard had grown and he felt he exuded a dank smell; a smell he could not himself describe but which had something to do with overheated clothes, disturbed sleep and too much whisky. The shutters were closed, there was no clock near him and his watch had stopped at a quarter past twelve. In front of him on the coffee table was a full glass of vodka. The bald man's glass was empty. It made him feel sick to look at the glasses, he pushed the quilt aside, rose and went to the window to open the shutters wide.

It must have been late afternoon. The sky was dark with clouds sweeping across at speed, and the first cars had already put their lights on. People on their way home from work were crowding into an entrance to the metro, a greengrocer sold the last bananas from his stall. In front of a café a paperboy cried his wares, the third edition of *France-Soir*. Was it five o'clock? Six? Seven? He looked around the flat to see if the bald man was asleep somewhere, but in the bedroom his bed had been made and there was a scent of freshly made coffee in the kitchen. In the bathroom he calculated that the bald man must have got up within the last half hour: his razor was still wet.

He was overwhelmed by the feeling that he was intruding, of finding himself in a place where he ought not to be as he wandered around the flat subjecting it to close inspection. To start with he did no more than glance at the big dusty piles of books along the walls, mostly American crime stories and books on film. The walls were crowded with posters of Italian westerns and in a doorway used for bookshelves were ranks of empty or half-full bottles of vodka. Mollerup had made himself respectable in the bathroom. He had borrowed the razor, the hairbrush and shaving lotion. He was about to borrow the toothbrush but confined himself to putting some toothpaste on his finger. So now he ought to leave. But he stayed on for a while, inquisitiveness getting the better of his sense of guilt. He couldn't stop himself taking a look into cupboards where there were piles of new sweaters, shirts and socks. He stayed away from the desk for some time but then could no longer resist the temptation to look through the papers on it, a synopsis of a script about the Italian partisans' struggle against the Nazis in Venice, a credit note from the Crédit Lyonnais, old cuttings of the hunt for members of the OAS glued on yellow sheets painted with large exclamation marks. On top of the papers lay pipe ash, unused metro tickets and some ten franc notes. There was also a small pile of amateur photographs. One of them was of the Italian woman. She stood on a beach in a bikini, her long black hair blew around her head and a pair of op-art painted sunglasses.

Underneath was scratched in green ink: *Je t'aime — Claudia.*

The following Saturday, after he had returned to a normal rhythm in which night was used for sleeping and day to phone news back to his paper, he met Lund. Every three months they had an hour's discussion of topical events in France which they recorded on tape at the French radio station and sent home to Denmark. For the first time Mollerup was looking forward to the discussion. He knew he would no longer have to defend himself against the ever self-confident Lund, that now he would be able to present his view of events without getting tied up in a web of self-contradictions. And everything went as he had hoped. His voice was clear, authoritative and penetrating as far as he could judge. When they had finished, he had definitely been the one who took the lead. Afterwards he went off with Lund. They had a beer at a bistro, but Mollerup took care to keep a distance between them, and he noticed that at intervals Lund looked at him with a mixture of astonishment and respect. Doubtless the dandyish Lund took note of the fact that his trousers were no longer baggy at the knees and his tie was unspotted. Perhaps, he thought — perhaps Lund was also impressed by the announcement of his forthcoming book which would appear before the one he was pretty sure Lund was planning. When they parted Lund again pressed him for a meeting at their old haunt, Chez Georges in the Rue des Canettes. He did not reply directly:

'One evening, you mean?'

'Yes, like old times . . .,' Lund replied hesitantly.

Mollerup looked at him as if he was a ghost from the past and wondered how he could ever have been afraid of this Danish Paris journalist whose floridly studied English appearance looked quite wrong in the fashionable French clothes. Then they went their separate ways. As Lund disappeared into a taxi he stopped looking back at the past. He lit a cigarette, he looked forwards: the Italian woman had suggested they should get together again when he phoned her to ask if he had left his pipe behind at her apartment. No, he hadn't, but he would be more than welcome to look in next Saturday. She was going to the outskirts of Paris with her writer friend. He was writing a new novel and wanted to study various districts, so if he was interested he could go along with them and maybe find material himself for an article on the Paris tourists did not normally see, the Paris of the oil drum towns, of the barrack-like high rises, the petrol tanks, motorways and supermarkets. The Paris of poverty. Red Paris.

They drove out there in the jeep, along the Autoroute du Sud. Mollerup sat in the back with a hand on his hair that was being whirled around by the wind. The crewcut writer was open and friendly from the start, as if they had known each other for a long time. Sitting at the wheel in a flying jacket overtaking one car after another, he turned round a few times and shouted into the wind that as far as housing and social conditions were concerned, Paris was at a stage that corresponded to that of Stockholm in the twenties.

'Yes, but I'm not Swedish,' replied Mollerup. In vain: the wind carried his words backwards.

The Italian woman wore a headscarf and put a hand over the windscreen to feel the air between her fingers. Then they turned off and drove into a small suburb Mollerup recognized because it was on the way out to Rolf Hauge's castle. They bumped over the cobblestones and out into open country again. Some way further, on the right lay a mass of miserable wooden shacks thrown up without any system, with television aerials on some of the roofs and washing hanging from roof to roof. Part of the area was fenced in with wire. Not far from where they parked, a bulldozer was levelling some of the huts to the ground while their owners ran in front of them screaming in despair, their hands full of possessions they had managed to rescue at the last moment. When they walked into the shanty town people looked at them suspiciously.

Mollerup had the uncomfortable feeling that he was playing the part of a housing shark hunting for building sites.

For the most part the residents were North African. The women wore veils when they went to the pump for water, and the children, who played in the dirt, were naked except for ragged tops. They all had those unfathomably dark eyes that could express everything from general curiosity to fear and the start of hatred of the white man's world. Everywhere transistors were blaring, their programmes clashing so French pop music blended with news bulletins from Algeria or Egypt or a passionate commentary on a football match between Real Madrid and Toulouse. The narrow paths between the shacks were full of holes and mud so the Italian woman had to jump over them the whole time so as not to soil her new walking shoes. Mollerup kept close to her so he could offer his arm. The crewcut writer sometimes disappeared to investigate something or chat to an Arab who invited him into his hut. In the centre of the shanty town was a small open space, not many meters each way, where an interim bar had been built out of old cardboard boxes and Coca-Cola placards. The bar customers were mostly older men, they squatted on the ground with strangely listless milk-white eyes, playing chess and drinking peppermint tea. When Mollerup looked up he caught sight of the tops of a row of high rise buildings and a jet plane coming down to land at Orly. Otherwise, they were in a world he had certainly heard about, knew to exist, but had never before dared approach because he had always been warned against going into the Arab districts. The children around their legs, the transistor radios, the washing that flapped against their faces when they bent down under it, the milk-white indolent eyes of the old people, the veiled women, the dogs plagued by fleas and the stench of latrine barrels, the blare and the dirty bodies.

The Italian woman started to play with some of the children. She had her pockets full of sweets to give them, but immediately four screaming mothers ran up and pulled the children away. A group of young men who were mending a scooter went towards her threateningly, but the crewcut writer appeared from behind a shack with an old Arab who offered them peppermint tea. The young men withdrew into a semicircle while they squatted down and drank out of battered old tin mugs. Mollerup kept glowering at the young men, he was very relieved when they finished their tea, and the writer said it was time they moved on. They left the settlement on the far side. Before them lay a large field where withered tufts of grass grew on heaps of rubble and over old cycle frames and prams. They crossed the field and went into an area of newly built high rise flats. The writer walked between them enthusing over how inspired he had been by the shanty town. The book he was writing was to be a crime story, but not a crime story of the usual kind. He was not interested in intrigue, but in all the inhuman big city settings his alienated chief character had to pass through in his flight from the system. He pointed up at the melancholy grey facades of the buildings, where fat pigeons slept on the French balconies, and suddenly let loose a stream of curses at a society that only housed a section of its inhabitants in a deserving manner and put up wretched wooden shacks close to modern high rise flats with all modern conveniences.

He grew more and more excited while frantically smoothing his scalp with its stubble of hair. After they left the high rise quarter and were walking along some quiet streets of luxury villas from the turn of the century, sheltered behind man-high walls with glass splinters sticking out of the cement on top, the writer brought his fist down hard on the bonnet of a parked Citroen 2 CV. The Italian woman tried to calm him down by taking his arm and giving him a shake. But his fury knew no end. As far as he could see there was only one way forward for modern society, and that was the way of revolution. He opened the door of the 2 CV and bent the handle of the horn upwards so it was pressed into the steel frame of the front window. They hurried off as the horn sounded, but then the crewcut writer caught sight of another 2 CV and repeated the operation by bending the handle of the horn up and jamming it fast. There was no stopping him although Mollerup and the Italian woman did what they could to quieten him down. He leaped from pavement to pavement every time he saw a new 2 CV and it was not long before a deafening din from about ten blaring cars made the residents of the villas open their windows and threaten them.

Mollerup was infected by the other's frenzy when he waved them down new side streets where all was peace and quiet, but where he immediately pointed out six or seven parked 2 CVs. If he found a car that was locked he gave it a furious kick on the front tyre. Gradually Mollerup let himself be drawn into the fun so he agreed to take care of the 2 CVs parked on the right hand side while the crewcut man dealt with those on the left. The Italian woman had caught the mood and walked between them in the middle of the road keeping an eye out for the police. An elderly man ran some way after them swinging a silvermounted cane over his head but they soon shook him off. They also escaped from a woman who had been out shopping and who threw potatoes at them, laughing at each other as the number of hooting cars grew steadily. The din they had initiated must be audible kilometers away, thought Mollerup. Then the police arrived. As they turned into a new road two gendarmes came towards them on bicycles at full speed.

They ran as fast as they could, back through the high rise district, over the field with the cycle frames and prams and grass-grown heaps and straight in among the Arab shacks. Mollerup thought he had never in his life run so fast, his legs worked as if they were on wheels, he splashed into big puddles and out again, he leaped over a couple of playing children, for some way a barking dog was at his heels, but he even outdistanced that. The crewcut writer ran in front, waving them on to run faster, faster. The Italian woman ran behind him, her shoes splashed with mud. Mollerup held out a hand to her, but she whispered hoarsely that she could manage. They did not see whether the gendarmes were at their heels as they rushed past the shacks. They ran across the little open space with the bar where the old Arabs still sat on the ground with their tin mugs, playing chess. Eventually they stopped in front of a certain shack and went inside. The Arab who had given them peppermint tea started up from his mat and asked in bewilderment what had happened. The writer, panting, put him into the picture, and when he mentioned the word 'gendarmes' the old man expressed himself ready to help and tidied up so they could lie down on his mats and regain their breath while he went out to fill a jug with fresh water.

They stayed in the hut for some time. When Mollerup had recovered he looked round curiously. Various pictures had been fixed to the walls with drawing pins; clippings from *Paris Match* and *Lui* among clumsy coloured drawings of naked women. A large photograph of Brigitte Bardot hung between two framed pictures, one of which showed Ben Bella attending a military parade in Algiers and the other President Nasser visiting the Suez canal. In one corner there was a television set covered with a cloth. The rugs on the floor lay on the bare earth, and all the Arab had in the way of a kitchen was a primus stove on a cardboard box, a dented saucepan and a little frying pan with weeks' old, burned margarine in it. The Arab did not speak to them. He offered them cigarettes and honey cakes and now and then went outside to see whether the police were about.

They could still hear the sound of horns in the background but it gradually grew fainter and fainter and finally stopped altogether to give way to the rowdy transistors in the Arab town.

The crewcut writer was in a good mood as they drove back to Paris. He whistled softly and patted the Italian woman on the head. Once back in town they parked by a bistro and had a beer each. Mollerup looked at the writer who now seemed perfectly normal, blowing at the foam in his beer glass. You would not know to look at him that he had just upset an entire district. With the same self-command with which he had exhibited his penis he leaned back and stretched out his legs, as if nothing really had to do with him, as if now he was merely playing the role of spectator. The Italian woman was still somewhat out of breath, and Mollerup's thighs were aching from the long run as he tried to recall what had actually happened. The afternoon had flown. Then he noticed the writer watching him over the edge of his glass.

'Do you work for a Swedish newspaper down here?' he asked.

'For a Danish paper,' he replied.

'And you've lived here ten years?'

The Italian woman must have told him.

'That's right,' he answered. 'It's coming up to ten years!'

The crewcut took off his glasses and rubbed his eyes.

'So you must have sent a good few articles home . . .'

'About a hundred a year,' he replied. After a moment he added: 'Now I've got a book coming out too. I thought it was about time I put some of my impressions together in a more *lasting* form.'

'A book! *Another* book on Paris!'

The writer started to laugh aloud, slightly scornfully, and went on:

'How on earth can you write a book about Paris? What *is* Paris?'

'Paris . . . it's this café, it's this street, the people, it's de Gaulle, it's . . .'

He knew he was about to dry up. It was impossible to explain to the other what his Paris book was about.

'I've just read one of these books on Paris written by a foreigner, by a German,' said the writer. 'Makes you clutch your head! Nothing but generalization heaped on generalization. You really can't write about Paris as it was done in the twenties when the Americans came barging over here with their whisky bottles under their arms swooning at the sight of a concierge. Paris — it is one great unreality, a violent mutation, a . . .'

'But,' he replied trying to sound polite, 'You're writing a book on Paris yourself . . .'

'Not that sort of book on Paris,' replied the other at once, 'Not on Paris as — 'Paris'.

He thought about what the crewcut writer had said about

the German's Paris book. It must be the same book he had taken two chapters from, and he was seized with a sudden despondency. The crewcut writer was right, of course: how can you epitomize Paris in a book of so many pages, divided into so many chapters? He thought of the visit to the shanty town, the Arab's hut with the rugs on the floor and the primus stove on the cardboard box, the stench, the transistors. He thought of the district with turn-of-the-century villas, of the high rise flats with pigeons on the balconies. He thought of the night club they had been to with the bald man and the painter with tufts in his nose. All these were Paris, fragments of Paris, but he had said nothing about them in his book. The table they were sitting at now was Paris, and the waiter with a cloth over his arm and clean nails was Paris. And so was the boulevard with its hysterical traffic. Paris was a window on the fourth floor where he caught sight of a white-haired old lady who sat looking down on the pedestrians. The old woman was Paris, her white hair was Paris. Paris was her flat that was hidden from his gaze in inpenetrable darkness: it might consist of one room, it might consist of ten rooms filled with mementos of a long life, faded family portraits in brown varnished wooden frames, conch shells from Tahiti brought home by her husband, who might have been a captain in the merchant marine. These family portraits, which he would never see, and the shells with their hollow singing sound of bygone times and oblivion were Paris. Paris was the chair he sat on and its seat and the individual plastic strips plaited together which formed it and the squashed cigarette end by his foot and the dust on his toe caps, all this and infinitely more was Paris, and none of it was in his book because it was impossible to summarize so much in barely two hundred pages that began at the beginning and ended at the end.

For a moment he counted himself lucky that the crewcut writer knew nothing about his work, his reporting, but especially the lesser articles he had written under the pseudonym of Monsieur Jean about the characteristics of Parisians, as if anything existed that could be summarized as 'Parisian.' He consoled himself by thinking that his book on Paris would only be read in Denmark where there was no wool you couldn't pull over people's eyes about the French — those 'weird' French people who traditionally were as remote from the English-snobbish Danes as Chinese or Brazilians. The book would serve as a timely boost for him on the home front. It would bring his name back into circulation so there would be no risk of his being called back to a job as education correspondent or television critic. Meanwhile he was already on his way to something new and quite different in a Paris that had nothing to do with the Paris he described to the Danish reading public. He would find new friends like those the Italian had introduced him to. He would acquire a completely new view of life, would have control over things, and maybe one day his dream of a house in the south of France would be realized; so that in a few years he could retire and enjoy life. He would have no more to do with Denmark, nor with the picture of Paris the people back home indirectly demanded he should tend and cultivate. He would not build images any more. He would be in the thick of it all, be a part of the life around him; in the winter he would be at the heart of Paris that was everything from the cigarette end by his foot to the white-haired old lady on the fourth floor, and in the summer in hot Aveyron or Provence with a million-voiced choir of cicadas and a shining blue sky and a sea he could swim in and rivers he could fish in.

'See you soon, I hope.'

The crewcut writer was standing up.

'Are you going already?' asked Mollerup.

'The book!' he said. 'The book calls! I can already envisage the whole thing, my 'hero' out in that shanty town, the stench of unwashed bodies, the peppermint tea — that *milieu*!'

'You're welcome to come home with me if you'd like to,' said the Italian woman, getting up as well and putting the money for her beer on the table.

'Me?' asked Mollerup.

'Yes, you! If you can make do with what I have in the kitchen . . . a little rice and meat and some peppers . . .'

She changed into casual clothes, a sweater and slacks, and told him he could sit in the living room and look at her books and newspapers while she cooked, but he preferred to stay in the kitchen and give her a hand. He washed up, dried and took the plates into the living room. When she had finished preparing the food she went into the bathroom for a moment and came back with her hair loose and eyebrows outlined in black. She lit a candle and put it on a small table with a red cloth. She switched off the main light and asked him to open a bottle of red wine.

'It's a nice place you've got here,' he said, feeling he had to say something, no matter what.

'D'you think so? I'm getting a bit tired of this flat . . . .'

They ate and he taught her to say 'Skål' in Danish, she might as well learn it now, as she was going to Copenhagen.

'I'm really looking forward to the trip,' she said.

'And I'm looking forward to going with you,' he replied.

She looked at him. He noticed she had put on the silver bracelet, or had she worn it all day and he had not noticed because so much had happened in the Arab town? When she had finished eating she took it off and held it up to the candle flame.

'I . . .'

She paused. Then went on:

'I don't think I thanked you properly for your gift. But you gave me such a *surprise* . . .'

He could feel something was in the air and thought about the outworn cliché 'something was in the air.' But if it was true that two people could send out inaudible signals to each other, without words, from body to body, from skin to skin, could suddenly be hedged in by an invisible circle so only the two of them existed in the world, existed for each other, then it was happening now. And it was happening in such a way that his blood started to run warm through his veins and a faint prickling spread over his skin, down his arms, out into his hands, down his thighs, out into his toes and from his neck into his scalp and from his shoulders down over his chest. He took her hand and caressed it and a little later rose and leaned over the table and kissed her so the hair on one of his temples was scorched by the candle, and all this took place without any intention on his part. He went round the table, put his hands under her arms and lifted her from her chair, and when she put both arms around his neck and ran the fingers of one hand through his hair he knew she would do it, that it was her natural reaction to his lead. He knew nothing could go wrong and that she would press her stomach to his and put her forehead to his shoulder and then kiss him on the neck. And he kissed her on the forehead, just above her eyebrow, he kissed the hollow beneath her ear, he bit her ear lobe, he held her around her loins and let his hands slide downwards and between her legs and held her bottom and lifted her up. She clung to him with her knees pressed to his hips. Her hair fell down over him and blotted his view and she put her lips to his neck. Then he put her down again and pushed her gently away so he could look into her eyes that had the same glow of excitement and red wine that he knew was in his own. But they could not look into each other's eyes for long. They had to touch each other again, feel each other. He had to pull her to him again and kiss her on the forehead and her soft eyelids and the tip of her nose and her mouth.

'Come,' she said suddenly, very low, almost inaudible. 'Come!'

She took him by the wrist and led him to a sofa, then lay down. He followed suit, first beside, then on top of her, and again they were carried away in a passionate embrace. His hands found their way beneath her sweater, which he tore free from her slacks, and he discovered she wore no bra, which seemed to him like a fresh affirmation that everything was happening as it should. He covered her breasts with his hands. He played with her nipples with two fingers until they emerged from their hiding place and grew hard and angular. Then he lifted her sweater right up above her shoulders and kissed her between her breasts and down over her stomach and in her navel until his lips stopped at the belt of her slacks. The next moment she was sitting on him, bending down to help him undo the zip of his trousers. She started to unbutton his shirt after he took off his jacket, and with each button she kissed him on the chest and played with his chest hair.

Then it happened, the thing he had been fearing the whole time. It was more than a month since he had last been to bed with a woman, at a brothel a few days after his mother had gone back to Copenhagen. So he was out of training and felt his penis starting to throb. He cautiously freed himself from the Italian woman, raised himself and sat on the edge of the sofa, feeling most of all like hitting out hard at something out of sheer mortification.

'Don't you want me any more?' she asked softly behind his back.

He didn't turn round. He looked at his shoes and heard how wrong it sounded. Perhaps she told herself that if he could not love her it was all the same to her. He looked round the room, at the neo-Surrealist pictures on the walls, the plain elegant furniture, the picture on the window sill of the crewcut writer sitting on the radiator of his jeep on some country road or other waving a Cuban straw hat. He looked at the picture for a long time but could not read what was written across it. First the photograph he had found in the bald-headed man's flat, inscribed *je t'aime — Claudia,* and now this picture which no doubt declared that the crewcut writer loved her. Maybe she made love to both of them at the same time. He felt her hand moving up his naked back, over one shoulder blade, back to his neck and up into his hair. He turned round and smiled at her, then lay down again beside her. She unbuttoned his trousers and he pushed off his shoes. Then she took off her own trousers and they lay naked. He kissed her softly on the cheek.

'Come into me hard,' she whispered.

Again he was seized with panic. When he had been sitting on the edge of the sofa he had deferred ejaculation for a moment, but now his penis started to throb again and he could only hold out at most for half a minute, perhaps only a quarter. He lay on her completely still while she grew impatient and he tried to control himself as he slid into her by concentrating his mind on everything but her. He stared fixedly over the arm of the sofa at the window sill and tried to count the number of flowers on the wallpaper. He reached 50 while the Italian woman forced him into faster and faster rhythm. As counting flowers wasn't much good he closed his eyes and searched his memory for something to concentrate on. He started to count how many chairs there were in the great hall of the Elysée Palace. Then he thought of de Gaulle's face, his little blinking eyes, his arrogant way of answering the female East European journalist who had asked about the French government attitude to the German voices claiming that the Munich agreement ought to remain in effect. Later, while the Italian woman moaned increasingly loudly and dug her nails into his neck and put her legs around his loins, he recalled a B-movie he had seen a few days before, he was on his way through the south of France at full speed in a Citroen DS, he pretended he was sitting at the wheel speeding up when some lights appeared in the back mirror. Then he lost that thread too and felt he would not be able to hold out any longer. He kept his eyes shut tight and in a last attempt to divert his attention he thought of his mother, of their breakfast together after the night when he had sneaked into the Spanish maid's room, he visualized his mother's wrinkled, liver-spotted neck and heard her reproachful voice that finally broke the painful silence.

But not even the thought of his mother could cool him down. Not even the thought of her liver-spotted neck. Suddenly he erupted. Something exploded inside him and a hot stream slid from him into the Italian woman who immediately thumped him on the back in irritation and went limp all over him while his penis shrank to the size of a snail. He opened his eyes. Luckily she was smiling at him. She said they could both try again. And her remark calmed him down.

'Is it a long time since . . . last?' she asked.

'I can't deny it is,' he replied and began to laugh at the comical aspect of the situation. He offered her a cigarette and they lay for a while smoking and looking at the ceiling. The next time it went better, he felt it from the start. Certainly he had to think of all manner of things between heaven and earth again but for shorter periods, gradually he fell into a rhythm in which he could love her without the fear of coming too early making him anxious. He even noticed a suspicion of stupid pride growing in him when she wanted to change position several times, to be loved from behind, while she sat on him, while he rose and took her on the edge of the sofa, and every time he managed to comply with her wishes. Eventually her orgasm came, she kicked out with her legs and pulled at the fabric covering of the sofa. She bit him hard on the shoulder and whispered he needn't worry about her any longer. But now he could not come. Now he grew nervous at being told he could ejaculate and dearly wanted to but could not feel it was on the way. And now he thought of everything that could excite him, of the striptease dives on the Pigalle where the dancers stood with a piece of the curtain between their thighs wriggling their bottoms at the audience. He thought particularly about a certain black dancer with an unnaturally large bum and big sensual lips. He groaned with exhaustion, from too many cigarettes, from the whole miserable lifestyle he had exposed himself to during the last few years, he felt he was really getting old, that his thigh muscles were no good, the cigarettes, the sleepless nights and the gallons of whisky had sapped his strength. Then the heat spread through his body and at about the same time white light shone behind his eyes and he fell happily relaxed on to the Italian woman.

They stood at the window, which they had opened on to the street. She wore a lilac kimono. It was getting dark and snowing. He was tired, a pleasant tiredness. He looked across at the doorway where he had stood some time before looking up at her lighted window, where he had caught sight of the bald man. Now he himself stood at the window. It was a November evening, an evening like thousands of others in Paris, an evening that chanced to be in the year 1964. Why 1964? Why this evening, this special November evening? He felt timelessness spread around him, the year 1964 could be 1937 when it was not de Gaulle in power in Europe but Hitler and Mussolini and Stauning in Denmark. The year 1964 could be 1966 or 1969 when de Gaulle might not be in power any longer and everything in the world seemed different, with the sole exception of the street he looked down on and which had looked the same for the last couple of centuries, and would stay the same for the next couple of centuries: the shabby walls with strong wooden buttresses supporting them, the small windows with small apartments behind them where people slept and ate and loved and quarrelled and died later on in the spring when most old people normally die.

'Do you never feel a foreigner in Paris?' he asked and knew that now it was time to speak more intimately.

'Paris *is* a city of foreigners,' she replied, taking his hand and squeezing it.

The dog scratching itself in the doorway opposite, as it had scratched for centuries and would scratch for centuries more, a fat old dog with matted tufts of fur and a floppy chest. The snow falling on the TABAC awning further down the street. The two American marines boxing each other to get warm. The television screen flickering blue in a room opposite. He felt like whistling. He kissed her.

CHAPTER SEVEN

Cigar smoke drifted through the editorial boardroom. Most of the newspaper's staff had come to participate in a discussion on the best way to launch a new campaign. In the new year the paper intended to take up the issue of allowing the dogs of Copenhagen to run loose in the city centre now the pedestrian street was a reality. Mollerup, who had spent most of the morning in the editor-in-chief's office receiving praise for his recent articles which — as the chief put it — documented that 'after a weak period' he again represented the paper in a suitable manner in Paris, had been invited to attend the meeting. He had actually intended to go straight back to Bahn's Hotel to wake the Italian woman, who was sleeping late after the flight. He could not resist, however, the temptation to walk with the editor-in-chief through the editorial office, with its ticking teleprinters, and into the boardroom, there to greet all his old colleagues from the time when he was a reporter in Copenhagen. He wanted to see how much they had changed, how much older they looked since he was last in town. One or two of them who used to hang out in the canteen far into the night had probably turned into alcoholics, others maybe had gone into hibernation in the suburb of Nærum, weighed down with wives, children, financial problems and ulcers.

One by one they came in. The sports reporter, cap under his arm in new tailor-made tweeds. The lanky poetry reviewer who had been editorial messenger twelve years ago when Mollerup joined the newspaper, but who after writing a feature article on T. S. Eliot in a Danish translation had worked his way up to being the leading authority in Denmark on modern Scandinavian poetry. The arts editor with a naval beard and black notebooks poking out of his breast pocket arrived with the 72-year-old theatre and film critic, one of the best known figures in Copenhagen press circles, loved for never uttering a disparaging word about any play or film. Three of the editorial secretaries came in in shirt sleeves with cigarettes in the corners of their mouths. Finally the educational correspondent walked in, an elderly writer of regional novels, who had earned his living for a short period in the Faroes as a supply teacher, on the strength of which he had been entrusted with everything concerning education, from the lowest to the highest. Mollerup received hearty handshakes from all, or a comradely slap on the shoulder. The only faces new to him belonged to three long-haired youngsters sitting by themselves with a pile of long-playing records, dressed as Tibetan monks. They were the editors of the newspaper's newly established youth culture pages, he learned from the editor-in-chief, who added in a whisper: 'You know, it's minors who rule up here in our little Denmark!'

When they had all sat down around the mahogany table, the door opened, and the cartoonist came in out of breath apologizing profusely for being late. For a moment Mollerup fervently hoped he could hide from him. The cartoonist was known for his hysterical adoration of everything French. In the evenings he would go round the small cafés of the city centre singing French military songs from the first world war, and the drawings he did for the paper all had the characteristics of late French Impressionism. He it was who had made sketches of Frenchmen in Alpine hats and French women with bottles of red wine and baguettes sticking out of their shopping baskets for Monsieur Jean's little columns, and he did all he could to look Gallic, with a cord-thin moustache and a striped French sailor's jersey under his suede jacket.

'Well, if it isn't . . .' he exclaimed.

Mollerup had to admit it was.

'Welcome home to the gloomy North! But tell me, what have you done with Monsieur Jean?'

'You need a change of style now and then,' replied Mollerup. 'I've laid Monsieur Jean to rest for a while . . .'

'I think that was *wise* of you,' interposed the poetry critic. 'Now, that sincerely engaged article you did yesterday about the Arabs' living conditions in the barrack quarter outside Paris. It made you feel that journalism can be just as valuable as, well, not as literature, but as *something* like that . . .'

'You have never had any understanding of France,' said the cartoonist.

'Oh, *haven't* I?' replied the poetry critic, sitting up straight and banging his paperknife on the table top.

'Your sphere is Germanic culture!'

A minor wrangle quickly developed between the cartoonist and the poetry critic. The latter accused the former of confusing superfluity with Gallicism, the former responded that if profundity was equated with modern Danish poetry then superfluity was a virtue. The education correspondent attempted to mediate but not until the editor-in-chief intervened and commanded order in the ranks did they subside. Cigars were lit, a couple of waitresses came in with traditional Christmas wine. Then the chief invited the gathering to present their ideas for the campaign to allow dogs to run loose in the city centre. The first to speak was the drama and film critic. He suggested taking a questionnaire out on the streets to ask the citizens for their honest opinion. Citizens from as broad a spectrum as possible, including a postman, a delivery boy, a priest, a professor, a dentist, a lawyer, should be questioned. Next came the sports reporter. He wanted to take the opportunity to put a word in for the introduction of dog racing in Denmark. Two of the editorial secretaries thought they should wait to start the campaign until some more inner city streets were turned into pedestrian precincts, while the arts editor offered to make his column available for a discussion of the subject in depth. The education correspondent thought there might be problems if children on their way home from school were savaged, but declared himself otherwise to be in full agreement with the aims of the campaign.

The editor-in-chief nodded amiably each time and made notes, while fishing with his left index finger for raisins and almonds in his glass. Then he turned to the editors of the young people's pages who had not yet put their oar in. All three declared at once that the campaign was pretty futile and they wanted to suggest instead that the paper should strike a blow to prevent folksingers in the city centre being arrested by the police when they took up position on a street corner and sang their peace songs about love among human beings.

'Perhaps we can take up that campaign another time,' replied the editor-in-chief. 'Not a bad idea! Free music in a free country!'

Then he turned to the poetry critic who had also kept silent and asked him for his opinion.

'Pop!' snarled the poetry editor.

'Admittedly!' replied the editor-in-chief. 'But on a big paper we have to think of all the readers, not merely the few who live in the kingdom of the spirit. Everything must be included from poetry to church and state!'

Mollerup noted with satisfaction that he was not to be questioned. It was obvious that the editor-in-chief took it for granted that as a correspondent from the great world on Christmas holiday in Copenhagen he was above concerning himself with Copenhagen trivialities. He calmly lit a cigar, one of the biggest, after carefully biting off the end and warming it over a match flame. He sipped his drink slowly and observed the others who were now all — with the exception of the poetry critic and the three youth editors — talking at once, bursting with eagerness to make good suggestions. There was something paltry about the group of journalists and reporters, he thought involuntarily, slightly against his will, with a touch of actual disgust. None of them had changed much in the last ten years apart from getting older; the sports reporter still lived up to his image of an English country gentleman, the arts editor still used the same black note-books that he ordered from the editorial caretaker, who in turn ordered them from an old firm in Jutland, for years he had lived for these notebooks, lived with them, sucked nourishment from them. And the poetry critic with his long, pale, somehow oily fingers clutching a half finished cheroot. And the education correspondent. Mollerup felt something like pain looking at him. His hanging underlip, his committed nod every time something was said that he thought significant and could go along with. And the boardroom, this boardroom that they all regarded as a kind of inner sanctum, a cerebral centre not only of the paper but of Copenhagen itself, the place where important persons made important decision while dead editors-in-chief looked down on them from their gilt rococo frames, hung on the striped fifties wallpaper among framed hand-written letters from celebrities, sent to the paper when it was young and aggressive and in tune with the European socialism that wanted to abolish the church, the military and the monarchy. The letter from Zola expressing his joy that people in Copenhagen had joined in his battle against reaction with curiosity and sympathy. The letter from Sarah Bernhardt that had faded so much over the years that no one knew any more what was in it. The letter from Henrik Ibsen sent while he was in exile in Germany, that too almost illegible.

Outside the snow fell in great wads and melted on a neon sign advertising sunlight treatment on the wall of the building opposite. He could not understand it. The whole thing seemed so small-scale. When he thought about Copenhagen in Paris it was as a big city like any other, something comparable to Amsterdam or Berlin. But now walking along Strøget for a moment, he found it hard to realize he was in a capital city. Compared with the Parisian boulevards, the Copenhagen streets seemed like streets in a provincial town. Was he in Holbæk? Behind him was Rådhuspladsen, the Town Hall Square, in front of him Kongens Nytorv, the King's New Square. If he spread his arms he could almost embrace it all, pick up the town and carry it off. The crowd of people out Christmas shopping with red cheeks and thick furs or lined suede coats all looked as if they knew each other. At least they resembled each other to an astonishing degree; the men with

their podgy faces and checked caps and large shapeless
shoes, the women with their terrible posture, their clumsy
gait, their white winter boots. And the children everywhere;
children in front of shop windows and milling around the
legs of a faded Father Christmas who stood with streaming
eyes and nose, carrying a board advertising a firm selling
clocks and watches, children in a line in front of the Metropole
Christmas show and children on their way in and out of
Thorngreens. The evening paper posters outside the Nygade
Theatre told of a scandal brewing in the newly established art
fund and of the interest being shown abroad in the Danish
orgasm debate: DANISH ORGASM SOLD ABROAD. The
banner for the Christmas collection for the homeless hung
across Strøget, customers crowded the bakers' shops. Outside, radio and loudspeakers in record-player shops played a
constant stream of Christmas carols. A carefree Lilliput community with sugar pretzels and horns-of-plenty cakes and
fizzy drinks for all. If he turned round he would glimpse
through the falling snow the Christmas tree on the town hall
square which he had always thought of as something high,
something infinitely high, but which now turned out to be
pretty insignificant. A man with a cap held out in front of
him, in a winter coat far too big for him, walked in front of
Mollerup, his breath making clouds around him and his arms
swinging in a coachman's cape:

> Copenha — a — gen you have everything
> that ca — a — aptivates my heart

In the kiosk in Jorcks Passage the previous day's foreign
newspapers hung on a stand. He leafed briefly through *Le
Monde* and *France-Soir*. In front of Gad's Bookshop he stopped
with a start when he caught sight of his book. A pile of copies
of *Paris From The Shady Side* were stacked up, others were
spread out in a fan. A photograph of himself, stuck to a piece
of tricolore-coloured cardboard, hung in the centre of the
window. It had been taken some time after he had received a
telegram telling him the book had been published, by a

photographer sent down to Paris by the publisher. He had not had a chance to see it before, and he was surprised to see how authoritative and self-confident he looked as he stood there on the balcony outside his apartment in the Avenue de Wagram looking over the rooftops of a Paris in October mist, with withering trees. He stood with his back half-turned towards the camera, straight-backed with a cigarette sending a thin whirl of smoke into the air. To the left of the picture he could glimpse the Arc de Triomphe.

Although *Paris From The Shady Side* had received quite positive reviews, even in the conservative evening paper Lund worked for and which was renowned for having the most disagreeable critics in Denmark, he did not want to stay by the window too long. The book was something that was over and done with, something he had needed to get off his hands at a low point in his life. He shuddered at the thought of having to read it with fresh eyes and be confronted with all the errors and all the generalizations he had been guilty of, either on his own account or because he had been influenced by the German correspondent's Paris book. He went on. He bought a sausage at a hot-dog stand and carried it down the narrow side streets off Strøget where new boutiques with teenage clothes had mushroomed since his last visit. Some way further on he found himself outside his mother's cinema. Unsurprisingly the poster advertised one of the many Gabin films she had ordered in Paris, and as usual reviews were on show in the showcases with red lines beneath the complimentary comments. In the vestibule the cleaners were washing the floor clean of the snow and slush brought in by the audience for the two o'clock show.

In the box office he caught sight of the manager of the cinema, a 60-year old unmarried lady with red permanent curls. She had worked at the cinema as long as he could remember and sat with her eternal cup of coffee and a cheroot, doing the accounts. He felt like putting his head through the window and saying hello to her, but knew she would be bound to tell his mother he was in town. And that was the last thing he wanted. Before leaving for Denmark he had made the decision not to see his mother so as to avoid getting involved in fresh exhausting quarrels with her. He particularly wanted to observe his home town with the eyes of an outsider. He threw away his hot dog paper and crossed to the opposite pavement. In his mother's apartment on the first floor, above the cinema, he could see a figure moving about the rooms behind the thick pre-war curtains. Was everything just the same in the apartment? The huge sofas with embroidered Greek myth designs that you sank into up to your waist, the tables whose cloths had meter-long fringes, the baroque angel hanging from the ceiling, the mirrors everywhere, in the rooms, in the corridor, in the pantry, the tapestries and bookcases with their first editions of Holberg and Baggesen that had belonged to his father. And in a little niche, the shrine, the urn with his father's ashes, with a mixed arrangement of fresh flowers and dried rosebuds from the 20s and 30s. No doubt everything was just as it had been for the last twenty years.

A small avalanche began to slide down a roof. In a moment the snow landed just in front of him with a muffled thud. He licked the tomato ketchup from his fingers and vanished round a corner on his way to Bahn's Hotel.

She had been out in town, she told him enthusiastically. She had guessed he would be late, would be involved in important discussions at the newspaper offices, so instead of lying about in bed she had gone shopping and taken a look at life in the streets. She really liked Copenhagen. The Danes seemed so friendly, so approachable, and in comparison with the Parisian shop assistants the Danish ones were sheer angels. And what beautiful complexions the Danish women had. Was it the climate? He could confirm that. The further north you went the more beautiful were the women's complexions, and when people said that Iceland had the world's most beautiful women, it was because of the cold up there and the air that was not yet poisoned by the big city.

'Are the Icelandic women really the most beautiful in the world?' she asked.

'It's true enough,' he replied with a knowing smile.

'Have you been there?'

'Once, many years ago,' he lied. 'The paper sent me to do a report.'

A picture of Strindberg hung on one wall in the hotel room. Had he once stayed in Copenhagen to produce a play? He knew the Danish writer Herman Bang had stayed there and probably Georg Brandes, the critic, too for a short while. But Strindberg, who hung there looking down on him with his wicked eyes and his neurotically bristling moustache? The room looked as if it had not been changed for fifty years, with reproduction rococo furniture and old-fashioned wallpaper. He went over to the window and looked down on the street where people walked through the snow bent forward, and darkness was falling. A stone's throw away was his mother's apartment with the cinema below it, where the audience for the four o'clock show would already be lining up, two stones' throws away was the newspaper with its gloomy view of backyards and narrow alleys. Behind him at an angle, perhaps four or five stones' throws away, was the Minefield, his haunt as a youngster after he had left home at the age of twenty and rented damp attic rooms and lived from hand to mouth, on sausages, pastries, instant coffee and hours of discussion with the local Bohemians. The long nights he had waited through with strung nerves for the morning papers to tell him whether he had had a poem accepted. The spring days when he played truant from the university which he hated more than anything else, and lay on a bench on Gammel Strand near the water drinking in the sun. And the summers then, with horses and carts in the streets and open windows reflecting the rays of the sun. Suddenly it all came back to him. But he could keep it at a distance. The past no longer meant everything to him, did not concern him with the same personal intensity as it had even a few months ago. He was a stranger in his own town and to his own earlier life. He was an observer. And he felt a warm surge of joy when he

heard the Italian woman whistling in the bathroom as she
turned on the bath taps. Her cases were on the bed only
partly unpacked. On the chairs were piles of dresses and
sweaters and trousers and underclothes. He picked up a
sweater and felt its soft luxury. He smelled it, buried his face
in it. He was going to have ten days in Copenhagen with the
Italian woman, ten peaceful days in this town where you only
had to offer a little finger to and it would drag you down into
emptiness and an endless gnawing hopelessness. Ten days,
and then Paris again.

'I'll soon be finished,' she called from the bathroom.

The water had stopped running, and he could hear her
splashing in the tub.

'Take as long as you like,' he called back.

'It's a lovely hotel you've found!'

'Glad you like it,' he answered and stuck out his tongue at
Strindberg.

It was difficult to decide on a decent restaurant. He pondered over whether they should eat at Fiskehuset, the Fish
House, at Allégade 10, at the Hotel Østerport or outside
town at the Lyngby Hotel. There wasn't much else to choose
from if he wanted to invite her somewhere he could be sure
the food would be more or less as good as in Paris. But
when they were on their way to the Town Hall Square,
walking along the street where his mother's cinema was, he
caught sight of a completely new restaurant. He had not
noticed it earlier in the day because he had been looking at
the cinema and up at his mother's flat. The door of the
restaurant kept opening and from the customers' clothes
he could see that it must be a good one. They went in. All
the small tables were occupied, and at the grill, waitresses in
yellow dresses and black aprons were busy giving orders and
serving meals. The restaurant was furnished in the French
style with small tables along the walls and a red-tiled floor,
and he recalled some articles he had read some months
before claiming that Danish restaurants were improving in

quality. They sat at a table not far from a loudspeaker playing English dance tunes from the thirties. From the start he could see how much his companion differed from the other women; her slender figure, her thick black hair compared with the others' broad build and fair curls set on top of their heads, her meticulous golden makeup beside the Danish women's red cheeks and over-emphasized black lines over their eyes. He recalled the first time he met her, at the reception at The Danish House in the Champs-Elysées, when she walked around among the tall ponderous Danes, her sunglasses in her hands, dressed in the thigh-length wine coloured dress. He couldn't help feeling quite proud at being her companion now and speaking in a language few in the restaurant understood.

'Why do they put so much on the plates in Denmark?' she asked when she had got halfway through her tournedos. She pointed ironically at the runner beans, the chips and the skinned tomatoes floating in a mixture of Béarnaise sauce and gravy.

'It's something to do with old habit,' he replied. 'You mustn't forget that Danish culture is above all a peasant culture with roots going back to a time when you had to eat as much as possible to put on enough weight to withstand the cold.'

She blew up her cheeks and punched herself clownishly on the stomach. Then she laughed.

'But this is a *nice* place,' she said after a moment.

He agreed.

'I've always heard that Danish architecture is some of the best in Europe?'

'That's maybe pushing it a bit,' he replied. 'But where interior architecture and design are concerned we can keep our end up.'

'But houses too,' she said. 'I have certainly read that.'

'Private houses, perhaps. But for large-scale architecture it's Finland that takes the prize.'

'Alvar Alto!' she said.

'Exactly!'

'Aren't the Scandinavian countries one big family?'

'A quarrelsome family!'

'You don't make many films in Denmark?' she asked soon after.

'We make a lot of *bad* films,' he replied. 'But of course there's always Dreyer.'

'Can you get me an interview with him?'

'I'll certainly ring him.'

'And your mother!'

'She's abroad. She is in Sweden, we have relations there.'

'Mais *non!*'

Her disappointed exclamation made a nearby couple whisper that they must be a French married couple quarrelling. He felt glad that his mother vanished like that while he was commented on as a Frenchman of Scandinavian descent. 'It *was* after all *Norsemen* who went ashore in Normandy, wasn't it?' a woman with prominent ears and a fringe asked her ten or fifteen years older husband. '*That* it was, Erna,' was the husband's response, 'and it's worth noticing that it's the Nordic type that de Gaulle prefers to have around him as ministers.'

As they were walking along Strøget looking at the shops after dinner Mollerup felt more and more of a foreigner. He noticed things that only a foreigner would notice. He looked at the town through the Italian woman's eyes, followed the direction of her gaze. The roofs of the houses. The neo-classical façades. The colour of the street signs. The numerous cycles parked in all the side streets, big black unwieldy machines with no hand brakes, chain-guards, baskets on the handlebars and overwide, frayed saddles. Then he pretended not to understand Danish and tried to pronounce the names and advertising signs on the shops. OSTE, on a cheese shop. OSTE. He repeated the word until it lost any meaning and was merely a word made up of an O and an S and a T and an E. Oste. Oste, Oste, Oste, Oste, Oste, Oste. It sounded weird, something like the name of a town or a vacuum cleaner or a drink. Oste. Then it was the word for shoes, skotøj, he played with. The O with a line through it. TØJ. SKOTØJ. SKO, SKO,

SKO, and then T and the O with a line through it and a J. Next there was BAGER for Baker, and in a doorway where there was a notice painted in white on the asphalt: NO THROUGH PASSAGE OF GOODS.

'What are you mumbling about?' she asked, taking his arm and looking inquiringly at him.

He was about to say the words, but realized she wouldn't understand if he told her about his little word game. Instead he said:

'That we need something hot to drink!'

It had stopped snowing. Melting slush gurgled in the downpipes of the gutters, and a gust of wind shook the branches of the trees around the Church of the Holy Ghost so big lumps of snow fell to the ground. They reached Illum's store.

'Oh, I must look!' said the Italian woman and pulled him over to the windows. 'They have much nicer things here than in the Danish shop in Paris, don't you think?'

'They are always five years behind at the Danish shop in Paris,' he replied. 'They think French taste is so bad they can sell them anything they like!'

They turned down a side street. Then they were outside the Drop Inn. It was very noisy inside, and when the door opened tobacco smoke wafted out. They went into the cloakroom where people crowded and pushed getting rid of their winter coats. Mollerup wanted to buy a pack of Gauloises from the cloakroom attendant and gave her five kroner.

'Nine kroner for the French ones,' said the attendant, with a reproachful look.

'Nine kroner! You can't mean that! Nine kroner for a pack of Gauloises. In Paris it doesn't cost two!'

'It's really not my fault, Sir. The price is what I told you.'

'Nine kroner!' he repeated resignedly, giving her the money.

'That's how it is when you come home from foreign lands,' a voice said behind him.

He turned round. He felt a shock of disgust.

'Ellesøe!' he heard himself say.

'Mollerup!' replied Ellesøe, looking him up and down. Mollerup returned his gaze and tried to look suitably superior. Superior and indifferent. As if he didn't turn a hair at standing face to face with this third-rate graphic artist who had wrecked a whole night in Paris for him. Ellesøe. Of all people he had to run into Ellesøe with his scanty hair, hollow cheeks and yearning expression.

'Claudia Benedetti,' he said, introducing the Italian woman.

'She obviously made an impression on Ellesøe. Mollerup saw an uncertain expression cross his face. Then a smile flickered over his lips. He cleared his throat, searched for words.

'Welcome . . . welcome to Denmark,' he said.

Then he straightened himself. Mollerup met his eyes again.

'Great, the bit with that nitwit Rolf Hauge!' he said with exaggerated jollity.

'Rolf Hauge?'

'Yes, making a right fool of him in your book. Bloody good!'

Three blacks in Black Muslim caps pushed between them. Mollerup grabbed the Italian woman's wrist. He wanted to seize the opportunity of getting away from Ellesøe and into the bar. But Ellesøe was there at once. He seized Mollerup's lapel with two fingers:

'One more thing. You write a bloody sight better than I'd expected!'

'I'm glad to hear that,' he responded, thinking he actually cared even less for the over-ingratiating Ellesøe than the aggressive and sly one.

'I didn't think you came here any more,' he went on. Just for something to say. Not to seem too taciturn. He remembered their conversation in Paris when Ellesøe confided that he had put his earlier Bohemian life behind him.

'Oh, well, you know . . . we can't all be as lucky as you.'

He looked at the Italian woman with an appreciative smile and went on:

'And sometimes — when it all slams down on you — you need a quick one. But I mustn't disturb you any longer,

Mollerup! You're obviously in the best possible company! Chiao!'

'Who was that?' she asked as they elbowed their way through the crush and reached the bar.

'Nobody special,' he said, ordering two *nagels*. 'Yes, actually. Do you remember the exhibition at the Danish House? Where we met for the first time? Do you recall the pictures of the dark, hunched-up people with their hands clasping their heads and sitting on flights of steps? Can you remember giving me quite a lecture on your dislike of Scandinavian art?'

'No,' she replied.

'Yes, you can!'

'Maybe. Now you mention it.'

'That was him. The one with the dark pictures.'

She laughed aloud:

'When you look like that, you couldn't make pictures in any other way!'

'A sad figure,' he said.

Someone gave him a push in the side. Then he fell alongside the bar so the hot drink splashed over his clothes. He had no idea what had happened. Suddenly he was lying on the floor staring up through a throng of legs shuffling about. He tried to get up and managed to lift himself on to his elbows, but then three drinkers fell on top of him so that the back of his head struck the floor hard and a something gave him a blow on his nose. The pain from his nose and the pain from his head rose into his brain, tears gushed from his eyes and he was temporarily blinded. But soon he managed to free himself and stand up. A violent fight was under way. One of the three black men was punching an American marine while the two others were involved in a fracas with a handful of bearded Danes. Tables were overturned, loud screams came from some of the women, and waiters in white shirts with the sleeves rolled up tried to separate the combatants, which only resulted in them being knocked down themselves. One of the waiters landed in a corner and knocked down a pile of boxes of empty beer bottles which rolled among the tables. Mollerup looked round for the Italian woman. He couldn't see her. He cautiously made his way through the crowd and out to the cloakroom where four police officers were on their way through the door with drawn truncheons. They grabbed him and said he was not to leave before he had given his name and address. He tried to break free but merely got a blow in the stomach with a truncheon. Then the Italian woman appeared from the restaurant. She shook the policeman vehemently and explained in broken English that they had nothing to do with the fight. The policeman looked at her suspiciously. Then he let them go.

Outside it was snowing again. All the parked cars had white blankets over their roofs and bonnets. Near Vartorv some black American soldiers threw snowballs at three laughing girls. The sound of tyres stilled and cyclists had to get off and push their cycles along on the pavement.

'Good Lord, you're bleeding!' she said, picking up a handful of snow and washing his nose with it. She put her arm round him affectionately and suggested they should go straight back to the hotel.

'And I thought Copenhagen was a peaceful town,' she went on.

'I thought it was too!' he replied. 'But it gets more and more wild every time I come back!'

They reached the hotel.

'Thanks for the help!' he said as they were about to go in.

'Nothing to thank me for!'

Her hand slid up his neck. He drew her to him and kissed her.

They embraced for so long that a leather jacket walking by on the opposite pavement shouted that that was enough. She laughed heartily at that when he translated it and gently stroked the snow off his hair with the edge of her hand.

They celebrated Christmas Eve at the hotel, with food and wine brought up to their room. Afterwards they lay side by side in bed and took it easy, she read an English crime novel, he had a pile of Danish newspapers going back over the past two weeks that he had brought from the office. They lit candles and put on a transistor radio they had borrowed from reception. Later on they put down the novel and the papers. She lay with her head on his lap looking up at the ceiling, he sat looking up at Strindberg with a pillow behind his head and an ashtray beside him for the ash of a Dutch cheroot. She questioned him about his childhood while she teased him by tickling his thigh with the tips of her unvarnished nails, and he told her about the outbreak of war when he was fifteen years old, about the German soldiers who were suddenly standing at Østerport Station with machine guns when Copenhageners were on their way to work and asking each other in astonishment what had happened. Then he asked her about her childhood. She lit a cigarette with the glow from his cheroot and said she could not remember a great deal. What she did remember did not have much to do with the war because her mother and father had managed quite well. She could remember the uniform of the Fascist soldiers, and she could remember Mussolini talking on the radio. She could also remember when the Americans reached Naples, where they were living at the time, and how her father went down into the street in a white suit wearing a straw hat to bid them welcome. But she could not remember much more. What made a far greater impression on her was her cat running away and not coming back for four days. One of its legs was missing, so it had to be shot.

'We had much too easy a time during the war. Just like you Danes! My father always kept on the right side. To start with he sided with Mussolini, then with the Americans and the Russians, and now he's on the side of the Christian Democrats. Tomorrow he'll side with the Chinese!'

He leaned down and kissed her. She took away the ashtray and snuggled close to him. On the windowsill a candle was nearly burnt out.

Next morning when they drew the curtains they were dazzled with white. Christmas Day in Copenhagen. Churchbells, no traffic, children playing in the street and Christmas trees in the windows of all the apartments. After breakfast he phoned a poet, a painter and a film director the Italian woman wanted to interview. She had no particular ideas of whom she should interview as she did not know anything about Danish art, so he described a selected few who were currently in fashion. From among them she chose the poet (he had read that he was the most revolutionary of all the twentieth century Danish poets), a painter renowned for having painted pixies for forty years and a young film director who (according to what he had read) was apparently an offshot of the French New Wave. He was unable to get hold of Dreyer for her. According to a woman who answered the telephone, he had gone to Paris to talk to an American producer about his Jesus film. As well as these, she had the names of some architects in her address book, names she had had sent by her newspaper in Italy. He drew maps for her on small scraps of paper so she could find her way to the various interview victims, and then she went off on her own.

For two days he walked around town alone until he met her in the evening on the Town Hall Square, in front of the newspaper centre as they had arranged. He went for long walks, on the first day down through Nyhavn, the New Harbour, over the big square of Amalienborg Slotsplads, the royal castle, and out to the tip of Langelinie, the harbourside walk. He went along the Strand Boulevard and out to the harbour at Svanemøllen, the Swans' Mill, where pleasure boats were laid up with ice on the rigging. He had lunch at a restaurant next to Svanemøllen Station and ended up having an argument with the eternal Danish waiter in his faded black suit rattling the coins in his pocket who refused to replace his open sandwich when he complained that the butter was rancid. Next day he walked over the Town Hall Square, out along Vesterbrogade, the West Bridge Street, to the right through the arch under the New Theatre, past the Cinema Palace and on past the lakes where elderly Copenhageners taking an airing after the Christmas orgies were feeding the ducks near the shore where the ice had been broken. He came to Sortedamsdoseringen, the Embankment by the Black Pond, and off Fugleøen, the Bird Island, he stopped where he could look over at the apartment in Østersøgade, the Street of the East Lake, where he had lived in 1937, when his father was on his deathbed. An intense feeling of melancholy seized him and forced him to go on, up towards Østerbrogade, East Bridge Street, and along a side street that to him stood for the sum of Copenhagen tristesse.

Nothing moved around him, no cars turned the corners, not a soul was on the pavements: only the almost untouched snow on the road and the pavements, the closed shops, the red barrack-like houses. A café far down the street and nothing else but the mirrors outside the houses in which old ladies caught sight of him, a solitary wanderer in a green coat who walked with his hands in his pockets, took out a cigarette, lit it, stopped, went on, glanced into a doorway, took a few drags of the cigarette and threw it away so it vanished into the snow with a faint hiss. A Christmas tree stripped of its decorations had already been put outside a street door, a few wisps of angel hair still hung on the branches with a single heart almost ripped in two with melted chocolate on the stem. He reached the café to find it closed. Through the dirty panes he could see the billiard table in a corner beside a pile of beer crates, the nicotine yellow pictures of King Christian X and Queen Alexandrine covered with fly mess, and the tables with green stained cloths. Some nearby churchbells started to ring for evensong, and soon afterwards bells were ringing all over the city. He pulled his collar up around his neck and lit a fresh cigarette, turned around and suddenly felt a violent urge to run, just run. And he ran up towards Østerbrogade where at least one or two cars were moving to and fro and a tram with a total of four passengers behind the misted windows was turning the corner from Øster Farimagsgade.

He cheered up in the evening when he met the Italian woman and they went out on the town to look at the night life. They visited various night clubs and finished up in Lorry which delighted her because she had never seen such a large dance floor before. They sat at a little table at the back, and she did not tire of admiring the decorative murals, not because they were beautiful or tasteful, but on the contrary so ghastly that they approached the sublime. Stars twinkled electrically in the sky above a lake with a rocking boat.

'Oh, it's wonderful,' she said and looked around her.

'I haven't been here since I was a boy,' he said, half to himself, pouring out his beer.

'What a scene for a film you could make with this decor and the orchestra as background, and the singer, and the people . . .'

Next day they went out to Dyrehaven, the Deer Park. They went in through the red gate and at once caught sight of a flock of fallow deer among the white-powdered trees. They went down towards Bakken, the Hill, and on the way she told him about her interviewees. She had liked the painter best, he had been so sweet, hopping around in a big glass-house wearing nothing but trousers, from one canvas to another. He wanted to hear her opinion of his pixies all the time, and when she left he kissed her on both cheeks and invited her to stay one summer. She thought the film director was nice too, but rather mediocre; he didn't have strong opinions on anything. He had only seen one Godard film, and the stills he showed her of his films were all about mysterious young Danes with long hair who sat on mattresses in dimly lit flats smoking hash. The poet had been more interesting but he could speak neither English nor French so they had had to speak each other by sign language and drawings. He lived in a big apartment with no other furnishings than a few foam rubber mats and lifesize nudes of his pregnant wife hung on all the walls. She did not care for any of the architects she had met. Although they could speak English they could hardly communicate like human beings, and all three of them looked exactly alike, with the same full beards, wearing the same health sandals and with wives in textile printed skirts who served tea in pottery cups.

Her cheeks grew rosy as they approached Peter Liep's House. She had on black gloves and a tartan trouser suit, and a little fur cap hid her long hair which she had put up on top of her head. She walked with little nervous steps and once almost stumbled over a stone. As she spoke, frosty breath came from her mouth, and small frost pearls had formed on her eyelashes. She stopped when she saw the deer among the treetrunks, but otherwise she seemed quite at home, as if nothing could surprise her. If they had gone to the Deer Park on their first day in Denmark she would certainly have looked around her with curious eyes, everything she saw would have been new and interesting, and she would have seized his arm to show him what she was looking at. Now it seemed as if she was expecting something, he didn't know what. Some kind of surprise. Something she could tell everyone about when she was back in Paris. Polar bears that suddenly rushed towards them so they had to run for cover behind the nearest trees? Peter Liep's house certainly did not hold her interest, even when he launched into a description of the old Danish style of building with thatched roofs and mud and wattle timbered houses.

'I can't forget the pictures that director showed me,' she said hesitantly. 'Don't the Danes do anything but sit around in flats . . . and . . . nothing?'

'Not a lot happens in Denmark,' he replied. 'Outwardly!'

He heard himself talking about the Danish culture that was based on the home on account of the climate, that everything went on between four walls and not on the street and in bistros and restaurants and so on as in Paris and Rome. He heard himself saying that in fact a great deal did go on in Denmark when people visited each other and got drunk and exchanged wives in a way no Frenchman in his wildest imagination would dream of. Not everything is visible on the surface, he instructed her, and heard how wrong it sounded for him to be — instructing her. That he should suddenly be defending something he had no wish to defend. But she was barely listening. She walked faster and faster as if she had set herself a definite goal. As they went through Bakken he told her what it was like there in the summer when Copenhageners went on the spree during the light nights, but he felt she wasn't much interested, it was so hard to describe atmosphere, all that was indefinable, the magic of the summer night, and when he suddenly started expanding on the poet Oehlenschlager's *Midsummer Night Play* he felt it was quite hopeless. He started well enough, indicating with assumed enthusiasm the shuttered stalls and the trees behind, he started with the onset of Romanticism, as he had learned it in the sixth form, but little by little he lost inspiration because she could not *feel* what he was telling her, the summer night, the laughter among the trees, the light sky. Was *sentir* the right word? Or the word *voir*? He tried them both but with no conviction, and finished by suggesting she should come in the summer so she could *feel* and *see* what it was he was trying to explain.

'I'm wondering what I should actually write in my articles,' she said quietly as they passed The Singer's Pavilion, as if she had not been listening to him at all. She bent down to brush snow from her trousers:

'I've promised the paper at least three articles in return for sending me up here . . . can't you help me? Isn't there *somewhere* we can go?

'We'll manage!' he replied, rolling a snowball and throwing it at a placard advertising hot dogs. He tried to sound merry and unconcerned.

They planned to tour the surroundings of Copenhagen and then drive north. He couldn't say there were any special sights they ought to see, but a famous American writer on architecture had recently said that the Copenhagen area was the most harmonious, the most beautiful and the most democratic in the world. They took a taxi when they got back to Klampenborg and drove around the residential district for an hour. Later on they drove up Strandvejen, the shore road, and every time the sea came in sight she leaned forwards.

'Oh, I love the colour of the Scandinavian sea,' she said and pointed to a sailing boat far out. 'That *grey* colour you see in Bergman's films . . .'

They spent an hour at Louisiana, the open air sculpture park and art gallery. There were a number of visitors there, mostly elderly couples, and a group of schoolchildren who ran from place to place playing tag. For the first time that afternoon the Italian woman seemed calm, she did not walk off as if she had to go somewhere, and she carefully studied every painting. He kept a step or two behind her all the time, looking through the glass walls at the snow-covered lawns that ran down to the Sound. When they had seen the galleries they had coffee and Danish pastries in the restaurant. They did not speak for a long time, she buried herself in the catalogue underlining names and writing in the margin, he made eyes at a small girl running through the legs of a gentleman a couple of tables away. Then the Italian woman shut the catalogue and looked at him.

'Do you think we could bring our departure date forward to tomorrow, so we get back to Paris for New Year's Eve?'

'We could ring and ask,' he said, surprised.

'You don't need to come with me if you'd rather stay here in Copenhagen.'

'If you go, I'll go too. I haven't anything to do here.'

On the way into town he thought over her remark. You don't need to come with me. She had uttered it in a strangely offhand way, as if to put some special meaning in the words, that she wanted to be free of him, simply, but did not want to hurt him because after all he had been kind enough to spend a whole week helping her in a strange town. Was she at this moment feeling forced to endure his company? What had really happened to cause this coolness between them, suddenly, without cause, why did she smile so mechanically when he pointed out Espergærde fishing village and said he had spent several summers there in his childhood, why couldn't they talk any more, either about trivial things or about everything important? He gazed at the driver's wrinkled neck and sensed a sinking feeling in his stomach. Should he do something mad? Leap out of the taxi at speed? Pretend to stick a revolver in the driver's neck?

'It gets dark early up here,' he said.

'Yes, it must be hard to live here all through the winter . . .'

She got out her cigarettes. He lit up for her so the flame illuminated her face and he could see bitter lines around her lips. When they reached the hotel he jumped out quickly to get to the reception and ring SAS. She mustn't think he was trying to get out of it, to pretend he had forgotten her question. 'It can't be done?' he said to the woman at the airline office and shook his head at the Italian woman, who turned and started upstairs to their room.

'You heard yourself there was nothing to be done,' he said on entering the room. 'The last two tickets were sold this morning.'

'There wasn't just one left?' she asked.

'They said it was full. Completely full.'

He wanted to embrace her but she pulled free and went into the bathroom to tidy up.

There was a hard frost on New Year's Eve and Mollerup slid about the pavement as he walked up to the Town Hall Square. A messenger from the newspaper had called at the hotel to ask if he would sign copies of *Paris From The Shady Side* at the bookshop beside the newspaper office in an hour's time. At first he refused but when the messenger said that the editor-in-chief wanted him to advertise himself a little and thus help the paper, he consented. He was greeted by the bookstore manager, a stocky man with big horn-rimmed glasses who led him to a small table covered with a green baize cloth. When he sat down he almost disappeared behind two big piles of *Paris From The Shady Side*, while the manager kept dancing around him smiling pleasantly. Soon the first customers were passed their copies, an old lady, a postman who announced with a stammer that in his humble opinion Monsieur Jean was Denmark's best journalist, and a middle-aged man who introduced himself as Mr So-and-so, a teacher from Østerbro Sixth Form College. To start with Mollerup took the trouble to write personal dedications. For the teacher he wrote that a good teacher occupied a more important position in the community than any number of peripatetic journalists. The postman took away a comment on how much it meant to a journalist abroad to be able to rely on the Danish

postal service. He paid tribute to the old lady for her youthful-
ness. But as time went on and more and more customers
turned up and the piles before him grew lower and lower he
limited himself to an *Amicalement* — *Votre M. Mollerup.* Just
before the signing time was up a man bent over him:

'Vagn!' he said with a strong whiff of mouthwash. 'Vagn
Schlütter! Don't you remember me from school?'

'Yes, of course, *Vagn!'* replied Mollerup with a false smile.
He picked up one of the last copies and wrote: To my old
classmate Vagn from his devoted Max Mollerup.

The other took the book and opened it with a smile that
swiftly stiffened:

'*Class*mate! I was bloody well three classes above you!'

'I'm very sorry,' he said, reaching for the book to change
the dedication.

'Yes, that's what I've always said, Jean de France, eh!'

Mollerup only half heard, and started to pack up his
things. He thought of going back to Bahn's Hotel but decided to wait till later in the afternoon. He felt tired because
he had not had more than a couple of hours' sleep. When
they went to bed the Italian woman had almost demonstratively turned her back on him, he was only allowed to kiss her
on the forehead and lay for a long time staring at the ceiling.
Later on he went and sat by the window because he could not
bear to lie beside her. She had placed herself right at the
edge of the bed as if she wanted to put as much air between
them as possible. He sat on the radiator and looked down at
the street and smoked three cigarettes one after the other.
When he went back to bed and crept under the double duvet
he managed to fall asleep, but then she woke him suddenly
with a push in the side because he was snoring. She made him
aware of it in a quiet and friendly tone, but nevertheless he
felt painfully humiliated. You snore! *Tu ronfles!*

He went up to his newspaper office where the porter on
duty wished him Happy New Year from behind his desk on
which was a little Christmas tree with electric candles. He was
the only man in the office. The office floors were covered
with old papers and teleprinter tape, a television screen

flickered emptily in one corner and smoke coiled from a half finished cigar in an ashtray. A big poster hung on one wall: REMEMBER TO BRING IDEAS FOR THE DOG CAMPAIGN IN THE NEW YEAR. A photo of a poodle hung beside it, a balloon issuing from its mouth: I TOO WOULD LIKE TO BE A FREE AGENT. The journalists had just left the office to go home and celebrate New Year, said the duty man, following him curiously everywhere as if he was a stranger who had to be watched. He shook him off and went into the canteen, but that was empty too and he could not get the beer he wanted. He sat down at one of the rectangular dining tables and leafed through the last newspapers of the year. Then he put his head on his arms and fell into a light sleep.

She had changed her clothes when he went back to the hotel. As he entered their room she went to meet him in a pale lilac thigh-length dress. She seemed less cool than he had expected, on the contrary she asked with slight anxiety in her voice where he had been so long. While he got out a dark suit and brushed it he told her how the signing session had gone, that it had been pretty irritating but was something authors had to do. Afterwards they drove out to No 10 Allégade where he had booked a table. The first New Year's fireworks were already sounding out in the streets and back yards and on the Town Hall Square a group of young people in dinner jackets and long dresses threw jumping jacks at each other's legs.

Their table was at the back of the restaurant. He sat on a chair, she on a red velvet sofa she sank right into. Though she smiled at him and said she looked forward to the dinner he knew he had to play his cards right, not to let his guard drop too much, not to believe that her friendliness covered much more than being resigned to celebrating New Year's Eve in Copenhagen, and she had told herself that she might as well get what she could out of it. There were a good many people around them, elderly couples from the residential district of Frederiksberg and some Americans he calculated must be from the American Embassy since they were discussing broken windows after a recent demonstration against the Vietnam war.

To begin with there was no change of mood. She was happy with the food, as was he. And they made an hour pass in discussing food, restaurants in Paris, food in general and French food in particular, which — she didn't know if he was aware, but she couldn't resist saying it every time French cuisine was praised — came from her native land, from Italy. He told her about the restaurant, it was one of the few acceptable ones in Copenhagen and had a history that was a piece of cultural history in itself: there wasn't a famous Danish actor or painter or poet who had not eaten here at some time or other. Suddenly he noticed that she was wearing the silver bracelet he had given her. That made him happy. Perhaps it signified something, that she had put it on. Perhaps it was her way of saying that she had not been herself for a time, like all women, but that now she wanted them to find each other again, for it to be the same as before. He felt warmth spreading over him, he felt alert, the food suddenly tasted good, so did the full-bodied burgundy. When they finished eating he called the waitress discreetly and asked her for two double Armagnacs.

'Ammoniak?' she asked, wrinkling her forehead.

'Armagnac!' he corrected her. 'It's a kind of brandy!'

When everyone had reached the coffee stage a door opened and the proprietor came in pushing a red wheelbarrow filled to the brim with paper hats and noses and crackers and streamers and bags of confetti. He furnished each table with a selection. Mollerup fumbled with a cardboard nose with cheap frames, unsure of what to do with it, but the Italian woman insisted he should put it on. She had on a clown's hat and was swinging a rattle and smiling. People at the other tables had put on their hats and noses too and were calling out to each other and throwing streamers and confetti. The restaurant proprietor stood in the middle of the floor nodding approvingly from table to table. Mollerup held the nose and glasses up to his face for a moment but would not put it on with the elastic: it was too childish. Instead he lifted his double brandy and toasted the Italian. As their glasses clashed together she held the back of his hand, and he felt he could read in her eyes that she was really sorry for . . . for turning her back on him. And he had to say something:

'I've been wondering. I don't know . . .'

No, that was the most foolish thing he could say. He shouldn't have opened his mouth at all, just accept her caress as a completely natural expression of fellow feeling. But he couldn't stop. He had wanted to ask her for a long time. Ever since they first slept together in her apartment and looked down on the Rue de Dragon with snow falling on an awning and the fat dog scratching itself.

'I've been wondering,' he went on, 'I've been wondering whether we might move in together when we get back to Paris . . .'

It irritated him to hear himself stammering and he tried to control his voice:

'If we need furniture I'll make sure we get it direct from Copenhagen. The Danish shop in Paris isn't worth three cheers, as we say in Danish.'

She took off her party hat and put it by her plate. She bit her lip. She raised her brandy glass and took a sip. Then she looked in her bag for cigarettes.

'And we were getting on so well,' she said, so quietly he could hardly hear.

With a sense of unreality he heard shouting and noise around them, heard the Americans tune up with Happy New Year and then a guitar being tuned. He sat with his back to the other diners hoping against hope he wouldn't be seen by a singer who had come in from the street and was starting on the first verse of a French soldiers' song. He knew the singer: the French snob who was the newspaper's cartoonist. But it was not long before the guitar sounded right in his ear and the cartoonist's face came in sight over his shoulder with 'Les Rues de Copenhague.' He put a big smile on his face and looked up slantwise into the cartoonist's happy ruddy face with the narrow moustache above the lips. He kept on smiling as he looked across at the Italian woman who was apparently thinking of doing something or other, no matter what, just something that could get them out of the situation they had suddenly been landed in. Her long fingers played nervously with a cigarette lighter, with the pack of cigarettes, with some breadcrumbs, a teaspoon, the bowl of sugar lumps. Wanting to get ahead of her, while the cartoonist went on to other tables, he took out a matchbox and put four matches in a square, a fifth as the handle of the square and inside the square a bit of sulphur. He moved three matches and only three. And in the right way, so that the sulphur was outside the dustpan.

'Like that?' he asked, still with the same big smile on his face.

She looked at him as if to express a certain disinterested satisfaction that he had at last learned how to do it.

PART TWO

O, capital infâme!

BAUDELAIRE

He was trying to spur himself into a sensible rhythm with work as the prime motive. As soon as he got up in the morning he went down to the nearest newspaper kiosk to buy the Paris papers, the latest weeklies and one or two political journals, to inspire new ideas for articles. He sat for hours at his desk leafing through an article on the topical problems of surrealism, then a survey of modern West African poetry, he read about the political situation in the Antilles, about the Swedish debate on sexual roles seen through French eyes, about Ben Bella's final moves in the attempt to shore up his hold on power and about the end of the world as seven French writers imagined it in a playful questionnaire. One of the seven was the writer with the crewcut. He thought the world would end some time in the twenty-first century when over-population was threatened in earnest and an all-destroying nuclear war would be the only disastrous solution.

Mollerup's fingers grew black with printer's ink, in particular the cheap print of the literary weeklies. He even read articles on subjects normally of no interest to him and needing constant use of the dictionary, from beginning to end. He stubbornly worked his way through the fine print of columns on 'language and objects' and the naturalistic fallacy in the philosophy of the young Sartre. He also studied the back page notes of the newspapers and so acquired knowledge of dog-training in Provence and the water shortage in Israel. If he came across well-known people who might be of interest to Danish readers, a young politician who came to a conclusion about de Gaulle's European policy and foresaw a new war between France and Germany, a film maker in dispute with the French censor or an agricultural expert criticizing the outdated Breton methods of pasturization, he jotted down their names on a list of possible interviewees. He cut out the most significant political and cultural articles and filed them in alphabetical order.

When he finally came to a halt he would walk around his study until he stopped by the window to look down on the Avenue de Wagram where the January rain was falling for the third day running, and the Spanish immigrant workers stood in doorways or behind the windowpanes of cafés playing the jukeboxes. He succeeded in keeping to his work programme for almost a week. The pile of newspapers mounted up beside his work table, the list of names to interview covered two closely-written sheets, the file of cuttings bulged and he had completed two long articles on the financial and social prospects for France in the coming year. But in the long run work could not drown out the awareness of his failure with the Italian woman. He could not forget himself in the African poem, the problems of the Antilles and the impending war between France and Germany. It was worst at night when he could not sleep and tossed and turned incessantly in his crumpled sheets and over and over again heard her repeat, softly and almost inaudibly, in a tone both disappointed and reproving: *And we were just getting on so well.* He recalled her dark eyes, their sudden change of expression, on guard against his next move. Did he dream of his defeat when he did at last fall asleep? He knew when he woke up in the morning with a dry throat and smarting headache that his dreams had been nightmarish. He had to hurry into the kitchen to put the kettle on for coffee to wake himself up and shake off the night and again lose himself in grinding away at French newspapers. And he cut out more articles, added more names to the list, until one morning he caught himself writing diary notes about what had happened in Copenhagen in the margin of *Les Lettres Françaises. Arrived before Christmas. All going well. Comfortable flight. Amazed at how small Copenhagen is. The dreary meeting with the others on the newspaper. But happy to be with her. She looks at Copenhagen with enthusiastic eyes and sings the praises of the Danes, the 'friendly Danes'. At the Drop Inn. The brawl. Ellesøe! But a wonderful night with her. Christmas Eve: wonderful again, relaxed. Between Christmas and New Year: suddenly she changes, wants to go back to Paris before the date we fixed. Turns her back on me in bed. When did this change begin and what caused it? She had seen the various people she wanted to interview. The Deer Park, Peter Liep, The Hill. Something happened in her, to her. But what? What? The days leading up to New Year: frosty, melancholy, no life in the streets. New Year's Eve!!!*

He picked up a piece of paper intending to expand the diary, write down what had happened hour by hour, if possible minute by minute. If he wrote a precise description of the stay in Copenhagen, with as many details as he could recall, surely he would be able to pinpoint the moment when things went wrong. There must be a reason. He started to write and came to Christmas Day and the day after Christmas when he walked around Copenhagen on his own. He resorted to his typewriter to be able to see what he had written more clearly. He added dates and times and after a while had written down everything he could remember. When he read through the account he came to a halt at the moment when they walked through the red gates and started to go down towards Peter Liep. When they got up that morning there had been nothing the matter, nor in the train out to Klampenborg. She had commented freely on the residential districts they passed and jokingly tried to pronounce the names of the stations, Hellerup and Ordrup in particular caused her problems. She did not even dare to try Klampenborg, she held a hand over her eyes deprecatingly as the train drew into the station. On the way to the Deer Park he had laughed heartily at her notion of the Danish language as something incomprehensible and inexpressible, something like Welsh or Breton.

But the change had come just inside the Deer Park: suddenly she put on speed and walked a couple of steps away from him when he tried to put an arm round her shoulders. What had happened during the few hundred meters from the red gates and a short distance into the park? It was probably not more than 25 or 50 meters. Ten perhaps? He put down the papers as a disturbing thought struck him. Had the poet she had interviewed said something unpleasant about him; that he was a rotten journalist, for instance? And later, when she went to see the painter and the film director and the architects, had she questioned them about him and had they all shrugged their shoulders and confirmed the poet's judgement? Had she, before she met the poet and the painter and the film director and the architects, been interested in him purely because she knew nothing about him, about his standing, had she regarded him as something exciting from an unknown country, but then had recalled the opinions voiced about him just as they walked through the red gates? And had she then looked sideways at him without his noticing and said to herself it must be right, what they said about him, that he was a mediocre journalist and an uninteresting person who was not worth spending more time on in a town that had nothing more to offer than cold, lifeless holidays with rowdy churchbells, a single pleasant dance hall and a few deer in a suburban park?

Or was he imagining all this? Did her behaviour merely reflect tactics? Did she want him to conquer her in the way southern women preferred, in contrast to Scandinavians? He convinced himself of this, folded up *Les Lettres Françaises*, went into the hall and put on his overcoat, then went down in the elevator. A dusting of frosty snow was whipped along the Avenue de Wagram by a strong gusty wind that whirled street refuse, cigarette stubs, pages of newspapers and withered leaves with it. Trees swayed in the wind, and an old lady fell over screaming in the middle of the road so the cars had to brake hard. Passers-by struggled vainly to fold up their umbrellas which the wind had turned inside out, and on a street corner not far from where his car was parked, a sign saying 'No admittance' had fallen over. The wind slackened slightly in the Champs Elysées, and when he came to the Left Bank it had dropped. He drove slowly down the Rue du Dragon and parked, and soon afterwards found himself on his way upstairs to the Italian woman's apartment.

He wondered what to say to her when she opened the door

or whether he should say anything at all and merely smile at her as if nothing had happened and it was the most natural thing in the world for him just to call. He was about to ring the bell when he heard voices behind the door: two men and one woman. He could clearly hear the Italian's and recognized one of the men as the crewcut writer. He stood with his finger close to the bell but was frightened when he heard loud scornful laughter. He thought he heard the Italian utter the word 'Copenhague', or maybe he imagined it. In any case he suddenly felt it would be totally stupid to ring the bell. Suppose she did not allow him in? He began to walk down the stairs, but at that moment a man came towards him from the street. He wore an ankle-length raincoat and ran upstairs two steps at a time. Mollerup turned and ran upstairs as fast as he could until he was on the floor below the top one. He looked down through the banister rails. Luckily the stranger had not seen him. He stopped outside the Italian woman's door and rang the bell. The door was opened and two female hands appeared, embraced him and drew him inside. Mollerup stayed where he was. Then an old woman came out of an apartment with a waste bin. Like a shot he bent down and pretended to tie up his shoelace, looked up and smiled at her. The old woman stopped when she came up to him so the stinking bin was just under his nose. A sour smell of cat and cod's liver came from her rooms.

'Do you *live* here?' she asked.

He straightened up.

'I'm going to visit someone,' he said.

'Who?!'

She wrinkled her upper lip in an inquisitorial manner so her moustache moved like a living thing and he could see her yellow teeth.

'A friend!' he replied and started to go down. He walked past the Italian woman's apartment. Now he could hear the sound of music.

'What is the name of your friend?'

'He is called . . . isn't this No 24?' he asked, going faster.

'This is No 34 — trente quatre, monsieur!'

He was out on the street with the old woman at his heels, she slammed the door after him in a loud demonstration. He walked up to the Boulevard Saint-Germain. He glanced at some books in the bookshop between the Café Flore and Deux Magots. He looked at shirts in a men's outfitters further down the street, but could not decide to buy one. The irritated assistant omitted to bid him goodbye. He bought a stack of Danish newspapers in a kiosk and went into a café to look through them. He read about Lommer's plans for the spring, about drug cases near St Nicholas's Church and an interview with a nude model who wanted to be a serious actress. He put down the papers, paid and went on. Soon afterwards he came to the restaurant where he had had kidneys and corncobs with the Italian woman. They were getting ready for the evening. The bald man sat in his black roll-neck sweater doing accounts while a transistor radio played in a corner:

> *Oh! oui, Chéries, on vous aime malgré tout*
> *Oh! ye-ye*
> *Oh! Oh! ye-ye*

Mollerup nodded.
'Thanks for that evening here!' he called through the open door.

The bald man looked up from his place behind the till and returned the greeting with two fingers to his temple. But he did not invite Mollerup in, and as he walked on he had to walk faster to keep warm. Each time he turned a street corner a cold gust of wind hit him. He went down to the Seine, crossed the Pont-Neuf, but turned round in the centre of the bridge and instead walked along the river to the Boulevard St.-Michel, where he went into a shooting gallery and won a teddy bear which he gave to an Arab boy at his heels. Later he bought a bag of toasted almonds, but could only eat two and threw the rest into the gutter. He went up to the Rue Champollion, but could not make up his mind to see a film in one of the four small studio cinemas with long lines of students at the box offices. He went into yet another book-shop, a record shop and a shoe shop where he upset another assistant because he did not intend to buy any of the shoes he tried on. He got back to his car as it was getting dark. He was hungry, but when he put his hand into his inside pocket he realized he had left his wallet at home. He spent his last change on yet another sheaf of newly arrived newspapers. You've got to work, he thought. It's the only way out.

But he could not concentrate. In the morning he tried out a small ritual. While he washed and shaved the coffee was heating. He had breakfast in the kitchen. Two slices of bread with salted butter and a large cup of coffee with cold milk. A cigarette. Then a short walk in the fresh air to buy news-papers. He put the papers in a pile on the right hand side of his desk. On the left he placed the cuttings file, in the middle the list of interviewees. He pushed the little typewriter table over to the writing desk. He settled himself. Filled four pipes which he placed in a row. But when at last he was about to start writing and reading newspapers he was seized with restlessness again, he fidgeted in his chair, stretched out his legs or pulled them in, got a pain in his neck and found his thoughts everywhere other than on his work. He wrote more diaries of what had happened in Copenhagen and each time came to the conclusion that things had gone wrong as soon as they had walked through the red gate.

The more he thought about the Italian woman, the harder it became to remember her. He could recall most of what she had said, in particular her tone of voice when she had talked of her childhood. He could hear her laughter, conjure up her perfume and her hair without trouble. He remembered her enthusiasm after she had been shopping in Copenhagen. Even the little drops of frost in her eyebrows when they were walking in the Deer Park. But when he tried to assemble all his impressions, he came to a stop. She turned into a shadow that vanished every time he tried to seize it, leaving a hollow place inside him. If he managed to think of something else she could suddenly take shape before his eyes. The impressions turned into a whole — to the image of a well-dressed, delicately built Italian woman who spoke French with a comical nasal accent and had long black hair and dark eyes and a face gilded by carefully applied make-up. Then she disappeared again. And he felt a greater and greater need to see her. If he stayed in the vicinity of her home he would be bound to meet her. But it ought to take place by chance, and when she looked up at him at a crossroads or in a restaurant he walked into and found a table near hers, or on the step of a bus she entered and he followed, he would feign total surprise and say: 'Oh, is it you . . . is it *You!*'

Just opposite the entrance to her block of flats there was a stairway. If he climbed to the landing of the third floor and stood on a chair that was in a corner he could see, through a narrow, very dirty window, across the street to her windows. To start with he did not actually mean to spy on her, just wait for the moment when she stepped into the street and then follow her at a suitable distance. But the temptation to watch her in her home was too great, and his heart gave a leap of excitement when he saw her behind the curtains, walking to and fro in the apartment, sitting at a little table in front of a small typewriter or walking through a door into the kitchen to make a cup of tea or coffee. He could only get a glimpse of her and he never saw her go right up to the window. Several days passed before he saw her go down to the street. He spent several hours on the landing every day, as a rule in mid-afternoon, waiting for her to go down. In the end he was on the point of giving up.

But one day the door opened. She was wearing a knee-length fur coat with a tight belt at the waist. She walked along the pavement and stopped at a post-box, then took a bundle of letters out of her pocket. She looked through them as if to check the addresses were correct, then posted them and vanished down a side street. He ran down the stairs and along the street until he reached the corner she had turned. She walked on the right sidewalk up to the Rue de Rennes. He stayed at least a hundred meters behind her and kept to the opposite pavement. Now and then she went into a shop but never stayed more than five minutes. Each time it was a shop selling wool and sewing requisites. Eventually she came out of a shop carrying a bag, and he thought now she had found what she wanted, some particular elastic or a certain colour of wool. If she looked towards the road he stopped at once and looked the other way or into a shop window where he could see her reflection through the traffic. Now and then she threw her head back in the habit she had of making her hair fall correctly over her fur collar. She walked purposefully, making her way deftly through the crowds coming towards her. Only once she was pushed aside when three North Africans refused to make way for her, she turned indignantly and grumbled at them, pulling at her shoulder to get her coat into place. Finally she arrived in Montparnasse and for some minutes he lost sight of her behind the booths selling flowers and fruit and sweets. He hurried over a pedestrian crossing to her side of the street. He increased his speed but slowed down when he was suddenly a few meters behind her. She appeared between the shoulders of two German marines. He turned promptly towards the edge of the pavement and placed himself behind a flower booth from where he saw her disappear into a garage. He stayed there, ignoring the booth owner, a skinny old man with an eye patch who told him excitedly that he had no right to stand there and not buy a bunch of flowers. Then he caught sight of her again. She drove out of the garage in her green sports car, looked to the left and the right and entered the stream of traffic, rounded a traffic island and headed at full speed back for the Rue de Rennes.

Next time he shadowed her she went shopping in the Rue de Seine. He had only just arrived at the window when she came out. She wore a raincoat with a hood and carried a shopping basket. To start with he kept to the usual hundred meters behind her, but slowly gained on her because she put the hood over her head and so could see little except straight in front of her. When she was shopping he went up close for a moment so he could hear her voice as she discussed the price of some cauliflowers with a street trader. But he felt that was playing with fire. If she turned round suddenly she would be face to face with him, and he felt that the time for their 'chance' meeting was not yet ripe. She would realize he had been following her. And he ran across to the opposite pavement and waited until she had finished shopping. She went from trader to trader buying carrots, apples, peppers and bananas. Then she checked her shopping list to make sure she had everything and turned round. She pushed off her hood so her hair fell free and kept changing hands, holding the basket. Ought he to take the opportunity of meeting her? Should he walk up beside her and take the shopping basket from her with a courteous: 'May I?' But before he could make up his mind whether to contact her or not she was back in the Rue de Dragon, and he gave up shadowing her, sat down in a café and ordered a beer.

Just as the waiter brought his beer he saw her again. She turned the corner of the Rue du Dragon and walked straight past his café to stand in the queue at the taxi stand on the corner of the Boulevard Saint-Germain and Rue de Rennes. Now she wore the knee-length coat with the tight belt. It was rush hour and there was a wait of several minutes between the taxis driving up to the stand. She bit one forefinger, fidgeted nervously at the edge of the gutter, ran her fingers through her hair and straightened her belt. Then she went up to the first person in the line and asked — as far as he could guess — if she could take the next taxi. The person she spoke to was a middle-aged lady who immediately started to fling her arms about in a fury. She had to go back and take her place in the line again, which meanwhile had grown to twice its length. She tried waving to one of the taxis that went by in the middle of the road, but as none stopped she let her arm drop and instead walked to a bus stop.

He quickly paid for his beer and buttoned up his coat. He could not stop himself from taking up the chase again, and before he realized it he had run after her and jumped onto her bus. He stood on the open platform with his back to her, looking down at the asphalt rolling away like a wide conveyor belt. Darkness was falling over Paris, the street lights had been lit for some time, and the electric signs whirled past his eyes. He stood clutching the greasy rail, bending forward slightly so the Italian woman could not recognize him by his neck. He looked in at the drivers of the cars following the bus. The people at the wheel all looked tired, cigarettes hanging loosely from their lips. In one car a man was quarrelling with his wife and he smiled because their mouths looked so comical, moving up and down as if in an aquarium, and he could not hear a word. In another car a mother on the back seat was giving her boy a hearty thrashing while her husband at the wheel beat himself furiously on the forehead. A motor-cyclist tried to get between the cars with the result that he crashed straight into a fruit cart sending hundreds of apples rolling over the road and exploding like electric bulbs under the front wheels of the cars.

Suddenly she got off. As the bus drove on he saw her walking along the pavement against the traffic stream with her hair swaying rhythmically over the fur collar. He leaped over to the step and unfastened the safety chain, turning so he faced the inside of the bus. The driver shouted at him to wait until the next stop, but he summoned his courage and jumped off. The road forced his legs into a hectic run and several times he nearly fell flat on his face. But as he came to rest, he ran more and more slowly and saw the bus becoming a distant lighted dot. Cars hooted at him because they had to drive around him, and a few furious yells from opened windows reached his ears. Then he stopped, out of breath, and stepped on to the sidewalk. He had lost sight of her, and when he regained his breath he started to run after her. When he came to a crossroads he looked to see if she had turned off. But there she was, just in front of him. She stood by a window exhibiting kitchen ware. Like lightning he crossed to the kerb making out he was waiting for a pause in the traffic so he could cross over. He had the feeling that she had the feeling that she was being followed by someone and wanted to find out who it was by looking at the window. But when he looked cautiously over his shoulder she had started off again. Finally she came to the Rue de Faubourg St.-Honoré and vanished into an art gallery. He approached cautiously and peered in. There were a lot of people inside with sherry glasses in their hands, absorbed in chatting together and pointing at the pictures on display.

He saw the crewcut writer among the guests. He stood in a corner with crossed arms laughing heartily at something an elderly woman in a crocodile coat was telling him. The Italian woman had gone up to a black-haired man he vaguely recalled as the man who had run up her stairs in the ankle-length raincoat the day he had been about to ring her bell. They gesticulated wildly. The Italian woman had unbuttoned her coat and kept clutching her head while she stamped the floor lightly with one foot. The man held a finger up in front of her as if rebuking her. As she refused to quieten down the black-haired man turned on his heel and left her. He took a glass of sherry from a small table in the centre of the room, downed it in two gulps, put it down and went back to her. This time he stretched out his arms in a conciliatory gesture, smiling all over his face, and immediately she calmed down and caressed the back of his neck. Various people near them followed the scene with interest.

Something told him he ought to go inside. It couldn't be a complete disaster. He had chanced by, had always been interested in modern art. Or he could even say that he had received an invitation as a journalist, and, as he had nothing else to do, had come along. He unbuttoned his coat and walked in. Just inside the door he picked up a catalogue. The paintings were by a Spaniard called Carlos Carlos who belonged to the group known as Nouvelles Figurations. His works showed nudes in surrealistic primeval forests. The people were painted in strong anti-naturalistic colours. One was tartan, another orange with blue teeth and green eyes, a third had skin like the American flag. All of them wore on their wrists the same scrupulously painted watch showing five minutes to twelve. Mollerup strolled round among the guests taking great care not to be seen by the Italian woman or the crewcut writer whose laughter resounded through the high-ceilinged gallery. He wanted to choose the moment for their meeting.

Most of the men looked as if they were in the diplomatic service or big business. They were impeccably dressed in dark pin-striped suits and, when they conversed, it was in the formal tones in which words were noncommittally slipped over the lips. The black-haired man had left the Italian woman and was greeting various guests. He constantly nodded with an assumed smile of modesty when the ladies clapped and praised the paintings. Mollerup guessed he was Carlos Carlos, the Spanish painter. *The Spanish painter.* Of course. Why hadn't he thought of it before? He must be the Italian woman's divorced husband. He had sideburns right down to his jaws, his nose was reminiscent of a boxer's broken nose and he wore a selection of gold chains on both wrists. Mollerup thought he also might be some actor or other in a Bunuel film he had once seen, and he was so occupied in studying him that he realized too late that he had come close to the corner where the crewcut writer was amusing himself with the lady in the crocodile coat.

'*Ah ha!*' exclaimed the crewcut writer, giving him a stiff smile.

He smiled back.

'Our journalist from Sweden!' the crewcut one went on.

'From *Denmark*,' he corrected and, going right up to the writer, gave him his hand.

'From Denmark, yes. That's true. I'd quite forgotten.'

'Denmark and Sweden are the same thing to the French,' he said, trying to sound casual and ironic.

'Not at all,' replied the writer. 'Denmark is the positive version of morbid Sweden. So I'm told.'

'Morbid and morbid. You should visit Sweden in summer.'

'Yes, the country looks quite different then . . .'

The writer was wearing the same bomber jacket he had on when they went to the Arab town, he was unshaven and looked very different from the rest of the assembly.

'How are you getting on with your book?' asked Mollerup.

'My book?'

'Yes, the detective novel you told me about.'

'Oh, that. I've got so many irons in the fire I can never sort them out. But I dropped the story you're talking about long ago.'

'Oh, you seemed so intrigued by what you saw in the Arab settlement.'

'Right. But later on I said to myself that it wasn't so interesting after all. Good God, there are so many shanty towns like that around Paris. And sociological criticism doesn't really appeal a lot to us French. The English and you Scandinavians are much better at that, shall we say, sentimental genre . . . .'

This time the writer seemed as chilly as he had been friendly last time they met, and Mollerup felt like going for him in some way or other, arguing with him, asking him painful questions, saying something about it being odd that France had had de Gaulle for so long that the intellectuals had not the remotest interest in improving social conditions. But then his heart literally missed a couple of beats: the Italian woman had come over to them. She put her arms akimbo under her fur and looked him up and down, not directly hostile but not especially enthusiastic either. Rather neutral, he thought. Neutral and yet slightly surprised.

'Isn't it . . . how did you get here?'

He was going to tell her the story of his getting invitations to most private views in Paris, as a journalist. But she apparently didn't expect an answer:

'It was interesting to get to know your country. I have already told my friends here in Paris about the dance hall we went to . . . what was it called?'

'With the painting of the boat rocking under twinkling stars?'

'Oh, yes, that's right!' She laughed.

'How are your articles on Denmark going, by the way?'

He looked her in the eyes, would not look away:

'You were going to write . . . wasn't it three at least . . . ?'

He was irritated at himself for floundering.

'Oh, those,' she answered, looking around her absently.

'There wasn't really anything to write about, so I agreed with my paper that . . . .'

The party was coming to an end, and she left him remarking that she had to say goodbye to people. The guests had thinned out, one by one or in groups and he was left there with the Italian woman, who was putting glasses on a tray, the crewcut writer who stood by a window hands in pockets, and the black-haired painter who was emptying ashtrays. The door on to the Rue du Faubourg St.-Honoré stood open. Almost like a direct reminder to him, he thought while faintly hoping that they . . . that they what? Would invite him to a restaurant with them? Or to the party they must be going to have after the private view? He walked slowly to the door and called goodbye to the Italian woman. She looked across at him, smiled and waved. The Spanish painter did not turn towards him but went on emptying ashtrays. The crewcut writer lazily lifted a hand: 'Ciao!'

He came to the Champs-Elysées, passed the cinemas, the cafés and The Danish House which had a new display in the windows. Big pictures of girl cyclists on the Shore Road had been gummed onto plywood and hung on fine steel wires. Beneath the photographs doll-sized Danish Life Guards went marching along with architect-designed knives and forks as guns. *Visitez le Danemark!* was painted on the windows in red and white letters. Then he reached the Avenue de Wagram. He went up in the slow lift and let himself into the flat just as the telephone rang. He rushed into the study, a faint hope rising in him, for she did have his number and would have worked out exactly when he got in.

But it was Copenhagen calling and in a moment the editor-in-chief was on the line, asking him to look up an Israeli spy in Paris whose brother had been thrown into prison in Cairo and condemned to death within a fortnight. He was to phone a certain number and get hold of the facts of the case so that Denmark could be the first country to start up a press campaign that would influence the Danish government to influence the Egyptian government to pardon the Israeli.

'You'll do this, won't you, Mollerup — and *fast*!'

He was to meet the Israeli in the Deux Magots, at the third table before the stairs leading down to the toilets. He would sit there holding a yellow periodical in front of him, in a grey winter coat with a red scarf. The Israeli also told him on the telephone that he had a sabre scar from his left nostril slanting down to his upper lip. With this information Mollerup easily caught sight of him when he entered the café a few days later. The Israeli sat as arranged at the third table before the way down to the toilets with the yellow periodical on the table. He was surprised at how wide the sabre scar was, at least a centimeter and with an almost blood-red stripe down the centre. How had he come by that scar? He guessed that the Israeli, who must be about 60, had got the scar in Germany at the end of the 1920s. After he sat down and introduced himself the Israeli bent towards him, looking around to see if anyone was sitting near enough to overhear what they said. Then the Israeli whispered that they must on no account talk about 'the case' at this table and in this café. He had a feeling he had been followed during the last few days, and now they must just behave naturally, chat about the weather, makes of car or the latest films. Had he seen the last American hit featuring the struggle between the Americans and the Mexicans in the nineteenth century?

Mollerup caught on at once:

'The one with Elsa Martinelli who gets shot at the end?' he asked so loudly that people sitting nearby could not help but hear.

'Elsa Martinelli?' said the Israeli looking blank. Then he smiled so his scar wrinkled:

'As far as I recall it was Claudia Cardinale . . .'

'No, it *was* Elsa Martinelli!'

'That's true. So it was. But it's so easy to confuse those two. They are both Italian, after all.'

They discussed other films, the inadequate heating system in French apartments and the signs indicating a renaissance of the Jugend age. Then the Israeli suggested discreetly that they should leave. On the way out he looked back over his shoulder. He took Mollerup by the arm and led him firmly round a corner, speeded up, turned another corner and pulled him into a doorway where hissing cats jumped down from the waste bins. He stood quite still for a while with his finger to his lips looking cautiously along the pavement. He wanted to find out if they were being shadowed. Then he initiated Mollerup into 'the case.' In a hoarse voice the Israeli described how his brother had been seized in the south of France and taken to Cairo in a trunk. The Egyptians had mixed up their names, and now his brother was about to be executed as a spy, without cause, without proof, solely on the grounds of name and false information. He himself could do nothing at all about it since he was the one they were after. A Danish friend had put him in touch with the Danish press and . . . well, he knew the rest, the Israeli emphasized while his little finger played with the light switch in the doorway. In short, now it was a matter of getting up a campaign in Denmark that would influence the Danish government and, in quick succession, the Swedish, the Norwegian, the German and the other European powers in Europe and the free world. The Egyptian government must be made to see that they had got hold of the wrong man. The Israeli looked hard at him: he must not reveal the source of his information, that was obvious. The Egyptians must not find out that the man they really wanted was in Paris.

Mollerup nodded and was handed a photograph the Israeli took out of his wallet. It showed his brother sitting in a garden in Provence, in swimming trunks with a drink in his hand.

They went out onto the pavement. The Israeli looked over his shoulder again, then pulled his collar up to his neck and the brim of his hat down over his eyes. Mollerup received a fervent handshake and was left holding the photograph as the Israeli disappeared in a taxi. Then he made his way to a cheap Chinese restaurant. While waiting for his meal, he realized the ludicrous unimportance of his own problems. How would it feel to have a brother about to be executed? How would it feel in fact to be a *spy*? He had never met a spy before, or anyone remotely like one, and their conversation seemed in a strange way to be unreal, something that had never happened, something he might have seen in a bad film. He took the photograph from his inside pocket. Had the man been kidnapped shortly after the picture was taken? Had two hands emerged from a bush just behind, where he sat screwing up his eyes against the sun with his drink in his hand, and had pulled him over backwards? Had he later been stuffed into a trunk with breathing holes and taken to Marseilles to be packed on board a freighter, destination Alexandria?

He put the picture back in his pocket and went over to a telephone in the corner of the restaurant to ring the Italian woman. The meeting with the Israeli had cheered him up even though he knew there was really nothing to be cheerful about. But for a while he had been able to forget himself, to escape from the circle he was caught in. Suddenly he was able to observe his situation from above, as if the meeting with the Israeli and his problems had been the push he needed. He was in love with the Italian woman, had run after her with his tongue hanging out of his mouth, undignified, childish. He had played his cards like a bumbling amateur — but so what? He would ring her. He would ask her out, cross out what had happened up to now, and if she accepted the invitation all well and good. If she declined he could soon find a new girl among the thousands of available girls in Paris, girls who would be happy to be invited to the cinema and to restaurants, whom he could sleep with and perhaps later on live with on a permanent basis.

When he had dialled her number he was assailed by doubt for a moment. There was no answer, but when he went back to his table he knew the doubt was not strong enough to stop him trying again in half an hour. She might be out shopping or on her way home from work or the cinema. He wondered how she actually did spend her day. What did he really know about her other than that she had had a protected childhood, that her father was well off and had supported Mussolini for a short while, then the Christian Democrats, that she lived in a little flat in the Rue du Dragon, that she had been married to the Spanish painter Carlos Carlos, that she occasionally wrote articles for an Italian newspaper and attended lectures at the Sorbonne? Was she in fact worth the trouble? He determined not to be quite so obliging and willing to let her take all the tricks next time they met. He would be slightly superior, friendly, of course, but not so much so that she thought she had him where she wanted.

He rang again. Still no answer. He rang a third time, a quarter of an hour later. This time she picked up the receiver, slightly out of breath, as if she had just come in and had not yet had time to take off her coat.

'*Alloo!?*'

He bit his finger. He lost courage and replaced the receiver. He drummed his fingers on the bamboo screen beside the telephone. Over the screen he caught sight of the Chinese waiter who was looking at him with a faint smile on his lips. Mollerup felt like making a face at him but controlled himself and smiled back. He lingered beside the telephone waiting for the waiter to look away, then rang again.

'*Alloo!? . . . A-l-l-o-o-o!!!*'

He realized he had bitten so hard into the flesh round his finger that he had drawn blood. He put down the receiver for the second time, excusing himself because he had to get out his handkerchief to stop the blood staining his clothes and dripping onto his shoe. He put his finger in his mouth, sucked the blood off, bound it up with the handkerchief and was about to ring again when the waiter turned towards him and smiled again. He smiled back. Then the Chinese smiled even more broadly, and his own smile stretched so he felt it was held with invisible elastic behind his ears.

When he passed a café with a telephone he decided that now was the time, now he should ring her and invite her out in a day or so. But every time the same thing happened: he asked the cashier if there was a telephone, and when he was told there was he went down to the basement and put a coin into the box, he heard the ringing tone and dialled the first letters of her number, LI, sometimes LIT, or else the whole number, LIT 3501, then he lost courage and replaced the receiver or actually flung it down in mortification. And then he was out on the pavement again, in the winter darkness, in the cold. He passed the Café Flore where the homosexuals sat with their carefully coiffed wigs drinking tea and rum. He glowered over at the Rue du Dragon and walked down towards the Rue du Bac, found new cafés he could ring from but now turned away just as he was about to go in. And he retraced his steps again to the corner of the Rue de Rennes and the Boulevard Saint-Germain, that village-like corner where he ran into the same people every time; people who spent the mornings sleeping in miserable hotel rooms and the afternoons and evenings on the pavement between the Deux Magots and the Café Flore. There were old ladies with lipstick smeared right up under their noses, hollow-cheeked American playboys with eyes dull from narcotics, seventeen-year-old girls with morbid white make-up chasing photographers who could make them famous and the usual untalented artists in old English uniform overcoats, paintings under their arms and overlarge sun glasses. He stopped in front of the Deux Magots and looked into the glass cage above the chairs and tables on the pavement. The paraffin stove had misted up the windowpanes. In one corner two black men were playing chess, in the other was the two meter-tall Swede who had made contact with him at the night club before Christmas. He sat with five empty cognac glasses in front of him and a sixth half full, his gaze wandering, as if expecting some acquaintance to appear and come and slap him on the shoulder. His eyes were bloodshot and his hair tousled, his shirt unbuttoned at the neck with his tie hanging outside his overcoat.

Mollerup hurried past. He went into the café and down to the telephone booths next to the toilet. He had to wait some time for a free booth. Each time the swing door of the toilet opened and closed he caught sight of two young men in front of the mirror combing each other's died sideburns. The attendant sat playing patience in a haze of cheap rose scent. At last a box was free. He would ring her for the last time, and before putting the coin in he ran a comb through his hair and unbuttoned his coat so as not to sweat too much in the booth which was hot after a long day's use. He dialled her number. His tongue was dry and his scalp smarted. His under arms and body grew damp but he held the receiver tight, would not break off. He closed his eyes for a second as the line connected and tore pages out of the directory, crumpling them up. But no one answered. Her voice was silent even though the receiver had been lifted. He put his hand to his free ear and had a feeling there was breathing at the other end. Shortly afterwards he heard whispering voices. He knew he only needed to say hello quite naturally for the mystery to be solved. But he kept on crushing the pages of the directory and moving his feet about in the narrow cubicle. And suddenly it struck him that at this very moment he might be falling into a trap. Perhaps the Italian woman had phoned the police or the telephone exchange and told them someone was tampering with her telephone, and they had told her that next time she should stay connected. Then he heard a sound like a door being slammed. Perhaps the crewcut writer or Carlos Carlos had gone out to the nearest telephone to find out who was ringing LIT 3501. Perhaps she was standing now breathing down the phone, biting her nails, afraid he would cut off so she could not find out who was badgering her.

It was with a slight feeling of malicious pleasure that he finally put down the receiver. Then he hastened upstairs and out of the café. He hurried down towards the Mabillon, constantly bumping into pedestrians. Suddenly he felt a hand on his shoulder. He had a shock, but to his relief discovered it was only the Swede, who had followed him:

'Hi!'

'Hi!' he replied, enveloped in the Swede's alcoholic breath. He made the excuse of being busy and dashed into a metro station. As the Swede came lurching after him down the steps he was obliged to buy a ticket and go onto a platform. There he managed to escape while watching one train after another drive past. After he had stayed on the platform for some time he went cautiously back and on to the opposite pavement. He reached La Pergola intending to go inside although he had no liking for this meeting place of good time boys and part-time prostitutes. Then he caught sight of the crewcut writer and Carlos Carlos. They drove down the Boulevard Saint-Germain in the crewcut man's jeep. They kept close to the kerb peering in at the cafés. Now and again, they stopped. The writer jumped out and went into a café, then came back shaking his head. Mollerup rushed down a side street where there was a taxi rank. He jumped into the back seat of a taxi and ordered the driver to drive off as fast as he could over to the Right Bank in the direction of Les Halles. The lights turned red as they reached the Boulevard Saint-Germain, and he crouched down on the seat. Then the lights changed, and, as they crossed, the jeep was stopped at the red lights on their left. The taxi went right past the jeep's bonnet, and when he turned round he thought the crewcut writer pointed in his direction. He told the driver to go even faster. When he felt it was safe he told him to stop. He got out, paid and found that he was not far from the Rue Saint-Denis. The big refrigerated vegetable lorries were parked in long lines, the tramps with their shabby perambulators were already searching the heaps of rubbish for discarded tomatoes and carrots, and a group of Americans in evening dress disappeared, laughing and talking, into an onion soup restaurant.

Girls on hotel steps, girls in cafés, girls on street corners. He went up and down the Rue Saint-Denis. If a girl approached him he smiled and threw out his arms, as if to tell her he might come back later. He calmed down on finding himself in a new and different district. It helped to be in company with German tourists and drivers who had come in all the way from Marseilles to speak sign language to the street girls behind the glass doors of the hotels pulling up their mini-skirts; to see one of the drivers go inside and come back fifteen minutes later with ruffled hair, buttoning his trousers; to walk from café to café and in each one have a glass of cheap white wine and chat to the girls mincing about at the bar counters or in the corner beside the juke boxes playing Sylvie Vartan and Claude François. He didn't like the look of all the tarts, some of them were over forty and wore thick make-up to hide the wrinkles, and had plump bodies bulging over their old-fashioned corsets. Others were too thin with hawk noses and black lines under their eyes. But among them there would suddenly be a girl who could well be one of the expensive prostitutes on the Champs-Elysées and the Avenue Franklin D. Roosevelt. He talked to one of these for a long time. She bore a slight resemblance to the Italian woman. She was about the same size, with the same long black hair, the same delicate mouth. When they had talked for a while and he had offered her a glass of whisky she asked him up to her room at the neighbouring hotel. Instead he suggested she should go home with him. He assured her he would pay whatever she asked. He knew it would not be all that much as the prostitutes in the Rue Saint-Denis were among the cheapest in Paris.

'*D'accord!*' she said, picked up her bag and walked with small steps in her high-heeled shoes into the street to pick up a taxi. Down the street he caught sight of three Arabs running after a man in a grey overcoat with a red scarf. For a moment he felt like going to help, but the man had already disappeared into a doorway. Soon he had convinced himself that the man in the grey coat could not have been the Israeli. He would hardly have been so foolish as to venture into areas where there were many Arabs.

'Avenue de Wagram,' he said to the driver, knowing it was an address that would impress the girl.

He aired the room, emptied the ashtrays, closed the curtains and put out glasses and a bottle of whisky. He tried to make conversation. She sat on the sofa in his study, he was in the armchair opposite. As it seemed heavy going he put on a record by Nat King Cole and she said she loved Nat King Cole. When he poured some whisky she told him she loved whisky. Soon after that he showed her a book with pictures of

Denmark, and she said she loved travelling and was sure she would love Denmark. But his desire for her had dwindled, she seemed to have changed. In the café in the Rue Saint-Denis she was in her own environment, now there was something timorous about her, although she had taken off her shoes and put her feet on the shelf under the coffee table, quite at home. He glanced at her toes in the nylon stockings and noticed they had not been washed for some days. Her make-up looked scruffy in the light of his lamps and quite different from how it had appeared in the mauve light from the café juke box, and on one side of her chin she had a scar that she tried to hide with several layers of powder.

'What do you do?' she asked him.

'I am a journalist.'

'Oh, I'd love to be a journalist,' she said, curling her toes.

'It's a great job, yes,' he said, finding it harder and harder to open his mouth.

'You must meet a *lot* of people!'

'Oh, I do. You meet a lot of people as a journalist.'

'Then you know Brigitte Bardot!!'

In the end it was too much for him. The scar on her chin, the dirty toes in nylon stockings, the shoddy clothes — and now Brigitte Bardot. He rose, collected the glasses and went into the kitchen where he stood for some minutes hoping she would take the hint and had put on her coat when he went back. But when he went into the study the first thing he saw was her clothes in a tidy bundle on a chair. She called to him from the bedroom where she lay on his bed dressed only in her bra and a pair of black briefs. He sat down beside her and tried to be friendly.

'What's your name?' he asked, staring at her scar.

'Yvette!'

'Listen, Yvette. It's not that I don't like you . . .'

She understood him at once. She rose, went straight into the sitting room and got dressed without comment. In the passage she looked in the mirror, tidied herself and put on a fresh layer of powder. She demanded at least a hundred new francs for her trouble and for the sake of peace he agreed, opened the hall door and rang for the lift. Later, back in the flat, he went to a window and saw her running across the road to a taxi rank. He sat down at his desk and at that moment the telephone rang. He went to pick up the receiver but something held him back. When he finally lifted it it sounded as if someone was breathing into the receiver at the other end.

'Hello!' he snarled.

The line was cut off and he thought of ringing the exchange to find out where the call had come from. But that would be making too much out of nothing, he convinced himself. Of course it would. It must have been a perfectly ordinary wrong number. He started to leaf through the pile of old newspapers, and his eyes caught the diary he had written in the margin of *Les Lettres Françaises*:

. . . *Between Christmas and New Year: suddenly she turns into someone else, wants to go back to Paris before the fixed time. She turns her back on me in bed. When did she change, and what was the reason?*

CHAPTER NINE

One day his newspaper printed a feature article on the crisis in the French left wing. It was based on the finding of Togliatti's will in a hotel room at Yalta and foresaw a reformation of international Communism on a parallel with the Reformation of 1520. The article examined the intense discussion that the will had generated in the French left wing between, on the one hand, the old-fashioned revolutionaries and on the other, the young revisionists who no longer held outdated revolutionary theories but foresaw that the day would come when the working class ceased to exist because all manual work would be taken over by robots. The article was entitled 'Year Zero', and it concluded: 'How can we stamp out the adverse influence of technology, alienation, and at the same time acknowledge that technocracy meets the needs of our modern age? How do we avoid the widespread hankering for the 'good old days' among the left wingers — and still preserve a modern progressive-democratic attitude? These are some of the questions preoccupying the serious French left. They are the questions of the future. The future that has already begun. We have already entered a new political age. In year zero. Will this soon be realized by the Danish left wingers who are usually twenty years behind in development and traditionally are more interested in petty intrigue and guitar music?'

Although this high-flown ending did not appeal greatly to Mollerup, he had to admit that the article was both well-written and informative, and it upset him, more than he cared to admit immediately after reading it: 'Year Zero' was by Munk, appearing for the first time in his paper, on his own.

He knew that hitherto Munk had lived on freelance work for minor newspapers in Denmark, one or two social democratic provincial papers and some sectarian weeklies, but now here he was suddenly in Mollerup's paper with his photograph on the front page, which was usually only included when the editors felt a feature article was particularly significant. Beneath the photograph the features editor had written: In today's feature article Mikael Munk, student, discusses the problems that really engross French people today.' Inevitably he interpreted that little 'really' as a concealed accusation directed at himself, as if the articles he sent home did not deal with the problems that 'really' interested the French. He knew the features editor was no special friend of his and had suggested a couple of times that the paper should have a younger correspondent in Paris, but had been shouted down by the others in the editorial inner circle who did not want to see the budget burdened with yet another salary.

The article ruined several hours for him. Then he flung the paper aside and tried to busy himself with something else. He went for a long walk down the Avenue de la Grande Armé, had lunch in the Relais de Venise and set his mind to prepare an important series of articles on France in the mid-sixties, to consist of features, general pieces and interviews with some of the names he had come across in his reading of French newspapers. If he could get hold of Mendès-France that would be something of a coup. If not, he could always go on and try to contact Gaston Defferre or Mitterrand. As the afternoon wore on he managed to master his chagrin over Munk's article and when he got home the first thing he did was to ring round to one or two French opposition papers to get the addresses and telephone numbers of Mendès-France and Gaston Defferre. In the evening he worked out the article series. A double feature would give a detailed description of France in which he would position himself between Gaullist complacency with the status quo and left-wing bitterness, the interview with Mendès-France would be followed by an interview with a Gaullist (he had still not given up hope of interviewing Malraux) and Tixier-Vignancourt from the far

Fascist right. He would conclude with a Sunday article on the Frenchman of 1965, the hotel proprietor, the bistro owner, the schoolteacher, the man in the street who lived from month to month occupied with human problems: the Frenchman with a wife and children and retired parents, with a sense for the good things of life and distrust of all the politicians and social prophets who courted his favour from right and left. A Sunday article the Gallic illustrator would amuse himself with in a dozen vignettes. Reassured by the prospect of this series he took himself to bed.

But next morning when the postman had been and he opened the newspaper he came across Munk's name again, this time as the author of an interview with Gaston Defferre. Munk had gone all the way to Marseilles to get the interview. It appeared inside the paper, on a page usually reserved for the regular correspondents. Was that a sign that the paper was grooming him as a coming Paris correspondent? Was the features editor about to force through his wishes?

He was seized by a feeling of powerlessness. Here he was helpless to do anything to prevent decisions about his future career being made over a thousand kilometers away. If he were in Copenhagen he could at least go into the office and merely by his physical presence influence things in the right direction, speak up for himself. But as long as he stayed in Paris he was out of sight, a correspondent sent here by chance; a pawn in a larger game, of no personal interest to those holding the strings of power. And this time he could not control his mortification at being confronted with Munk's name in the columns reserved for him, he smoked one cigarette after another, he thought of making a pot of coffee and put the kettle on, but switched it off shortly afterwards because he didn't really want coffee. He went into the bathroom and turned on the bath taps because he could generally think calmly and sensibly when he was lying up to his chin in scalding water, but when the bath was half full and he was enveloped in steam he let the water out again. He walked up and down the room and started on his usual pedantic tidying, the newspapers in a separate pile, the latest bills in another pile under the letter scales, letters awaiting an answer in a third pile on the coffee table. He lit another cigarette. He threw it away after a couple of drags. He filled a pipe. He put down the pipe, found a cheroot instead. Finally he went to the telephone and rang Denmark, the newspaper. He asked for the editor-in-chief and his secretary came on the line.

'Good morning, Mollerup! What's the weather like in Paris?' came the secretary's chatty tones. 'We've got a good seven degrees of frost up here.'

'It's just above freezing down here,' he said, looking out of the window as he put the receiver into his other hand.

'Who do you want to speak to?'

'The editor-in-chief.'

'Is it *very* important?'

'Yes, it is.'

'I hope it is, for your sake. You know they are in an editorial meeting at this time of day. But hold on a moment, I'll try. Goodbye, Mollerup.'

He heard the town hall clock strike twelve. Then the editor-in-chief was on the line:

'Have you got hold of de Gaulle, or what?'

'I just wanted to ask something.'

'*Ask* something. Didn't my secretary tell you I was in a meeting? Well, what is it you want to ask, Mollerup?'

'About the articles by Mikael Munk in today's paper . . . and yesterday's, I mean yesterday and the day before yesterday, of course the papers are delayed a day here . . . if they . . .'

'Yes, what about them?'

'I thought . . .'

'What? Get on with it, Mollerup.'

'Isn't it usual for a journalist to be informed if articles in his sphere of interest are accepted? I am about to do an interview with Gaston Defferre myself, I have spent a lot of time getting hold of him and arranging a date and then . . .'

He felt he was getting under way:

'And then I suddenly discover you have already published an interview with him. Well, that was what I wanted to say. I really think that was going behind my back a bit.'

He heard the editor-in-chief clear his throat, light a cigarette and blow the smoke down the phone. Then his reply
came, hard and swift:

'You say it is customary for correspondents and so on to be
sent the manuscripts and so forth. But tell me — since when
has it been the custom for you to phone home for a good
word? Don't you know we have a strict budget that does not
permit telephone calls at the newspaper's expense any old
time? And just one more *small* thing, Mollerup, now we are
about it. That story about the Israeli — what happened to
that? Did you ever search him out as I asked you to? Well, it's
of no consequence now. Luckily the Israeli made contact
with a Swedish journalist who immediately wrote a long
article so the Swedish government is now working at the
highest level to get the Israeli's brother released. Goodbye,
Mollerup, for now. Give Defferre a miss and do something
on . . . well, on some other big noise instead.'

As he replaced the receiver he realized the editor had hit
a really sore point: he had completely forgotten to write the
article on the Israeli's brother. He visualized the situation: as
the clock struck the last stroke of twelve, the editor-in-chief
was going back into the boardroom to where the other
editors sat wreathed in tobacco smoke, sitting down at the
end of the rectangular mahogany table and dropping a
comment about that addle-brained Max Mollerup who had
phoned from Paris merely to make a fuss about — what was it
now? — an interview with Gaston Defferre. And the others
would puff at their pipes and suck on their cigars and cheroots. The education correspondent would nod weightily
with his pendulous underlip, and the features editor would
take the opportunity of airing his wish to have a younger and
more enterprising Paris correspondent. Perhaps the whole
thing was a prearranged game between Munk and the features editor? Perhaps the features editor had told Munk to
fire away with his articles so at some point he would have to be
given a permanent post? Mollerup wiped the sweat from his
hands off the receiver and strode about restlessly. One morning, he thought — one morning there would be a letter from

the editor-in-chief. *On account of unforeseen circumstances we are obliged to make certain changes so that from the first day of next month you are to take over the post of television reporter in Copenhagen, while the position of Paris correspondent will be filled by another reporter.*

There was only one thing to be done. He must cast off all sense of shame and lose no time in seeking out Munk for a confidential talk. He decided to go out to the Cité Universitaire where he knew Munk had been living for the past year. He would be friendly and receptive with Munk and, as he was the older, he had better ask him out to a restaurant. Then he would make it clear that under no circumstances would he tolerate articles being published behind his back. If Munk wanted to get articles accepted he should bring them straight to him. He would say that he had nothing against collaboration, on the contrary there could be situations where it was necessary for two men to be on a job. But Munk must realize who was the paper's accredited reporter in Paris, who decided on what was to be written and how. It was useless for him, Mollerup, to spend several days contacting Gaston Defferre only to see all his work had been superfluous. Yes, he could voice his opinion to Munk in various ways and, when, after going to a film and having dinner, he went out to the University he felt as good as certain that he would be able to outmanoeuvre him.

Music came from a few open windows in the Danish students' lodgings. Inside, the hall was decorated and a few couples were dancing in the main room. The carpets had been rolled up and laid along the walls, a little bar made of old planks with a cardboard awning painted like the Danish flag was arranged in one corner. After lengthy negotiations he got past the porter at the entrance who had to see that only the residents and their friends joined the party. Outside a group of French and Moroccan students were wailing and hooting old car horns, offended at not being allowed in. Once in the hall he glanced into the room where the dancing was taking place. Then he went over to the bar for a beer but could not see Munk and, when he inquired for him, received vague answers. Yes, he had been here an hour ago. Probably.

'He always keeps himself to himself,' said one.

'We never know where he is,' came from another.

'But try his room,' said a third. 'He always works at night, he *reads* so much . . . .'

He went to the porter's lodge where there was a house telephone. He made out Munk's name and number on a list of the residents. But when he rang there was no answer. And he walked up and down the hall, pushed aside by two students who came up from the basement with a crate of beer while he read the notice board that announced that such and such a Frenchman in the sixth arrondissement was going to Scandinavia and could give a Danish girl a lift if she paid for half the petrol. Other notices publicized a programme on Vietnam at the American Students' House, a Scandinavian evening on the coming Saturday with readings of well-known Swedish writers and songs and that the service at the Danish Church on the Champs-Elysées had been cancelled next Sunday because the minister had stomach trouble. The door of the director's apartment was open, and the director sat in an armchair playing rummy with his wife. Mollerup moved to one side so as not to be seen. Some years before he had had a violent quarrel with the director because he had interviewed two youngsters who complained about the strict rules of the house, and he had no wish to meet him again. Soon afterwards he went down to the basement where some girls were making smørrebrød with pâté and Italian salad on rye bread. But he could see no sign of Munk and was about to go up again when one of the girls approached him. She wiped her hands on her apron having sucked the pâté from her fingers, tossing her head to get her hair out of her eyes.

'I didn't get the part after all,' she said, smiling at him.

'Oh, you didn't?' he said, totally uncomprehending.

'Yes, *you* know . . . I rang you the other night to tell you.'

'You didn't get it?' he asked again. Then it began to dawn on him. He remembered a girl at the artists' party at Rolf

Hauge's castle asking him to dance and suggesting he should write a back page story about her because she was going to play a Swedish girl in a French film. But he found it hard to recognize her. She had grown fatter in the face and had bleached her mousy hair.

'No,' she said. 'I didn't get it. That's what I just said. And isn't that *typical*: I didn't get it because the producer only wanted to sleep with me, and I didn't want to . . .'

'That was too bad . . . .'

'Yes, that's how they are, these Frenchmen. I do wish you would write an article about it. I could tell you plenty about the methods they use to get themselves into bed with us.'

At that moment another girl with bleached hair came running down the stairs and across to them.

'They're here! They're here!' she cried, exploding into giggles.

The first girl quickly explained the situation to him as she took off her apron. They had been pursued for several months by two Moroccans from the Moroccan students' house nearby. Every time they went into Paris the Moroccans were at their heels, confronting them in the metro and in cafés and shops. Now they wanted to teach them a lesson. They had invited them to visit them, so they could pay them back by chucking them out. As they could not get in by the door they had suggested they should fetch a fire ladder from the back garden and crawl in through a window.

'They must have found one,' she said, pulling him along.

'What?' he asked though he knew quite well what she meant. But it was all happening so fast he was confused.

'The ladder, for God's sake!'

They asked him up to their room so he could see with his own eyes how the swarthy chaps behaved with Scandinavian girls. Then he could get ideas for his article, he was told. But first there was the little problem of how to get him upstairs. The porter was on watch in the hall the whole time, between the staircase that led to the men's section and the one to the women's. But at a moment when the porter was looking into the reading room where dancing was still going on and more and more people crowded round the bar, the girl beckoned to him, and suddenly he was running hell for leather up the stairs. He did not really want to go but wanted to wait for Munk to turn up. But he might as well pass the time with the girls as down in the hall. On the way up another girl was summoned so they could make up three couples. The girl who had invited him to join them knocked on the door of a room and called out that there was a party in number fourteen. He was just to go along, he learned, together with the new girl, and share a bottle of wine. Then they entered a room. The girl who had fetched them was already standing by the open window gesticulating, and when he approached he saw the two Moroccans down in the garden. They were dressed in dark suits with white shirts and silver-grey ties and polished winkle-pickers. They were battling with a long ladder trying to get it in place against the window sill. Finally they had it in place and started to crawl up and, soon afterwards, climbed in through the window. Mollerup saw they were not too pleased to see him. In particular one of them, the darker of the two, measured him from top to toe in a hostile manner, but the two girls explained that a third girl would soon join them so they could have a proper party.

'You must have fun as long as life lasts,' said the girls in broken French.

'That's what we say in our country,' said one of the Moroccans, winking happily to his companion who was brushing pigeon muck from his trouser leg.

Soon the door opened and the third girl came in. She wore a flowered dress with bare arms and white ski socks in a pair of Norwegian slippers. Mollerup guessed she must be about thirty and could hardly be a student. She had coarse hands and looked more like a potter or weaver. The two Moroccans sat on the edge of the bed and were given wine in tooth mugs, the curtains were drawn and a couple of candles lighted. He sat on a rocking chair in a corner looking around the room that was simply furnished, with an abstract carpet, a poster on the wall above the bed of Wonderful Copenhagen with the policeman stopping the traffic so a mother duck and her ducklings could cross the road. Three Kay Bojesen monkeys in different sizes hung by the arm from the bookcase which held various new collections of Danish poems, a couple of novels by Ulla Ryum and some handbooks on potato prints in striped covers.

'What are your names?' the first girl asked the two Moroccans.

'Amar,' said one, holding out his glass for more wine.

'Ali,' said the other.

'Amar and Ali! How nice!'

They put a record on, and the girls asked the Moroccans to dance. Mollerup moved closer to the third girl and tried to start a conversation with her. What was she doing in Paris? Nothing! she replied, biting her fingernail. She had intended to study art but she couldn't stand the French, they were so unfriendly. 'But you must do something,' he tried. 'No,' she replied. 'Why should you do something if you don't feel like it.' 'How did she pass the time?' She read newspapers, made collages and slept.

'You get so sleepy in Paris,' she said, starting on the next nail. 'It must be the air, don't you think?'

'There is a lot of diesel smoke in the air,' he replied.

'Yes, there is, isn't there?'

He moved away from her a little, put off by the smell of sweat and because she was looking at him pleadingly, as if she expected him to ask her to dance so they could be among the four others who were dancing cheek to cheek, closely entwined. He smiled to himself because the Moroccans only came up to the Danish girls' chins. Then the girl he had met at Rolf Hauge's reception pulled her dress down over one shoulder, wiggled her hips and threw her head to and fro so her hair fell over her face. The Moroccans clapped delightedly, took off their jackets, unbuttoned their shirts at the neck and loosened their ties.

'You're fools,' she said to them and pulled her dress down over the other shoulder.

'Quoi?' asked the Moroccans together.

'You're dumb as hell!'

'Quoi?' the Moroccans smiled uncomprehendingly.

'What a pair of scruffy idiots!' she went on.

'Shut up,' hissed the other girl. 'They can understand that last word, it's the same in every language!'

'What are you saying?' asked the Moroccans and, seizing the girls' wrists they pulled them close and kissed them on the neck and under the ears.

'Oh, my friend says she can't resist your sort. She says black-haired men are much better lovers than Scandinavians.'

'That's true enough,' chimed in the Moroccans, trying to kiss the girls on the mouth.

But now the girls played hard to get. They eluded the two men, ran around the room, took off the record and put on the light again. The Moroccans blinked and tried to switch off the light, but the girls placed themselves in front of the switch with their hands at their sides.

'Now we're going to bed!' they said in French, putting their hair straight.

'Already!' said the Moroccans.

'We think Amar and Ali should go home to bed now,' they went on, adding in Danish: 'It's not good for little boys like you to stay up late.'

Mollerup rose. He wanted to leave. To start with he had been amused at the girls' manoeuvres, but now something almost painfully mulish had come over their faces, as if they knew they had gone too far and could not retreat. The third girl stood up as well, clearly feeling uncomfortable. She looked at him the whole time as if she wanted him to intervene and take control of the situation. He went towards the door. The Moroccans pulled at the girls so one of them fell on to her side. In her fall she crashed into the bookcase so the three Kay Bojesen monkeys came loose and landed on the floor.

As he was about to leave the room the door was opened from outside and he was confronted with the director. He could walk past him nonchalantly. He could apologize. Say he had come to the girls' section by mistake. He could tell a lie. Explain that he was going to interview one of the women residents about Danish girls' experience of impertinent Frenchmen and had got involved in a party by accident. There were plenty of ways he could get himself out of the tight spot. But he couldn't hit on the best one, on a suitable explanation, he merely stared at the director who stared back, sucking his teeth.

'*You!*' said the director, wrinkling his forehead in surprise.

'Oh, you see, I'm only here to . . . .'

He tried to walk around the director, but the man gave him a slight push so he found himself once more in the middle of the room about to tread on one of the monkeys and crush it. One of the Moroccans shot up from the floor where he had flung himself on top of the girl who had fallen down. The other ran over to the window, tore aside the curtains and already had one leg over the sill when the director grabbed hold of his collar. Almost lifting him into the air, he carried him to the door and threw him into the corridor. Then it was the turn of the other Moroccan. He ducked as the director lunged at him with flat hands, then got a kick from the rear so he fell on his nose in the doorway. The other Moroccan ran back to help him up, and together they vanished along the corridor and down the stairs. One of them had left his jacket behind, the director fished it off the floor with two fingers as if it was infectious and, with every sign of disgust on his face, threw it into the waste paper basket, stamping it down with his foot.

'You'll be hearing from me later!' he said to the two girls who were smoothing their dresses down over their hips.

He went over to the window and caught sight of the ladder. Mollerup could see the ladder rocking. The two Moroccans must have reached the ground and run around to the back garden to take the ladder away with them. But the director had opened the window and was holding it firmly:

'*Fichez-le-camp!!*'

Mollerup couldn't quite understand why he did not take the opportunity to get away. Perhaps he didn't want to sneak out with his tail between his legs. He did not want to give the director the chance to make it known around the Danish colony that he had caught him out one day in the women's section, after which he had taken to his heels like a burglar.

'Did they really come in through the window?' he asked stupidly.

The director did not reply. He pointed at the tooth mugs on the bedside table with dregs of wine in them and ordered the girls to tidy up. Then he turned and went out of the door. That was almost the worst thing. That he just left Mollerup standing there. He followed the director at a suitable distance. In the vestibule the director reprimanded the porter for not keeping a better watch. The porter threw his arms out as if to indicate that he really could not do anything about strange students climbing in through windows. Some of the dancers came out of the living room with beers in their hands and made an inquisitive circle around the director and the porter. As Mollerup crept down the last steps he caught sight of Munk in the group. In one hand he had a French girl, in the other some literary magazines. He hugged the wall trying to get by him unseen. He could always have a talk with him some other day. He got as far as the door. Then he heard the director calling. But he did not turn round and, as he set his hand on the door handle, the director sent a comment in his direction that made the young people laugh aloud. The words struck him on the neck almost like something physical, and a tickling feeling of unease spread down over his shoulderblades, his spine and right down to his coccyx. He did not turn round but he knew that the parting shot would stay in the young people's memories to mark him out as a dimwit, and that they were looking scornfully at him through the glass doors as he ran down the steps and with hurried steps made for the way out of the university. He could hear the director's remark echoing through his head:

'Mollerup! At *your* age . . .'

Several articles by Munk appeared in his newspaper. Interviews, feature articles, pieces in various sections of the paper. Munk dealt with a wide range of subjects, the women's movement in France, French abortion laws, the crisis in French film and the lack of places at the Sorbonne. He also wrote short notices for the back page, whenever a young Danish painter had had an exhibition praised by the critics or a cinema had put on an evening of shorter Danish films from the 1940s. Once Mollerup had the misfortune to have an article rejected by the editor because Munk had got in first with the subject, and every morning he expected to find a letter from the editor-in-chief telling him he was being recalled to Copenhagen to take up a minor post. Perhaps as a local editor in Århus or Ålborg where the paper sent reporters it wanted to get rid of without too much trouble. It would not have surprised him if within a fortnight he found himself in a cramped office with a view over Århus Town Hall with an article on cattle shows or professorial quarrels at Århus University in his hands. But the first of February passed without a letter summoning him home as he had feared. His pay cheque arrived as usual. And now there was a brief pause in Munk's output: a whole week passed without his name appearing in the paper. With some relief Mollerup thought that Munk had perhaps been making a guest appearance and would soon be writing for other newspapers. But then he was there again, in the Sunday edition, with a whole page interview with Michel Simon. The interview was also adorned with Munk's own photographs of the old actor feeding his monkeys or sitting in a high-backed basket chair with a patched, porridge-stained coat over his knees.

He was unable to write like that. He could not get going on his planned series of articles on France in the mid-sixties because he did not know if it would overlap with forthcoming articles by Munk. He did not want to risk having articles rejected again and he resolved to remove Munk from the scene by harassment. He could not do it directly. After the episode at the students' residence, Munk's position was too strong for it to be possible to meet him in conversation. But perhaps he could ferret out something unpleasant about Munk in the Danish colony. Perhaps Munk had made a fool of himself in some way, made himself unpopular. Perhaps he had borrowed money and not paid it back. Surely it must be possible to get hold of something, and he started in a café near L'Étoile which was a meeting place for Danish photographic models. He approached his subject with caution, talked to the girls about their work, comparing photographs in the French illustrated papers with Danish ones. Then he casually made mention of Munk, had any of them seen him lately? 'No,' they replied, as if they had never heard of him. From the café he went on to the Danish House, through the courtyard restaurant and up to the Danish Club where the minister was busy airing the room and emptying ashtrays after a meeting the previous evening. He asked after the minister's stomach trouble and whether his services were well attended, then dropped a comment on Munk: did he see much of him? The priest closed the windows and lit a cheroot:

'Occasionally. And every time we have a chat it irks me as a professional churchman that the *best people* never belong to us but are always on the other side of the 'fence', if I can put it like that.'

'Yes, there's a long tradition for that,' Mollerup replied.

'In Denmark! Not so much here in France where the Catholics can claim supporters like François Mauriac and Robert Bresson. Those are *names* for you.'

The minister relit his cheroot, which had gone out. 'Perhaps there's a subject there for a discussion evening for our au pair girls? 'Catholicism and Protestantism?' How would you like to introduce that? I mean, last time you were here you were a great success . . .'

Mollerup thanked him politely and walked towards the exit. The minister accompanied him and, at the door, laid a hand on his shoulder and looked him in the eye:

'Try and get to one of my services! I know you are on the other side of the fence too, but still . . . .'

'I'll come along one day!' Mollerup replied, smiling as best he could. 'I'll try and make time one Sunday very soon . . .'

The sour smell of the minister's cheroot accompanied him along the Champs-Elysées. Then he called in at the Danish shop behind L'Étoile. The lame proprietor went up to him as soon as he entered and started to upbraid Monsieur Jean for not having written the open letter confirming that the goods in the Danish shop had regained their high standard.

'It's on the way,' he reassured the man. 'Either I'll write it myself or perhaps Munk can do it . . . .'

He looked at the proprietor hoping that the name would say something to him. Perhaps he had been dunning Munk for money he owed, or he had annoyed the man in some other way. But the proprietor looked at him blankly:

'Munk? Who's he?'

'Oh, never mind.'

He caught sight of the round table with orange tiles that the Italian woman had been so taken with. In order to leave the shop in the best possible way he asked for the table to be sent to her address. He realized that it would cost him far too much, but as soon as he had settled the business of Munk he would visit the Italian woman again and sending her a fine gift would be bound to have a good effect. He offered his hand to the proprietor, who put down his stick.

'Just send the bill to me!'

It was somehow against his will that he found himself crossing the Champs-Elysées on the way to the Danish Embassy. He had gradually come to realize that he was not going to discover anything to Munk's discredit and that he had been acting in an amateurish manner. Suddenly Paris had shrunk down around him. He no longer heard French but Danish. Danish from morning to night. His Parisian horizon was again surrounded by the Danish Student Residence in the University City, the Danish House on the Champs-Elysées and the Danish Embassy, which he was now purposefully approaching. He thought of turning round. Going in a different direction, down the Champs-Elysées, mingling with the French. But now he was embarked on his search he might as well bring it to a logical conclusion and, on the way up the embassy's carpeted staircase, he again speculated on how he could introduce the subject of Munk this time. He would have to be careful in what he said to the press attaché, who knew everything about the various Danes in Paris. No doubt the press attaché had already noticed Munk's articles and would quickly guess how things stood if he blurted out too much. Should he go straight in to him? He decided to spend some time in the embassy reading room first, going through the Danish newspapers from the last couple of weeks. He picked up a pile of issues of the paper Lund worked for to see whether Munk wrote for that as well. He did not. All the material from Paris was signed Lund or Monsieur Dupont, Lund's pseudonym. Nor were there any articles by Munk in the other papers.

Mollerup lit a cigarette and drew the smoke deep into his lungs. He put the papers down and cleaned his nails with a broken match. Then the press attaché suddenly entered the room:

'Why, it's you! I was just thinking about you. Are you going home soon?'

'Home?'

'I've had a letter from your editor-in-chief asking me to help this Munk to get a press card. Is he going to take over your job?'

Mollerup had no idea what he replied or what he did with himself. But suddenly he found himself in the press attaché's office. There was a flickering before his eyes as he quickly ran them down the letter from the editor-in-chief that the press attaché handed to him with a smile he could not interpret, which perhaps expressed malice, perhaps merely ordinary sympathetic friendliness. He did not read the substance of the letter and made every effort to remain unmoved. He went over to the window, buttoned and unbuttoned his jacket, ran a hand through his hair, scratched his neck. He rocked on his toes, cleared his throat and pointed to the other side of the street where a building had been pulled down and four bulldozers were loading bricks and earth onto lorries. He heard himself chatting about Paris that was growing more and more inhuman to live in, that was no longer a town but a Ragnarok, an asphalt jungle, a nest of madmen. As he grew more and more heated he felt an increasing anxiety that the press attaché, who had come to stand beside him and was polishing his bald pate with his hand, could smell he was sweating profusely: under his arms, down his body where the sweat made him itch, on the palms of his hands and his neck just where it touched his collar.

'A Ragnarok, you're right there, Mollerup. But you've written about that so many times, haven't you, that . . . .'

'That what?' he asked, irritated to hear his voice rising.

A crane was brought into place at the demolition site. A large ball of lead hung down from it on a chain. The crane driver made the ball slowly start swinging by driving one meter forward and one back, with small abrupt movements. Gradually the ball was swinging 180 degrees and finally it struck the end wall of a six storey house with a crash. Cracks appeared in the wall which soon collapsed, tearing wooden floorboards with it. In a couple of minutes a huge cloud of dust enveloped the place where the wall had fallen, and spread across the pavement so the people walking past had to press their handkerchiefs to their faces.

'Incidentally, I had Fouchet on the telephone this morning,' said the press attaché in a different, more friendly tone. 'He said it straight out: we cannot govern this town any more! It's getting *savage*!'

He found himself in a metro and suddenly he was at the Porte de Vincennes. He crossed over to the opposite platform, got into a new train and rode all the way back across Paris to the opposite terminus. He stayed sitting there for some time looking at the empty carriages being ranged on the rails alongside. Then the driver went walking past on the platform and knocked on the window with his biro to remind him the train was not going any further. Shortly afterwards he was in a new train that was about to leave. When he reached the city centre again he changed to a different line. Sometimes he went through one or two stations before jumping out and finding his way to another train going in the opposite direction from where he had come. He passed through stations he had never come across before: Buzenval, Tolbiac, Bolivar, Picpus, Ourcq. He stood up most of the time and was tossed to and fro when the train rounded a sharp corner. To start with there were hardly any other passengers. There might be an old woman with spittle dribbling down her chin or an old man with a wooden leg or artificial arm on one of the seats reserved for the disabled from the 'Great' War. A couple of Africans might stand in a corner with their hands in their pockets mumbling in a language he did not understand a word of. Otherwise, he was as good as alone. The platforms were deserted, at most a man with a broom might sweep cigarette stubs off the platform edge. Trains going the other way emerged from the darkness at intervals and vanished again leaving all the points rattling because they were not weighed down by a normal number of passengers. And all the time DUBO DUBON DUBONNET painted in white on the walls of the tunnels, DUBO DUBON DUBONNET. But as time went on more passengers appeared and suddenly, in no more than a few minutes, there were crowds of people on the platforms. They pressed forward to get through the automatic doors and stood right on the edge of the platform when the train he was on drew in. Rush hour had started and he decided to go out on to the street.

While he was riding around in the metro he had tried not to think about Munk. It calmed him to ride along below ground. Every time his thoughts turned to the press card the press attaché had been asked to get for Munk, he left the train at the first possible station, as if mere physical action could keep thought at bay. He ran as hard as he could to get on to the next train that was arriving. But now he was out in the fresh air, in gently falling rain with a faint scent of the coming spring, not knowing where to go or where he was. There was just a small square, a few trees, a café and a newspaper kiosk. He remembered again what the press attaché had said to him with his indefinable smile. He could no longer hold off the thoughts and went into a café, ordered an espresso and leafed through an old *France-Soir* on the zinc counter. He grabbed one of the hard-boiled eggs from the holder on the counter, knocked off the top on his heel and bit into it, but spat it out because he discovered the yoke was purple-green with age. The bar was generally grubby, with a faded Michelin calendar hanging from the dirty mirror behind the counter, a damp soiled wooden floor and tables and chairs that looked as if they were never cleaned. The bistro owner looked offended when he threw down the egg. The coffee tasted of dishwater.

Soon afterwards he was out on the square. He had no idea where to go, where the various roads that led from the square in a star shape would lead. He had a vague feeling that he was on the Right Bank and that a street sloping steeply down towards a wide boulevard led in the direction of the Seine. But what did it matter that he did not know where he was. The last thing he wanted was to go back to his flat in the Avenue de Wagram. He was sure that the letter ordering him to move back to Århus or Odense had arrived by the evening post and was sitting on the mat with a pile of bills and the mass of advertisements that came daily. He started to walk in a desultory way. He went along narrow streets without any shops or cafés, streets with gloomy facades that reminded him of those in the most desolate areas of Østerbro in Copenhagen. Then another square opened out with a shop selling birds, a café and a labour exchange. He stopped in front of that and glanced through the various scraps of paper offering jobs for drivers, domestic help and nurses at an old people's home that were stuck to the window with tape. A youngish man was sitting in the office in a pin-striped suit with his feet on the desk reading a weekly paper. Mollerup knew it was a mad idea to go in and ask if there were any other jobs than the ones in the window. He stood before the man in the suit who did not even bother to look up at him but went on reading. He was about to turn round and go out again. If he wanted a job he would certainly not find it here. But he stayed there until the man behind the desk put down his paper and looked up at him:

'We are closed!'

'But the door was open!'

'Don't know anything about that.'

He heard the man shutting the door with a bang behind

him as he crossed the square and made for the café. He ordered another espresso and soon afterwards yet another. His stomach started to rumble, his heart beat too fast. The café was just as scruffy as the previous one, the owner leaned on the till chewing a cigarette stub and listlessly watched a television screen that hung from the ceiling in one corner. In another corner a group of North Africans were playing mini football. He ordered another coffee although he knew his stomach could not take any more, but he felt an urge to fill himself with no matter what so long as it was strong and kept his circulation moving. Then he was pressing his knees against the counter, clenching his jaws so hard that his ears were singing and pushing a finger into a crack on the edge of the counter where one or two small nails were protruding. He kept pushing his finger into the crack until it began to bleed. Then he stopped, put down the money for the coffee and left the café because suddenly he could not stand it any longer. He walked down more side streets, over more squares, sometimes he collided with passers-by and for a while he followed a woman with long black hair whom he mistook for the Italian woman. He went right up to her, passed her but then discovered she was at least fifty and merely tried to make herself look younger by wearing her hair loose and stiletto heels. He crossed a busy boulevard and suddenly found himself in front of the *Le Monde* building. The coffee was still rumbling in his stomach and he badly needed to go to the lavatory, but instead he went into the building, found the editorial assistant on duty, introduced himself as a visiting correspondent from Denmark and asked to speak to one of the editors.

The whole thing took less than five minutes. He was shown along a long corridor and into a corner room. A small man in a sleeveless sweater rose from his desk and came towards him with outstretched hand. A bottle of sherry and two glasses appeared. A packet of cigarettes was opened. Mollerup explained that he represented a certain Danish newspaper and in reply heard that Denmark was a friendly country which journalists on *Le Monde* were always happy to visit. Later on he asked if the paper was well supplied with Scandinavian material.

'Don't you think it is?' came the response.

'Well, yes, . . .' he said.

He heard that his suggestion of himself as editor of the Scandinavian items that came in from the press offices did not fall on specially good ground. The little man in the sleeveless sweater, whom he guessed must be a kind of sub-editor, put down his sherry glass and threw up his hands, as if to say politely that the paper had no opening for that. But he was welcome to leave his address and telephone number. It was always good for the paper to know there was a Scandinavian expert on hand if a particular situation arose; for instance if Denmark and Sweden suddenly decided to join the Common Market. And after he had written his name, address and telephone number on a pad the little man handed him, he was accompanied to the door with a smile and an 'au revoir, Monsieur', walked down the corridor, past the editorial assistant and down to the street where he did not know what to do next. Whether to go to the Pigalle and get drunk, really legless, or merely see a couple of films in quick succession — problem-free films that would take him away from it all. He didn't want to go home. He knew he had not the strength to confront the letter recalling him, not tonight at least. He smoked one cigarette after another, his knees shook under him and after having yet another cup of coffee in a café he felt his stomach was about to explode.

When it was past eleven o'clock he went into a small hotel. He was shown to a room on the third floor overlooking the street. He turned down the coverlet at once, lay down and fell asleep, but woke up only an hour later. A woman was groaning in the adjoining room. At first he thought she was ill and sat up in bed and was about to knock on the wall and ask if he could help her when he heard a man groaning frantically too. Soon afterwards the woman screamed aloud while the man's groans turned into half-suffocated grunting. Then they quietened down and he could hear them whispering. He tried to fall asleep again, but now all the coffee he had drunk took its effect in earnest, every time he fell asleep his stomach rebelled. His heart beat faster and faster, his temples throbbed and he started to sweat all over, and kicked off the heavy bedclothes until they lay crumpled at the foot of the bed. He tossed and turned, tried to sleep on his stomach with his arms under his head, on his side and on his back with his arms along his sides. Now and again a refrigerated lorry on the way to or from Les Halles thundered past his window so he felt as if it went right through his head. An electric sign on the wall above his window flashed unceasingly and threw a mauve light over the basin, the bidet and the plastic mat in front of the shower. He got up and hung the bedspread over the window, but every time he went back to bed it fell down again. Finally he opened the window and tried to hit the sign with the soap which he tied to his belt. He climbed on to a chair and swung the belt with the soap into the air and towards the wall, but it stayed ten or fifteen centimeters from the bottom of the sign. Down in the streets a newspaper blew along the pavement and across the street. The newspaper slowly fell apart. To begin with, the first and last sheets came away and whirled up into a tree, then the middle pages were spread over the street as far as he could see. A solitary man walked along just under his window. He held a handkerchief to his forehead and now and then almost collided with a tree. Then he sat down on a bench, took off his shoes and ranged them beside him, and fell asleep with his head nodding against his shoulders.

There was no letter awaiting him when he let himself into his flat at midday, only bills and printed matter, but he knew it must be only a matter of time before Munk took over his job. Nothing indicated that the newspaper intended to keep him in Paris, so he felt he might as well take precautions and, with his scrapbook of the latest articles he had written under his arm, he called on numerous Paris papers and publishing houses during the next few days. *L'Express* told him that they would bear him in mind if the paper should suddenly need a

Scandinavian expert. He had the same result at *Le Figaro*, and he left his address and telephone number in both offices. At *Combat* he was told that the paper's finances precluded any new staff appointments, and that the paper had a contact with a journalist in Stockholm who sent regular reports on happenings in Scandinavia. *L'Aurore* told him he was welcome to interview Dreyer, possibly Bergman, but there was no question of regular employment. He also visited one or two popular evening papers, but they showed not the slightest interest in Scandinavia.

He gave up visiting editors and instead began to ask publishers if they could use a Scandinavian adviser. Despondency took hold of him and he had to struggle against an increasing hatred of the French, unassailable behind their big mahogany desks. Everywhere he went he received a friendly but definite rebuff: none of the publishers he called on were in a position to employ a Scandinavian expert. At each place he was offered a cigarette, perhaps a glass of sherry or vermouth, and listened to words of praise for Hans Christiansen Andersen's and Søren Kierkegaard's fatherland. But it always ended with him being accompanied to the door where a secretary was waiting to show him the last part of the way to the exit. He knew that the slip he had left with his address and telephone number was torn up and thrown into a waste bin the moment he was out of sight. Gradually his hatred of the French was mixed with hatred of the language whose slave he was and which was understood by a nation of only four or five million people, and, in Paris, by only a few hundred with the ambassador, Rolf Hauge, Lund, Munk, the press attaché, the director of the Danish shop and the Danish minister at their head. He went back again to the Saint-Germain district, walked to and fro along the little stretch between the Café Deux Magots and the Café Flore, met the American junkies, the homosexuals, the old ladies with lipstick up to their noses, the artists with paintings under their arms and the photographic models chasing photographers. He caught sight of the two meter-tall Swede in the glass cage of the Deux Magots with his empty cognac glasses and he hurried across to the opposite pavement and into a bistro. He had gradually come to see that it was no good visiting publishers either. Sitting in the corner of the bistro with his scrapbook on the table before him, he felt like one of those despised artists he normally waved away in irritation when they went up to him and opened a portfolio of mediocre etchings. He could write the most excellent articles but no one in Paris could read them. He could place his most successful reports in front of a Parisian editor-in-chief knowing that it was on a level with those in the French papers, but all he achieved would be the quarter minute of the editor's time it took for his eyes to slide over his text as if it was written in Chinese, throw out his arms, offer him a cigarette or a glass of vermouth, walk with him to the door and then tear up his address and telephone number the moment he was out of sight.

In the end he decided to go and see the bald writer at his restaurant. Perhaps *he* could help him get some job or other. Paris was the city of connections, he might as well acknowledge that. But when he reached the restaurant he heard the owner had gone to Venice. Soon after that he decided to call on the Italian woman. Now she must have received the table with the orange tiles and could hardly fail to welcome him. And she must know a lot of people in Paris who might help him to get going. But she was away too, he learned from the concierge who was in the courtyard throwing herring heads to a few skinny cats.

'You don't know where she has gone?' he asked.

'Venice,' the old woman replied. 'She left at least a fortnight ago, Monsieur.'

As he went back through the gateway he caught sight of the table with the orange tiles in a corner. The corrugated cardboard it was wrapped in had been torn and one of the tiles was broken. For a moment he thought of taking the table away and returning it to the Danish shop to avoid the considerable expense. But he was too tired to put the idea into action and, when he came to the Rue des Canettes to buy a calvados in the epicerie Chez Georges, the only thought that came to him was that spring was on its way. The first tender buds swelled on the trees, and the rain that began to fall again was faintly scented with iron and warm earth.

Of course he should have told himself that Lund would be sitting at the bar playing dice with a guest. The fact that he had not himself been to Chez Georges for the past six months did not mean that Lund too had given up their old haunt. But it was too late to turn round when he first appeared in the doorway, and when Lund beckoned him over, he at once ordered two calvados; one for himself and one for Lund. He put the scrapbook down remarking that he had been round to two hundred stationers to find one like it but without success: the particular kind he always had must be out of stock. And then they played dice and it was Lund's round.

'There certainly is some *go* in youngsters these days,' said Lund, looking at him.

'Yes,' he replied listlessly. 'But there was go in us once . . .'

'*Was* . . .?'

'Oh, well, I mean . . . .'

'I was only thinking of that chap Munk,' said Lund. 'He certainly works at it!'

Mollerup felt Lund was after him. But he did not react, and as luck would have it he threw three sixes so Lund slapped him on the shoulder, impressed.

'By the way, I actually got Ussing on the phone the other day,' Lund went on soon afterwards. 'I managed to get hold of his number.'

Mollerup watched Lund throw. A two, a two and a five. He did not know what to reply to Lund's remark about Ussing. Suddenly it seemed an endlessly long time since he himself had set store on getting hold of him. At this moment nothing interested him less than that vanished Danish correspondent spoken of by everyone in the Danish colony now and then as if he was supernaturally great. But he could feel Lund had more up his sleeve. His smile revealed it. His self-assurance even if he was consistently losing the game.

'He was furious with you, by the way.' Lund pulled his cuffs out of his sleeves and straightened his gold cufflinks. 'Something about your book. I don't know what it was. But shall I find out for you? The old nincompoop has promised me an interview one day soon . . . .'

This time Mollerup had to control himself so as not to show anything. Something about your book. He dared not give voice to the thought that came to him and tried with all his might to preserve an expression that said nothing in the world could affect him, except the dice he rolled between his palms. He threw three sixes again. Lund scratched his temple:

'Devil take it!'

He found a hotel not far from St Mark's Square. Although it was springtime in Venice there were not many tourists, and when he went down to the large dining room for breakfast only the seats at the end of the long table were occupied. For the first few days he kept to himself. He did not like the look of the other guests; an elderly German couple, some Catholic priests from Ireland and an American with a wart on one side of his nose. Every morning the American greeted him heartily, trying to make contact, but Mollerup sat down as far away from him as possible. He ate his breakfast hastily so he could get out. He then spent most of the day wandering around Venice, in the little alleyways behind St Mark's Square, along canals, over bridges, along new alleyways and out to the working districts of the town where there were hardly any canals and where many of the ramshackle houses seemed to have been jerry-built within the last fifty years. He did not have any brochures or guides, he was not interested in seeing the famous places, knew nothing about the various churches, squares and statues. He merely happened to be there by chance, in a town reeking of sewers and stagnant water, far from Paris, even further from Copenhagen: a town where he heard neither French nor Danish but a language of which he understood only fragments. There was no singing at the windows, as he had expected in Italy. The people who passed him on the bridges or steered small dinghies with outboard motors on the canals were on the whole dark-haired, but did not look especially Italian. No more Italian than the French. Most of them were anonymous working people in blue overalls on their way from one place to another, their features marked by fatigue. Venice? Where was the Venice he had always imagined? Something lightly floating, something contrary to nature, something oriental, something with gold and silver and precious stones and distinguished white women's profiles at its windows. He was in a town in which the houses resembled houses in so many other parts of the world, where the people were not at all different and where the gondolas, moored under the bridges waiting for the summer influx were merely clusters of misshapen variations of normal rowing boats.

Venice? Romantic Venice? True, the air was warmer than in Paris and Copenhagen. No doubt there would be between five and ten degrees of frost in Copenhagen and, at most, plus five in Paris. But only a couple of days after he arrived in Venice he was able to take off his coat and carry it over his shoulder. He found a little restaurant where the proprietor was putting tables and chairs outside. He ordered escalope Milanese and sat at a table with a view over most of St Mark's Square, which the police were cordoning off because a film was to be made. Each time he had crossed the square he had noticed a mass of lights and cables being laid among the columns. Now shooting was about to start, there was shouting from loudspeakers, technicians ran to and fro on the square and a group of soldiers stood at ease waiting for orders. The soldiers were in white windjackets and old fashioned skiing caps. When a detachment of SS soldiers came into sight Mollerup realized that the film was set during the Second World War and must be about the struggle with Italian partisans. He became so absorbed in what was going on that he sprinkled grated cheese outside his plate: four men in ankle-length winter coats came running out of one of the alleyways, across the square right into the arms of the white-clad soldiers. They managed to get away, only to be surrounded by the SS who had hidden behind the columns. Hand to hand fighting broke out, two of the partisans were knocked down, the other two got away. Just as they were running into the alleyway they had come from, the SS and the Italian soldiers opened fire with their machine guns. The shots could be heard over most of Venice. Curious people came rushing into the square from all directions so the police had to shepherd them back with yells and flailing arms.

The scene was shot three times, and by and by Mollerup lost interest. Instead he grinned at the thought that his newspaper might be trying to get in touch with him. Perhaps the letter recalling him had come, perhaps it was intended that Munk should take over his flat soon. But no one knew where he was! No one, either in Copenhagen or in the Danish colony in Paris, would have the least idea that he was in Venice, that at this moment he was eating an escalope Milanese watching the making of a film about the Second World War in St Mark's Square. Everyone in the Danish colony would be phoning each other, the press attaché would — after a call from the editor-in-chief — phone Lund, and Lund would ring up Munk or the Danish minister who would ring the director of the students' residence who again would phone Rolf Hauge. But no one had seen anything of him for the past few days, and in the Danish colony they would get more and more worried. They would ask each other nervously if he might have had an accident and perhaps a deputation would be sent to his apartment. If he was to be recalled from Paris it would certainly cause them trouble — if they succeeded in recalling him at all. Something told him he ought to hold on to the idea of contacting the Italian woman and the bald man, that they would be able to help him find some job or other in Paris. And a couple of days after his meeting with Lund he had set off. He was unable to concentrate on anything at all in his flat, and if he went out he always went over to the Left Bank, where he went round in circles and met the same eternally restless Bohemians. He needed to get a long way away and he felt he was bound to come across the Italian woman if he went to Venice. He had stayed a night in Milan, and now he was here. He would not rush around searching for her. He did not even bother to look at the telephone directory to see if she had a number. He knew he only needed to stroll around the alleyways and along the canals for a few days more, then he would bump into her by chance when she was out shopping or in a restaurant or a pavement café near St Mark's Square.

He rose, paid and went back to the hotel. He would have a drink and take a siesta. The two Irish priests sat in the bar on one of the deep leather sofas with a jug of fruit juice, looking at brochures spread out on the floor. He sat near the German couple. The man, engaged in putting a film in his camera, at once asked him how he was, if he did not think Venice was a city that called out secret powers in a Northerner and that, by the way, he had noticed they were making a war film.

'Ja, ja!' beamed the German, closing his camera. 'Auf dem Markusplatz!'

His wife nodded agreement.

'Ach so!' replied Mollerup, gulping down his drink. He slid down from the bar stool and went up to his room. He closed the curtains and set his alarm to ring an hour later. But just as he was dropping off he was woken up by a knock at the door. When he opened it the American with the wart on his nose stood outside apologizing for disturbing him. He just wanted to ask Mollerup to come and have a drink out in town. Mollerup agreed to go with him, without really knowing why, but suddenly he had no objection to company, and when they were outside heading for the nearest café he questioned the American about various things with increasing curiosity. Was he on holiday in Venice or on a business trip? Did he often visit Europe, had he been to Denmark? The American seemed happy to answer questions, and for the next half hour he talked away, scratching the wart on the tip of his nose with his little finger. He was tall and ungainly, with large brown leather shoes and a light suit under his raincoat. He was on holiday in Venice, he explained. He did not want to stay in America. He lived here and there in Europe. He was a writer of science fiction but had not written anything for the last year or two. He lacked ideas and besides was so nervous of letting his imagination loose that he did not want to write any more books. He lit one cigarette after another and sucked in his cheeks like a film star every time he wanted to emphasize a point. Mollerup wondered when it would be his turn to be questioned, but apparently the American was only interested in talking about himself. When they left the café to go for a walk he went on complaining about how lonely he was. He could write a book but the loneliness remained, he could get married but the loneliness remained, he could travel all over the world but loneliness was there the whole time like a shadow beside him.

'You know . . .,' he sighed and lit another cigarette.

'I know,' replied Mollerup although he knew the American was not in the least interested in his opinion.

During the days that followed he was with the American from morning to night. At breakfast time the American sat down beside him as if they were now old friends, shiningly smooth shaven and each day wearing a new suit with a fresh colourful shirt. The American was always bursting with energy when they left the breakfast table and related his bad dreams in minute detail. The dreams were always about how he stood looking down into a bottomless abyss while someone tried to push him from behind. He often laughed so hard that he started to hiccup, laughed at his bad dreams and his loneliness. And when he started to walk he took gay little dance steps when he recounted something specially horrible. He described why he did not dare to write any more science fiction novels: everything he wrote suddenly became more real than reality itself. If he wrote about the year three thousand when it was possible to make artificial human beings, he was *in* the year three thousand, among soulless remote-controlled human robots who looked at him with cold lifeless eyes, had moon-pale skin and were dressed identically. And if he wrote about the collapse of the solar system, he did not dare go outside for several days because the whole time he had the feeling that the sun was slowly nearing the earth to burn it up. He could even feel the air gradually getting hotter and hotter, first the leaves of the trees started to curl up, then the gardens steamed, the mountain tops started to melt and people dropped to the ground like hot wax.

'Do you know how one's thoughts can be more real than . . .

reality?' he asked, cavorting a few steps again. 'Do you know that everything takes place in *here* . . .'

He tapped his skull with a finger:

'Then your head feels like bursting. Then you feel everything in the world is made up purely of mental processes . . . .'

Hours could pass during which Mollerup did not need to open his mouth. The American talked, laughed, hiccuped, danced, scratched his wart, lit one cigarette with the other and sucked in his cheeks so you could see the shape of his skull when for a moment the stream of words stopped. Mollerup suspected he could not be a very good writer, perhaps he had not even published a book. His laughter grew more and more disturbing, and if Mollerup had found a certain pleasure in his company to begin with, had found him entertaining, with his loneliness and his mad fantasizing, now he wished to be rid of him, and regretted having made his acquaintance in a weak moment. The American had started to relate his life story from the beginning, when he was a boy growing up in the South, and later had gone to New York as a young man, lived a Bohemian life, married and got divorced and married again and divorced again, up to when day by day, as if some unknown force had him in its power, he was pushed into a way of life in which he no longer had anything to hold on to, nothing to believe in or to live for. He could never stay in one place for more than a month at a time. If he was in Paris he dreamed of Copenhagen, if he was in Copenhagen he dreamed of Venice.

'You see!'

As a rule they finished up at a nightclub behind St Mark's Square. It was there one night that Mollerup made up his mind to put an end to it. From the next morning he would shake off the American somehow or other. They sat in a corner of the night club not far from the bar where a row of girls in shabby dresses waited for male guests to come up and offer them champagne. The American ordered a bottle of whisky and drank three almost full glasses immediately. Leaning over a glass table with a miniature fountain in its centre, he explained in a voice grown hoarse over the past two days that whisky was the only thing that could keep the ghosts away. He had never gone in for drugs, he did not even want to try hash. But whisky! Good old whisky! He caressed the neck of the bottle, sniffed the cork and then kissed the label. Mollerup watched him getting more and more drunk and then starting to run out of words. The American looked at him wide-eyed as if wondering who he was drinking whisky with. Mollerup tried a friendly smile and started to talk about the dinner they had had together, how good it had been, with just the right amount of spice. A little later he winked at the girls by the bar so two of them came to sit at their table, but the American waved them away loudly, as if they were infectious. As the girls stayed where they were smiling invitingly the American stood up and pushed them away. He stood there for a while swaying to and fro and flipping irritatedly at the fountain so it splashed Mollerup in the face and down his tie. Then he staggered on to the stage, grabbed the microphone from a singer humming South American tunes, coughed into the mike, tapped it with his nail, scratched it and swung it round by the wire, gabbling about Venice being a rotten town and its inhabitants lazy wretches. Then he started to sing in a hoarse voice, a blues song.

'Come up here, you dirty Dane!' he suddenly shouted in the middle of his song, and Mollerup felt even more pained at being seen with him. The members of the orchestra beckoned two waiters on to the stage, and as the American almost fell over backwards more than once, they jumped up, seized him by the upper arms and carried him outside. Mollerup had to pay the bill.

On the way to St Mark's Square, the American kept on repeating that everything consisted merely of mental processes. Mollerup held on to him to stop him from falling, and when anyone came towards them he shouted abuse at them. As they were crossing the square, Mollerup let go of him for a moment. Suddenly he caught sight of the bald man and the Italian woman in between two of the columns. The bald man had a meter-long striped scarf wound around his neck several times. He was talking to some of the film technicians. The

Italian stood a little apart from him with a manuscript under her arm. She was in a grey suit with a raincoat hanging loose from her shoulders. Mollerup wondered how he could get away from the American who was now slightly ahead. But the man kept on shouting to him, and after he had fallen face down with his arms at his sides Mollerup was obliged to go the whole way to the hotel with him, take him up to his room and help him to wipe the blood off his nose and go to bed. The American turned over in bed whimpering like a small boy: he had a headache, he was going to be sick. He kept on saying he did not want to be alone.

'Stay with me, just till I fall asleep,' he begged.

Mollerup backed away, towards the door. Then he whispered goodnight, rushed downstairs and ran as fast as he could to St Mark's Square. Just before he turned into the square he slackened speed and straightened his clothes. But when he reached the place where he had seen the bald man and the Italian woman, they had gone. He looked out over the square. There was nothing to be seen but one man walking along, and the wind whirled a paper bag up into the air where it hovered before coming to rest on a ledge of the Doge's Palace.

He could not sleep. After having a whisky in the bar and chatting to the two Irish priests he went up to his room and undressed. On the other side of the wall he could hear the American still whimpering. Footsteps echoed on a bridge not far from the hotel. For half an hour he concentrated solely on falling asleep. He tried to cut himself off from his consciousness, but gradually found himself slipping into the sphere between sleeping and waking when every possible thought and impression come rushing in. He thought about the Italian woman and the bald man and about Lund's remark in Paris that Ussing was angry with him. He thought about Ussing who was even now preparing to attack him over his Paris book, and perhaps at this moment was with Lund, who was eagerly noting down everything he said. He thought about the press conference in June and heard laughter coming from somewhere in the background of the hall in the

Elysée Palace. Then he visualized the Italian woman again, in the Danish shop in Paris, in the Deer Park with frost on her eyelashes or walking to and fro in her apartment in the Rue du Dragon that he could see into from his hiding place.

He had a strong feeling that he had lost the chance of meeting her. He heard more footsteps on the bridge and an aeroplane flying low over the roofs of the town. And he wondered what he was actually doing in Venice, in this hotel room at the beginning of March as spring approached drawing a long summer with it which he might spend somewhere in the south of France; or perhaps — and the thought made it even harder for him to fall asleep — in Copenhagen, in the editorial department, in a small back office or perhaps in Århus or Ålborg in some or other dreary two-room flat with a view over a men's outfitting shop and a cinema showing five-year-old Danish comedies every night. The blood seemed to rush to his head, hot, boiling, as if carrying the thoughts with it so he could no longer hold them at bay. Mental processes, he thought. Mental processes that again were nothing more than chemical processes; than the blood that rose to his head and caused the electrical chemistry of his brain to undergo constantly new processes; lured out the memories and predicted an uncertain future that made him afraid and the sticky sweat run over his forehead and down his neck. He sat up in bed and held his hands to his temples, then squeezed as hard as he could to press the blood away. Then he went over to the basin and plunged his head into ice-cold water, trying to concentrate his attention on the objects immediately in front of him. Neutral things without hostility, the tooth glass with Venetian decoration, the tube of toothpaste, the soap, toothbrush and the contact for the electrical shaver. The American was still whimpering, but less loudly and at longer intervals. The two Irish priests went by, along the corridor, talking together; and below his window a young girl's laughter rang out. Venice. You are in Venice, he thought, and for the first time in your life. But that was no help. On his way back to the bed he knew, walking over the cold mosaic tiles that sent shudders up through his feet, that it would be another hour or two before he could fall asleep, and for a moment he wished he could do what the old Tibetans did: bore a little hole in his skull to ease the pressure of his thoughts.

He lay down under the quilt, but then he started to feel freezing cold and he cursed the hotel that only supplied heavy bedclothes. He grabbed his jacket and spread it over the quilt, and at last fell asleep when the birds began to twitter.

He woke to find the American standing right beside his bed head, freshly shaved, in a new suit, smiling all over his face. He wanted Mollerup to go out walking in Venice again and suggested that from now on they should take life a bit less seriously. Last night had been a gloomy business, he said, half jokingly. Mollerup sat up on the edge of the bed and excused himself, saying he felt unwell. Upset stomach. Hangover. After the American had departed shrugging his shoulders, Mollerup dressed slowly, and, after breakfast, he went to St Mark's Square, where he found the filming was under way again. When he had stood for some time watching a scene in which the white-clad soldiers and the SS herded a group of townsfolk beneath the columns to body-search them, he again caught sight of the bald man. He was in the middle of the square, a loudhailer in one hand. Mollerup guessed him to be the director, and suddenly recalled the time when he had stayed the night in his flat, and in the afternoon had looked through his papers and found some loose sheets from a shooting script. He looked round for the Italian woman. At first he could not see her, then she came out of a shop, with some newspapers under her arm. She was wearing the same grey suit as on the previous evening and a headscarf. The wind kept lifting one corner of it. She made straight for the bald man.

There were various ways in which he could approach them. He could walk past without taking any notice of them in the hope they might recognize him and call to him. Or he could go straight up to them. Or he could take his place in the crowd of curious onlookers. He chose the last approach, and when several minutes had passed, the Italian woman looked at him. She started, looked away, looked at him again wrinkling her forehead. He did not dare go up to her, not even when she smiled faintly. She whispered something to the bald man who at once beckoned to him to come closer.

'What are you doing in Venice, then?' she asked.

'Bit of a holiday,' he replied. 'I suddenly had to get away from work, the daily routine, away from Paris . . .'

They were in a restaurant. After finishing the scene the bald man called a halt, and they took one of the fast motor launches over to the Lido. The Italian woman's friendly attitude reminded Mollerup of the first times they had met, before the ill-fated Copenhagen visit. She was wearing the silver bracelet he had given her and looked at him the whole time with a friendly expression, leaning her head slightly back and winding a lock of hair between finger and thumb. For a moment he felt that it might have been yesterday they had first gone to bed together in her apartment. But nevertheless she had spoken to him formally and something told him that he must not on any account try to get too close to her, that she was keeping a distance between them, and that she must be living with the bald man here in Venice. Now and then she spoke to him about everyday matters as if they were married: she reminded him he should not smoke too much, and he asked her not to forget to get his shirts from the laundry while blowing cigarette smoke from his nostrils and sketching camera moves for a future scene on a napkin. Mollerup wondered what to do. He rolled up the end of his napkin and ate too much of the bread the waiter had brought. He could not make out why the Italian woman had been so friendly.

Then the bald man suddenly came out with it. From the moment he had seen him in the crowd of spectators he knew that *he* was the man. The one to play a leading German spy who comes into the Casino here at the Lido to find an

Englishman on a secret mission The bald man went on and laughed heartily, as if trying to apologize for his offer. He must come along wearing an ordinary suit of English cut and generally do everything he could to look as unlike a German as possible while at the same time leaving no doubt as to his origins. The German who does not want to be a German. The German who tries to behave like an English or French aristocrat. Then he would walk among the gaming tables looking for the Englishman on a secret mission. To begin with he had no idea who he was looking for, but a red-haired, slightly curly Leslie Howard type in sunglasses would soon attract his attention. He would then sit down opposite him and in a short time would challenge his English sporting spirit by constantly playing for higher stakes. In the end the Englishman — who incidentally spoke German and tried to look extremely German in a wool-mix suit — would forget himself and utter some curse or other in his own language because he had lost all his money. This would give him away. The Englishman grew nervous and drew his revolver, but the German had already beckoned four SS men over to the table. They handcuffed him and dragged him out of the room while the other guests nervously mumbled and screamed. There was only one problem, the bald man went on. Did he object to having his hair dyed? Mollerup smiled deprecatingly, but the bald man maintained it was necessary so people could see from the start that he *was* a German dressed like an Englishman.

'You must do it,' said the Italian woman, getting out her script and marking off the scene so he could read it through.

He guessed she must be the continuity girl for the film. And he wondered why he had come all the way to Venice. So that she and the bald man could get him a job? If he refused to play the part of the German he would risk getting no help later on. He accepted and was told that the scene would be filmed that very afternoon.

He walked round among the tables with a Dunhill pipe in the

corner of his mouth. Festively dressed ladies in long dresses and gentlemen in dinner jackets sat at all the tables. The four SS men stood along one wall. The scene took place at night so black paper had been stuck on all the windows to keep out the daylight. The bald man had told him precisely which route to follow. At each table he passed he was to put down a small sum on red. Then he would slowly move on to the table nearest the camera and sit down opposite the Englishman who would have piles of gambling chips in front of him and a self-assured smile on his face.

As Mollerup walked around with one hand in his pocket and the other full of chips, he was constantly nervous of doing something wrong so the scene would have to be retaken. He was afraid of falling over his feet or colliding with one of the middle-aged society women who walked towards him carrying long-stemmed champagne glasses and wearing silver lamé dresses from the forties. But after the first few minutes he felt quite sure of himself. The bald man stood a little way away from the camera watching him intently and nodding his satisfaction. Then he reached the table where the Englishman sat with his huge winnings before him, making discreet professional notes on a pad with an antique silver pencil. He waited until a seat was free just opposite the Englishman, sat down and did exactly what he had been told. He took the Dunhill pipe out of his mouth and tapped the burned tobacco into an ashtray. The camera came slowly closer. The moment it stopped he took a gold cigarette case out of his inner pocket. He put a Craven A between his lips, after tapping it on the lid of the case. Then he lit it with a lighter, also gold, and drew the smoke deep into his lungs, expectantly biting one cheek. For a minute he observed the Englishman's play, as if to calculate his technique. Each time the Englishman bet on number twelve, on the evens and on the first dozen, every time or every other time the stunned croupier announced that number twelve had won. Mollerup stole a quick glance down at the wheel in which the ball never fell into the number twelve hole at all. The bald man had explained the technique to him: later on they would take some close-ups of a specially made roulette wheel in which a magnet ensured that the ball would fall into the right numbers; first the Englishman's and then his own.

At one point the Englishman seemed to be getting tired. He took off his sunglasses, rubbed his eyes and called a waiter, who went over to him with a towel wrung out in warm water for him to wipe his face with. The Englishman counted the money he had won and prepared to leave while his luck still held. Then it was time for Mollerup to place his first bet on number thirteen, odds, second dozen. Number thirteen came up. The Englishman frowned. Mollerup smiled at him, and he smiled back. Again number thirteen came up, again Mollerup had a big win. This time the Englishman did not smile at him. He suddenly sat up straight as if he had just arrived, the tiredness in his face had vanished. He lit a cigarette and bit the side of his little finger when, for the third time, the croupier announced number thirteen. As the pile of chips grew in front of Mollerup, the Englishman decided to play again. Once or twice the ball fell on a number far from twelve and thirteen, but then thirteen came up again, twice running. The Englishman grew visibly nervous and started to move his bets around. He covered four numbers in the third dozen, two in the first dozen and two in the central one. Number thirteen came out once again. Mollerup noticed the other players at the table looking admiringly at him. For a moment he forgot he was acting in a film. The Englishman opposite him took out his sunglasses again, polished them and put them on. He clutched his silver pencil with one hand, calculating new systems which might defeat his opponent, and this was real life. He felt the Englishman was in the same situation, he too had forgotten he was in a film; and although he had looked admiringly at him when he first won on number thirteen, now hatred was growing in his pupils behind the sunglasses. The sweat breaking out on their foreheads was not produced by the fierce heat from the spotlights but by the tension of the game. As the minutes passed the Englishman's pile of chips diminished while Mollerup watched his own grow and grow. Finally Mollerup staked all his winnings on number twelve, evens, first dozen. The Englishman immediately seized his chance and put his last chips, three in all, on number thirteen, odds, second dozen.

'Twelve,' came indifferently from the croupier.

'Damn it!' exploded the Englishman.

Mollerup looked at him stiffly, as he had been told.

'English?' he asked, with dangerous mildness.

'Nein!' replied the Englishman, starting to rise. He already had his hand in his pocket reaching for his revolver. He pushed back his chair and now Mollerup was looking straight into the muzzle of the revolver while the Englishman took off his sunglasses and backed away towards the exit. Mollerup snapped his fingers, and the four SS men came rushing up and knocked the revolver out of the Englishman's hand, grabbed him and handcuffed him. All the gamblers had left the tables and fled screaming.

The scene was shot again, and this time Mollerup was eager to play his German with every nerve in his body. He straightened his back as he walked among the tables and tried to assume an ice-cold expression; when he pulled at his Dunhill pipe he exaggerated, as a German who had never smoked an English pipe before would do. The bald man nodded energetically at him to indicate he should go on just as he had begun, and when he sat down opposite the Englishman, put down the pipe and took out the gold cigarette case, he started humming a bawdy English war song. Then the roulette started up and everything happened as before. He won and won while the Englishman lost and lost. And again he had the feeling that he was not in a film but that everything was happening in reality.

'Damn it!' said the Englishman.

'English?' he asked, even more dangerously than the first time.

'Nein!' replied the Englishman and at once Mollerup was looking straight into the muzzle of the pistol. The four SS men came rushing up.

'Nehmen Sie ihn weg!' shouted Mollerup, pointing at the

Englishman, then getting up while he stubbed the English cigarette out in the ashtray with deep disgust. He could actually feel the English disguise slipping off him and the German taking over, and he felt the lack of a monocle to put on. All the same, he was slightly nervous in case he had overdone the act and his improvised order to the SS men would annoy the bald man. But when the scene finished, and the Englishman had been dragged outside, the bald man came straight up to him and slapped him on the shoulder, while the Italian woman gave him a significant wink. She handed him one of the biggest chips as a symbolic reward for his achievement.

'You're a real actor!' said the bald man, scratching his neck and offering him a French cigarette.

Mollerup took the compliment with a smile. He could not hit on a suitable reply. Should he come out with the usual claptrap about it 'not being anything much' or that 'it was fun' and he had done just 'what had come to him'? He decided to say nothing, it would make a good impression if he just left and met them again in a day or two. The Italian woman closed the script when he gave her his hand. She turned her head so he could kiss her on the cheek. Then she in turn gave him a kiss, a very neutral kiss, but still a kiss as if there had never been anything painful between them.

'You did it so well,' she said.

'Glad to help,' he replied and wondered if she meant it when she spoke to him with a little more intimacy. He went on: 'It was just what I'd been expecting when I came to Venice — that I would meet you people and take part in a *film* too!'

'We're having a little party this evening,' she said, 'if you'd like to come . . .'

He woke up clear in the head. From the mood he was in he knew he had not had the usual bad dream. He dressed feeling cheerful, and when he left the hotel with the note in his hand and asked the way to the address it bore, he did not feel the usual pressure on his neck. His arms hung down relaxed, and a faint hum of well-being spread over his body, as if he had slept soundly in one position for a whole day and night. The cigarette he lit suddenly tasted of cigarette, and he even played football with a flat stone. After flipping it around the narrow alleys he took a run at it and sent it with the toe of his shoe out into a canal where with zigzag movements it sank into the murky water until he could no longer see it, and the final ring it had made on the surface was broken up at the edge of the canal. Then he found his way to the address the Italian woman had given him. He went down a blind alley and stopped in front of a house with balconies outside all its windows. To get into the house he had to cross over a little marble bridge. The door, adorned with carved baroque angels, was open, and as he went inside the Italian woman came down the stairs and showed him up to the first floor. She was in tight black slacks, flat shoes and a high-necked Japanese silk blouse. She told him the apartment belonged to one of her women friends who was in America on a study tour, and that she and the bald man had borrowed it for as long as it would take to make the film. She took him by the hand and led him round the various groups of guests, as if he was a specially important person she wanted everyone to meet, while she enthusiastically described how he had been a huge success that afternoon in his role of a German officer. She straightened her back, put on a hard expression and said in a deep voice:

'Nehme Sie weg!'

The guests roared with laughter.

'Nehmen Sie *ihn* weg!' he corrected her with a smile.

'*Ihn*, yes,' she replied. 'I'll never learn to speak German! Kra, kra, kra!'

She put a welcoming glass in his hand and went on explaining to everyone who was listening that he was the son of the world-famous Danish actress Marianne Mollerup.

'The apple doesn't fall far from the tree,' said one of the guests.

'Oh, a marvellous artist,' said another man he soon recognized as his adversary from the casino. He had taken off his

Leslie Howard wig and spoke French with a clear Italian accent:

'La grande Marianna! Mother to my trouncer!'

'Marianne,' he corrected, nibbling the slice of lemon on the rim of his glass.

He sat down on a sofa covered with thick green velvet and noticed he was the centre of the guests' attention. They sat down one by one opposite him and asked him if he was on holiday in Venice and what he otherwise did with himself. He replied that he was a correspondent in Paris and had been in need of a holiday, and as he had never been to Venice before, that was what had made him decide to come — before the tourist season was under way. The guests were mostly young, well-dressed and relaxed. He guessed most of them must be Italian, while the only older person, a stout silver-haired American with a gold ring on his little finger and a cigar in his mouth, must be the film producer, because the bald man kept asking him if there was anything he wanted, if his glass was full, if he wanted something to smoke and if he was getting hungry. The American signed with his hand over one shoulder that he was quite happy, and Mollerup had to answer various questions about his mother. The American wanted to know how old she was, when she had last been in a film and if he would be able to meet her when he went to Scandinavia for a short holiday soon. To start with Mollerup gave his answers politely and slightly unwillingly, but when he noticed the interest of the people around him in his stories about his mother, he quickly served up all the anecdotes about her career he could remember. He described the time she had been on the stage of the Comédie Française. He told them about 'the false Marianne Mollerup'; about her tireless energy and her daily occupation as director of a cinema in central Copenhagen. He felt her becoming two people again — the mother he had endured for over forty years and an international celebrity he happened to know a lot about. Each time he finished an anecdote the American leaned forwards, slapped his thighs and burst into high-pitched laughter that made the others laugh too.

'I *like* your Danish friend! Very funny man!' he said to the Italian woman.

Some of the others wanted to know about Denmark and the Danish sense of humour they had heard so much about. As the Italian had left them again he told the old stories about the way the Danes had behaved towards the German occupying power. He felt ashamed to dish up again the anecdote about the German soldier on guard outside the royal palace of Amalienborg in an armed guardhouse on which someone had scrawled 'he has no trousers on', but could not resist the temptation to score with it. After he had entertained the guests with several more stories of that sort, a discussion of Germany started up. The American said he intended to make a blockbuster that would reveal the German slave mentality in earnest; an episodic film from Luther to Walter Ulbricht. When the discussion switched over to Italian, with excited gestures, Mollerup rose and went out on to one of the balconies. Some gondolas glided along on the canal below. In the first one was a young bridal pair, the girl in white with a long veil, the man in evening dress, while a gramophone with a large speaker attached played mandolin music. The parents were in two other gondolas. The cool of evening had fallen over Venice, it was getting dark and a Caravel about to land had already lit its landing lights.

He stood there for a quarter of an hour with his glass on the ledge of the balcony. He was in a neutral mood. The world around him had suddenly come to rest, no longer did things come towards him as if to force him backwards. For a moment he felt that the object of life was merely to go on. One moment everything could be turned upside down, the next everything was peaceful and undisturbed. The sun rose and set, the days succeeded each other and all the things he had thought of as violent events around him were really only certain unfathomed mental processes, just as the American at the hotel had asserted. Mental processes, chemical processes. The mountains did not melt, the solar system did not burn out, human beings did not dissolve into hot wax. He threw a piece of paper from the balcony so it whirled through the air and landed on the water in the canal and was carried away by the current, in the direction of the three gondolas now turning off into a side canal. He lit a cigarette, turned round and inside the apartment caught sight of the Italian woman, who was intently watching the bald man's attempts to flirt with a young blonde in a poppy-red low cut dress. The Italian woman bit her knuckles and tried to preserve an unconcerned smile. In a strange way Mollerup did not feel attracted to her in quite the same way as before. Although she looked more lovely than he ever remembered seeing her, in the black slacks and high-necked Japanese silk blouse, it was as if he could suddenly and for the first time see her as she really was: a woman on the wrong side of thirty-five, divorced and clearly afraid of not being attractive enough. Which French poet had said that, to a woman, age is an illness? The beginnings of bags under her eyes, her thick black hair, piled up youthfully with a slide at the neck, but with the first hint of grey. He looked at her for a long time and wondered if he had ever really seen her properly. Was she as beautiful as he had always imagined when he was not with her and recalled her as something almost too graceful? Had he been attracted to her just because she was a type he normally had little contact with, because she was — southern? The mere fact that he always thought of her as *The Italian Woman* and not as Claudia. The Italian woman! The Dane's dream of the Italian girl! Had he fundamentally behaved in the same way as the Italians who ran after Scandinavian girls just because they were long-limbed and fair-haired? He could not help smiling scornfully at the thought of all the time he had wasted chasing her around Paris, as if happiness lay merely in being in her vicinity, in glimpsing her as she walked about her apartment. The trip up the Rue de Rennes when she was going to fetch her green sports car from Montparnasse. The bus ride when she was going to the art gallery in the Rue du Faubourg St.-Honoré. And his panicky and childish attempt to telephone her from café telephone boxes. And then everything that happened after that. Munk's articles that upset him purely because he was unbalanced. The visit to the Danish students' residence. The visit to the press attaché. And the begging calls on Parisian editorial and publishing offices. What were the forces that had played havoc within him since Christmas? Forces that had led him all the way to Venice, to take part in a weird film as a German of the deepest dye, and then to this party where he was interrogated about his mother's career by a swaggering American and now stood on a balcony looking down at a canal of dirty water with three gondolas disappearing from view? He had come here to get the Italian woman to help him find a job and he knew that this was the best moment to make the request. She and the bald man would undoubtedly help him so he was not left with nothing when the letter came from the editor-in-chief. But *what* letter? Who said the newspaper was going to fire him at all, to call him home to a job as local editor in Århus or television reviewer or whatever it was he had been imagining? Who said the paper had any idea of appointing Munk as Paris correspondent? And what had really been wrong in Munk sending a few articles to his newspaper to earn a little money and that he had asked to have the French press card that opened all the doors that otherwise were closed?

He stubbed out the cigarette against the ledge of the balcony and flicked it out over the canal with his index finger. Obsessions, the thought rushed through him, nothing more than obsessions! For a moment he felt slightly shaken because he could see himself as one person sees another. Agitation spread over his body and caused a nervous prickling to run down his arms and out into his hands. Here he stood, outwardly calm and relaxed; a man who had nothing to do with the person who had rushed wildly around Paris on the track of the Italian woman and later from editor to editor and from publishing house to publishing house, and finally in a narrow circle in the sixth arrondissement. Could a person be split in two? Banal, he thought. All the same, he looked at his hands in surprise and moved his fingers in the air, as if he was about to pull on an invisible pair of gloves. He bent his knees. He pulled his shoulders back and breathed in deeply so the air reached the tips of his lungs. He was master of his body. He was a different person from just a few days ago. At this moment he was the cool observer who knew exactly what he was doing. The world lay around him like a scene he could move about in, naturally, without preconceived opinions, without fear. Far out on the horizon, hundreds of kilometres away, yet no further than he could throw a stone, that was how he felt it. A place on the other side of the theatrical roofs and towers of Venice, under the evening sky that was now almost completely black, with the first stars, behind fields, valleys, rivers and mountains lay Paris, a city of almost ten millions, power centre and mirage at one and the same time. In that city was an insignificant colony of Danes. And he had believed that colony was the same as Paris. He could not understand it. He could not understand himself, the way he had behaved until this moment when suddenly everything had released itself inside him and around him and the pressure of his thoughts had eased, as if he really had a Tibetan hole bored in his skull.

He longed for Paris again, for the boulevards, the cafés, the traffic and the heavy diesel smoke-laden air. For over a week he had seen nothing but gondolas and motor boats. The prickling nervousness vanished. Instead he felt a happy urge to get going again. The Danish royal couple were about to pay an official visit to Paris. Although normally he did not give much thought to the monarchy, he would use the opportunity to write a series of well-written and lively reports to make amends for the neglect of his work since Christmas. Perhaps he ought to write an explanatory letter to the editor as well, directly apologizing for not having written enough of the sort of articles the paper wanted, and he would try to explain the affair of the Israeli. It would soon be spring in Paris. The protective windows would be taken down from the pavement cafés, the banks of the Seine would teem with young lovers, and summer fashions would be on display in the couturiers' windows. And in the afternoon the sun would lie in big squares on the floor of his apartment while the Spanish workmen down on the Avenue de Wagram would doff their dark winter coats. Suddenly he felt as if he had been on a long much-needed holiday, and that the Paris he was going back to was a town that just lay waiting for him to take possession of it once more. He smiled. He smiled because he knew well enough that his calmness and self-assurance stemmed from his success in the part of the German. Was that all it took? But he was happy to realize it. On that issue as well he was able to see through himself.

He decided to leave the party and went inside. He thanked the bald man for an enjoyable evening and went over to the Italian woman who was talking to the silver-haired producer while continuing to glance in the direction of the bald man to see if he was flirting with the blonde in the poppy-red dress.

'Going already?' she asked.

'I'm planning to go back to Paris tomorrow,' he replied and heard how controlled his voice was. He enjoyed seeing the Italian woman look at him with slight uncertainty, as if she could not understand his leaving just when he was at a party surrounded by amusing young well-dressed Italians. She went down the staircase with him.

'I'll ring you in Paris,' he said. 'When you are back too . . . .'

'Oh, yes, you really *must*,' she said. She pulled the silk blouse down and rounded her lips to receive his kiss. For a moment he wanted to embrace her but he controlled himself and contented himself with kissing her gently.

'I owe you a good dinner after all you did for me in Copenhagen,' she said as he made ready to leave. 'Bon voyage!'

'Take care of yourself,' he replied in a rather too fatherly tone, squeezing her hand.

He walked around for a little while. It was midnight. The orchestras on St Mark's Square were packing up. The waiters went around the café tables picking up tips. He thought of going to the night club he had visited with the American with the wart on his nose. For a moment he felt like having a fling, quite alone, with a couple of the bar girls. But he knew that he did not have enough money on him for that and, after strolling along a few canals and over various bridges, he went back to his hotel. The American was in the bar playing ludo with the German couple. He ate a handful of salted almonds and played dice with the bartender. Then he went up to his room and packed everything except his toilet things. When he lay down he knew he would have no difficulty in falling asleep. He glanced round the room, wondering why he had not studied it closely before: the ceiling decorated with themes from Greek mythology, the heavy dark green silk curtains, the antique bedside table, the cream-coloured telephone and the old Venetian tooth glass on a glass shelf above the basin in which a ray of moonlight was reflected. For a second he was suddenly uneasy because he recalled Lund's remark that Ussing was angry with him. It seemed there had to be *something* to disturb and irritate his newly acquired serenity. But then he pushed the thought away. Happiness is never perfect, he thought, again looking forward to Paris, to the apartment in the Avenue de Wagram soon to be warmed by the first afternoon sun of springtime.

After paying the bill he asked the hotel to order a taxi motorboat at three o'clock; an hour before the plane left for Milan and then to Paris. He told the porter he was going to sit in St Mark's Square and asked for a page to come and fetch him when the taxi arrived. Then he went into Venice and spent most of the morning buying new clothes. He supplied himself with several shirts, two pure wool sweaters, orange socks, a pair of shoes, a summer cap with airholes in the sides and a light raincoat. With his last Italian money he bought a suit in a gentleman's outfitters on St Mark's Square and, when trying it on, involuntarily saluted himself in the mirror. His dyed hair made him look at least five years younger. He had lost weight, too. The plumpness in his cheeks had gone, and he recalled the day in late summer when he was in a café in Paris with his mother and caught sight of himself in a mirror that reflected his profile in another mirror. Then he had been shocked at himself, now he could not restrain the feeling that after all he was not so bad looking. The thought of his mother made him buy a postcard and send it to her. *Am on holiday, having a great time, the Italians more than friendly, Venice splendid.* She loved him to write to her like that.

After lunch he sat at a café table on St Mark's Square from where he could see the page coming from the hotel. He put all his parcels down in front of him and lit a cigarette. In his hand he had the chip the Italian woman had given him in the casino after his successful acting. He tossed it into the air, caught it and started whistling. Tonight he would be in Paris. Tonight he could stroll up and down the Champs-Elysées again, have one of the ice creams he loved at the Pub Renault, drink a calvados, buy the latest French evening papers. He might also feel like a little trip up to the Pigalle, to La Belle Ondine, the bar with the Vietnamese girls he had not been to since the night with Ellesøe. And tomorrow he would get going on articles, on his work. There was nothing to hinder him any more, nothing to stop him from living life as he wanted, sensibly divided between work and pleasure.

When the waiter came he ordered tea with lemon, he wanted to be quite clear in the head for flying. A newspaper vendor walked past in the middle of the square, with Danish, Swedish and German morning papers, and a group of newly arrived Dutch people proved that the tourist season was now in full swing. Soon the Danish tourists would be here in swarms too. So it was just right for him to be leaving today. He beckoned the newspaper man over and bought a two day-old Danish paper. He crossed his legs, stirred his tea and for a moment watched a flock of pigeons coming in to land after a uniformed man with a wheelbarrow had sprinkled corn for them in the middle of the square. Then he opened the newspaper and read about the cold weather in Copenhagen, about the winter that would never end, about the Copenhageners who were escaping south with the clergyman who had started up an airline, and the travel firm Simon Spies, and about the empty cinemas in town. Suddenly his eye lit on a sizeable headline on page three:

WELL-KNOWN DANISH PARIS CORRESPONDENT
ACCUSED OF PLAGIARISM

His eyes clouded over as he read that a German publisher had demanded that *Paris From The Shady Side,* by the well-known Danish Paris correspondent Max Mollerup alias Monsieur Jean be withdrawn because at least two chapters had been taken almost word for word from one of the publisher's own books, written by a well-known Paris correspondent for a Hamburg newspaper. At first he thought it was a joke. Some journalist he had once had a few beers with wanted to tease him. He went on leafing through the paper and pretended not to have seen the article at all. Instead he tried to concentrate on a piece about Greenland girls in Copenhagen who ended up as prostitutes. Then, as he turned back the pages, he nourished some inexplicable hope that something quite different would be in the place where he had read the German publisher's demand. It was not. The article was not a hallucination: something he had imagined with everything else he had imagined during the past year and which he had thought he was rid of. There it was, covering three columns, black on white, but with no picture of him. *Well-known Danish Paris correspondent accused of plagiarism.*

In the distance he caught sight of the page running towards him shouting that the taxi boat had come. He stood up. He put down the paper. He gathered up his parcels. His ears sang.

CHAPTER ELEVEN

In Paris, Denmark was the order of the day. The Dannebrog flew beside the Tricolore on the Place de la Concorde, and in most of the shop windows on the Champs Elysées there were photographs of the smiling royal couple with the princesses between them. An armoured train filled with Danish works of art valued at ten million kroner had been sent on the Scandinavian express. On the occasion of the official visit of King Frederik and Queen Ingrid, de Gaulle had ordered five rooms at the Louvre to be available for an exhibition of Danish art and craft, from the Vikings up to the twentieth century. In the rooms, furnished with pale curtains and decorated in pastel colours, visiting Parisians would be able to make the acquaintance of Christian VI's enamelled gold chalice from Fredensborg Castle Chapel, the coronation chair from Rosenborg Castle, the gilded altar from Ølst, a bronze horn, silver and gold bracelets, rings and chains from the Viking period and Pilo's painting of Frederik V on horseback, as well as paintings by Weie, Giersing, Lundstrøm and Rolf Hauge. The latter would be represented by the eight meters-wide and four meters-high 'Light over Saint-Aubin du Cormier' which he had completed six months earlier and which was inspired by the battle between the Bretons and the French in 1488. At the Danish House on the Champs Elysées there was an exhibition of modern Danish jewellery. The exhibition was 'arranged in surroundings as light and cool as the Scandinavian summer night,' as a leading Jutland gold-smith put it in an interview on French television. The small studio cinemas on the West Bank were advertising *Day of Wrath* and *The Word*, and a group of Danish women students in red skirts and white blouses cycled round Paris giving out free tickets for a prize of a midsummer journey to Northern Greenland. Some French journalists who had been to Denmark by invitation of the Danish Ministry of Foreign Affairs had written of their impressions of the fairy-tale kingdom whose king was to visit the president of the fifth republic. *Le Monde* wrote about Denmark's transformation from an agricultural to an industrial country, *Le Figaro* about the Danish social services which France should learn from, and *Combat*, in a series of articles, 'Denmark 1965, or Bourgeois Socialism', drew attention to the newly established arts foundation and wondered why the workers were so intensely opposed to it: 'One wonders what the Danish workers would say if, instead of using money to improve conditions for artists, the state used it for atomic weapons,' the paper concluded, aiming at de Gaulle.

When Mollerup returned to Paris, preparations for the royal visit were almost complete. Flagpoles had been erected along the boulevards, and when he walked up the Champs-Elysées, photographs of the Danish royal family were already in the shop windows, twined around with Dannebrog-coloured crepe paper. In the display windows of the Danish House jewels had been arranged on red and yellow bricks as a taste of what the exhibition on the second floor had to offer. Meanwhile, the doll-sized Danish guard with the architect-designed knives and forks had been placed slightly in the background. It was just past nine o'clock and the prostitutes had come out from the side streets. He asked for the latest Danish newspapers in all the kiosks along the road to the L'Étoile, but they were sold out everywhere. Finally he got hold of a copy of his own paper. He looked around him to see if anyone he knew was about, then quickly leafed through the paper. At first he felt relieved because his portrait did not meet his eyes as he had feared, beneath some hard-hitting headline: *The Mollerup affair develops*. Then he realized that naturally the newspaper would not want to deliver up one of its own employees in that way. If he wanted to get a true impression of what had been written about him, he would have to read the other Danish papers and first and foremost the one Lund worked for.

Suddenly he felt certain that the whole thing originated from Lund's interview with Ussing. It was Ussing who had been the evil spirit: Ussing who for over twenty years had lived in isolation near the Pigalle and who had reappeared now to show himself to the Danish public and say he had been irritated for many years by his successor as correspondent in Paris. And Lund had willingly noted it all, in particular Ussing's 'discovery': that two chapters in *Paris From The Shady Side* had been copied from a German book, and some time later the news had reached the German publisher. Mollerup tried to control himself. For a rational moment, as if the whole thing was like a game of chess in which he had merely made a few foolish moves, he regretted that instead of going to Venice he had not set his sights on finding Ussing after the night he met Lund in the Rue des Canettes. Then he could no longer keep himself in check, either in thought or movement. He went behind a tree because he felt someone had noticed him. He knew that Lund loved to sit for a couple of hours after dinner in the cafés near L'Étoile, with a coffee and brandy.

He stayed behind the tree for a minute or two, but then people really did notice him. They turned towards him, whispering to each other, shook their heads as if they thought he was having a pee like some barbarian. He rushed across to the opposite pavement and went past the drugstore where he had long ago spied on the Italian woman. He walked the whole way round the Arche de Triomphe and down the Avenue de Wagram. And with every step bringing him closer to his street door his stomach contracted more and the pains in his neck increased. He reached the door and was about to go in when the sweat trickled down his palms so the door handle slipped when he tried to turn it. Suddenly he had not the strength or courage to take the lift up to his flat and open the front door so the week's mail would be pushed across the mat: if he had imagined before that there would be a letter from his editor-in-chief recalling him, now he was quite sure that it had arrived. It would be impossible for the paper to keep him in Paris any longer now he was compromised. How many days would he have left in the city? Would the paper insist he travel home immediately? Was Munk the officially accredited correspondent of the newspaper already? He went on along the Avenue de Wagram looking at the shops. In a radio shop Danish stereo equipment was on show in front of a life size photograph of King Frederik as conductor. Then he found a taxi and told the driver to drive him around Paris — anywhere. He passed the Place de la Concorde, the National Gallery, went along the Seine with the illuminated plastic boats that sailed past with their spotlights searching out young lovers on the banks. He let the driver go where he wished and looked out at Paris flickering past the windows. Finally he asked the driver to stop at some hotel.

He had been amazingly calm on the plane and had whiled away the time by chatting to a French business man who was interested in investigating the possibility of selling Algerian pipe tobacco to Denmark. He explained to the Frenchman that Danes preferred English tobacco mixture. He grew really absorbed in the conversation and constantly made the Frenchman laugh aloud when he described the Danes' persistent efforts to ape the English. Although his ears went on singing and his neck hurt, he could still not believe that what he had read in the paper was true, that he had been accused of plagiarism. Again he told himself the article must be an illusion although he knew that was foolish. But he could not accept the idea that he could be in trouble over something so trivial as letting himself be rather too inspired by a German book that ridiculed the French. As if he had committed burglary. As if he had stolen a valuable object from a museum. As if he had actually *done* something or other. As the plane tilted down towards Paris and he could see thousands of street lights and the cars pulling long postcard-like trails of light behind them, he still felt he was watching a world that offered countless possibilities and which could not possibly be closed to him merely because once, six months ago, he had played his cards wrongly. And as he parted from the business man he asked him for his address and telephone number so he could invite him to dinner. The man handed him a card and smiled all over his face, and they agreed it would be really pleasant to meet regularly. He took the card, convinced he had gained a new friend, and on the airport bus in to Paris the world around him had looked perfectly normal. The Paris he drove into was the same Paris he had longed for on the balcony in Venice.

But the pain in his neck was still there, everything had really gone wrong, and, as he stood on the Champs Elysées, the truth struck him again. When he fumbled in his pockets for notes, his hands trembled like those of an old man: the driver asked sympathetically if he could help him with anything. The driver already had one foot on the pavement and was indicating that he would carry his suitcase for him, but Mollerup put on an artificially cheerful smile, took the case and walked into the hotel. He got a room with a view of one of the best known Paris stores, and for some reason or other, perhaps because he wanted to make a good impression and did not want the proprietor to attach any importance to the fact that his hands were shaking, he paid the 45 new francs at once; all the French currency he had, exactly. When he had undressed he searched for some sleeping pills so as not to lie awake all night tossing and turning. He had a hot bath, took exaggerated pains to be clean, as if that might help. He cut his toe nails, washed his hair with the hand soap, scrubbed his neck. Then he lay down, grateful for the effect of the pills. A sensation of heaviness spread up his legs. Although he was able to keep the worst thoughts at bay he was still — but as if they were nothing to do with him, as if inwardly he did not care — wondering if he had *really* been accused. If that meant a court case and all that. Would the German publisher be satisfied if *Paris From The Shady Side* was merely withdrawn? Would he be liable for damages?

He looked out of the window, though at intervals his eyelids closed. A gigantic photograph of Princess Margrethe was being hoisted up the facade of the store opposite. First Margrethe's permanently waved curls appeared, then her forehead, her eyes, her nose and her mouth until the picture covered four floors. He smiled sleepily, his eyes closed completely: the picture of Princess Margrethe was at least five years old.

Next day he went straight to the Danish embassy. He made sure to get there in the lunch hour so he could go up to the reading room unnoticed and there be confronted with the whole truth, as it appeared in the papers that did not need to spare him because of internal considerations of prestige. As he approached the Embassy he waited on the opposite pavement for the press attaché and his secretaries to leave the building on their way to a nearby restaurant, then crossed over. When he entered and the guard asked what he wanted, he showed his press card and hurried upstairs to the reading room. He put his suitcase in a corner and seized a pile of back numbers of the newspaper Lund worked for. He leafed through the previous days' editions until he caught sight of what he was looking for: the interview with Ussing. It was given an important position, with a three-column wide portrait of the elderly Ussing at a bistro near the Pigalle. Ussing was leaning on the bar counter with his elbows pushed back, a glass of red wine in his hand and a stub of Gauloise in the corner of his mouth. His nose was bulging and porous, and, compared with earlier pictures Mollerup remembered, his hair was white. Lund had obviously taken great pains to get the right tone into his rushing torrent of speech. For the first one and a half columns Ussing recalled his youth in the twenties and thirties, when the talk was 'European' and Paris was ruled by hideous neo-nationalism. He talked about the hectic days of the Popular Front, about meetings with the serene André Gide and the young Malraux fiercely eager for life. Then he went on to make a violent attack on de Gaulle, but finally warned people in Denmark not to confuse Gaullism with the true spirit of France. In that connection, he wished to take the opportunity to express his disapproval of what certain young Danish journalists wrote home from Paris: was it impossible for them to discern the genuine charm of Paris behind superficial Americanization? In particular he expressed his dissatisfaction with a book on Paris by a certain Monsieur Jean: could this Monsieur Jean ever write anything *positive* about the French, about Parisians? What did he mean by publishing a book that was a vitriolic attack on Paris? Did not Monsieur Jean realize that the French had a habit of unseating their government every ten years and that a revolution would be bound to knock de Gaulle off his pedestal at the end of the sixties? To Lund's question as to why he — the best known of all Danish Paris correspondents — had withdrawn and kept silent for twenty years, Ussing replied that he merely wanted to be himself; an anonymous Parisian. That was the end of it, and Mollerup folded up the paper with a faint wonderment that grew into relief. So Ussing was only angry with him because he did not like Paris enough! He felt like laughing aloud at the whole situation, but then the relief vanished and he leafed nervously through more papers until he saw the announcement of the German publisher who demanded that *Paris From The Shady Side* by Max Mollerup alias Monsieur Jean be withdrawn. The announcement had been sent through Ritzau's Bureau and apparently had no connection with the interview with Ussing. It was in the other Danish papers as well, but only in the midday paper he had bought on St Mark's Square was the word 'accused' employed. The others merely wrote that *Paris From The Shady Side* should be withdrawn. Then there would not be a court case? Could he allow himself a slight feeling of relief?

Suddenly he heard voices in the corridor. He leaped up not sure where to go. Then he slipped behind the door. A moment later when it opened it hid him completely. The press attaché came into the room with his train of secretaries. A strong scent of expensive after shave emanated from him and reached right into Mollerup's hiding place. The press attaché was in the middle of a long lecture he must have begun on the way upstairs: he had to receive the royal Danish couple when they arrived at Orly tomorrow, and the Embassy messenger had still not fetched the new suit that was ready for him! And why had not all the passes for the reception at the airport been delivered to the Danish journalists? And who was the bungler who had not seen to it that the 25 crates of specially produced Carlsberg were delivered to de Gaulle's ministers, but were still taking up room down in the vestibule? He walked around the table where the papers lay. And who had left these newspapers in such a mess?

The secretaries looked at each other in bewilderment. One promised the beer crates would be sent off this very afternoon. Another that she herself would fetch the press attaché's suit. The third, blushing, started to tidy up the newspapers. At a point when the press attaché stood looking out of the window and the secretaries were all occupied in making notes, Mollerup crept out of his hiding place and into the corridor. But one of the secretaries caught sight of him and called out, asking who he was. In sheer fright he started to run and as he went down the stairs the press attaché ran after him. As he reached the hall he heard his quick steps behind him. Could he see who it was? He pushed his collar up to his neck thinking it was a bit of luck he was wearing the new suit he had bought in Venice. He ran past the astonished Embassy guard who fortunately had not had time to notice his name on the press card. Then he reached the door. Behind him he heard the press attaché: 'Qui-est?! Qui-est!'

He ran on along the pavement and into a back yard where he leaned against the dustbins to get his breath back. His bronchial tubes whistled every time he drew breath and he felt his knees would splinter at any moment. He had to squat down. Then he punched one of the dustbins with all his might: of course he would have to leave his suitcase in the embassy reading room; before long the press attaché would be sure to find out that he was the one who had run away like a thief. For a moment he thought of going back as if nothing had happened. And if the press attaché asked him if he had been there he would appear totally surprised. But he knew he was in no state to carry out that manoeuvre, and in the end he decided to go home. At some time or other he would *have* to let himself into his flat. Would *have* to open the letter from the editor-in-chief.

He sat down at his desk with his raincoat on. He put aside the bills, among them a bill from the Danish Shop for the table he had had sent to the Italian woman's address. He put three letters from his mother unopened into a book, the first one had been posted the same day as the announcement from Ritzau's Bureau appeared in the papers, the other two letters on the two following days. Before he opened the letter from the editor-in-chief he poured out a big glass of whisky and drained it in one gulp. His hands shook again, and the whisky increased the singing in his ears. Then he ripped open the envelope with his index finger, trying to calm himself by thinking that it could not be so bad but that in some way or other he could find a way out of the dilemma. Involuntarily he thought of all those who were in a worse situation than his. Of the millions of starving Indians. Of the clochards under the bridges of Paris. Perhaps at this moment a mother had lost her daughter in a traffic accident. A father his son. At every minute of the day people died in the traffic or were maimed for the rest of their lives. What had he to complain about? A simple paragraph sent from Ritzau's Bureau? Wouldn't he be sure to get out of it? But he could not feel uplifted for long, thinking of the starving Indians did not help him in his own situation, even if he was confronted with the sum of all human suffering, he could not take the letter from the editor-in-chief lightly, he had still not taken it out of the envelope. And he spun out the time and looked out of the window and suddenly felt a stab of envy. A young man embraced a girl on a street corner, in the bright spring sunshine. The young man had thrown down the books he had been carrying under his arm and the girl had put down her shopping basket and put her arms round his neck, pushing one leg between his. On a bench nearby, two elderly men in straw hats with sticks between their knees laughed at something. The Spanish workers in small groups were playing boules under the trees whose crowns had taken on a pale green shine. He stared out of the window for a long time, poured out more whisky, then summoned his courage and pulled the letter out of the opened envelope. He only read every other word. *That wasn't so good, Mollerup. Consideration for the prestige of the paper is all important. A serious situation like. But come home soon — very soon — and let us talk it over. We must find a way out. Yours sincerely.*

We must find a way out. Did those words indicate that the editor-in-chief did not mean to be too hard on him? He rose and walked round the rooms with the whisky glass in his hand. He stumbled over a carpet, and the whisky splashed out of the glass and on to one of his abstract paintings. He was still in his raincoat and, even though the spring sunshine warmed the rooms, he was so cold that he felt like wrapping himself in a blanket. Then he went into the dining room and switched on the television in the hope that some serial was on, but the flickering screen only showed the time. Now the whisky began to take effect in earnest, he felt nausea and the beginnings of a headache. He rushed into the bathroom where the sight of his dyed hair in the mirror made him jump. He ran his fingers through it, irritated, then sat on the edge of the bath with his head over the lavatory pan. But the whisky would not come up, it went round and round in his empty stomach. Instead he turned on the taps to the basin and splashed his face with water. Then he dried himself carefully on the hand towel, went into the kitchen and opened a tin of pâté. He downed it in three large mouthfuls. Who could say that with time people would not forget he had copied a couple of chapters from some German book on Paris? Now, if he openly and honestly admitted he had *blundered*, that he had done something *wrong*, and if he took care to write a long series of good articles of his own — wouldn't he get himself out of the scrape in a natural way? He went into the study, hung the raincoat over a chairback, cleaned the typewriter and took out some paper, so that everything was ready when he started to write his reports on the royal visit.

Next day he went to a barber's to get the dye out of his hair. The sun was high in the sky. The springtime was almost summery, the trees were even greener and all the tables at the pavement cafés were full. There were more and more sight-seeing buses packed with American tourists. Along the Seine the quays were filled with students shirking lectures. After the barber he went straight out to Orly. There was still an hour before the royal couple arrived in a military plane, and he spent the waiting time having a glass of red wine at a snack bar and reading *France-Soir* and *Paris-Presse*. He wanted to be in the front row when the reception took place so he did not miss any details and could make his first report as lively as possible. Around him policemen were already milling, either uniformed or all too recongizable in their identical raincoats and check caps. A teacher was instructing a score of children on how to wave the Danish flags they had been given, and Danish silver was on display in the display cabinets. On the front page of *France-Soir* there was a gigantic picture of King Frederik with a bare torso so all his tattoos were visible. In the accompanying text the newspaper described the king of Denmark as one of the least regal and most democratic rulers in the world: he could be seen every day on his bicycle in central Copenhagen. He had once laid a friendly bet with Michel Simon on which of them had most tattoos. However, it was doubtful whether His Majesty would pay a visit to Monsieur Simon this time, concluded the article. *Paris-Presse* had a picture of Princess Margrethe on its front page. It had been taken on a slant from below so her thighs were well revealed. The caption said that Princess Margrethe was not accompanying her parents on this visit to de Gaulle because she was hunting for a prince consort in England. But this is how Denmark's future queen looks, not quite as graceful as her French sisters but straightforward, not snobbish, ready to get going.

He put down the papers and swallowed the rest of his wine, but when four female Danish journalists came past he seized *France-Soir* again and hid his face behind it. Shortly after that he caught sight through the glass doors of the press attaché getting out of an Embassy car, in a dark suit with an umbrella over his arm. Mollerup hurried to the nearest lavatory. At the urinal he thrust his hand into the rays of light emitted by the photocells so the water ran in little coughing jerks. When a pilot came into the toilet he quickly took his hand away and went over to the wash basins. He combed his hair and discovered in the neon lighting that his hair was slightly darker than it had been before it was dyed, but not so that anyone would notice. He stayed in the toilet until he felt the press attaché had gone by.

Passes? He repeated the word and searched his pockets. No, he did not have a *pass* on him. The two gendarmes with machine guns over their stomachs looked at him accusingly and said that they could not admit him to the pavilion where de Gaulle was to receive the Danish royal couple when they left the aeroplane. He showed them his press card, but that was definitely not enough, they told him. A press card! Anyone could get hold of one of those! He looked from one gendarme to the other as a mass of thoughts rushed through his head. The press attaché. It was him. He had personally crossed him off the list of journalists to cover the royal visit and stopped all invitations to him. For a moment he was seized with despair, the singing in his ears started again, he was weak at the knees and he looked at the gendarmes with a mixture of agitation and hopelessness, exasperated that he was completely in their hands; that they could see he was in a painful situation, and obviously found it amusing. The way they gave each other resigned looks as he still did not take himself off. The way one pulled out a packet of Gitanes, offered it to the other and passed the packet right in front of him on its way back to his trouser pocket. When a group of journlists and photographers with passes in their hands came up to the gendarmes he finally hurried away. He was back where he started: he couldn't even get the opportunity to rehabilitate himself by normal reliable work.

Or could he? He suddenly regained his energy: he would not let himself be crushed! He might as well face the fact that in future he would be harassed countless times in great and small ways, and there was nothing to do about it but resist until the day people would start to forget what he had done. And before he was aware of it he was up on the spectators' platform pushing his way through the crowd until he reached the barrier from which he could see de Gaulle receiving the royal couple. A small glass pavilion had been erected in the middle of the cement runway, ringed by soldiers. All over the airport, as far as he could see, on hangar roofs, on the runways right out to the horizon, were security men and gendarmerie. Two cars drove under the wings of some stationary planes and stopped at the end of a red carpet running from the pavilion. Out of the cars stepped first Messmer, the minister of defence, immediately after him came Pompidou. They wore grey, and Mollerup noted down that Messmer had red socks. That was the sort of thing that spiced a report. Both were bare-headed. He noted that too. Shortly afterwards a long limousine drove up, out stepped de Gaulle. He too was bare-headed. He walked down the red carpet closely followed by his two ministers. All three faced the flag and listened to the Marseillaise played by a military band. Then they went into the glass pavilion where a large gathering was already assembled. Among them Mollerup thought he could glimpse the press attaché's bald crown. Was he talking to Lund?

It was one minute to three. De Gaulle came out of the glass pavilion and walked back along the red carpet. Madame de Gaulle came in sight, her car had been driven behind the soldiers. Just behind de Gaulle walked two Danish ministers with Messmer and Pompidou, the Danish ambassador and his wife and the press attaché. A military plane had landed on one of the runways and was slowly approaching the red carpet from the right. At the same moment as de Gaulle and his entourage reached the end of the carpet the plane came to a stop. The door was opened, the steps pushed into place and King Frederik and Queen Ingrid appeared. A tremendous shout of excitement went up around Mollerup: the schoolchildren he had seen before waved their Danish flags and shouted in unison 'Vive le Roi!' and 'Vive la Reine!' Queen Ingrid, in a coarse-weave navy blue coat and an emerald green hat, waved to the children. While King Frederik and de Gaulle inspected the guard she got into Madame de Gaulle's car: it had suddenly started to rain. But neither de Gaulle nor King Frederik seemed to worry about the change in the weather, they walked calmly towards the glass pavilion and vanished inside. The retinue hurried after them, with the press attaché bringing up the rear.

'Ooh, the Danish king is much taller than de Gaulle!' said one of the schoolchildren.

'Charles doesn't like that,' said another child, giggling.

'Charles *de Gaulle*,' corrected the teacher.

The schoolchildren went on waving, and Mollerup ran down to the vestibule. A little later he met a couple of French journalists who had just left the reception. He asked them what de Gaulle had said in his speech of welcome. 'The usual thing,' they grinned: 'that Denmark is a country that is at one and the same time faithful to the past and engaged in the future.' Then he drove into town. At the Porte Orleans an honour guard stood beside a ceremonial cannon. The lion by the Denfert-Rochereau was occupied by half a dozen spectators who could not find a place below it. It had stopped raining and the sun made the asphalt shine like silver. He drove down the Boulevard Saint-Michel and parked in a side street. Then he joined the crowd on the Boulevard Saint-Germain and waited. After fifteen minutes he could hear bursts of cheering in the distance, then he caught sight of de Gaulle and King Frederik in the first car of the cortège. People leaned out of all the windows waving their handkerchiefs and paper flags. In the car after de Gaulle's were Queen Ingrid and Madame de Gaulle, then came the ministers, the Danish ambassador and his wife and finally the cars carrying French and Danish journalists. In the last car was Lund with the press attaché. They leaned back and smiled at the spectators. Then the whole procession had passed and Mollerup hurried back to his car and drove home. He ran up all the stairs because the lift was out of order, let himself into the flat and put the kettle on for coffee. He pushed away every thought, all he wanted was to get the report of the first day of the royal visit off his hands as quickly as possible. It took him an hour to write, and after he had read it through and corrected it he was quite proud of the result, the sentences connected smoothly. He had included everything, from Messmer's red socks to the colour of Queen Ingrid's dress and the sudden shower that fell as King Frederik set his foot on French soil. He rang through to Copenhagen straight away and asked for the call to be given express treatment. An editorial secretary took the call.

'Mollerup, Paris,' he yelled as the connection faded for a moment. Then he lowered his voice: 'I have the first report here.'

'The first report?'

'Yes, from the royal visit.'

'But we *have* it covered.'

He did not reply immediately. The receiver stuck to his hand and in the distance he could hear the town hall clock strike six.

'Can I speak to the editor-in-chief,' he said after a moment.

'For heaven's sake, Mollerup. He hasn't *time*.'

He put down the receiver without saying goodbye. He got up, walked round the table, then went into the kitchen to find he had forgotten the kettle. The water had long since evaporated, the bottom of the kettle was red hot and the whole kitchen smelt of burnt iron. He poured cold water into the kettle which hissed and steamed, and when he shook it he could hear that all the lime scale had come loose. It was as if he realized the truth for the third time: at this moment he was in his flat, he was well and everything around him looked normal: the pictures hung as they should on the walls, the furniture was where it usually was. But in a few days? He would have to go home as soon as possible, as the editor-in-chief had demanded. Would he ever come back to Paris? To this apartment? He grabbed the book in which he had hidden his mother's unopened letters. He felt a sudden need to be confronted with all the unpleasantness at once.

Dear Max, ran the first letter, *is it true? Your Mother.* The second letter was equally brief, *Max, answer me!* The third letter was typewritten, it took up one and a half pages. *Dear Max, I don't know what I'm going to do with you. Today I received a postcard from you, from Venice. You write that you are having a good time and enjoying life. Knowing you as I do, that doesn't surprise me. And meanwhile all this is happening. Of course I saw the last time I was in Paris with you that you do not worry about anything at all. It will take a long time before I forget that afternoon at the café when you would not help me get a glass of water to ease the pain in my back. Nor have I forgotten the night when I surprised you with your Spanish maid like any . . . no, I refuse to make use of that word. But I thought your crisis was merely temporary. And I was proud — proud, Max — when your book came out (even though you did not even trouble to send a copy to your old Mother). But in the last few months I have noticed that you have not made yourself felt at all in the newspaper. While some Munk, quite unknown to me, writes masses and masses on Paris. That's the kind of thing people notice here in Copenhagen. And now this — this scandal which is dragging the name of Mollerup through the mud. Do you know what that is like for me? Do you know? I don't see anyone, Max, because I will not listen to them. You know how people* talk *in Copenhagen. I do not even meet with my regular bridge group on Thursdays any more, and the sorrow you have caused me is like the sorrow in a Greek tragedy. Do you remember the 'false Marianne Mollerup'? Perhaps that will help you understand why I despise cheating. But — and here I come to what I want to say — you are my son. And let us try to cross out the past together.*

One thing you must know: your Mother's love for you is unflagging. Do you know the story of the boy who killed his mother and cut out her heart, then ran with it and fell and it rolled out of his hand? Do you know what the heart said? 'Did you hurt yourself, my boy?' This letter, dear Max, is written in a fateful hour. You have to know that THIS is what I feel. You have fallen and hurt yourself for the rest of your life, and you have dropped my heart that you were holding, that heart that will ALWAYS be with you. Whatever happens, and your career as a Paris correspondent is definitely finished, your old home, which you have so often looked down upon, is open to you. Your old room is still yours. You know I love you. You know I shall always love

you. THAT is what means most, Max, in spite of all the misfortunes
that afflict us.
  Your Mother.
  PS. When you come home please remember that picture of your
father which you have. I noticed you did not have it on your desk the
last time I was with you. But that picture means so much to me.
Mother.

He tore up the letter and then the report of the royal
visitors' reception and rushed out of the flat. On his way
downstairs he almost collided with the concierge who was on
her way up with a message for one of the tenants. She looked
at him in amazement as he seemed about to fall down. She
asked if he was ill, he looked so pale. He hurried on and was
about to call up to her not to worry about him when he
realized she had disappeared from view.

He chatted up a fur-clad prostitute in the doorway of a
hotel. She had a silver poodle with a golden collar. He asked
her price and learned that it was a hundred francs for fifteen
minutes, plus the room. He asked how much she wanted to
bring a friend with her. Then of course it will cost twice as
much, she replied, took his arm and smiled. After a moment
he asked how much it would be if he insisted on her wearing
rubber boots. She thought about it, drew down her mouth
suspiciously so he could see the fillings in her teeth. Then she
smiled again and tried to pull him through the door into the
hotel: fifty francs more, she whispered, wheedling. He did
not know what had induced him to mention rubber boots.
The idea of making love to a woman, even a prostitute, while
she was wearing rubber boots, had never occurred to him.
But he felt like seeing how far he could go and asked if she
also had an oiled raincoat and a southwester. The girl nodded in agreement, the hotel where she worked would do
anything for the clients! She lifted up the poodle, put it
under her arm and patted its head. In the end the price had
gone up to six hundred francs plus room and tips for the staff.
He made it clear that he wanted at least half an hour, that he
wanted her and her friend fully dressed in rain clothes and

that he also wanted them to dance for him while he lay in bed. Then he bolted. At once the prostitute started shouting abuse at him so passers-by stared at him in disgust.

He went along the Rue du Faubourg Saint-Honoré and among the parked cars in front of the Elysée Palace he noticed those of the press attaché and the ambassador. There were lights in all the rooms of the palace. When he went through the doorway with his hands in his pockets he was chivvied away by the police. It did no good to explain he was a Danish journalist and that he had forgotten his invitation to de Gaulle's dinner for the Danish king and queen. He had really no right to even stand there and look in through the windows. He moved on and shortly afterwards stopped in front of a shop selling television sets and radios. All the sets were tuned to the Danish director Carl Dreyer's *Gertrud* and spectators had already gathered in front of the window. But as there was so much dialogue in the film, and the subtitles filled most of the screen, they went away one by one.

The Restaurant Pré Catalan in the Bois de Boulogne could accommodate about a thousand guests for a reception. All the Danes in Paris had received an invitation to meet the royal couple. Mollerup had an invitation as well. At first he thought it must be a mistake. When he read it after it arrived with the morning mail he had not intended to act on it. He drank half a pot of coffee to wake himself up. The wanderings of the night before had taken him from the Place de la Concorde and on along the Seine, towards the Place de la Bastille and up towards Montmartre from where he finally took a taxi home. He could still feel all over his body that he had gone for a tramp for which he had neither stamina nor age. Least of all did he feel fit to go out to the Bois de Boulogne and meet the entire Danish colony who would undoubtedly whisper about him in corners the moment he stepped into the restaurant. But as he gradually woke up after his coffee he found an intense defiance growing within him. No doubt most of the Danes would not think he had enough courage to turn up. They thought he would stay at home to lick his wounds. It would therefore be doubly challenging if he went out there, in fine form, smiling, perhaps with a brisk retort on his lips, just as if nothing had happened. Didn't he have enough acting talent to spend an hour or two in the company of Parisian Danes?

As he drove out to the Bois de Boulogne he thought several times of turning round, but each time defiance triumphed over doubt. Nervousness pricked him under the arms. As he parked in front of Pré Catalan and went up the steps, he felt the skin of his face stiffen and nerves prickling his scalp just in front of his ears. He scratched his underlip, straightened his jacket, polished the toes of his shoes on the backs of his trouser, lit a cigarette and let it hang in the corner of his mouth. He had received an invitation with two red lines running from the top right hand corner. That meant, according to a note on the back of the card, that he would be admitted to only one of the two rooms allotted to the meeting of the royal couple with the Danish colony; the room where far the greater number of guests would stay while the king and queen together with the best-known Danish residents would be in the other, smaller one. As soon as he was inside he went over to a long table with antique Danish silver dishes of cocktail food and ships' decanters of sherry and whisky. He poured out a large glass of whisky and walked round among the guests. In the other room the press attaché and Rolf Hauge were enjoying themselves with a world-famous Danish ballet dancer while the ambassador stood by himself practising the speech he was to make when the king and queen arrived. Mollerup felt relieved that the press attaché was so far away and that he knew only a few of the other people standing in little groups fanning the cards with red lines on to give themselves air in the scrum. But all the same he intended, at some point, to see that the press attaché, who now let out a roar of laughter at something the ballet dancer said, took note of his presence.

Suddenly a middle-aged lady came towards him. He thought at first she must be a widow seeking male acquaintances. Her dress was reminiscent of the fifties, and she was holding the latest issue of *Paris-Match* with Queen Ingrid in eskimo dress on the front cover.

'Ah, doesn't this suddenly make you feel what it means to be *Danish?*' she said.

'What do you mean?' he asked, drinking his whisky.

'You *know* quite well what I mean! A warm spring day in Paris like today, with the Dannebrog flying on the Place de la Concorde beside the Tricolore, with our king and queen in all the shop windows . . . It's really not being chauvinistic . . . but the Danish flag: is there a more beautiful one in the whole world?'

'No,' he replied. 'That white cross against the red background.'

'Yes, that's right, isn't it! And have you *seen* what the French papers say about Denmark? About our democracy, our social services. I must say . . . when you have lived in France for over twenty years as I have, you suddenly see Denmark in a quite different light . . .'

He looked around him, but there was no means of getting away from the woman. Some Danish children were playing tag among the trees outside. They were all in party clothes, and now and then a mother called out to them that the king and queen would come soon and they must not get their clothes dirty. Their French governess kept an eye on them too. Further off some youngsters played shuttlecock. There was not a cloud in the sky.

'What is your name, by the way?' the woman asked. 'I think I've seen your face somewhere . . .'

'Mollerup,' he replied, annoyed that he hadn't thought of saying Randrup or Ellesøe or something else.

'Oh, is that who you are? . . . Oh, forgive me, I didn't mean . . .'

She looked uneasy and he noticed her fingers clutching *Paris-Match* so Queen Ingrid's face wrinkled. The woman smiled sideways at him, gave him her hand and said it had been nice meeting him, then hastened over to the table to get a glass of sherry. When she had gone he looked around the various groups. Most of them were talking loudly about how good it was to be a Dane abroad: one always met with trust and frankness, in the shops, restaurants and over important deals.

'It's remarkable,' said an elderly man in pinstripes. 'But if you say you're Danish you're immediately seen as someone who wears the emblem of trustworthiness in his buttonhole. I remember well from my time in Chicago . . .'

'And then we haven't been at war with France since 1814 when Napoleon ruled the whole of Europe,' said a lady with piled-up hair and big African ear rings.

'I think you're wrong there,' said a third. 'We were on Napoleon's side!'

'That's what I mean,' the woman replied, laughing wildly. 'The French can never forget that!'

Suddenly he caught a remark from a group further away:

'Apparently right back at de Gaulle's last press conference he behaved oddly, to put it mildly . . .'

He approached the group. A young officer was speaking:

'It seems he wanted Malraux to say something, but no one knew what he really wanted, and to start with he just sat and stared up at de Gaulle so of course the old chap had to shake his head in despair . . .'

'How old is he?' someone asked.

'Who, the general?' said the officer and went on: 'Oh, *him*. My age. Around forty. A bit older, perhaps . . .'

Mollerup went right up to the group so the officer could not fail to see him, and suddenly the conversation switched to something else. The officer cleared his throat and lit a cigarette and began to expand on his increasing anxiety about the future of NATO. Some mothers looked at their children playing outside and discussed upbringing: what was the right thing, a boarding school in Denmark or a French school? Mollerup stood there until the group slowly dispersed. Then he thought he could hear another group discussing him and he repeated his manoeuvre, approaching it so a nervous silence spread. A little later he thought he heard his name in a third place, then a fourth, a fifth. Each time he went from one group to another he took care to pass the drinks table and fill up his glass. Gradually, as he grew more and more drunk, he started to move with long strides to and fro in the room reserved for guests with red-striped invitations, as if he wanted to stop everyone from talking about him. He kept feeling their eyes on his neck, and then he would turn sharply, fix his eyes on a guest who was whispering something behind his hand and paralyze him.

He knew everyone was watching him from the adjoining room, including the press attaché and Rolf Hauge. Whenever he demonstratively went over for more whisky he had to smile because so many eyes followed his every movement. He managed to pour four fifths whisky and one fifth water into the glass, which made two elderly ladies near the table put their heads together. He enjoyed the knowledge that he had slowly put a damper on the party. Should he tap his glass, ask for silence and call for a toast to old Denmark?

He grew more and more drunk. When he looked out of the windows at the youngsters playing shuttlecock among the trees and the children playing in the foreground with their French governess, their movements seemed to be in slow motion. He had trouble staying upright, and when soon afterwards he caught sight of his paper's snobbish French artist who arrived with Munk and kissed some ladies on the cheek, he threw both hands in the air and greeted them so loudly that people hushed him. The officer made straight for him and asked if he wanted to be helped outside for a moment before the king and queen arrived. He merely stared at the officer, feeling his eyes were already bloodshot. Then he saw the lame proprietor of the Danish shop coming towards him after leaving a group of young potters:

'Now, you haven't forgotten our little account, have you!'

'Which account?' he asked, swaying.

'The table! The table with the orange tiles . . .'

'No, no,' he snarled, feeling like giving the man a shove on the shoulder so he was knocked backwards and fell down taking the officer with him: 'No, no!'

Suddenly silence fell, the royal couple arrived in a big black limousine provided by the French government. King

Frederik and Queen Ingrid went straight into the room where the ambassador and his wife, the press attaché, the ballet dancer, Rolf Hauge and his French wife and other well-known Paris Danes were waiting. While the ambassador asked for silence so he could give his short speech of welcome, the rank and file guests pushed over to the doorway into the V.I.P. room. Everyone wanted to get a close view of the king and queen. Two of the embassy staff, who stood in the doorway, tried to keep them back, assuring them that they would be able to hear the king's speech over a loudspeaker. For a moment the crowd subsided, the ambassador stammered his speech, but then those behind pushed forward so violently that the crowd started to move forward again and the staff members were pushed aside. A lady screamed that she had dropped her handbag on the floor with her pass and money in it, one or two children whimpered down among the grownups' legs, but there was no stopping the crowd who quickly pushed through and made a close circle around the royal couple. Mollerup found himself in the front row and he had to push back with his shoulders the whole time so as not to crush the queen, who glanced nervously around her, smiling politely. She sent an imploring glance to the press attaché who threw out his hands in despair as a sign that he could not do anything. But the king smiled happily and then started to make an improvised speech about the happiness it always gave him and the queen to meet Danes abroad; Danes who were faithful both to their old fatherland and the new one. Mollerup could feel the whisky making him nauseous, or was it the queen's perfume? He looked back over his shoulder, but it was impossible to get away: the most he could do was move his feet a couple of centimeters. Behind one of the queen's shoulders he caught sight of Rolf Hauge who looked stiffly at him with his watery blue eyes. If he looked to the right he met the eyes of the press attaché, which were fixed on him too. To the left, squashed between some students, stood the director of the Danish student residence with an indefinable smile on his lips. No matter where he looked there were eyes staring at him while the king finished his speech. Rolf Hauge in particular continued to stare him out, and Mollerup involuntarily recalled the chapter in *Paris From The Shady Side* in which he had made fun of him and depicted him as a pompous prophet.

The nausea turned into dizziness, and again he had to resist with his shoulders so as not to be pushed against the queen, who had calmed down a little and nodded each time the king said something she could applaud. Most of all he wanted to put a hand to his face so he could avoid being stared at by one pair of eyes after the other, cold, indifferent, speculative eyes with pupils like rifle muzzles or like . . . no, he gave up trying to find the right simile. His throat contracted, and then his knees started to shake while the breath of the people behind him tickled his neck. Then the king ended his speech, the crowd clapped energetically, and finally the dense circle of listeners thinned out. Some returned to the first room, others went outside to stretch their legs and enjoy the spring weather. One or two guests wanted to shake the king's hand but were prevented by the press attaché who explained that their majesties preferred to be left alone as they had a taxing programme ahead of them. Mollerup drew breath by an open window, but the fresh air and the sight of a relaxed Munk playing football with some children only made his nausea worse. He knew it could only be seconds before he vomited and suddenly he started to run through the restaurant to find the toilet. He slackened speed as Rolf Hauge came walking towards him with a small knight's cross in his buttonhole he had not noticed before.

'Serves you right!' hissed Hauge after him when they had passed each other.

He thought of retorting with 'Dimwit, Celtic nincompoop' but he was already in the toilet. Five fingers down the throat? The floor rose to meet him vertically, the mirror seemed to be melting, and when he coughed everything around him moved in crazy little jerks. When he left the toilet he went out of the restaurant at once. He walked across the gravel drive to his car. On the way he met the press attaché walking with Lund.

'Your suitcase . . . Monsieur Jean!' the press attaché shouted after him. 'You must have left it when you made your some-what informal visit to the Embassy!'

He made no reply, did not even turn in the direction of the press attaché. He felt Lund craning after him inquisitively as he got into his car, turned the key and drove off so the gravel crackled under the tyres. His temples throbbed, he knew it was mad to drive in the state he was in, but when two policemen on motorcycles, who had concealed themselves behind some trees, started after him he did something still crazier: he increased his speed, crossed over a red light, suddenly turned down an unknown side street as he approached Paris, almost ran over an old lady at a pedestrian crossing and grazed a fruit cart with his rear mudguard. In one place there was a crump under his front wheels as if he was running over a cat. But he told himself it was just a parcel. A parcel of old clothes, fallen off a lorry.

He finally succeeded in shaking off the police, but he felt pretty sure they had taken his number. He ended up in a district he had never been in before, inhabited by Portuguese immigrant workers. Then he reached the inner boulevards and soon afterwards parked in front of his street door. He rushed in, frantically pressed the lift bell and then remembered it was out of order. So he ran up the stairs and went into his flat. The first thing he did was phone the Italian woman. Perhaps she had returned from Venice. He did not know what made him suddenly think of her, but he had to call her, had to hear her voice, had to hear French. When the receiver was lifted he felt the old terror of the telephone rise in him again. He heard the Italian woman asking again and again who was there. She clicked the phone and groaned in irritation. Then he plucked up courage.

'It's me,' he said.

He asked if she had received the table with orange tiles. Yes, she had. And she had been *so* surprised when she arrived back from Venice that morning and saw it in the doorway.

'Thank you,' she said, in a tone he could not place. 'Thank you!'

Then he came to a halt. He had been going to ask her if she

happened to know someone who knew someone who could help him get some job or other, but instead he said they must get together soon. She agreed, still in the same tone of voice. At last she said he had been really good in the film and they might ring him about taking part in another scene which was to be filmed here in Paris.

'Yes, do ring!' he said with an artificial laugh. 'I'm always ready!'

After he had put down the receiver he did not know what to do. He had to do something. In some way or other he had to get his thoughts to calm down. He felt as if they grew out of his head like climbing plants twining around his arms and legs and preventing him from moving freely. For some time he just sat staring at the old-fashioned telephone with its extra receiver and the dial on which numbers and letters were almost obliterated. Then he walked around the flat and, when he reached the bedroom he suddenly started to pull all his clothes out of the cupboards. He threw them anyhow into his suitcases. When he had finished he put the cases in the hall. Then he started on his books in the study. He tore them out of the shelves so they fell in heaps on the floor. Then he picked them up and put them into random piles, French novels with uncut pages, dictionaries and political books and complimentary copies of *Paris From The Shady Side* jumbled up together. He tied them up with string and carried them out into the corridor where he put them beside the suitcases. He took the paintings down and wrapped them in old newspapers. In the kitchen he collected up everything he owned; tea spoons, casseroles, chopping board, knives and forks, and threw them into plastic bags. In the sitting room and dining room he pushed all the furniture against the walls and put the chairs on the tables, then rolled up the carpets. Gradually he began to feel that being active relieved the state he was in. Only when he suddenly straightened up after bending down did everything go black for a moment behind his eyes.

Next day he went on clearing out. He woke late with the sheet rolled up around his feet. He had a splitting headache. But after taking a handful of pills he slowly came to. He drove straight out to the flea market and contacted a trader who was willing to take all his furniture, kitchen equipment and books — even the Danish ones. Later in the day he found a used car dealer who was glad to buy his car. He knew he was getting a poor price for it but he did not want to embark on long-drawn-out negotiations and agreed when the dealer offered a thousand francs. Then he drove home in a taxi. He had arranged to meet the trader at twelve o'clock. He explained to the concierge that he had to go back to Denmark in great haste — he had been offered an important post at his editorial office in Copenhagen. Then the trader arrived with an assistant and in a couple of hours all the furniture had been carried down to the street. While all this was going on he felt everything was a dream; one room was cleared, then the other, quickly, efficiently, but nothing to do with reality. And before he knew it he was walking alone around the flat with white squares on the walls where paintings had hung. He could not even remember what the trader and his assistant looked like, they had just been two men in blue overalls with burnt out cigarettes in their mouths, they had not had a beer together or coffee or even talked. When they had finished, he had been handed a bundle of notes he had not even bothered to count: he knew he had been cheated but he didn't care. All that was left in the flat was a mattress on the bedroom floor, a few nails in the walls, the suitcase with his clothes in the corridor, the cardboard box with Ussing's porno magazines and old textbooks and the day's mail that still lay on the floor opposite the front door. The day's mail: the previous day's Danish newspaper in its yellow wrapping, some printed matter and a letter from the Scandinavian institute at a university in the south of France asking him to give a lecture on modern Danish literature. He threw away the printed matter and the letter, tore the wrapper from the paper and read Munk's report of the first day of the royal visit. The report was in large print on the front page and he had to admit that Munk had put in all the details correctly — apart from the fact that Messmer's socks had suddenly become yellow. Then he put down the paper and opened the cardboard box containing the *International Who's Who*. The smell of mouldy pages. Of the past.

He put the book back and went out of the flat and down the stairs. He walked up the Avenue de Wagram, crossed over at L'Étoile and went down towards the Seine. The royal visit was over, and workmen were taking down all the flagpoles. The photographs of King Frederik and Queen Ingrid had disappeared. Spring was turning into early summer, the café clients wore open-necked shirts, and cars had their windows down. When he reached the Seine he sat on the quayside and looked across at the other bank. On the right was the Eiffel Tower with the spotlight circling the whole horizon to warn planes not to fly too low, on the left the National Assembly. The traffic on the other side of the river was an endless stream of cars and lighted buses. A young couple walked along behind him with a transistor radio playing a Wagner opera. Even though he had taken the pills his headache was slowly coming back. It felt as if it returned in jerks.

CHAPTER TWELVE

Winter came back again, after a few days of sudden spring had coerced Copenhageners out into the fresh air. Travellers coming home from Mallorca with a sun tan caught colds the moment they stepped out of the charter planes at Kastrup airport. In suburban gardens the first spring flowers died of cold. Mollerup was in an office on the fourth floor of the newspaper building. It was almost midnight and the paper had just gone to press with a big front page picture of the powdery white Town Hall Square. The text noted that in Paris the temperature was twenty degrees. In Rome it was twenty-two and in Berlin fifteen. He put the still warm first edition aside and looked down into the courtyard where piles of newspapers were being loaded into vans. The snow melted in big lumps against the window and he had the heater on at full power. He really ought to go home to bed. But he was not sleepy. He had drunk a pot of very strong tea during the last two hours to help him finish the article he had worked on all day. He knew the result was unsatisfactory. Most of the article was a quotation from police rules on how to walk your dog in the street. His own text was restricted to a few ironical comments. He checked the quotation for correctness once more:

> It is illegal to allow dogs on a street, road or square without having them on a lead, which must be of a length that keeps the dog close to the owner. However, this rule does not apply outside the boundaries mentioned below, providing the dog is with a person who has full control of it:
> Strandvænget, from Kalkbrænderihavnsgade, following the S railway line to the boundary of Frederiksberg, following this to

Vesterfælledvej, Ingerslevgade, Tietgensbro, Tietgensgade, Bernstorffsgade, Ved Godsbanegården and Kalvebod Brygge as well as the Amager line Øresundsvej, Englandsvej, Peder Lykkesvej (from Englandsvej to Røde Mellemvej) and Grønjordsvej.

When he arrived in Denmark he had reported at once to the editor-in-chief after taking a room in a small hotel in a street off Vesterbrogade. The meeting was quite different from what he had been expecting. He had been sure he was going to be fired and that the editor-in-chief would not bother to see him. But on the contrary, the editor-in-chief seemed friendly, rather too friendly, perhaps. He did not say one word about 'the affair', but it was somehow understood in everything he said. Mollerup could not rid himself of the feeling that the editor-in-chief spoke to him like a specialist to a patient. The reassuring hand on his shoulder. The knowing smile. And the eyes that kept distractedly looking for a remote resting place. The meeting lasted a quarter of an hour, and when he emerged from the editor-in-chief's office into the corridor where the two editors of the youth pages suddenly came by, hidden in their Tibetan cowls, he had been given the task of doing something about the dog campaign, which had been in abeyance since Christmas because of staff illness.

He stood in the corridor for some time before going straight into the editorial offices where all the journalists greeted him with a cheery 'Hi!' It seemed as if everyone on the paper had arranged to treat him as if nothing had happened. He was promised his own office very soon but for the time being he was to work in other staff members' offices when they were free. The one he now occupied with its view over the courtyard belonged to the aviation correspondent. On the walls there were photographic trophies showing the correspondent as a young man on one of the first flights across the Sound in an open two-seater machine, up to the last one taken at Cape Kennedy with a rocket ready for launching in the background.

The rotary press made the building vibrate like a ferry gliding out of its berth.

After staying at the hotel for some days he rented a room in a house in the residential suburb of Hellerup. Whenever he worked late he would take a taxi home. He felt that Copenhagen was small enough for him to be able to taxi from one place to another. When he was down in the street he went straight to a taxi rank on the Town Hall Square. He went into the house. Two families occupied it. On the ground floor was a police sergeant with a wife and three children, on the first floor an unknown cabaret artist with his father and mother. He had rented a room from the cabaret artist that was so small there was room only for a bed and a table. In one corner was a wash basin with big rust marks from the taps, in the opposite corner he had piled his suitcases on top of each other. In a way it suited him to have such a small room. It was easier to keep tidy. From the moment he landed at Kastrup airport he told himself that orderliness was the best defence against what was awaiting him. Order in big things, order in small things. Order in finance, order in the papers he would have in his hands, order in his daily rhythm. And no credit from traders on Strandvejen. The more orderly, the more anonymous he could be.

He knew how little it would take for everything to disintegrate around him, and the first thing he did when he got up in the morning was to make his bed carefully, air the room and see if his bag of washing was so full that he needed to visit a launderette. He thought he would circulate around four different launderettes because he did not want to be recognized with his dirty underpants and shirts. The exaggerated helpfulness of the blue-aproned assistants reminded him of a nursing home. He also alternated with four different grocer's shops and preferred to buy his pipe tobacco at Hellerup station where the assistant did not take much notice when he stood in line. When he got home in the evening he crept upstairs to avoid attracting attention and confronting the sergeant or the cabaret artist, and this evening he crept extra carefully so the snow in his trouser turn-ups did not slide off and leave a row of wet spots all the way up. When he got into his room he checked that everything was in the right place. His typewriter the only object on it, was in the middle of the table, his shoes were in a straight row under the bed and on the shelf above the basin his razor, shaving cream, toothpaste and nail scissors lay in their allotted places. He turned the bed down at once and folded up the bedspread at its foot. He opened the window slightly but closed it again because the snow came filtering in. In the adjoining room he could hear the cabaret artist entertaining some guests with old Danish songs.

He arrived at the newspaper offices just before eleven. Then he did not risk meeting too many of his colleagues. Most of them got there after twelve. He went to the porter and was told he could not use the aviation editor's office any more. He had just got back from going round the world. But he could have the poetry correspondent's office, he had gone to an inter-Scandinavian cultural congress at Helsingfors in Sweden. Mollerup was handed a key and found his way to the narrow, smoky hole of an office, overlooking a beauty salon in which girls in pastel-coloured overalls ran to and fro behind the blinds. The first thing he did was to thoroughly investigate the office. It made him feel at home to know exactly what its hiding-places held. Then he studied a long row of photographs of well-known Danish poets from the forties to the present, stuck close together on the longest wall. He recognized some of them from twenty years ago when they were not yet established and had haunted the Minefield. Then he looked through the papers on the desk and on the window sill among discarded millimeter-slim volumes of verse with graphics on the jackets. He knew it was wrong to go on sniffing around like this, but only when he had reached the bottom of the piles did he sit down at the desk and begin to search for ideas for the dog campaign. He had delivered the article on police rules to the editorial office, now he needed to get on. He reread a letter the editor-in-chief had handed him with the remark that it was 'very relevant and worth thinking about.' The letter was briefly signed 'A friend of Denmark': *As an American visitor to Denmark I immediately felt at home because so many things are the same as in the USA — for instance, the high standard of living and the high taxes. Nor was I surprised to find the portions in your restaurants over generous — nobody, unless they suffered from starvation, would be able to finish — but as I love dogs I was disappointed to discover that the idea of the "doggy-bag", for taking leftovers home for the dog — is unknown. This is a serious shortcoming on Denmark's part. It is a tax-free custom that gives the restaurant proprietor an almost philanthropic feeling, is free and brings happiness to both dogs and humans. In an affluent society it should no longer be necessary for dogs to live a 'dog's life.' Give them, Danish proprietors, a "doggy bag".*

Suddenly spring seemed to be coming back, thawing snow slid down from the roofs, landed at intervals on the pavements and there was a gurgling from all the gutter pipes. He felt he had better wait before phoning the Copenhagen restaurants to hear what they thought about the letter-writer's suggestion. Instead he composed the long questionnaire with a lengthy list of questions asking Copenhageners for their views on stray dogs in the city centre. Then he noticed it was past twelve o'clock. He was hungry. But he did not want to go to the journalists' canteen where everyone knew him. Instead he left the office and took a route he had worked out soon after arriving from Paris: he took the elevator up to the fourth floor, from there went across the loft past the reproduction plant, in through a little door to a short corridor that led to an iron stairway. The stairway was outside the building and when he had descended seven steps he came to a door that led into the composing room. He walked through that, from there through another door, down some steps which led to the technicians' canteen where no one knew him. There he could eat in peace at a table to himself — he had three open sandwiches and a light beer. Then he went all the way back with a tray holding enough coffee for the rest of the afternoon. The moment he closed the door behind him in the poetry reviewer's office, the telephone rang. It was from the editorial office, asking him to look in.

'Well, Mollerup, your article on the police rules for dogs is great. But don't you think it could do with a bit more *meat*?'

It irked him that there were so many journalists in editorial. Most of them turned to look at him as the sub-editor took him to task.

'Then we'll put it through the machine once more,' he replied, trying to sound unruffled. Perky.

'I really think it's about time you got going on the questionnaire and did some proper fieldwork,' the sub-editor went on, lighting a cigar.

The others were still looking at him, inquiringly, curiously, as if they expected him to crack at any moment. His temples throbbed when the sub-editor bent over his work as if his words were an indisputable law. After a few moments the sub-editor looked up again and said as if astonished:

'Are you still here?'

He took a couple of steps backwards. He crumpled up the rejected article, threw it into a wastepaper basket and left the editorial office with a prickling feeling in his back. He felt an urge to turn round to stop them grinning at him behind his back, but he had already reached the lobby where the porter told him there had been three telephone calls for him during the last hour. An elderly lady had phoned him, but would not give her name.

'Did she have a very deep voice?' he asked.

'Sort of rusty,' replied the man, busy sorting mail.

After putting on his coat he went down to Strøget. The sun had melted the snow in earnest and passers-by had unbuttoned their coats and loosened their scarves. He tried to turn his thoughts away from his mother. He was determined not to contact her. He had been hoping she thought he was still in Paris and intended to write forthcoming articles under a new pseudonym. But she had obviously ferreted out that he was back. He walked down the street and went straight up to an elderly couple emerging from a baker's shop. Assuming a friendly expression he asked:

'Excuse me, but do you have a dog?'

The couple looked at him angrily:

'What's that to do with you?' said the man.

'I was just asking,' he replied in a tone he could hear was far too jeering. He smiled:

'I am going to carry out a questionnaire.'

'For *television*?' asked the pair in unison. Now their faces lit up.

'No, as you can see I don't have a camera. My newspaper wants to find out whether there is a majority of Copenhagen people in favour of allowing dogs loose in the city centre.'

'There certainly is!' said the wife, shaking her husband's arm, 'isn't there?'

'Yes, I suppose so,' he replied.

'May I ask you directly: so you are in favour?'

'Yes, we are,' the wife replied. 'You can be sure of that, . . . Mr?'

'May I also ask your name?'

'Heimburger, office manager,' answered the man, raising his hat in farewell.

He wrote down the name and put a little plus sign beside it. Then he contacted more passers-by. He deliberately avoided young and middle-aged people and singled out those over sixty. It might not be exactly the way the paper would want it done, but he knew it was the only method which would enable him to collect a sufficient number of answers. Often the elderly couples looked at him as if he was a drunk coming to pester them when he approached, nodded and asked them if they liked dogs, but each time he mentioned the word questionnaire they were responsive. Some dictated long-winded replies that took up a couple of pages, others were content to smile and nod to express their positive attitude. After a while he had taken down so many names and replies that half his pad was filled with his shorthand. Every time the thought rose in him that this was the most absurd commission he had ever been given in his journalistic career he reminded himself of the decision he had made at Kastrup Airport: to be orderly, above all orderly in his work. But disgust kept welling up in him. It only needed another drop for it to spill over. He lit one cigarette from another, and every time passers-by glowered at him as if he was a Jehovah's Witness on the hunt for souls. He bit his cheeks. The drop came a little later in the form of a remark he could not help overhearing. He was questioning yet another elderly couple when two full-bearded young men came by.

'That's the one from Paris . . . with the book, you know . . .' one said to the other.

They were both smiling as they went on along Strøget. He kept looking after them and hardly heard the elderly couple asking why he wanted to know if they liked dogs. Then they went on their way looking offended, and he walked down a side street where there were only a few people. A tramp on some basement steps raised his beer and toasted him, a young couple passing by sniggered when he stepped aside and messed up his shoes in a puddle, and a woman in a salmon-coloured petticoat waved at him with a teasing smile from a fourth floor window. When he reached Gammel Strand a sizeable procession was going by. In front were a dozen mini-skirted mothers with prams, then some young men with placards urging the Americans to leave Vietnam. Bringing up the rear were four long-haired fellows carrying a gallows and a life-size effigy of Johnson. He calculated there must be about a hundred of them and when they all struck up with 'We shall overcome' he involuntarily joined in.

Soon the procession reached the American Embassy where hundreds of demonstrators had already assembled. Two lines of police in steel helmets were ranged in front of the Embassy. To begin with all went peacefully. A writer made a speech in which he sharply condemned American imperialism and pledged support for the other America. The author called on all those present to demonstrate in a fitting manner, in conformity with the non-violent philosophy of Martin

Luther King, but then the first stone was hurled at a window in the Embassy and soon afterwards the police had to duck to escape being hit. The prams turned out to contain cobblestones and groups of demonstrators formed chains in Japanese fashion. The officers still held back but when one of them was hit on the shin by a stone they were ordered to charge. Soon an ambulance siren could be heard in the distance, the first wounded demonstrators were already lying on the cycle tracks writhing in pain, and one or two prams were broken up. Mollerup found himself standing in the middle of the road and when two policemen ran towards him with their truncheons at the ready he held his hands in front of his face to avert the blows instead of running away.

'I am a journalist!' he heard himself shout aloud. Far too loud.

'Ugh!' snarled two girls nearby involved in a struggle with three officers. 'Some excuse!'

He reached the pavement opposite the Embassy, but the two girls who had freed themselves from the policemen came after him. They called several of their friends who all formed a circle around him.

'Are you *for* or *against*?' asked one of them, a young man with frameless glasses and long fair hair.

'I'm with you!' he replied, trying to smile authoritatively and convincingly, as if to say that it was really pretty stupid of them to even doubt him. 'Can you be anything but opposed to the American way of waging a war?'

'God knows what *you* can be,' one of the girls replied.

When more police came running towards them, the group quickly split up. Mollerup took the opportunity to get away. He went over to Lille Triangel and quickly turned left down Øster Farimagsgade. It was getting dark, the first cars put on their side lights. He could barely make out the buds on the bare branches of the trees against the overcast sky. On the Avenue de Wagram the trees would be fully in leaf now, he thought, and the next moment thought he would not think of Paris any more. He walked on and felt a slight pleasure in just walking and walking, in knowing that despite everything his legs obeyed him as they should. Finally he reached the newspaper building. He waited on the opposite pavement until six o'clock when most of the staff went home for dinner.

The coffee he had brought with him from the technicians' canteen was completely cold, but he put the cup to his mouth and drank to get rid of the sandy taste that had covered his tongue during the afternoon. He lit a cigarette, wiped his sweaty hands on his thighs and began to look through his notes. He could read the first few pages, but then his writing deteriorated and the last pages were quite unreadable. Finding he could not make out what he had written threw him into a panic. He walked to and fro in the narrow space, glanced at the endless row of poets, looked over at the beauty salon where a cleaner was working, leafed through a few poetry books, lit a fresh cigarette. Then he sat down at the typewriter. After writing down the first answers to his questions that people had given him, word for word correctly, he made up several more. He invented a long list of new names. Jørgensen, teacher, Virum. Viktor Borge, artist, Valby. André Fontaine, translator, city centre. He took care to see that all of them — in different ways — expressed themselves in favour of loose dogs. The questionnaire took shape. He headed the list with Heimburger the office manager, and when he read through what he had written he inserted — for the sake of balance — a nameless sergeant and a photographic model of southern extraction who were both hostile to dogs.

The sub-editor weighed the manuscript in his right hand:

'Honestly, Mollerup, how on earth could you?' He sucked at a cigar end and went on:

'I really don't want to be hard on you . . . but isn't this a bit much?'

'What do you mean?'

When he got back to his room after dinner he found a message from the cabaret artist saying the newspaper had phoned him about an important assignment. To start with he decided to ignore the message, he had a right to a free evening after the afternoon's work. But he could not keep calm for long. He tidied up and tried to get the rust marks off the basin with scouring powder. He lay down and filled in a form for the tax office calculating how much he expected to earn in the coming year, but after half an hour he put on his coat, walked up to Strandvejen and found a taxi. On the way into town he kept on telling himself that there could not be anything wrong. Perhaps he was going to be sent abroad as a reporter, to Stockholm, Berlin or . . . Paris? All the same his heart beat far too fast, and the moment he entered the editorial office and saw his manuscript spread in disorder over the sub-editor's desk beside an open telephone directory and a road-finder, he saw what had happened. But he was here now. He couldn't just turn round and run away. And he repeated, almost inaudibly and with a little smile that angled for sympathy:

'What do you mean?'

'What do I mean?' hissed the sub-editor, spitting the cigar butt on the floor: 'You know very well. Heimburger, office manger, well and good. He really exists. The next on the list, all right as well. But just tell me: who is this . . . what is it you call him? Viktor *Borge*? I don't know any artist of that name. And what do you call your translator? *André . . . Fontaine!* Come off it, Mollerup! One of your café chums from Paris?' — '*Paris!*', shouted the duty man in the doorway. 'Shall I put him through?'

The sub-editor nodded and picked up the telephone:

'Yes, yes . . . it's me . . . speak a bit louder, Munk, it must be a bad line. — Malraux, did you say? To the orient? Yes, that's a real scoop. I'll put you on to the telegram desk so you can phone in the article. Give Paris my love! And don't forget that bottle of calvados when you next come home on holiday . . . .'

Mollerup heard Munk cackle at the other end of the line. Was he ringing from the students' residence or had he got his own flat with a phone? While the sub-editor continued to chat about calvados he went over to the notice board with the list of staff telephone numbers and private addresses pinned up. His own address in Paris had been crossed out and his new one in Hellerup written in in biro, with a note that he did not have his own phone but could be reached through the cabaret artist. Immediately below him was Munk, also in biro: 7, Rue de Chezy, Neuilly sur Seine, France, own phone in about three weeks. He stood there reckoning that Munk must be getting a larger regular salary if he could afford to live in Neuilly. Did he live in a modern block? In a residential district? Neuilly-sur-Seine. View over most of Paris. Sacré Coeur. Pavement cafés open until long after midnight. People. Masses of people on the boulevards. Noisy traffic. The scent of toasted almonds, of cats, garlic, petrol. The metro. Didn't the new metro with rubber wheels go to Neuilly? Or had Munk already got his own car so he could get into the centre of Paris in ten minutes and cross over from the Champs-Elysées to the Place de la Concorde and over to the Left Bank? The Left Bank. Rive Gauche. The plane trees, with gratings round their feet, the Rue de Dragon, the kiosks at the Deux Magots with newspapers and journals from around the world. Spring in Paris, summer in Paris. The sunshine on the Seine, guitars, the scent of thyme from the restaurants with open stoves right out to the street. The Spanish workers on the Avenue de Wigram who had left off their dark winter coats long ago . . .

'Mollerup, this article,' came from behind him. The sub-editor sounded slightly more friendly now: 'Try again, then we shall both feel much better.'

It was only when he had reached the Town Hall Square that he actually realized how patronizingly he had been spoken to. 'Then we shall both feel much better.' That was how a doctor talked on his rounds. He came to a halt. Should he go back and tell the man there was no need to speak to him like that? He wasn't a child. He wasn't a hospital patient. No, he knew it was impossible to stand up to the sub-editor, there was still only one way he could get himself out of the scrape: by producing something that would impress the man. He walked around the square for a while, was accosted by a male prostitute, waved him away, went down to the underground toilet, had his shoes cleaned, went up again into the air. No pavement cafés, no real warmth in the air, only this dark grey sky above a little square area which could easily fit into a corner of the Place de la Concorde, with dirty yellow trams and buses and bent figures with faces smeared with sourness. A hotdog stand, yet another hotdog stand. Some scraps of paper full of ketchup flew past his feet. A couple of fat pigeons, a couple of lost tourists. He went down Strøget keeping close to the walls on the right. A rowdy jukebox from a dance restaurant on the first floor. A newly equipped milk bar. Music shops with people silhouetted in front of the lighted windows. Exalon. Bar-dot. The darkness grew ever thicker, Strøget more and more deserted. A couple of workers from southern lands swung their arms like coachmen in a doorway and in front of the kiosk by the Nygade Theatre four elderly men stood leafing through the porn magazines on show. He started looking at the magazines and for a moment thought of buying a whole suitcase full to take to Paris and sell at three hundred percent profit to the Arab traders in the Pigalle, but the mere thought of turning up with a suitcase and asking the dried up old lady behind the counter knitting a pale pink baby's bonnet to fill it with a selection of the most explicit mags was enough to terrify him. She would look at him as if he was the worst type she had to deal with. And the other customers would look at him. People passing by would crowd around him, whispering and giggling and turning their eyes to heaven in disgust. A whole suitcase full! He must be destitute! When he had leafed through the topmost magazines on the counter and started to dip into the piles, the woman looked at him, then put down the half-finished bonnet:

'Do you wish to *buy* something, sir!?'

They were out to harass him, no doubt about that. The pleasant way he had been greeted by the editor-in-chief and the rest of the staff when he arrived back was nothing but camouflage. They wanted to provoke him. And he suspected they were carrying out a definite plan. They were only waiting for the moment when they could get rid of him. Doutless the porter and the messengers had been told to treat him conde-scendingly. Why else did they only greet him with a short indefinable nod when he said good morning? And why did the porter look so maliciously pleased when he told him he could not use other staff members' offices any more because they were all in use, but would have to write his articles on one of the free typewriters at the back of the editorial office where the trainee journalists usually sat?

He would avoid the newspaper. Since they were all deter-mined to make him uncomfortable anyway, and the editors had agreed among themselves not to use his articles, he might just as well stay away. And for a day or two he spent the afternoons wandering around Copenhagen. If he sensed one of the journalists was coming to meet him he quickly took refuge in a doorway or a pub where he was accosted by unemployed men whose breath reeked of meths and cheap beer. He walked through streets he had never been in before. Suddenly he was on Amager island in an area being cleared. Then he was in the streets around Toftegårds Plads. The spring grew steadily more springlike. He took off his coat and slung it over one shoulder, unbuttoned his shirt, bought sunglasses. He did not like going back to his room because he had a feeling that the cabaret artist and his wife had started to watch him. The bathroom was kept locked so he could not use it without asking permission. He was banned from the kitchen, was not even allowed to make coffee, obviously because the cabaret artist had suddenly got the idea that he was stealing from the larder, something he had only done once or twice and only for a spoonful of sugar or a filter paper for his coffee. But after a while he grew tired of walking around Copenhagen, through streets that were all alike, people who pushed him or snapped savagely if he happened to push them. Instead he shut himself in his room from morning to evening, only going out up to Strandvejen when he wanted food. He had a key made to fit the door so the cabaret artist could not burst in on him. He sat quite still at his desk or lay on the bed and when the cabaret artist knocked at the door and shouted for the umpteenth time that there was a phone call for him from the newspaper he did not reply. He was not at home.

He started to make paper aeroplanes. He made a big pile with A4 paper and put them on the desk in front of him. At first he made an ordinary rocket-like model, later he experimented with more complicated models that could stay longer in the air when he launched them out of the window. He tried to get them to fly up over the telephone wires but no matter how hard he threw them they always flew underneath. Some of them went into a spin and landed next door, others reached no further than the garden hedge. He hit on the idea of putting elevators on them and when a favourable gust of wind blew, he succeeded in getting one to rock gently over the wires. He drew national symbols on the wings, German swastikas and the rings of the Royal Air Force. He sent the German machines off first. Some of them landed on their backs or noses and so were disqualified, but most landed as they should. Then he sent the English machines after them and every time one of them flew just above a German machine he made believe that the English had bombed the Germans. After half an hour all the German machines were destroyed. He made more models and furnished them with landing wheels from two buttons he tore off his shirts and fastened them to two matches with sewing thread. He glued the matches under the wings and when an aeroplane landed on the road it looked like a real machine: it jolted along the asphalt, slackened speed, then came to a stop with its nose in the air and the tail pressed to the ground. He tried propellers too. He cut them out of cardboard and put an elastic band around the middle. He strengthened the body with split pencils, pulled the elastic underneath it and fastened it around the tail. But he could not make the propeller turn properly. Instead he sent off the planes with a long elastic as a sling so they rose almost vertically into the air and landed in the gardens on the other side of the road.

He grew more and more absorbed in the game, his room was a factory, hangar and repair shop in one. The models stood in rows on the desk, the German ones in front and the English ones that were to chase them at the back. Eventually he had used up all his paper, a whole tube of glue, four pencils and a box of matches. When the cabaret artist thundered on the door and shouted he was wanted on the telephone he did not reply. He put his ear to the door and heard irritated groans from the corridor. Later on the police sergeant came up as well. He rattled the door handle and said that if he did not open the door it would be broken down. He heard a third voice in the corridor too but could not recongize it. When the police sergeant repeated his threat he opened the door so the draught made the paper planes go whirling up from the desk and around the room like a flock of frightened seagulls. The cabaret artist brushed one of them off his irritated face while the police sergeant craned his neck to look into the room. The third person was a messenger from the newspaper, who told him he had been sent round by the editors to tell him to go into the office immediately.

He only half listened. He let the sub-editor run on: what did he mean by just staying away for several days without even leaving a message? Did he realize that they would have to cancel the dog campaign now because another newspaper had sniffed out the idea and was going to start a similar campaign? The paper had given him a chance, the paper had gone on 'forgetting' his mistakes! The sub-editor was running out of breath, his cigar kept going out. The journalists stopped working, they wanted to listen, and Mollerup could hear them whispering together when the sub-editor paused in his lecture. But he would not let them worry him. He looked out of the window telling himself that it was all just a question of *shutting off*. Finally he was told to go and review an indifferent Danish film because the film and drama critic was ill.

'At least we can use you for *that*,' said the sub-editor.

On the way to the cinema he was smiling at the thought that his tactics were proving effective. The sub-editor had not succeeded in wounding him. Words were nothing but words, things that slipped out of people's mouths, vowels, consonants, strange sounds, throaty sounds, whistling through the teeth. Words were not primed weapons, they hit you only if you gave in to them. He sat in the cinema, in one of the back rows where some Arabs were already sitting. It was a pornographic film about a shapely young woman who picked up men in the street every day, took them home and went to bed with them before the eyes of her impotent husband. A few people in the audience left the film a quarter way through, one or two elderly ladies audibly protested, young people laughed. An Arab sitting beside him scratched his crotch and got so excited that he masturbated openly. Just before he ejaculated Mollerup moved away. He sat on a gangway seat and thought of his paper planes. He had glue on his fingers that could be peeled off in big skinlike flakes. Should he buy some finished models in a toyshop instead of bothering with his own?

When the film had finished he hurried back to the newspaper. He ignored the porter, did not look around him, walked purposefully into the office which was half empty because it was lunch time. He sat down at a typewriter and wrote a brief review. *As usual a feeble example of Danish celluloid ribbon. Bad sound, hideous actors, limp story-line, weak production. It seems we shall never learn how to make films in little Denmark. M.M.*

He put the review on the sub-editor's desk. At that moment the sub-editor came in wiping sauce from his mouth with the back of his hand. He cast his eyes over the review:

'Do it again!'

'Do it again *how?*' he asked.

'That is not how we treat our readers. They need a proper description . . . !'

'In France we always dispose of bad films in three lines,' he replied arrogantly, looking out of the window. He pretended the sub-editor was air.

The silence lasted up to one minute. Then the sub-editor walked right in front of him so he could not avoid looking straight at his face with the English moustache, scruffy red fringe and a razor cut on his chin. The veins in his temples pulsed:

'*Don't* you think you should give France a rest?' he whispered, desperately attempting to control himself.

'Provincial hole! Yes, this is nothing but a *provincial hole!*' he replied in a loud, clear voice.

He didn't know what had come over him, how he summoned up the courage to answer back. The sub-editor's face contracted like rubber, his eyes flickered to and fro, a clutch of nerves quivered beneath his moustache, and the razor cut looked as if it would split at any moment. When one or two of the other journalists got up and approached as if they thought a fight was brewing, Mollerup grabbed his coat from a desk and left the room. On his way home he seemed to be floating lightly, and at one point he started whistling so people turned round and looked at him. He walked all the way. He nodded to passers-by a couple of times and near Tuborg he pulled out his wallet and offered a lady walking her dog a hundred kroner note. When she started scolding him loudly and threatening to call the police he hurried off. He turned down his street. The moment he walked in he bumped into the cabaret artist who had come running downstairs to meet him. He was ordered to move out at once. As he was walking upstairs still whistling in an unconcerned manner, the cabaret artist seized him by one arm, but he shook him off, went into his room and stood facing the window. He let the cabaret artist go on talking in the doorway in the same way as he had let the sub-editor go on. He did not listen. And yet he heard the man meant what he was saying: he must be out of his room by noon the next day.

Around midnight he went out and walked about the little streets around Hellerup harbour. Two o'clock passed, then three. Later he went up to Strandvejen and walked north towards Klampenborg. Gradually the traffic stopped altogether, only occasionally a sports car drove off with young people going home from a party. A police car crept round a corner, a couple of cats howled in a back garden. Mist lay over the Sound so ships had to use their foghorns. He went right out to Klampenborg and down to Bellevue beach. He sat on the sand until his seat was damp. When he returned to Hellerup it was nearly morning. He caught sight of a single faded copy of *Paris From The Shady Side* among innumerable illustrated travel books in a bookshop window. Obviously the bookseller had forgotten to take the copy away when the withdrawal order came. One of his paper planes with German markings lay in a gutter and he wondered listlessly how it could have got there. Had it flown by itself or been found by a boy who had played with it? He felt dirty. His beard had grown, his scalp kept itching, and his feet were alternately too hot or too cold and damp. The traffic started up again. The spring sun was already high in the sky. Seven o'clock and then eight passed and he was still on Strandvejen. He kept walking to and fro in front of a telephone box. He felt his stomach had been pumped out, he was hungry.So hungry his knees shook.

At first he didn't want to ring. Then he decided he would after all, but then he had forgotten her number. It was getting on for a year and a half since he had last phoned her, when he came home for a week's holiday. He felt it was a warning that he had forgotten her number: he ought not to ring. But when he had come some way from the telephone box and was watching the beer lorries driving out of the brewery the number suddenly came back to him. Now the sun was really warm. He went back to the telephone. He put in a coin. In a moment he was speaking to his mother.

CHAPTER THIRTEEN

Nothing in his old room had changed. The check coverlet was on the bed. It might have faded with the years. All the textbooks from his first years of university were in the bookcase. His mother did make use of his little laquered writing desk to store her unused flowerpot holders on, but neither the tattered rag rug on the floor, the dark curtains at the windows or the van Gogh reproductions on the walls had been replaced. He sat down at the desk, moved aside the flowerpot holders and caught sight of all the places where he had scratched his signature. Then he took some books from the shelves: Frithjof Brandt: *Psychology I and II*, Frithjof Brandt: *The New Philosophy*. Names underlined in red, psychology and philosophy definitions in blue, dates in yellow. Caricatures of the professor and students in the margin, abstract patterns, telephone numbers. In *The New Philosophy* he found a little yellowed scrap of paper: *remember the party on Saturday in the Bispekælder — won't you?* The handwriting was not his. Had a girl written it and passed it to him during a lecture? Hadn't there been some farmer's daughter from Jutland who had set her cap at him in his first term at university? Elsa, Else, Else-Marie, Marie, Marianne? He vaguely remembered her. She was quite plump, almost shapeless. With national health glasses and a battery of pimples on her cheeks. Else-Marie was her name. Now he remembered it. Later on she left university. Domestic science college?

His mother was busy in the kitchen. She had still not said a word about the debacle over his book. When he rang her, her voice sounded exaggeratedly warm. I'm expecting you, she had said. I knew you would ring. The moment he feared most was when she opened the door. But she merely smiled, stretched out her hands and pulled him to her so he should kiss her on the neck. She had tea ready, with home-made biscuits to go with it. As they were sitting at the big coffee table he knew the effort she was making not to comment on his unshaven and scruffy appearance. She smiled the whole time, spoke very little and kept offering him biscuits as if she took it for granted that he must be hungry. After tea he slept for an hour or two and now dinner was almost ready.

He went into the bathroom to wash his hands. One of his mother's wigs was on the laundry basket but otherwise everything was painfully tidy, just as in the old days. The soap with a rubber cloth round it, the tube of toothpaste rolled up from the end. The big wall mirror over the bath looked as if it had been polished with spirits, and on the window sill were a score of boxes of powder and perfume bottles beside the first aid box with the name Falck on the lid. Everything was as he remembered it; the scent of powder from the window sill, the scent of the particular soap his mother had used ever since he was a boy, the smell of spirits from the wall mirror. When he had tidied himself up he went through the dining room to the living room, over to the niche with the shrine holding the urn containing his father's ashes. He carefully opened the lid so the heavy scent of dried roses hit him with an almost physical strength. The rosebuds lay in a heart around the urn, around the shrine itself were four vases holding fresh flowers. He was just about to lift the lid of the urn when his mother called from the kitchen that dinner was almost ready. He quickly closed the lid and waved his hands to spread the scent of roses around the room. He went over to the bookcase and took down a leather-bound book at random. Christian Winther, *Poems Old and New*, sixth edition. Copenhagen. C.A. Reitzel Publishers, 1862. There was a dried four-leaf clover in the book and on the inside of the jacket was his father's ex libris: an owl on the top of a collection of books with a typewriter in its claws and a big cigar in its beak.

'Oh, you're reading, are you?' said his mother as she entered the room. 'Weren't you in the bathroom just now?'

'Yes,' he answered.

'Washing?'

'Yes,' he replied, wondering what the question meant. Did she mean to keep a constant watch on him?

She had opened a bottle of white wine. In the middle of the table she had placed one of the two large silver candlesticks that normally stood on a bureau in the living room. As she brought in steamed fillets of fish with hollandaise sauce and parsley on boiled potatoes, she hummed good-humouredly and smiled at him again. Although he was not in the least fond of steamed fish he expressed gratitude: he knew how much care she had taken over this meal. Before they sat down she patted him tenderly on the cheek, saying nothing was too good for him. Otherwise they did not talk. He had two helpings to please her, thinking about their breakfast in Paris when, after surprising him with the Spanish maid in the middle of the night, she had maintained total silence, as if nothing had happened. The big English clock in the corner of the dining room struck seven. When he suddenly looked up at her she immediately averted her eyes and began to crumble white bread. He could hear the audience arriving at the cinema below. There was a clattering of seats and then the Metro-Goldwyn-Mayer lion roared.

'Is the cinema doing well?'

'Ah, Max . . . you know . . . .'

'I thought you didn't show American films?'

'You get so *tired* of Gabin,' she said, looking up at him. 'And then Hollywood has really got so much better than it was in my youth . . . .'

The false Marianne Mollerup, he thought. Now she'll tell the story once more. But she held back. She was no doubt thinking of the letter she had sent him comparing him with the false Marianne Mollerup and didn't want to bring that up again now. He could even see how she bit her tongue when she passed him the sauce-boat. They continued eating. After dinner, he made an attempt to help her clear the table. He rose and piled up the plates, but at once she took them from him saying that he shouldn't do anything this evening, he must relax, feel at home, really at home. Later, after a few days, he could help her with this and that. In the living room she served coffee, and the biscuits came out again. It was still difficult for them to talk and as he sat in one of the big armchairs embroidered with mythological designs he noticed she had grown older since she had visited him in Paris. Not much. Not in any way you would immediately notice. She still didn't look much more than sixty or sixty-five. But her hands had started to shake and some liver-coloured patches had appeared on her neck. He couldn't really see if her hair was any whiter as she wore a wig, but could it be she had acquired a hearing aid? Wasn't she fiddling with something or other beneath the big black shawl that fell right to her waist? He did not dare to ask her about it. Maybe she had had the hearing aid the last time they were together and he had not noticed it.

'Max . . .'

'Yes.'

'You aren't saying anything.'

'You always say that!'

He looked up at the gilt baroque angel hanging by a cord from the ceiling just above the coffee table. Then he caught his mother's eye. He felt she was about to get worked up over his abrupt tone and he quickly took a box of matches out of his pocket and put five matches on the table, like a dustpan with a bit of sulphur in it. He explained to her that she had to take away three matches and arrange them in a different way so the dustpan faced the opposite way and the sulphur was left outside. He was successful in getting her to concentrate on the puzzle, at first she worked at it distractedly, as if to say that it couldn't be so hard to get the dustpan to face the opposite way, but gradually she grew agitated, she tried one way, then another, then a third without result. She put her head on one side as if she thought it would help to look at the matches from a new angle, she rose and walked round the table, sat down, tried again.

'No, I can't do it,' she said in a harsh voice.

'Try once more,' he said. 'It's not very difficult.'

'Yes, Max. It *is* difficult! You know very well it is, it's just that you know how to do it. Now tell me what to do!'

'Another time,' he said.

She rose. Was she offended? She went into the dining room and was gone for some minutes. But then she came back, pushed the coffee cups and cake plates aside and put a Scrabble board between them. She explained the rules to him quickly. Then she refilled his coffee cup, settled herself and took seven letters. At once she put down six to spell *coffee*. That gave her twelve points. He could only put an o above coffee, which gave him four points for the word *of.* After picking up four new letters she spelt the word *coffeemaker,* the new letter he took was a d which he put in front of her a, but she rejected that. Then he put the d above her o in *coffeemaker* and added three points to the four he already had while his mother already had over twenty. As the game progressed he was on the point of starting an argument several times. She went on using outdated spellings but firmly refused to accept his objections. She would spell as she had always spelled! He didn't get anywhere either when he complained about her compound words. She made *coffeemaker* into *coffeemakerkit,* and when he finally managed to put down a longer word, *shoemaker,* she immediately added *boy* and then *rain,* and insisted on that: *shoemakerboyrain* was when it poured in torrents. 'Got *pour,*' she triumphed and put a p and u and r with the o of *boy.* He gave up objecting, not least because she started to fiddle with the hearing aid under her shawl, so she obviously could not hear what he said and because she was keeping the score. He allowed her to win with 480 points against his own 200. When the game was finished she packed up the board and passed him the score sheet so he could see with his own eyes that she had calculated correctly. The Metro-Goldwyn-Mayer lion began to roar again in the cinema below.

'That was a good game!' she said.

'You're certainly a wizard at it,' he replied, trying to strike the right ironic tone.

'You'll soon get better at it.' She rose and brushed some crumbs from her skirt: 'But now it's bedtime!'

'Bedtime?'

'It's late, Max.'

'It's just after nine . . .'

'I always go to bed when the nine o'clock show has started.'

There was no way round it. Of course, he could stay awake in his old room, he could read or do something else, but he was not to stay in the living area any longer. She told him she had to economize with everything, including the lighting and besides, she didn't want him to make a mess. He promised to keep just one light on and sit quietly in a corner with the day's newspapers, but suddenly she started to switch off all the lights. She went out with the coffee things. Soon afterwards she came back from the kitchen and called him from the doorway. After kissing her on the forehead he went into his room. He lay on the bed and felt the bulges in the mattress that were exactly the same as fifteen years ago. He put one hand under the edge of the bed and got hold of a lump of chewing gum. It was so dried up he couldn't get it off. The ceiling: the same old patches like the outlines of an elephant. The windows: the blind cord that hung down in the middle and swayed lightly in the heat from the radiator. And the smell, like musty apples.

She woke him at half past seven. When he asked if he could lie in for an hour or two longer he was told that was out of the question: breakfast was ready. So he got out of bed, shuffled sleepily to the bathroom, splashed his face with cold water, cleaned his teeth and ran his fingers through his hair. When he went into the dining room his mother was halfway through her breakfast. She looked up at him and he saw she was restraining herself from criticizing him because he still looked tired. Breakfast consisted of weak tea and crispbread with margarine. When he asked if she had any real butter she put her cup down with a bang and lectured him about butter how it was unhealthy and fattening, bad for the heart and slowed the circulation. But margarine prevented hardening of the arteries and left the brain intact.

'How do you think I keep so young?' she asked.
'Not by eating *that*,' he replied, pointing at the margarine.
'Yes, Max, that's how!'
'Can I buy my own butter in future?'
'No.'
'That won't bother you, surely?'
'Yes.'

He could only eat one piece of crispbread and the tea tasted like boiled water. She had not even put out one egg or a glass of fruit juice. After breakfast he went out and found a restaurant where he had coffee and rolls and butter. He was glad his mother had not succeeded in getting him worked up, she would never succeed in that. He would treat her in the same way as he had the sub-editor and the cabaret artist. Like air. He was just obliged to stay with her now he had been thrown out of his room in Hellerup and fired from the newspaper with only the small pension he had contributed to during the past ten years. But he would be sure to find somewhere else to live soon, and if he went on shutting himself off from other people and did not take the words that slid out of their mouths as dangerous weapons, no one could get at him any more. He was convinced of that.

He kept to the smaller side streets. Some of them were directly reminiscent of Paris, especially the ones with deep kerbs, cafés and antiquarian bookshops. A certain street curved in the same way as the Rue du Dragon, a small square with trees resembled the Place de Furstemberg where Delacroix had his studio. When he pressed two fingers to his eyelids so everything swam he was in Paris for a moment, with its grey houses, balconies, café noise. Below him the metro rumbled along. Above him the sky was blue. If he went round a corner or two he would be beside the Seine. If he went through an entrance gate he would walk into a hotel with a moustached old lady at the reception desk and a cat that came to brush against his legs. He took his fingers from his eyes and found himself in front of a dairy. He went inside and bought butter and rusks. Then he bought some coffee in a grocers. Later on he bought a kettle and a jug. He went home in the late afternoon. He let himself into the hall cautiously, crept along the passage and into his room. He put the jug and the kettle under the bed. He put the butter on the outside window sill to keep fresh, and stored the rusks and coffee in the flowerpot holders on the desk. Then there was a knock at the door and his mother came in. She pursed her lips and wrung her hands before scolding him for staying away most of the day without saying where he was going, without even phoning home. In future he must tell her exactly where he was going or at least when he would be home. He smiled. He said 'Yes, Mother,' and 'I will, Mother.' That confused her. She had probably reckoned on him answering back so she could subject him to a really thorough telling off.

'Do you hear what I say, Max?'

'Yes, Mother!'

Dinner consisted of roast pork with boiled cauliflower in white sauce. He knew she knew he didn't like that kind of dish. But he didn't make a fuss. He even said he didn't often have anything so delicious. After dinner he let her win at Scrabble again. He deliberately didn't make any effort, only put down two and three-letter words. Then he retired when the lion's roar sounded below. He kissed her with exaggerated politeness on both cheeks, went to his room and took out the rusks.

Next day she asked him to help her. There was to be a full-length television film featuring her life and career, so she needed to get the albums of her old photographs out of the bureau where she had stored them and put them in the correct order so the television crew did not show pictures from the Queen Kristina film while Mary Stuart was being discussed. He helped her all day. He could just as well do that as anything else. He willingly let himself be ordered about and the only time he protested was when she forbade him to smoke his last French cigarettes.

'It hangs so in the curtains!' she said. 'I don't care what they say about them being better for you than Danish cigarettes!'

Every time he felt like a cigarette he went to the toilet or his room. But he went straight back to her and by the end of the afternoon he had arranged the old photographs in twenty big heaps on the sofa, the ones from the most important historical films in front. He put the theatre pictures in a pile on a chair, he could not get them in order. When his mother inspected his work she expressed great appreciation. She had been looking through old papers, letters and envelopes full of amateur photographs. When he asked what she had found she said that was nothing to do with him. She put the letters, papers and envelopes back in the top drawer of the bureau and locked it. When she thought he was not looking she put the key on top of a door.

'Which role do you think I am best in?' she asked, coming over to him.'As Queen Kristina? As Catherine the Great?'

'Leonora Kristina,' he said, pointing to a picture of her standing in the Blue Tower prison looking out of a grimy window with the first manuscript chapter of Queen Leonora Kristina's book *Memoir of Woe* on a stone table in the middle of the narrow cell.

'Nonsense!' she growled. 'In that one the producer did everything he could to make me look as ghastly as possible. He ended up fraternizing with the Germans, anyway . . .'

Suddenly she put down five matches in a dustpan shape. Then she put a sprig of dried heather that had been among the film photographs in the dustpan:

'Do tell me the trick!'

'Another time,' he replied.

'You said that last time!'

She was irritable for the rest of the afternoon. He went on being polite and friendly, helped her wash up, made the coffee, let her win at Scrabble once more. He knew she had been racking her brains over the puzzle since he had set out the matches the first time but that until now her pride had kept her from pumping him again.

After she had gone to bed he tiptoed into the living room. He found the key above the door and opened the top drawer of the bureau. He put the drawer on a chair and took out the first letters. There were four big bundles of fan letters, from his mother's first film in 1910 right up to the year she retired from the theatre. Most were from Danish admirers, known and unknown together, from sixth form students, doctors, working men, from directors gamely offering her marriage and from fellow actors asking for advice on how to get a foot in the door of the film's 'exciting new world.' There were brief notes of homage from Georg Brandes, the scholar-critic, and Otto Rung, who offered in a postscript to write scripts for her. Many of the letters were still in their original envelopes, some with neatly drawn hearts on them, others with her name and address in filigree, all with the stamps cut off. Then there were letters from abroad, mostly from Germany and France, a few from Austria and Hungary, two from Serbia. One letter had been written by a whole regiment of German soldiers from the trenches of Flanders.

When he had looked through the fan letters he put them back in their original order and began on the letters from his father. Love letters. Timid, apologetic, shy, later on — after their first night together — sprinkled with quotations and declarations of love. After they were married the letters grew more matter-of-fact. Many of them had been written abroad. Now his father was lecturing at Uppsala (on the heroic war hero-priest Kaj Munk), now in Norway, Finland or Germany. *All this Heil-ing! It seems to me that Hitler is of a far more dangerous cast than Mussolini, who after all has done much good for his country. 1933, 1934, 1935. Kiss Max for me. Tell him he can look forward to going to school and finding lots of new friends instead of the ones in the back courtyard. And tell Skrutmikkel I have bought him some new clothes, quite impossible to get in Denmark.* Then suddenly letters from the mid-twenties. Three of them were from Paris after his father and mother had lived there for nine months. *What shall we call him? Something with M. Mikael, Mads, Max? Or Mauritz, or is that too Swedish? And if it's a her she will be Mikala, Marie-Louise or — Marianne the Second. Ha! — Come back soon, I am really fed up that you had to go home for a while. I sit and mope every night in my little hotel room with its view of the Luxembourg Gardens, but at our restaurant they do all they can to cheer up this poor old grass widower. The other day I had frogs' legs! Yes, you may shudder! And I've found a mass of new material in old newspapers in the Bibliothêque Nationale. I think the thesis is beginning to take shape. Love you, love you, love you.*

Then there were big gaps, the next letters were from the end of 1936, from a health resort in Czechoslovakia. The tone was resigned and sad. In some letters his father attempted to make a joke of it all. He described the plump nurses who sat at the end of his bed in the evenings to hear him talk about Hans Christian Andersen, walks in the mountains, balls at the local community halls *(or whatever those places are called in Czech)*. But also he wrote of the Czechs' increasing anxiety about the new Germany. *Looking forward to getting home to our new apartment in Østersøgade, but most of all to the summer in North Sealand. Then I'm going to whitewash the shed. Love you. Say hello to Max and tell him not to worry over having to stay in bed with his ear trouble. He'll be up and about in a few days — and my goodness, he'll soon be getting his own room. It will be worse (between ourselves) if he goes and fails his exams! Once more, love you.*

There were letters from himself as well. Letters from the boarding school he was sent to after his father died. 1938, 1939, 40, 41. *It's so idiotic here and I feel quite alone among the others. They keep on calling me Theatre Rat after that evening when you read poetry in the gym. But it will soon be spring and I shall have a fine holiday. There is one person here I really like, and we have arranged to go on a biking trip to Jutland. You wouldn't mind, would you? The headmaster goes on touching us on the thigh when he gets the chance, and some of the older boys say he likes boys. There's nothing more to write. Your Max.* Then came a letter from the trip to Jutland. There were letters from the summer he passed his entry examination and took his first long trip abroad to England and Scotland, then a gap until the mid-fifties when he went to Paris. The first letters filled over five typed pages each and described the various cheap hotels he stayed at, the books he read, the films he saw, people he met, among them a Danish girl who *I shall probably move in with. I am sure you will like her. I met her quite by chance, bumped into her on a street corner and when I said 'pardon' she replied with a scared 'undskyld' and then we felt we might as well get together. Enclosed is a photo of us on the Pont-Neuf. We have been to the pictures and seen a beautiful Polish film and are on the way to a restaurant we've heard a lot about, where they serve the best sauce in Paris with pommes frites. She works for a French family, more and more Danish girls are doing this. They don't get paid much, but it's a good way of learning French. She might come home with me for Christmas. Could she stay with us? Well, I must run. I'm going to meet her in half an hour by a certain bookstall beside the Seine and I'm late already. Say hello to Copenhagen for me. Am writing masses of articles, you'll see them in the paper, I expect. Now I must really run! Your Max.* The next letter was written a month later, there was only a single page. *Don't really know what to write. Perhaps you've already read about the accident in the paper. I was going to meet her, and it was just before we were moving in together. Had already found a flat. And then I heard it from Madame (I forget her name), the one she worked for. The only consolation in such a situation is that it was over quickly and she did not feel anything. If that is any consolation. I have already written to her parents, but was just as lost for words as I am now, writing to you.* After six months the letters were longer again, one of them reported that he had at last been promised an interview with Sartre. *I don't know whether you like him, but from a journalistic point of view an interview with him is a coup. Sartre is simply the hardest man to get hold of, everyone pesters him. But I went on and on. I rang his secretary every day for a whole month and now I am going to meet him. I may even get Simone de Beauvoir as well — you know, she's the women's movement one.* In a later letter he complained that the interview did not come to anything after all. Then there were more big gaps. Didn't he write home at all in 1959? From the beginning of the sixties the letters took on a fretful tone and only recorded basic details. *It's winter down here. It's spring. Now it will soon be summer, and I expect I'll go south.* The letters from the last couple of years, five in all, were more concerned with telling his mother to stop sending him lectures than with Paris. The last letter had been written just over a year ago. *I'm glad you are coming to visit me at last. The spare room is ready, and I have a Spanish maid to cook. I think you will find Paris greatly changed since you were here in the twenties and thirties with Father.* Finally he found the postcard he had sent from St Mark's Square. *March 65. Am on holiday, having a great time, the Italians more than friendly, Venice splendid.*

When he had finished with the letters he searched the drawer to find the photograph of him with the Danish girl at the Pont-Neuf. But it was missing. Had his mother torn it up? Had he forgotten to enclose it? But he found other photographs. His father and mother in Paris in 1925. They sat on the hexagonal radiator of an old Renault, his father in white trousers with spats, his mother in a short dress, cloche hat and buttoned shoes. His father by himself walking in Montparnasse with trolley buses in the background. His mother looking at theatre programmes on a poster, autumn, Rond Point, *Le Figaro's* offices on the left of the picture. Pictures of North Sealand. The view from the summer cabin down to the Sound. His mother making jam, a portable gramophone beside her. His father in a deckchair wearing only bathing trunks, with an open book over his face to shield it from the sun. Paris again. The early thirties. His mother's guest appearance at the Comédie Francaise. A section of the audience with his father on the first row clapping enthusiastically. The end of the thirties. The apartment on Østersøgade. The view from the study of Sortedamssøen with the birds' island in the middle. Then he found a bundle of letters. Letters of condolence. He left them alone. More dried rosebuds. A letter from a lawyer. A pocket game of chess. A paper knife. A bundle of unused ex-libris with the owl and the typewriter on the pile of books. An old banknote. A 1940s patriotic badge. A pack of prewar cigarettes. The obituary notices for his father, stuck on to black card. One of his father's unpublished manuscripts, *Kaj Munk, Greatest Dramatist Of Our Time.* A book with a silk cover in a pale blue slip case. Baby Record Book. The pages were illustrated with drawings of red-cheeked babies with fair curly hair. Among them, on dotted lines his mother had written all his details. 'A stork gave me to Mummy, and so you see/Here begins the story of "Me". I arrived. Greetings to baby. How heavy? Gifts. How big. My locks. My first time out. My diet. Mother's notes. Max Mollerup. Nine Pounds. Nine pounds, four hundred grammes. Eleven pounds, a hundred grammes. 11 Nov. 1925. A bankbook from Aunt Sane, a christening gown from Aunt Eva. Sixty-three centimeters. And then a lock of his first hair, fair and downy, entwined with pearl thread. 29 Sept. 1925: I was ever so good, and I had to shout/When I saw the sun on my first day out. *Max started to coo at two and a half months, and had great fun with the sounds he produced, and a few days later he discovered his hands and lay looking at them, moving his fingers. At six months he gave a real chuckle.*

There was nothing left in the drawer. Were there any other drawers, other hiding-places? He grew restless, left everything lying around on chairs, tables and the floor. It was after four o'clock, and the silence was almost tangible. Water ran in a waterpipe somewhere. Was that a mouse scrabbling behind a panel? The baroque angel above the sofa table turned slightly. A drunk man belched down in the street. Was that a row of chairs creaking down in the cinema, was a tap dripping? He stood in the middle of the room and slowly turned his face around so he caught sight of the tapestry on the wall with Caesar wooing Cleopatra, the Romanesque crucifix, the niche with the urn holding his father's ashes and the fresh flowers. One of the heavy curtains moved slightly because a window was half open. He felt cold and realized his mother had turned off the heating. Then he could feel the whole house, from the cinema up to the attic. His mother turned over in bed with a faint whistling from her nostrils. In the box office the telephone rang, probably someone had dialled a wrong number. In the flats people slept either alone or in double beds, their hands under their cheeks or along their sides. One of them woke up and went into the kitchen for a glass of milk. A cat jumped down from a bookcase and lay down beside a radiator. He could sense more than the house: the street, the streets. The drunk had arrived home. He was on the way upstairs to his flat, fell down between the second and third floor and crawled the last stretch. Behind the dark windows thousands of alarm clocks were ticking and waiting for the moment when they would explode and chase people out of bed. The moon moved slowly over the rooftops. Time did not exist. Time became one with empty space with the planets circling around the suns. He still stood there unmoving, in a chance room on the dark half of the earth, among heavy curtains and immovable furniture. The sun illuminated the other half of the earth and in Rio de Janeiro or in New York people hurried along the pavements or rode in crammed metros. Lunchtime, midday heat. Or was it in Hong Kong and Peking that it was day? There was no spot on Earth he could not sense. The sound of waves on the beach in South Africa. An avalanche in the Alps. A ship's bow on the way into morning in the middle of the Atlantic or into sunset in the Pacific. Light pushing at darkness and darkness pushing at light. The slow shift from night to day and from day to night around an infinity of suns placed in the midst and around and above and below in that space of timelessness and infinite night where there was neither anything called midst or around or above or below. The chairs creaked again in the cinema. The mouse scrabbled again behind the panelling. Dripping from the tap. Footsteps in the corridor. Footsteps that came nearer and nearer. But he stood still, did not hide. He was strangely indifferent about his mother surprising him. She was already in the doorway, her hand on the handle. The tousled chalk-white remnants of hair on her scalp. The net of wrinkles on her face. She wore the frayed Japanese kimono.

'What *are* you doing?'

He did not know how he got past her. But suddenly he was in his room. He seized the chair by the writing desk and put it against the door with its back fixed under the door handle. He let his mother get more and more frantic in the corridor, just lay down on his bed fully dressed with his hands under his head. He slept for a couple of hours. When he woke up it was late morning. His mother was shaking the door handle as if she had been standing there outside the door ever since he fell asleep. But he did not react. Not until he had boiled water, made coffee and eaten four thickly buttered rusks did he take the chair away. His mother stood before him, fully dressed, in her wig. She asked him to come into the living room with her for a 'serious talk', but he pushed her gently aside. As he was about to leave the flat she held a letter before him. He read it through without interest. It was from the manager of the Danish shop in Paris reminding him that he still owed for the table with orange tiles. If the money was not received within four days legal proceedings would be instituted against him. The letter had been sent to the editor-in-chief who had readdressed it to his mother without comment.

'Is it too much to ask for an explanation?' she asked.

'It's just a bill,' he replied and went down to the street.

At first it was the sounds. A sports car's three-toned horn. A bicycle bell, footsteps, a jet plane flying low over the rooftops. The whine of trams around corners, pop music from the gramophone shops' loudspeakers, roadworkers hammering cobblestones, the diesel engines of taxis, belching sounds from buses. He heard all the noises together. Burmeister & Wain. The thunder of factory machinery. Flames licking at refuse disposal plants. The conversation of passers-by. A pile was hammered down in the harbour, in another place a house was demolished, and the final wall fell to the earth with a crash. Underground trains moved off below Nørreport with almost the same sound as the metro in Paris. The hooting of ships' sirens, the bridges groaning as they were raised or lowered. Out in the suburbs beer bottles clinked at topping-out ceremonies. Even the quietest whisper in a classroom could he hear. And the demented clattering of desk lids in another classroom where the teacher had no control over the situation. Bells. School bells. Factory bells. Roaring lions in all the Metro-Goldwyn-Mayer films. A pane of glass knocked out of an open window on a fourth floor that fell to earth and broke into a thousand pieces just at the feet of an old lady. The tick of teleprinters in editorial offices, the hum of oil boilers in basements, the dog-whistle squeaking of rats in the sewers. Later on it was the colours of the city. Red colours seemed to be fighting with orange, blue writhed under the embrace of green. Amongst them neutral gray of all shades from the white-grey of clouds to the dark-grey of asphalt. There was the yellow of trams and buses, the black of taxis, the red of letter boxes and the verdigris of roofs and church spires. There was the painting on gables and the silver and gold in jewellers' windows, there was the first fully opened leaves on treetops. He only noticed them now when spring was becoming early summer, and the sun suddenly pushed the clouds away so the sky was every shade of blue with the black dots of birds and confetti-like multicoloured letters behind a sports aeroplane advertising a certain brand of television set. Cars of every colour. Dresses and coats and hats in every colour. The white lines on the asphalt. The blue pedestrian crossings. The red signs for no entry. Sunblinds. Ochre-coloured sunblinds. Coke-coloured sunblinds, red-and-white-striped sunblinds. And the first coloured umbrellas of the summer in front of one or two restaurants that dared to put tables outside. And then the smells. They came a little later. The smells that blended in with the sounds and the colours. Perfume. Cheroot smoke. The smell of underarm sweat from passers-by, of eggs from the sea, the stink of the sewers with their squeaking rats, the smell of steamed potatoes and breaded cutlets from canteens and caféterias. But everything smelled differently from Paris, just as the colours and the sounds were different from Paris, where the cars went around without silencers with two or three exhaust pipes, and the bells rang from the rear platforms of buses when they started off from the bus stops. The telephones had a deeper, more humming sound and the colours were stronger, the red more red, the blue more blue, and there was no smell of cheroots and beer but of Gauloises, and even the sweat was different because there was a hint of garlic in it. Only beside the lakes did he feel he was in Paris for a moment. He put his head on one side and looked over the water that reflected the grey facades with balconies and little towers on the rooftops. Then he put his head down between his legs so he was looking at everything upside down. The lakes were the Seine. The Lake Pavilion at the end looked like a plastic boat rushing towards him full of American and Danish tourists. He kept still for a while feeling the blood rushing to his head. An old woman stopped to look at him. A couple of children started to giggle on the grass slope. A postman passing by up on the pavement shouted at him:

'Got a headache, chum?'

He let the old woman look and the children giggle and the postman shout. Not until they had all disappeared in various directions did he straighten up and start to walk back towards the city centre. On his way upstairs he almost stumbled over some cables. The hall door was ajar and he heard voices from the living room. He opened the door cautiously and saw his mother sitting in one of the big armchairs in the corner just beneath the wooden Romanesque crucifix. She was in a dark dress with a pearl-embroidered silk shawl. She wore the wide Indian silver bracelet, and her wig was pushed slightly up from below so she looked almost girlish. In front of her on a stool sat a young woman holding a manuscript. There was a camera on a tripod and four technicians went to and fro carrying cables and arranging lights. He closed the door again and went downstairs, where he met the daytime manageress of the cinema. She was underlining in red photocopies of enthusiastic reviews for the showcases. They had been showing the première of a new American film about an English consul in Paris who loses his two sons because he neglects them in favour of his decadent French lover. The manageress smiled and said it was nice to see him again, and he replied that it was nice to see her. She offered him a cheroot which he declined.

'Oh dear,' she said. 'I can well remember you when you were so high!'

She stretched out her hand a meter above the floor.

'Nice to see you!' he said.

She looked at him, surprised:

'You don't need to say it twice . . . .'

'Oh, no,' he replied and thought how easy it was to confuse other people just by letting some chance sounds pour out of your mouth.

'I think I'd like a cheroot after all,' he said.

'I'd be surprised if you had suddenly stopped smoking! You've always liked the good things of life so much!'

He lit up. He drew the smoke deep into his lungs. Then he smiled again:

'Nice to see you!'

She turned round, went into the box office and sat down to arrange the tickets. She did not look up at him, and when the telephone rang he went upstairs to the flat again. They were having a break in filming; the technicians and the female interviewer were out in the kitchen having coffee. He greeted them briefly and went into the living room where his mother immediately ordered him to make himself useful and hand the cameraman the old photographs in the right order. That was all she said. And she said it without so much as looking at him. As if it disgusted her to address him. When they began filming again he placed himself over by the table where the pictures lay in the order he had arranged them in. He noticed that the bureau drawer had been furnished with a padlock.

'Now we come to your first visit to France and you received deserved homage,' said the interviewer. 'Wasn't that in 1921?'

'Yes, that is about right!' his mother replied, smiling straight into the lens with her head coquettishly on one side. 'And *that* certainly didn't please the Danes! Before 1920 I was — as everyone who knows anything about cinema history knows — extremely well known in Germany and Austria-Hungary. But that didn't count here in Denmark. Oh, no! Not until the French recognized my talent could the Danes reluctantly follow suit! There is an old saying that runs, 'when Paris takes a pinch of snuff, the whole world sneezes . . .'

He fumbled with the padlock and noticed his mother stiffen in front of the camera. After a few moments he moved over to the shrine, and that made her still more nervous.

When the technicians and the interviewer turned towards him he just smiled as if nothing had happened. He handed them the pictures they wanted in a friendly way. Mary Stuart. Catherine the Great. But each time the camera was rolling he did some little thing or other which made his mother frantic. He saw the sweat form on her forehead and run down her make-up in little streams. Then he kept still and let her talk in peace, and she smiled again and grew calm, recounted anecdotes, laughed at them herself, made the others laugh, threw out her hands, shook her head indignantly in anger at some long-dead producer and lit an Egyptian cigarette, not to smoke but so that the smoke could drift up in front of her face like a mysterious veil. Not until she came to her old age towards the end of the filming did he go to the shrine again and move as if he intended to open it. Suddenly she dropped her actress persona, shot up from her chair, dropped her cigarette and ordered him to leave the room immediately. He went to his room and started playing with the flowerpot holders. He built a tower with them until the pile almost reached the ceiling. Shortly afterwards he could hear his mother's relaxed laughter from the living room. The filming must have finished, the technicians must be packing up their camera. What sort of eternity did she think would remember her through this broadcast?

At that moment the pile of flowerpots fell over, and he started picking up the pieces.

She did not speak to him over dinner. The flat was itself again. The heavy curtains seemed back in their old folds. There was no trace of the television recording. The smells were the old ones again, of mouldy apples, dried flowers and dust that had gathered for decades in sofas and chair seats, so deep down that no vacuum cleaner could cope with it. Dinner was grilled cutlets with French beans. Up to now he had been given a light beer, but now there was only a jug of water without ice on the table. And there were no candles, only the cold chandelier in which three bulbs had gone was lit. His mother had taken off her make-up, she wore the kimono and had left her wig in her bedroom or the bathroom. When she chewed he could hear her jaws crack, when she breathed in there was a hollow sound in her throat, and now and then her hearing aid gave a faint electrical pinging and she fumbled irritably at her stomach for the button that regulated it. He could smell her as well. Old skin, powder, lavender soap. After dinner she grunted when he offered to help clear away but still said nothing. When he opened out the Scrabble board and took seven letters for each of them she put it away again at once and went to sit in an armchair with the evening paper.

'You're not saying anything,' he said. He wanted to see how far he could drive her with his random sounds. 'You haven't spoken a word all evening!'

She made no reply. He tried again:

'Have you lost your voice?'

Still she didn't answer. Then he fell silent too. He listened to the sounds in the flat. Was the mouse still there, somewhere behind the panelling? The English clock ticked and ticked. The creaking of the floorboards when he walked over them. Then he concentrated on the smells. He felt her eyes following him uneasily when he put his nose up close to the curtains, down in the plant pots, down in the chair seats and into the niche with the urn, sniffing demonstratively. But still she failed to react as he had anticipated. She turned page after page of the paper and it sounded as if a microphone had been placed right under it. Then he gave the baroque angel a light tap so it swung to and fro. And suddenly he could not stop. He gave all the pictures a push so they hung askew, he fingered the curtains, opened the windows so the curtains blew inwards almost horizontally, pushed all the lights on the chandeliers so they swayed and plaster started to fall from the ceiling. He sent a couple of sofa cushions rolling across the floor and let the saucers under the plant pots follow them. Gradually everything in the room was in movement. And his mother was running from one corner to another. She bent down to pick up the saucers, stopped the baroque angel swinging until he gave it a fresh push, closed the windows, stopped the cushions with her feet and stretched vainly to reach the chandelier which was still making plaster drift down and pile up in little heaps on the carpets.

'Max!' she shouted in a voice that cracked. She stood and put both hands to her temples, staring at him:

'You are quite *mad*!'

The ants were moving over the ceiling in a long winding column. Then they went down the wall, over the mirror above the basin and on to the shelf. They marched past the tube of toothpaste, the razor and up the shaving brush to gather in clusters in its bristles. They gnawed at the dried foam and from a distance the brush appeared to be alive. Then they marched back again by precisely the same route. They had done this ever since he moved in. Twice a day, at nine in the morning and seven in the evening, they came from under the ceiling and made purposefully for the shaving brush. They stayed in it for one hour. Not fifty minutes or seventy minutes but exactly one hour. He pondered again on how to get rid of them. He did not want their dead bodies lying about the room. If he killed them while they were marching over the ceiling they would fall into his hair and his bed. If he killed them while they were in the brush he would rub them into his skin when he shaved. He would make enquiries at various shops to see if he could get some insect killer which acted slowly. Then he could spray them as they marched back, so they did not die before they had left the ceiling. He had to go into town anyway for pins with green and red heads, and a new door handle. He had gradually organized the whole room as he wanted it. He had found a wooden bed that exactly suited him, a bedside table to go with it and an old bentwood chair. He had painted everything white and had even changed the screws in the mirror, but there was still something the matter with the door handle. He couldn't say what it was. Something or other.

From his room on the third floor of the villa he had a view over most of Paris. He had stayed at hotels for some weeks.

But everywhere there was something wrong. Sounds, smells, colours. In one place he heard Danish in the adjoining room, accompanied by the usual stupid Danish giggling, in another there was a stink of urine, in a third the colour of the furniture made his eyes hurt. Or the hotel proprietors scowled at him or the guests pushed him on the stairs. Or there was something very wrong with the view over a narrow backyard. But in the end he found, through a letting bureau where they had been astonishingly friendly, a quiet elderly couple with a room to let. The fact that they lived in Sceaux was nothing but an improvement. He knew there were certain districts and residential suburbs he could not live in purely on account of their names. If he were to live in Enghien-les-Bains or Kremlin-Bicêtre, where the letting office had first offered him rooms, he would be aware every day that he lived in Enghien-les-Bains or Kremlin-Bicêtre, unpleasant names made up of wrong sounds that were either too soft or too hard. But Sceaux sounded of nothing, of something casual and meaningless. The place was peaceful, without too much traffic. And the elderly couple left him quite to himself. He only saw them occasionally and they had no objection to his exchanging the furniture in the room for the pieces it had taken him several days to track down in the flea market. Now he only needed a new door handle. And everything would be as he wanted it.

He took the Ligne de Sceaux train to Luxembourg soon after eleven. That was his usual time for going in to Paris. There were not many passengers on the train then, and he often had a whole carriage to himself. When he arrived at Luxembourg, the midday heat blazed down over Paris, the dust blended lazily with the petrol fumes, and passers-by had big sweat patches under their arms. He walked down the Boulevard Saint-Michel. The shooting galleries, the stalls selling toasted almonds, the kiosks with newspapers hanging from coat hangers: DEFFERRE AS PRESIDENTIAL CANDIDATE. WILL DE GAULLE RISE AGAIN? Suddenly he took a left turning down a side street. He had come to be able to sense far ahead if someone he knew was approaching. He did

not know whether it was Lund or Munk or perhaps the press
attaché on an afternoon off from the Embassy. But it was one
of them. Fifty meters, perhaps only forty or fifty meters ahead
he would come across one of them if he went straight on. He
hurried down the side street and only slackened speed when
he passed a small boy spraying a hissing cat with a hose. A
couple of blacks hanging about a stairway laughed loudly
when one of his trouser legs got splashed by mistake. The boy
promptly threw down the hose and tore off as if he took it for
granted Mollerup would give him a clip on the head. But he
just brushed off the water and made sure he showed no
emotion to the blacks. A drop of water on a hot summer's
day! When he had offered the blacks cigarettes with exaggerated politeness he went on and entered a bistro where he
bought a postcard. Curtly and succinctly he wrote to the
editor-in-chief that in future his pension should be sent to a
certain bank in Sceaux. Then he found a post-box. Heard the
little plop as the card fell on top of other mail. That was the
last Denmark would hear from him.

The dust settled in his throat, the petrol fumes and heat
made him dizzy. He made his way to a shop and bought a
white plastic handle. Then he caught sight of a haberdasher's
where he could buy pins, but as he approached it a voice
inside told him to turn round. There was something wrong
about the shop. They would be sure to treat him unkindly and
perhaps would not even give him the pins even if he had paid
a lot for them. He turned off, went down more side streets,
down to the Seine and over to the Right Bank where he found
another haberdasher's.

'C'est pour vous, Monsieur?' asked the lady behind the
counter as she put fifty green and fifty red headed pins into a
bag. She looked inquiringly at him as she scratched one
nostril.

'Oui!' he replied firmly.

He stuffed the bag into one of his trouser pockets and
hurried out. The heat was worse than ever. Ice creams melted
in people's hands, children cried and were smacked by their
mothers. Old people on benches groaned, and in the parks

people were lying on the grass asleep: the men with newspapers over their heads and transistors broadcasting the
latest news of the Catholic Popular Republicans' refusal to
support Gaston Defferre's presidential candidacy, the women
with their flowery dresses pulled up over their thighs so you
could see their swollen veins and salmon-pink petticoats. It
was quite the wrong day to have come into Paris and he grew
more and more tired because he constantly had to make
detours when he got the feeling that people he knew were
approaching. If he started to go down into a metro he
suddenly turned round in the middle of the stairway. If he
went into a park he hurried out again because he had a
feeling that a handful of Danish students from the university
were close by. Then he calmed down: he was in streets where
no one knew him. But in front of a cinema he again sensed he
was going to meet an acquaintance. When he looked at the
photographs in the showcase it was himself he met. One of
the pictures showed the inside of the casino in Venice. He
saw himself in profile, with the dyed albino hair as a German
in English disguise. Opposite him, also in profile, sat the
Englishman with the Leslie Howard wig, dressed as a German. The croupier was gathering in the chips. He stood there
for some time watching the audience coming out of the
cinema and his eyes misted over. Luckily there were no other
pictures of him and, as no one recognized him, he reckoned
that his appearance in the film could only last a few minutes.
Nor was his name mentioned in the programme he bought
and immediately afterwards dropped into the gutter.

By taking one bus and changing to another and later to a
third he reached Luxembourg without being recognized. He
took the last train before the start of the rush hour. As he let
himself into his room he felt a surge of relief. He had closed
the curtains before leaving to keep out the heat. He began
straight away to exchange the black door handle with the
white plastic one. He could feel to his fingertips that everything in the room was now as he wanted it, chalk-white and

cool. Next he took out an old map of Paris which he had bought in a bookstall by the Seine. He fastened it carefully over his bed with four drawing pins. First he found Munk's address. Rue de Chezy, Neuilly-sur-Seine. He calculated the route Munk would take daily to get to the city centre and marked it off with seven red headed pins. Nor must he go into the area around the Rue de Rivoli. That was where Lund lived. And Ussing lived in the Pigalle. Then he worked out the press attaché's route on his way to the Danish Embassy. In one place, in the middle of the Champs Elysées, Lund's route coincided with Munk's who again coincided with the press attaché at L'Étoile. That made him put an extra number of pins on the Champs Elysées. Next it was Rolf Hauge's turn. He mostly stayed in his castle in the suburbs, but when he was going into Paris he would have to take the Autoroute du Sud. Four red pins. The lame proprietor of the Danish Shop, the Danish minister, the director of the students' residence. He did not know much about them. But he might as well mark off the places around the Danish Shop, the streets near the back entrance to the Danish Church and the route along the Boulevard Jourdan-Avenue du General Leclerc-Denfert-Rochereau that the director of the students' residence must take on his way to the city centre. In the sixth arrondissement it was above all the Rue des Canettes with Chez Georges, Lund's regular café, he should be careful of. And then, of course, the Place Saint-Germain-des-Prés where he would be sure to meet Danes as on the Champs-Elysées. He also put a red pin in the middle of the Rue du Dragon where the Italian woman lived. And he found the street where the bald man's restaurant was. He could not recall the crewcut writer's address, but he would doubtless be where the Italian woman and the bald man were. He suddenly remembered the night-club he had once visited with them. Yet another red pin.

He put the first green pin midway between the e and the a in Sceaux. From there the green pins would spread out over the map, in and out among the routes marked by the red ones. Each time he had been in a district where he could be in peace he would place a green pin in the centre of it when he got home. One day perhaps there would be more green pins than red. But for the present it was vital for him to know exactly which streets, squares, metro stations and whole arrondissements he must avoid. He stepped back when he had finished placing the pins. They were the only coloured points in the whole room. He smiled with satisfaction. Went over to the basin and washed his face in cold water, damped his hair and made a neat parting. In the wardrobe were the clothes he needed, a single suit, a sweater, underclothes, socks. In a cupboard, built in under the window, were some tins of pâté, sausages, salt, bread. What more did he need?

The ants were there again. They had gone all the way over the ceiling and were on their way down the wall. He was annoyed to have forgotten to buy the insect killer. As the ants reached halfway down the mirror he squashed the first one with his index finger. At once the whole column stopped. It kept still for a minute. As the first ant still did not move, all the ants began to cluster around it. They started to repair it and after a while it came to and ran round in a circle as if it was drunk. Then it took its place at the head of the others who again formed a long winding marching column. Now the ants moved up the mirror, the wall and disappeared under the ceiling. He looked at them until the last one had gone. Was that really all it took? Would they really stay away now? In a little while he went to the window and looked out over Paris. Sacré Coeur, la Tour Eiffel, l'Arche de Triomphe. He could just about see masses of red pins sticking up from the streets. Soon green ones would mix in with them. Masses of green pins. He stayed at the window. It would soon be dusk.

For the first time he felt he could take possession of life. And he was happy.

BOOKS BY THE SAME AUTHOR

THE MAN WHO WANTED TO BE GUILTY
Translated by David Gress-Wright

This short startling novel, set in Denmark in the not too
distant future, concerns a man who, in a moment of passion,
murders his wife. He is met with the cloying sympathy of
psychologists and social workers eager to 'help' him.

The result is failure and loss: this manipulative and plastic
society cannot accept individual responsibility and negates
all emotion and humanity. He is denied truth and integrity,
any memories of his wife are wiped out, and he loses custody
of his son. He is deprived of the basis for existence and slowly
goes insane in his attempts to prove his guilt to 'the helpers'.

Acclaimed by Anthony Burgess as 'a novel in the tradition
of Swift and Orwell', it depicts and indicts the good inten-
tions of a society where enlightenment becomes
institutionalized and divorced from real human feeling. The
'staff of life' — whether it be guilt or joy — is rationalized and
therapied away.

'(*The Man who Wanted to be Guilty*) is a brief, witty, deeply felt,
biting and finely imagined assault on the workings and psychological subtlety of oppression — an awe-inspiring attack on
the modern enlightenment.'   *Book Choice*

'. . . an experience conveyed with great power.'   *The Times*

'. . . the near-actuality of Stangerup's book chills more than
anything I have read in years.'   *Anthony Burgess*

THE ROAD TO LAGOA SANTA

Translated by Barbara Bluestone

In 1833, the young Danish prize-winning naturalist Dr P.W. Lund made a journey into the jungles of Brazil from which he was destined never to return. For ten years Lund struggled against suspicious natives, endured bouts of ill-health, the hostile climate and the bloody retributions of tribal lore, aided only by his black workers and his faithful companion, artist P.A. Brandt. Then, suddenly, at the age of 44, he stopped working and sank into a profound depression bordering on insanity, which was to last until his death in Brazil at the age of 79.

What really happened to Lund? Henrik Stangerup's discoveries are embodied in this historical novel in which he skillfully uses an epic sweep to evoke the wonder of the Brazilian landscape and Lund's passionate, obsessive character. He explores the methods by which the nineteenth-century world picture was put together, with man taking an unsteady position at the centre of his newly discovered universe, shattering the concept of the Divine Plan of Creation. Lund's life — and Stangerup's novel — are both deeply informed by the work of his great contemporaries, Kierkegaard, Darwin, Cuvier and Humboldt.

'(*The Road to Lagoa Santa*) is a superb novel and a fascinating adventure story — clean and vivid prose, admirably translated.'   *Library Journal*

'Has a suitably stormy quality, morose and turbulent — a highly original novel.'   *The Guardian*

THE SEDUCER
It is Hard to Die in Dieppe
Translated by Sean Martin

The death of Peter Ludvig Møller in Dieppe, worn out, syphilitic, high on coffee, wine and ether, marked the end of a career that was remarkable not only for its brilliance but also its profligacy. As a bright child and promising theology student, Møller's career in the world of Danish letters seemed assured, but his great passion for life and literature, his obsession with the realities of God, sex and death, sent him chasing wildly across Europe where his life rapidly burned itself out as he hurtled from triumph to disaster.

An associate and sworn enemy of Søren Kierkegaard, whose book *The Seducer's Journal* he inspired, and the man who encouraged and made the reputation of many writers, Møller achieved great influence as a critic and became an acute observer of Baudelaire's Paris. Stangerup's fictionalized account follows its subject all over Europe, through the highs and lows of passion, inspiration and ambition towards the final depths of despair and his pathetic death in Dieppe.

Described as a masterpiece by the Danish press, *The Seducer* is a stunning biographical novel in which Stangerup has infused the spirit of a gothic romance, transforming Møller's life into a ceaseless pursuit of perfection which can only be realized once he has attained the impossible; which is to write himself into his own work.

'*The Seducer* cannot be ignored. We are all somewhere within this novel.'   *The Independent*

'. . . an extraordinary entry into the mind of an obsessive man.'   *The Times*

BROTHER JACOB
Translated by Anne Born

In the sixteenth century, Brother Jacob, younger brother of King Christian II and son of Queen Christine and King Hans of Denmark, is studying in Paris as a Franciscan Grey Brother. As the forces of the Lutheran Reformation topple his family from the throne, Brother Jacob is driven through Europe by his acceptance of God's love and his hatred both of the cruelty of the established Catholic Church and the self-denying sterility of the new Reformed religion. Fleeing to Mexico in search of his Utopia, he founds monasteries and hospitals there and champions the religious rights of the Amerindians. In return for this he is ordered to do a penance of silence and dies at the age of 82, honoured as a saint by the Indians.

Henrik Stangerup is the winner of the Amalienborg Prize, the Queen of Denmark's personal literary prize, the Danish Critics' Prize, and the Grand Prize of the Danish Academy of Letters.

'Old and new worlds, hatreds, miracles and a dream of tolerance form a memorable, powerful mix.'   *The Tablet*

'*Brother Jacob* is an inspired book, enthusiastic, angry and visionary.'   *Le Monde*

'Without doubt (*Brother Jacob*) is the most exciting novel on the discovery of the New World.'   *J.M.G. le Clézio,*
Le Nouvel Observateur